D0837628

STAR WARS REBELS

1

Based on the series
Star Wars Rebels created by
**Dave Filoni & Simon Kinberg
& Carrie Beck**

Based on Star Wars created by
George Lucas

Art by
Akira Aoki

Lettering:
Phil Christie

This book is a work of fiction. Names,
characters, places, and incidents are the
product of the author's imagination or are
used fictitiously. Any resemblance to actual
events, locales, or persons, living or dead,
is coincidental.

STAR WARS REBELS, VOL. 1
© & TM 2020 LUCASFILM
First published in Japan in 2019
by LINE Corporation 4-1-6 Shinjuku,
Shinjuku-ku, Tokyo, Japan.
Produced by LINE Coporation 4-1-6
Shinjuku, Shinjuku-ku, Tokyo, Japan.

Yen Press
150 West 30th Street, 19th Floor
New York, NY 10001

Visit us at yenpress.com
facebook.com/yenpress
twitter.com/yenpress
yenpress.tumblr.com
instagram.com/yenpress

First Yen Press Edition: November 2020

Yen Press is an imprint of
Yen Press, LLC.
The Yen Press name and logo are
trademarks of Yen Press, LLC.

The publisher is not responsible for
websites (or their content) that are not
owned by the publisher.

Library of Congress Control Number:
2020944894

ISBNs: 978-1-9753-1766-9 (paperback)
978-1-9753-1765-2 (ebook)

10 9 8 7 6 5 4 3 2 1

WOR

Printed in the United States of America

STAR WARS™ REBELS

Based on the series Star Wars Rebels created by

Dave Filoni & Simon Kinberg & Carrie Beck

Based on Star Wars created by

George Lucas

Art by

Akira Aoki

1

CONTENTS

Story 1. The Boy from Lothal I ———— 3

The Boy from Lothal II ———— 43

The Boy from Lothal III ———— 87

Extra. Lord of the Sith ———— 143

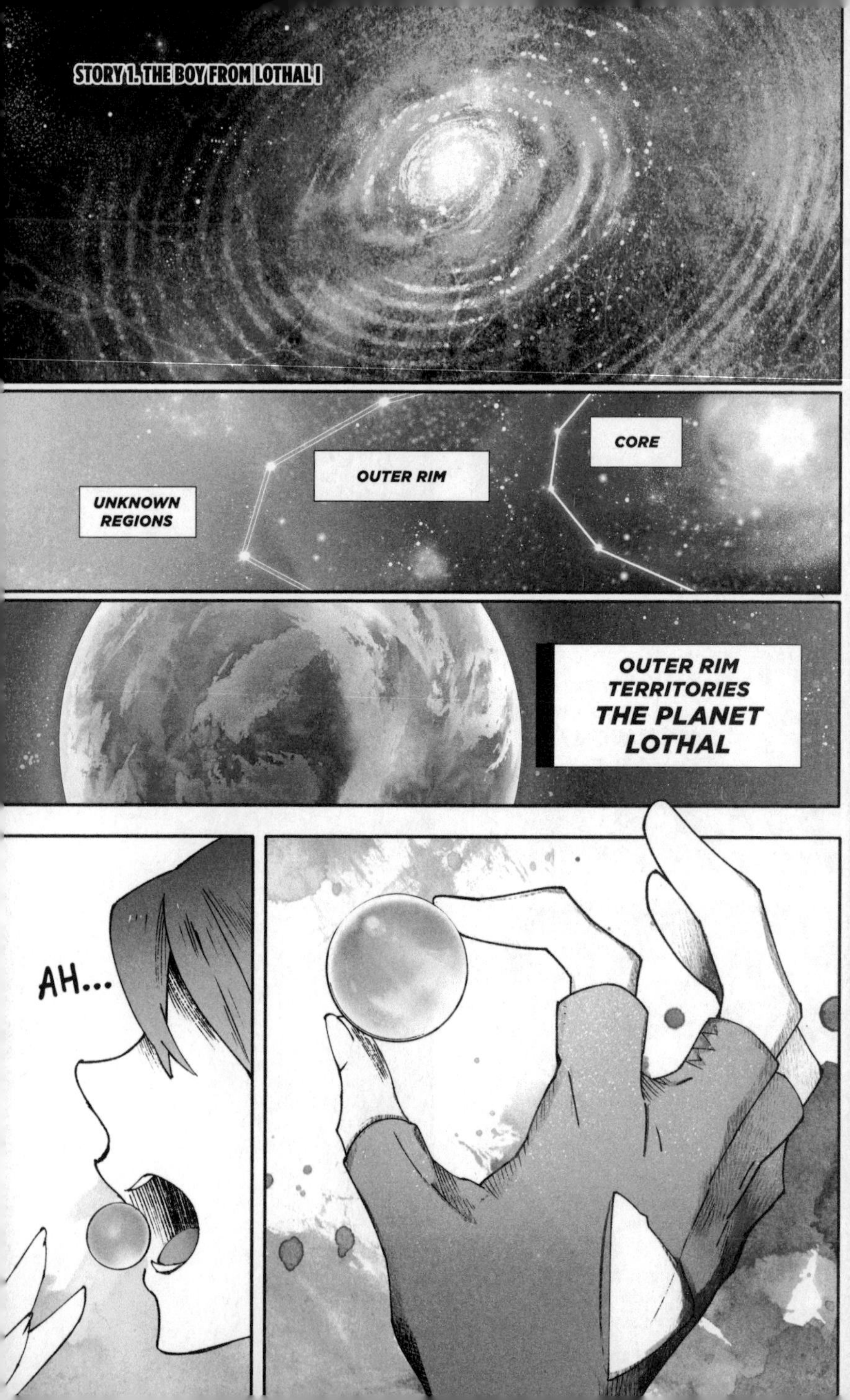
STORY 1. THE BOY FROM LOTHAL I
CORE
OUTER RIM
UNKNOWN REGIONS
OUTER RIM TERRITORIES THE PLANET LOTHAL
AH...

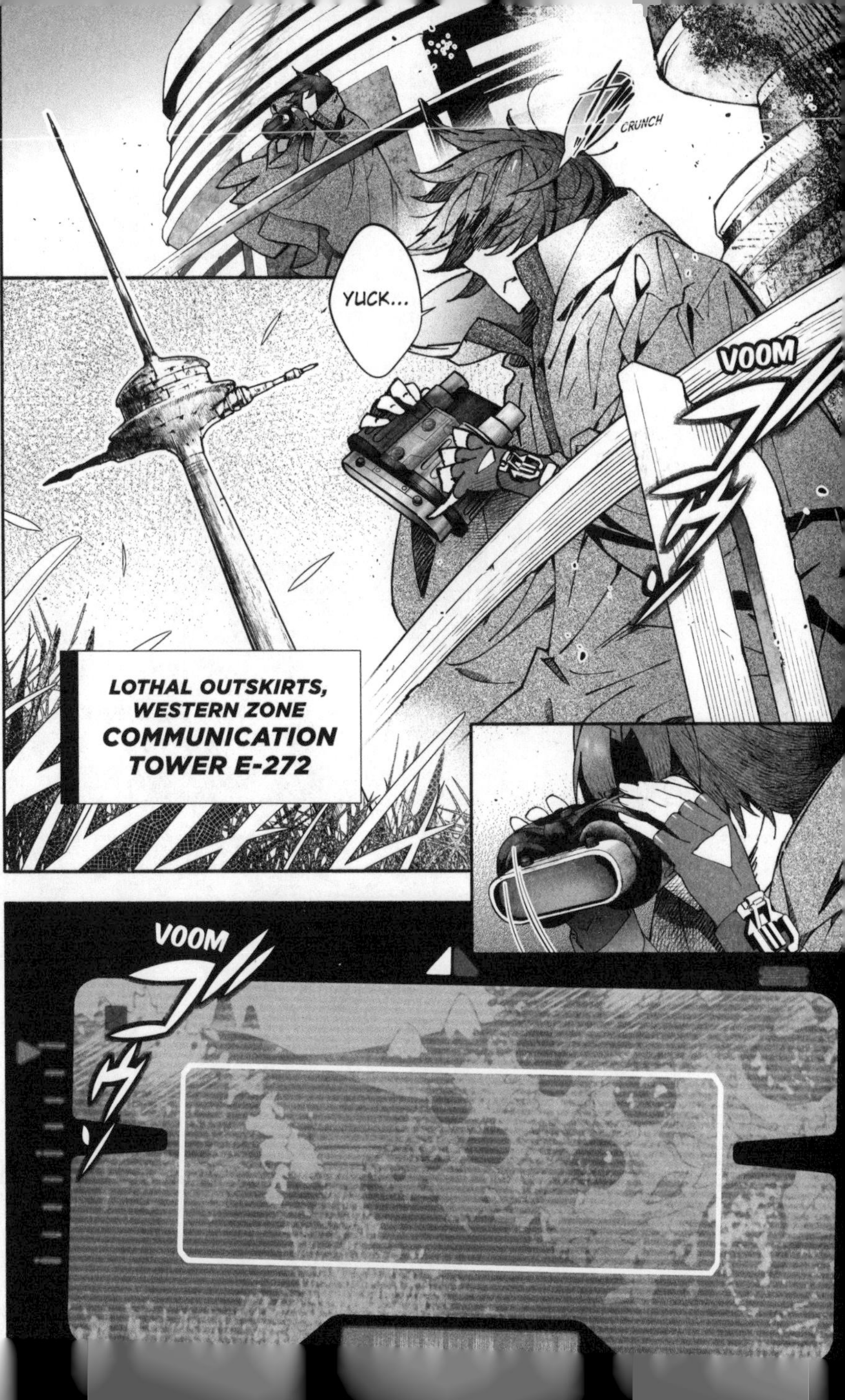
CRUNCH
YUCK...
VOOM
LOTHAL OUTSKIRTS, WESTERN ZONE
COMMUNICATION TOWER E-272
VOOM

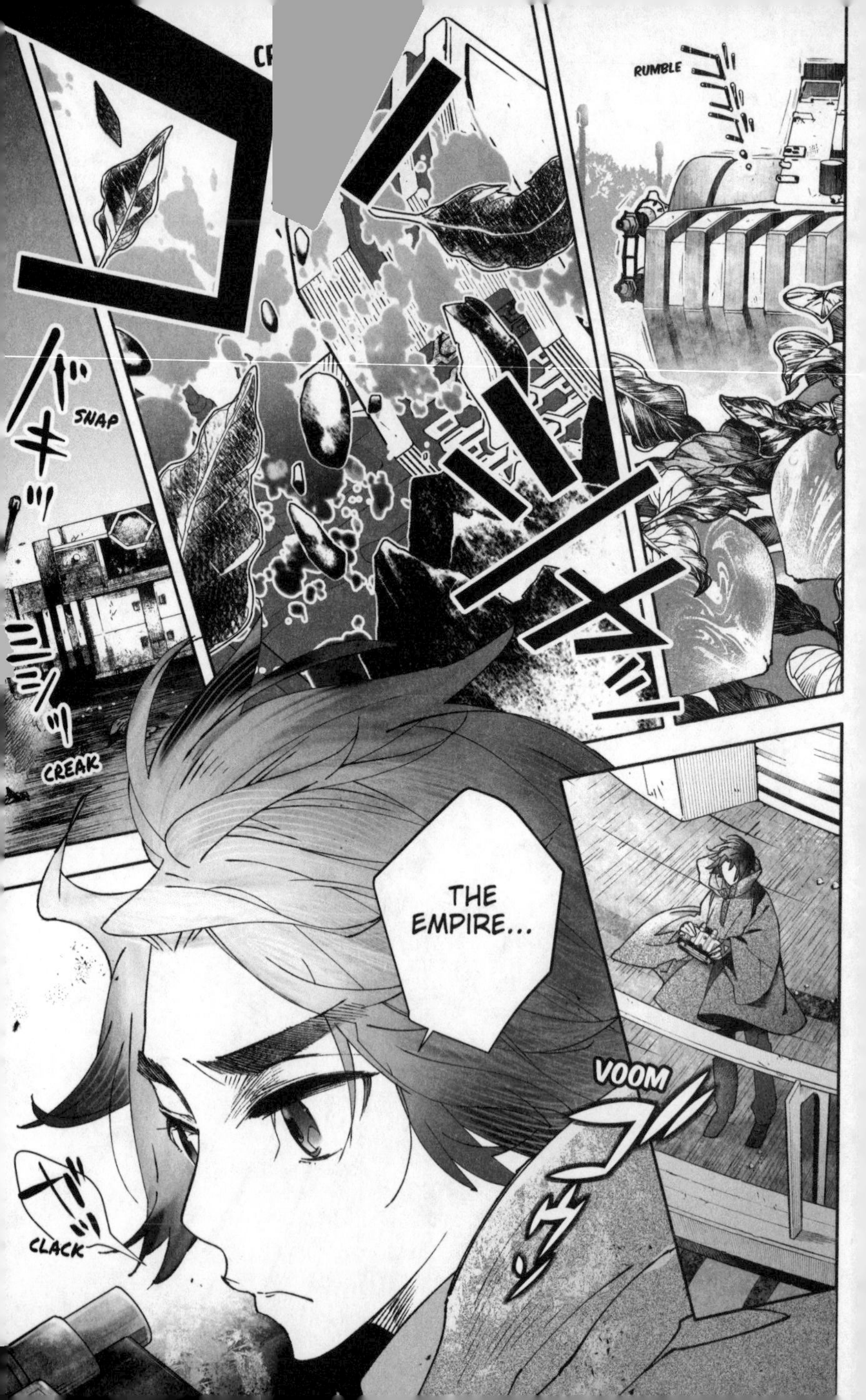

RUMBLE
CR
SNAP
CREAK
THE EMPIRE...
VOOM
CLACK

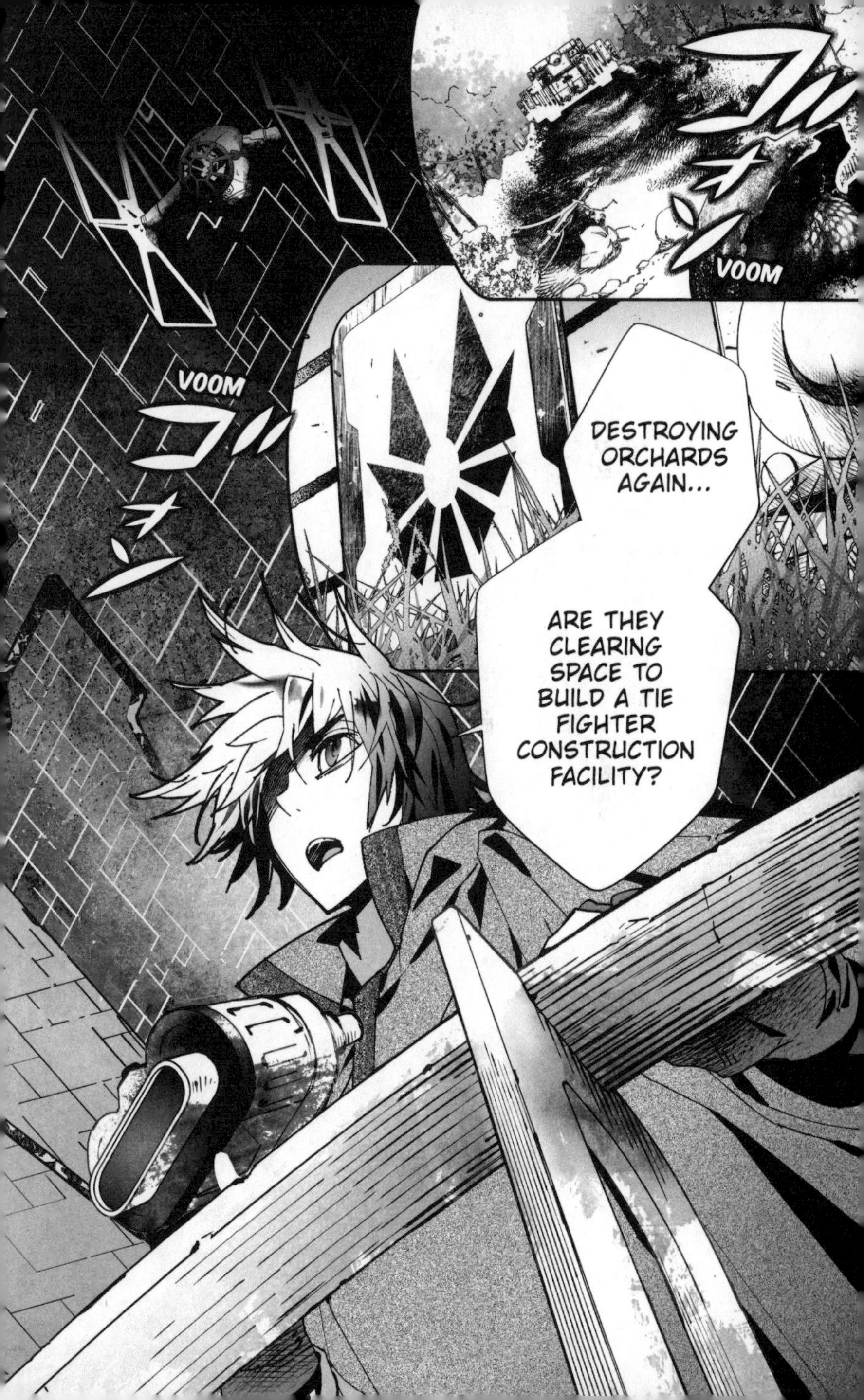
VOOM
DESTROYING ORCHARDS AGAIN...
ARE THEY CLEARING SPACE TO BUILD A TIE FIGHTER CONSTRUCTION FACILITY?
VOOM

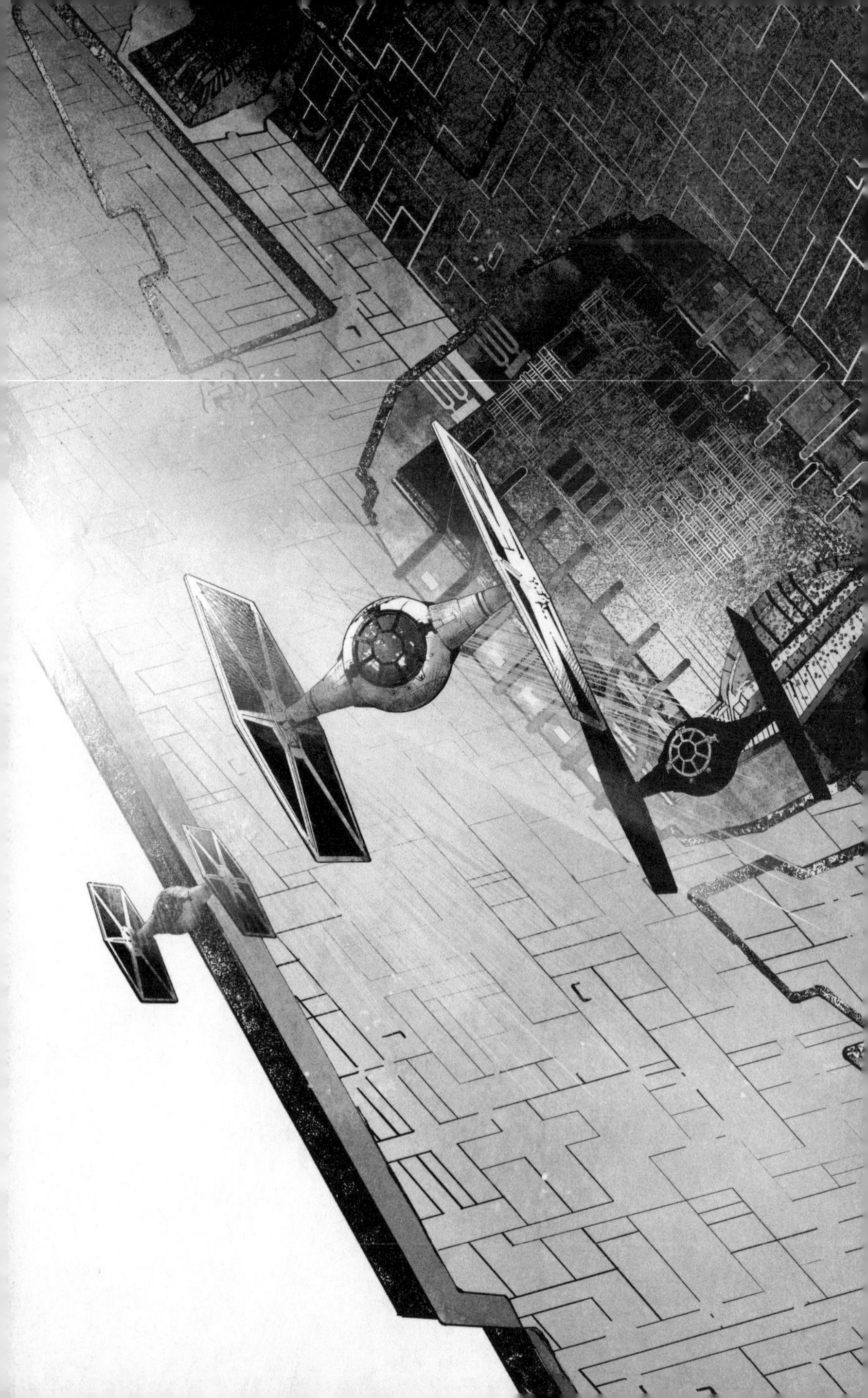

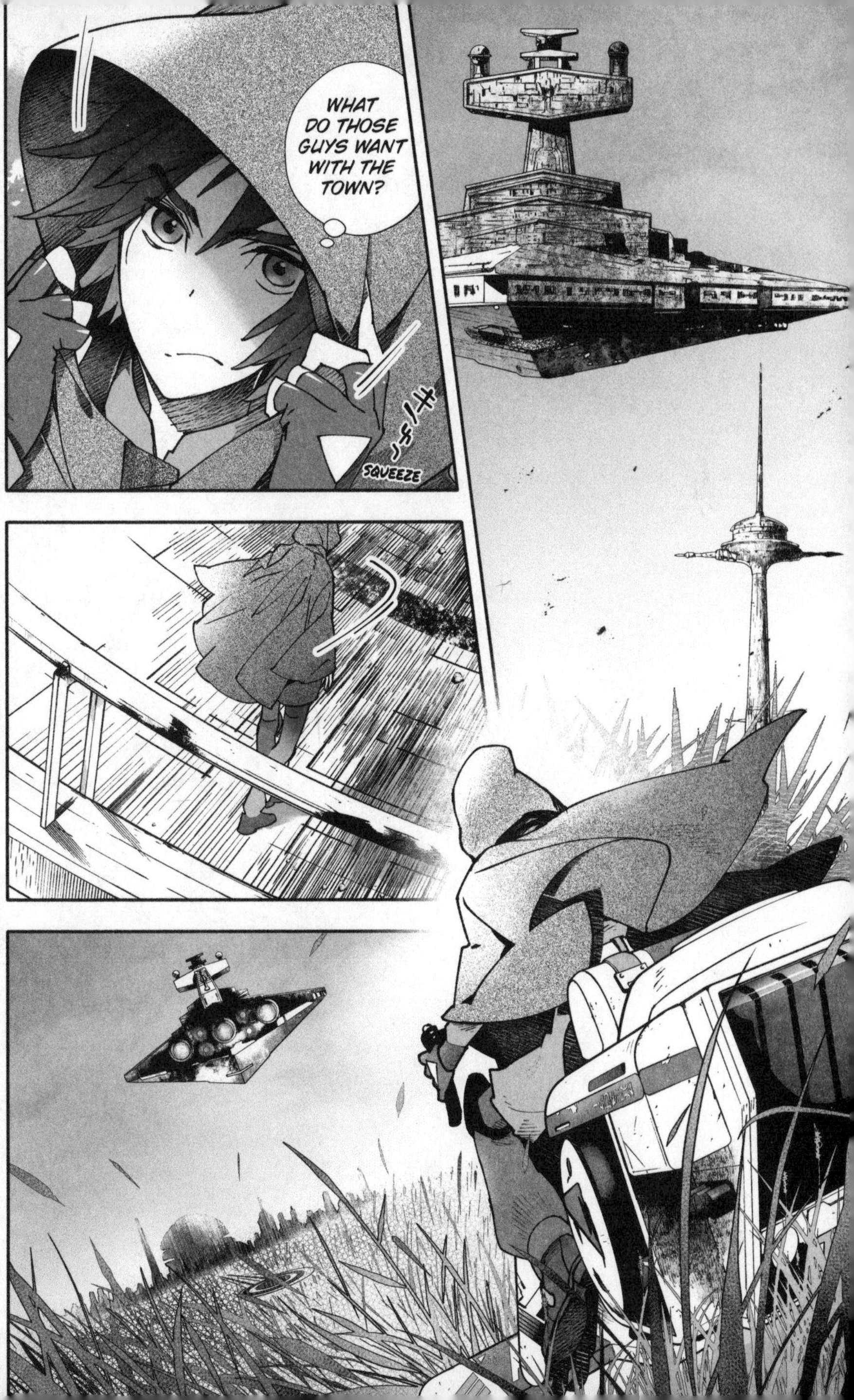
WHAT DO THOSE GUYS WANT WITH THE TOWN?
キュッ
SQUEEZE

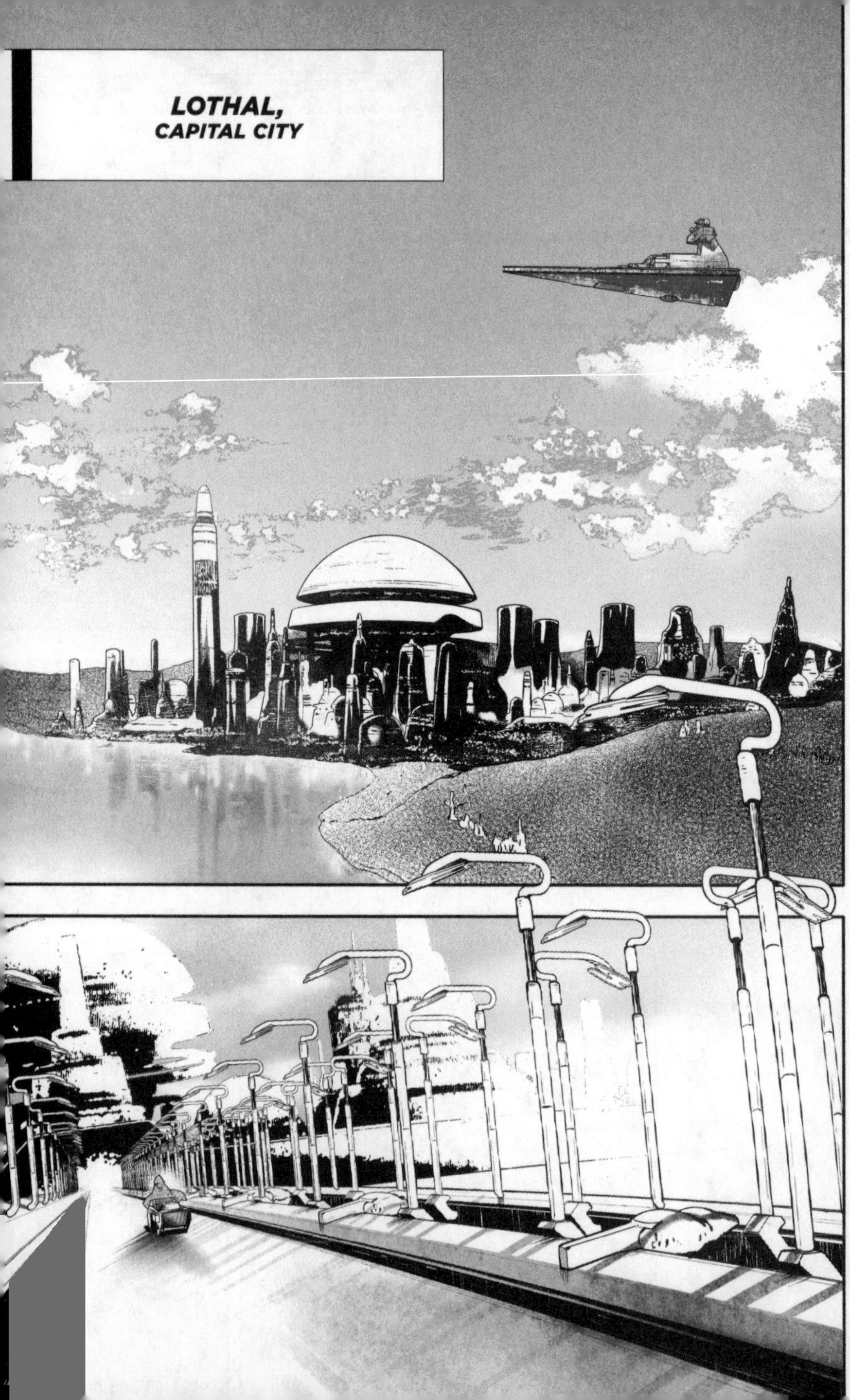
LOTHAL,
CAPITAL CITY

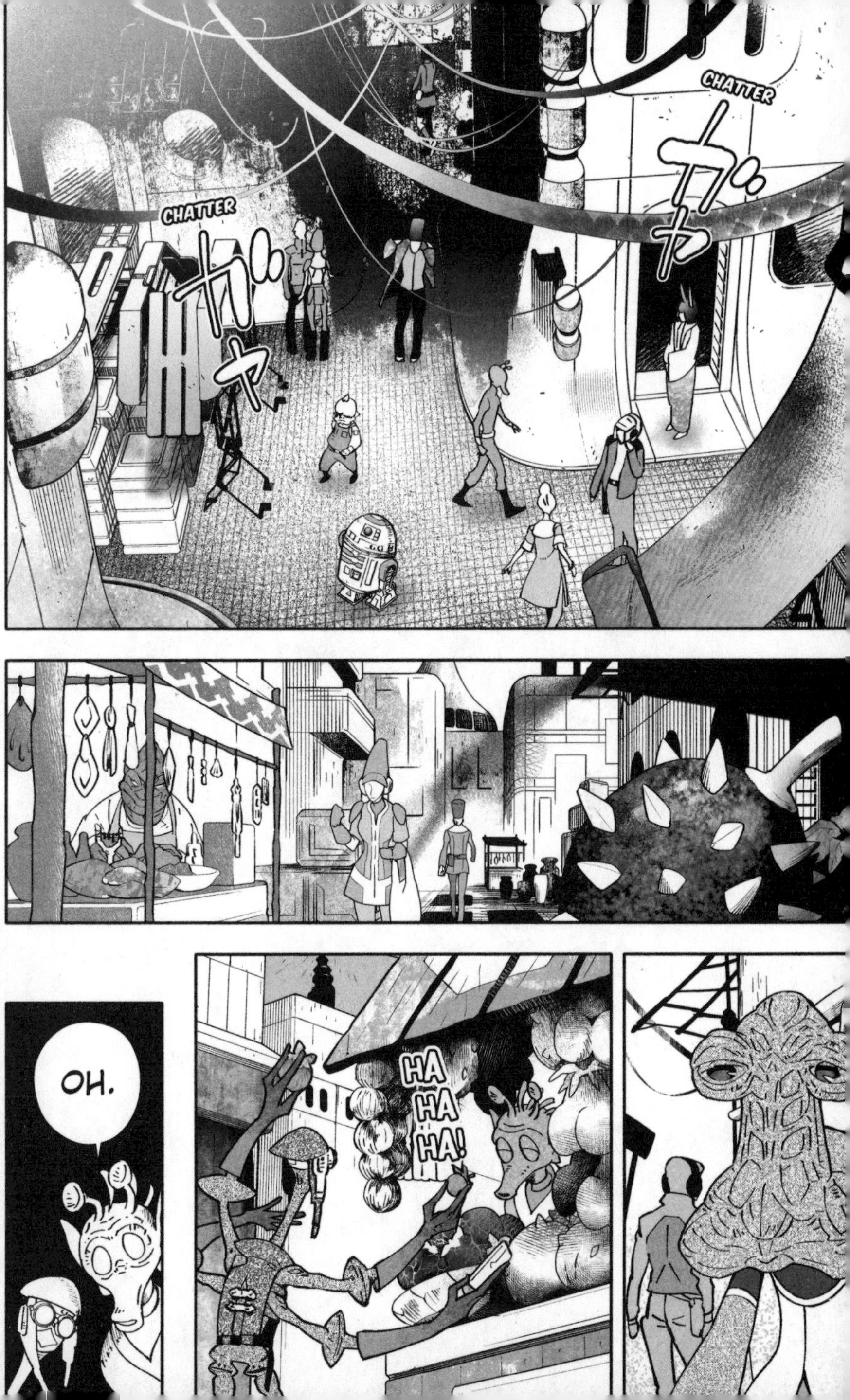
CHATTER
CHATTER
HA HA HA!
OH.

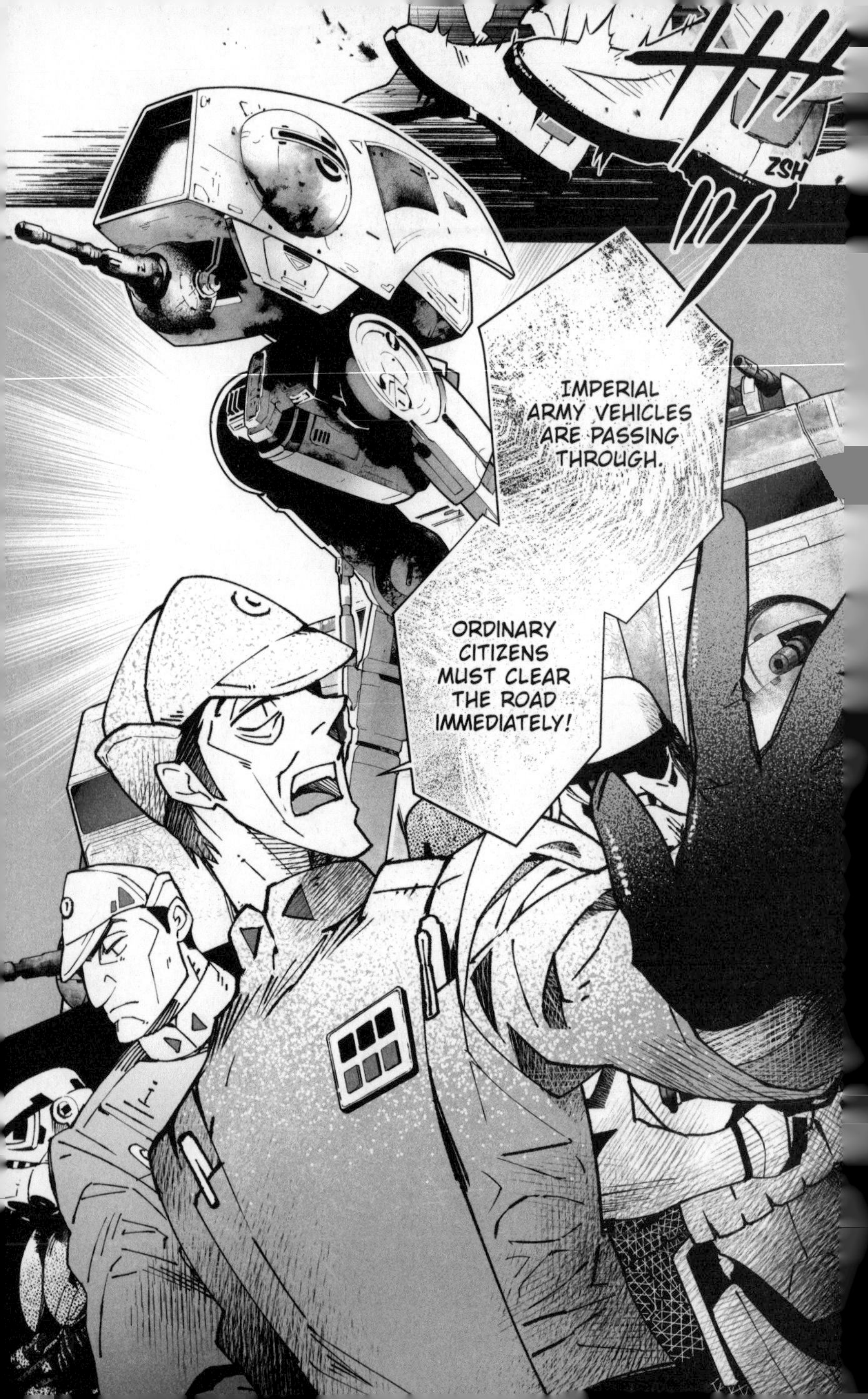
ZSH
IMPERIAL ARMY VEHICLES ARE PASSING THROUGH.
ORDINARY CITIZENS MUST CLEAR THE ROAD IMMEDIATELY!

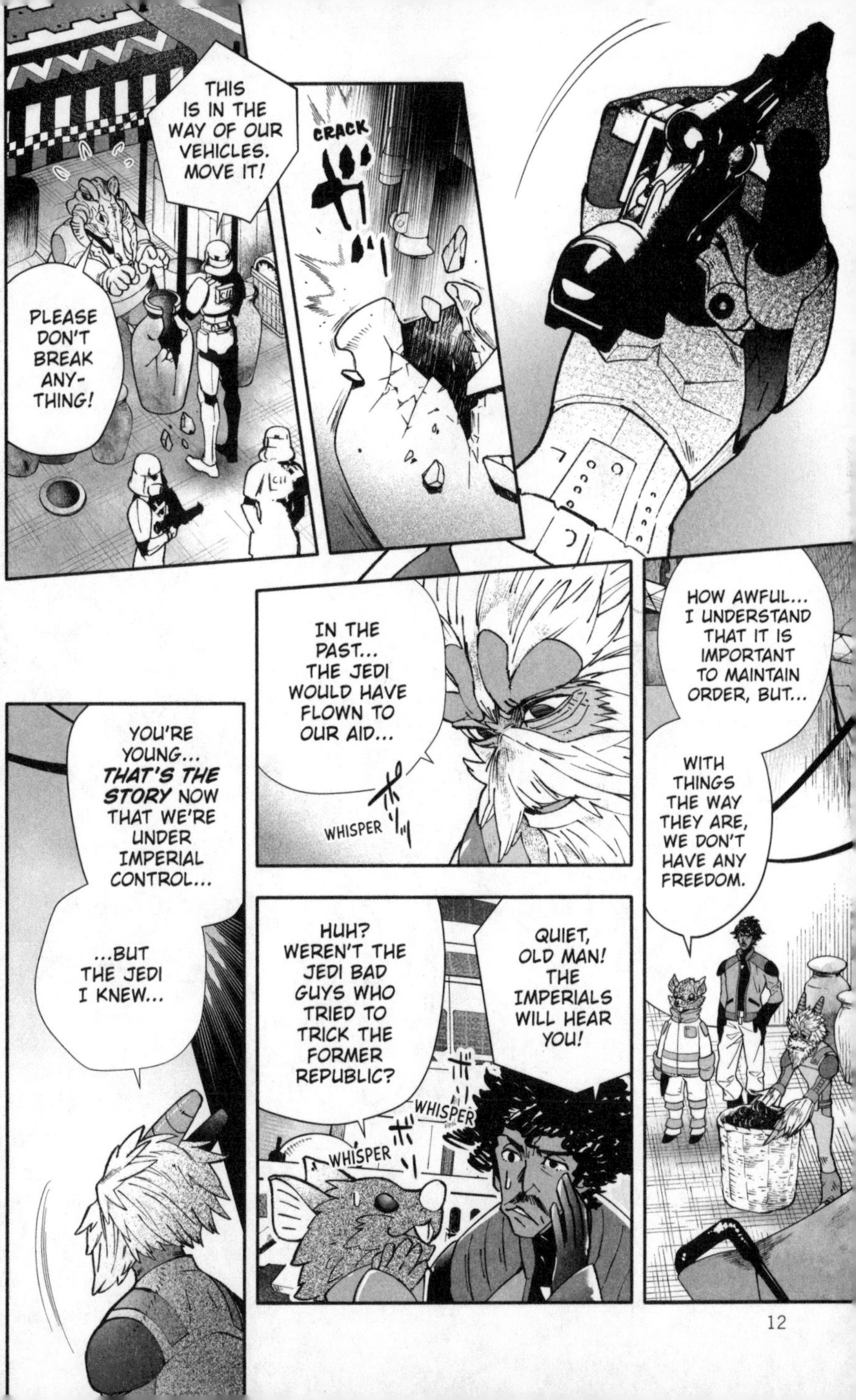
CRACK
THIS IS IN THE WAY OF OUR VEHICLES. MOVE IT!
PLEASE DON'T BREAK ANY-THING!
HOW AWFUL... I UNDERSTAND THAT IT IS IMPORTANT TO MAINTAIN ORDER, BUT...
WITH THINGS THE WAY THEY ARE, WE DON'T HAVE ANY FREEDOM.
IN THE PAST... THE JEDI WOULD HAVE FLOWN TO OUR AID...
WHISPER
QUIET, OLD MAN! THE IMPERIALS WILL HEAR YOU!
HUH? WEREN'T THE JEDI BAD GUYS WHO TRIED TO TRICK THE FORMER REPUBLIC?
WHISPER
WHISPER
YOU'RE YOUNG... ***THAT'S THE STORY*** NOW THAT WE'RE UNDER IMPERIAL CONTROL...
...BUT THE JEDI I KNEW...

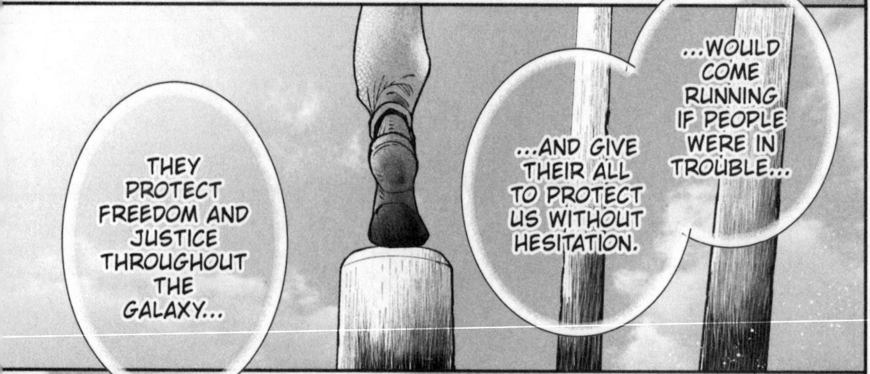
...WOULD COME RUNNING IF PEOPLE WERE IN TROUBLE...
...AND GIVE THEIR ALL TO PROTECT US WITHOUT HESITATION.
THEY PROTECT FREEDOM AND JUSTICE THROUGHOUT THE GALAXY...

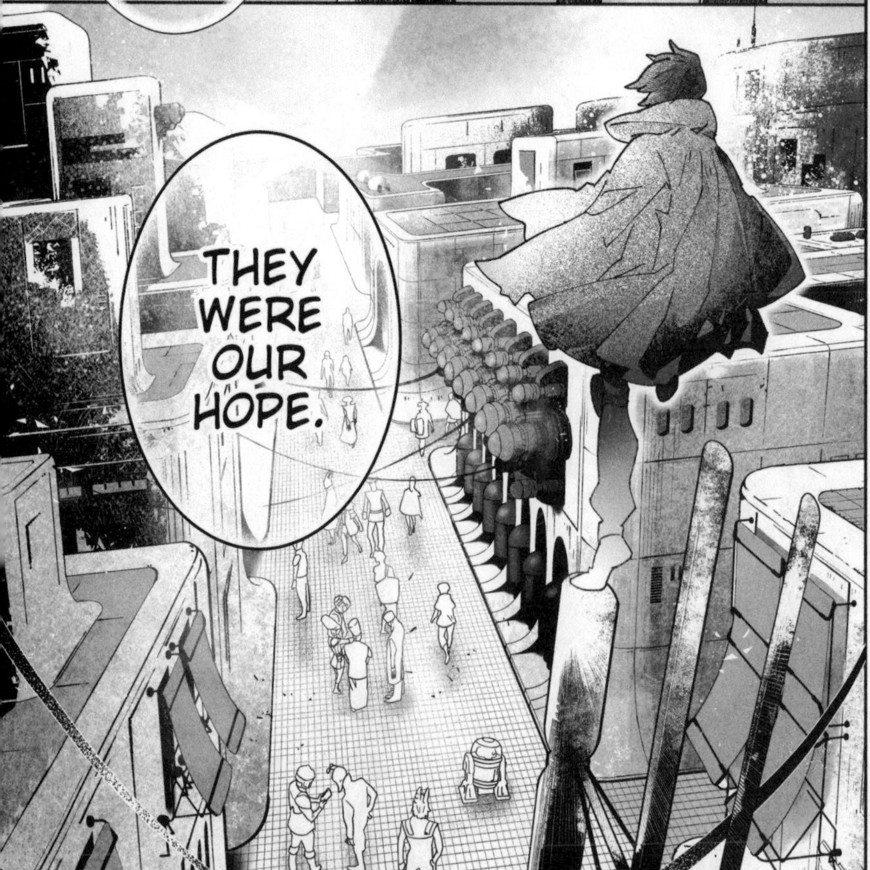
THEY WERE OUR HOPE.

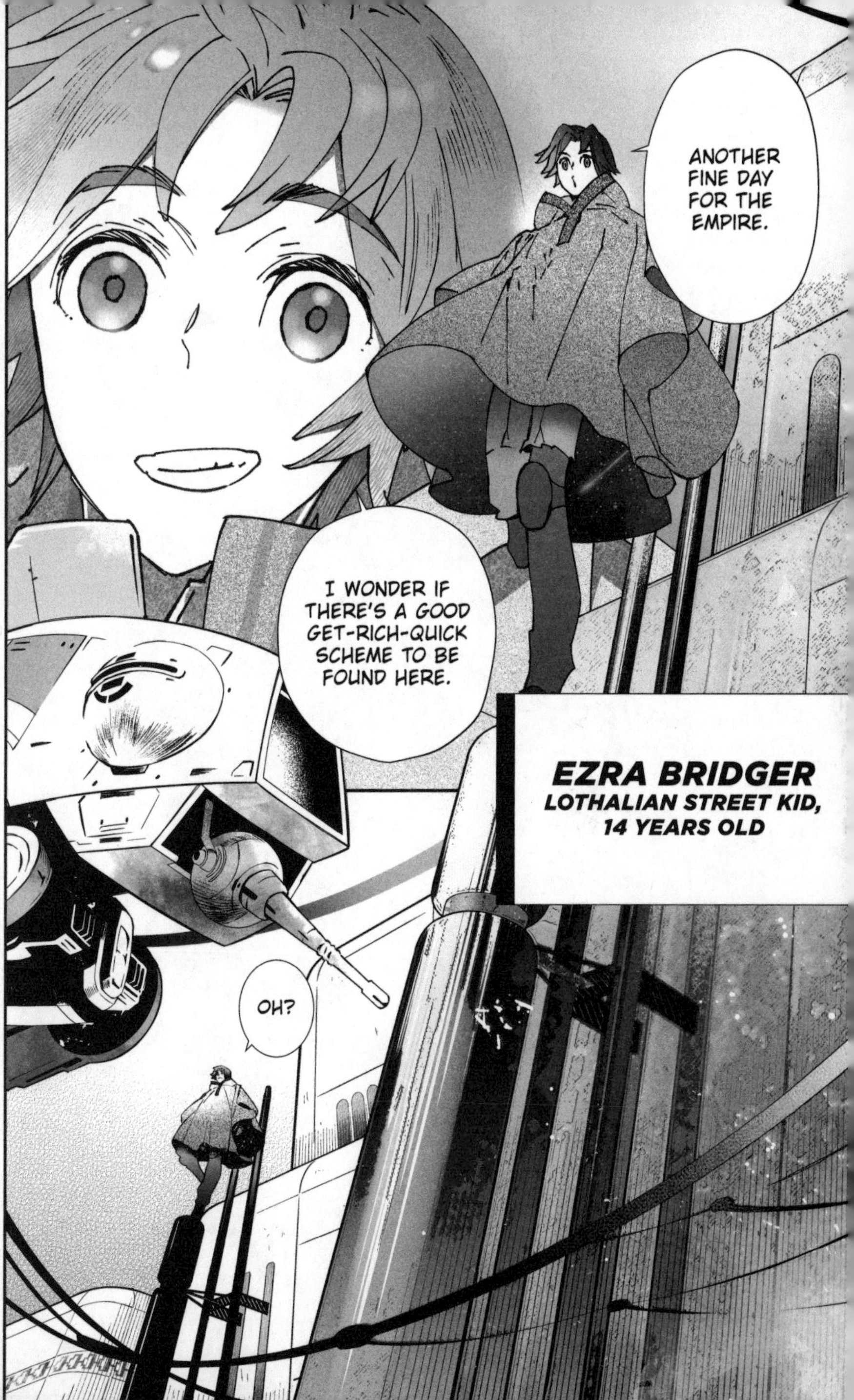
ANOTHER FINE DAY FOR THE EMPIRE.
I WONDER IF THERE'S A GOOD GET-RICH-QUICK SCHEME TO BE FOUND HERE.
EZRA BRIDGER
LOTHALIAN STREET KID, 14 YEARS OLD
OH?

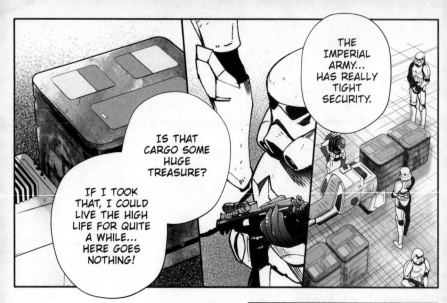

THE IMPERIAL ARMY... HAS REALLY TIGHT SECURITY.

IS THAT CARGO SOME HUGE TREASURE?

IF I TOOK THAT, I COULD LIVE THE HIGH LIFE FOR QUITE A WHILE... HERE GOES NOTHING!

HMM?

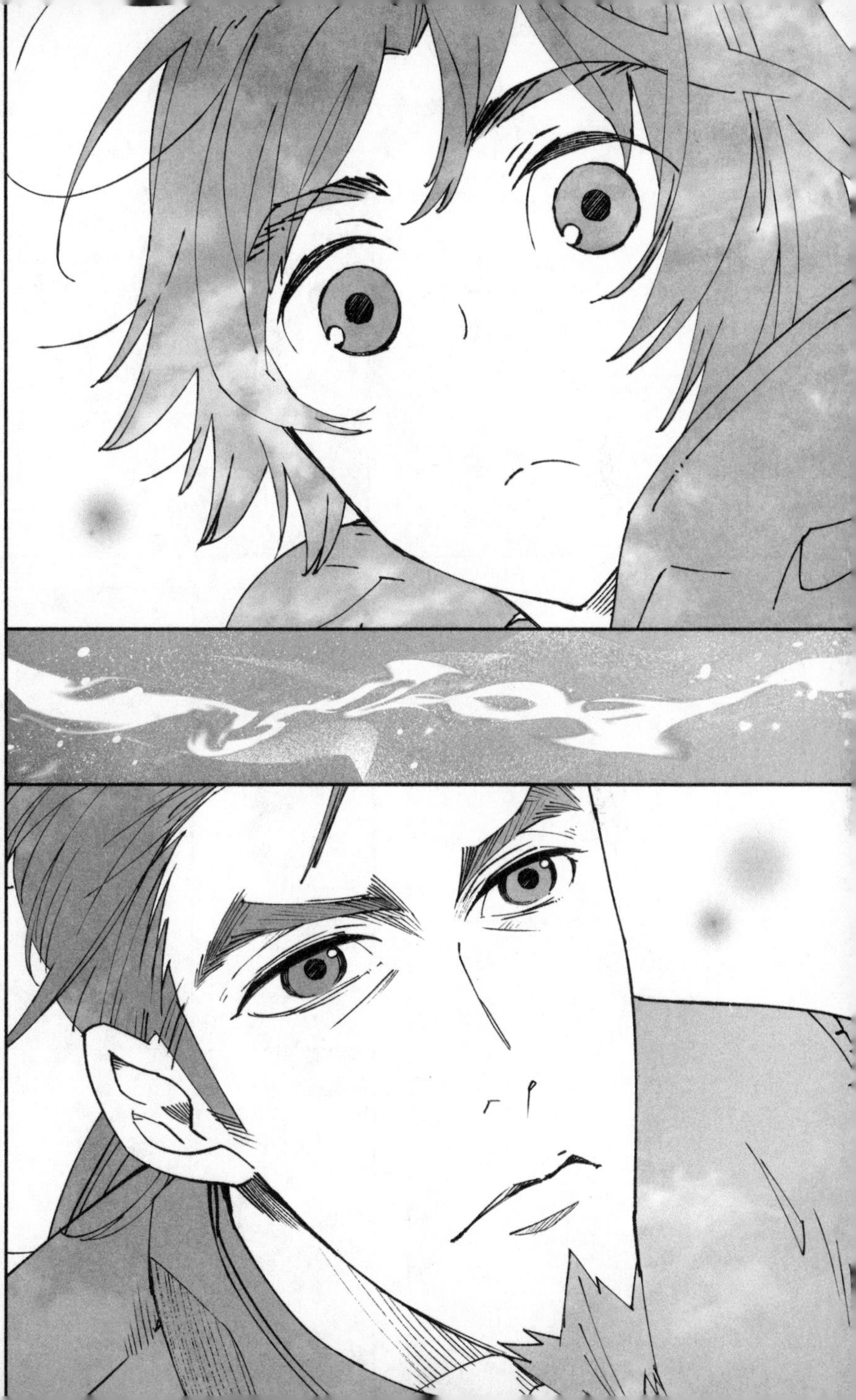

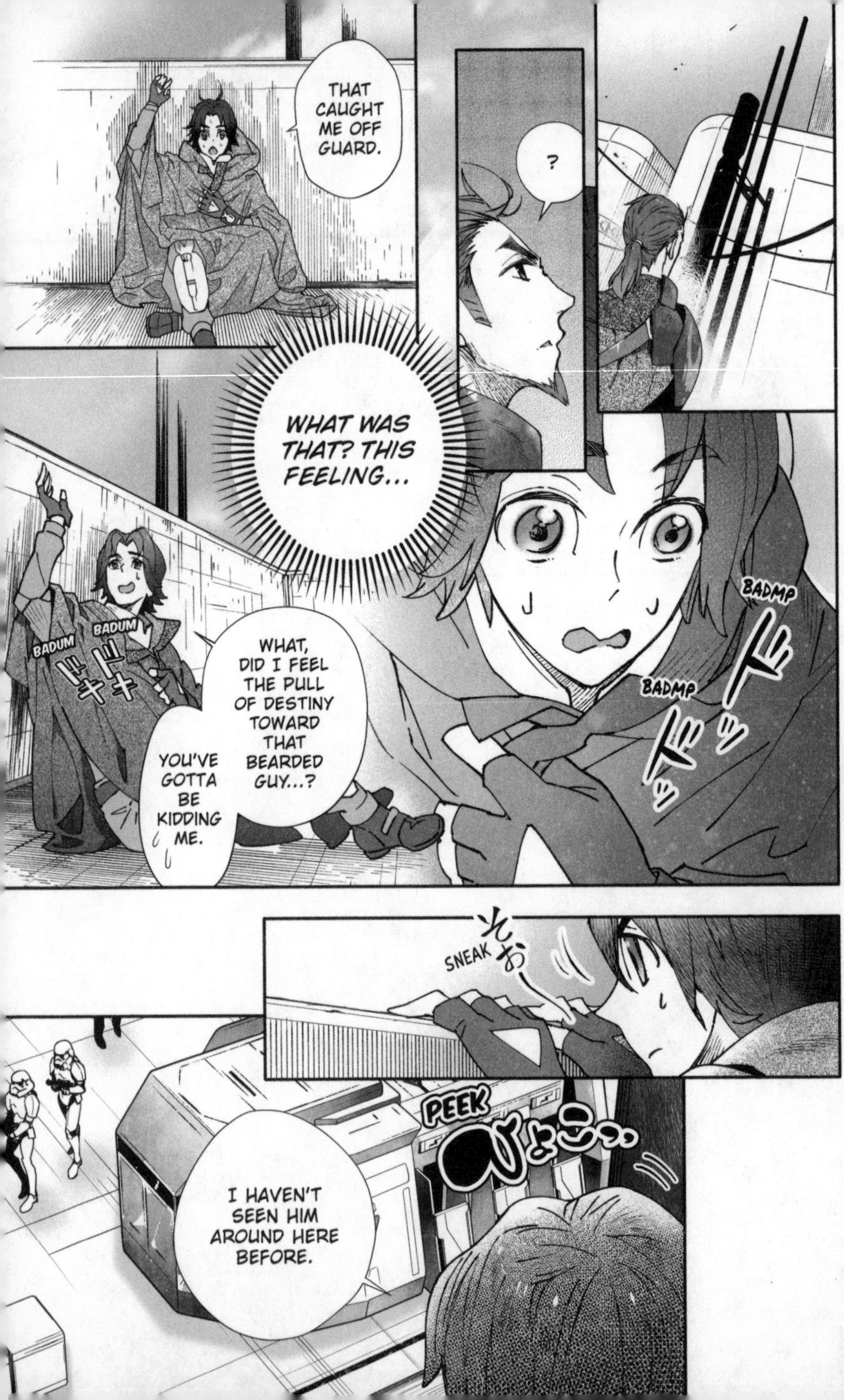
?
THAT CAUGHT ME OFF GUARD.
WHAT WAS THAT? THIS FEELING...
BADMP
ドッ
BADMP
ドッ
BADUM
ドキ
BADUM
ドキ
WHAT, DID I FEEL THE PULL OF DESTINY TOWARD THAT BEARDED GUY...?
YOU'VE GOTTA BE KIDDING ME.
SNEAK
そぉ
PEEK
ぴょこ
I HAVEN'T SEEN HIM AROUND HERE BEFORE.

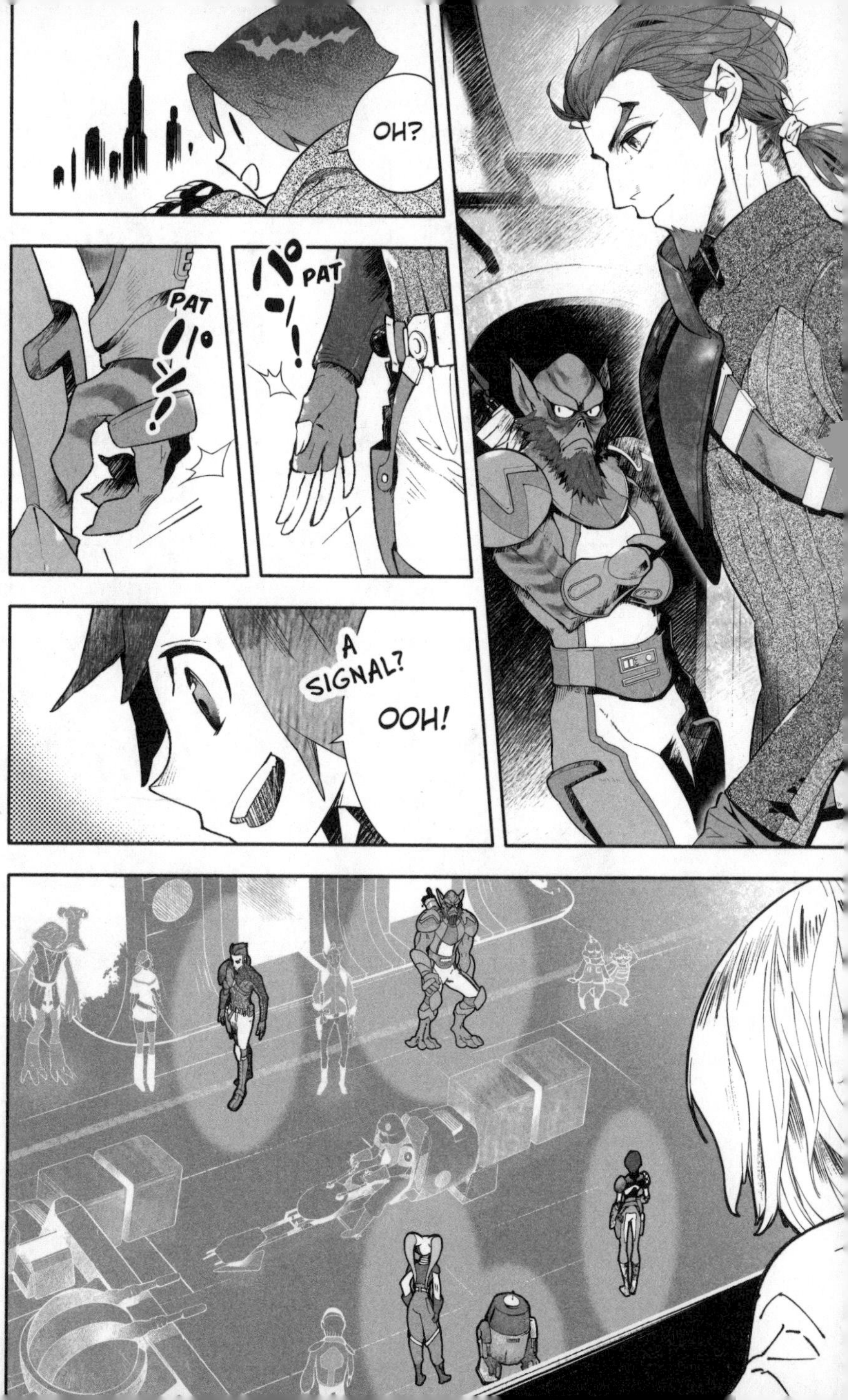
OH?
PAT
PAT
A SIGNAL?
OOH!

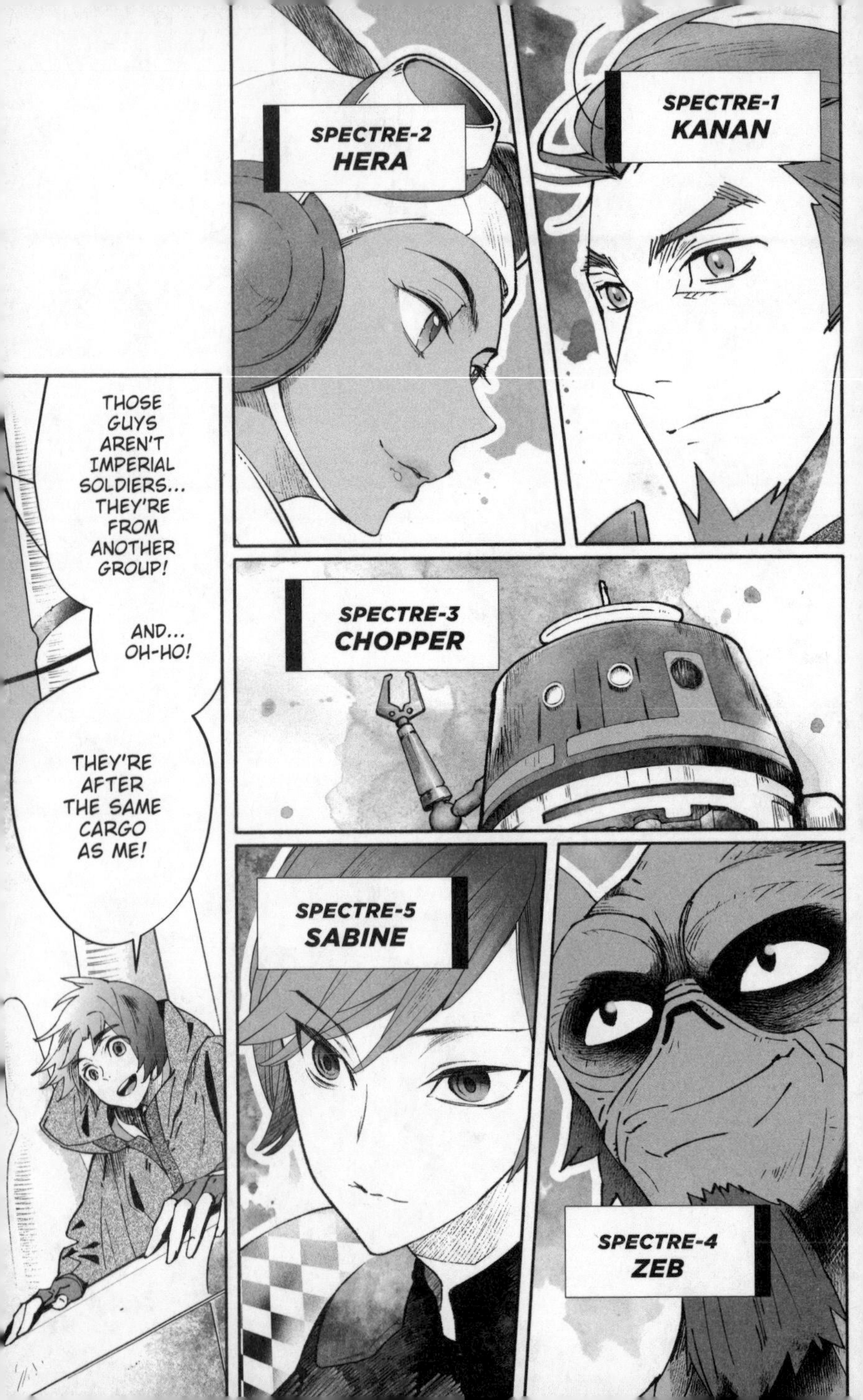
SPECTRE-1
KANAN
SPECTRE-2
HERA
SPECTRE-3
CHOPPER
SPECTRE-4
ZEB
SPECTRE-5
SABINE
THOSE GUYS AREN'T IMPERIAL SOLDIERS... THEY'RE FROM ANOTHER GROUP!
AND... OH-HO!
THEY'RE AFTER THE SAME CARGO AS ME!

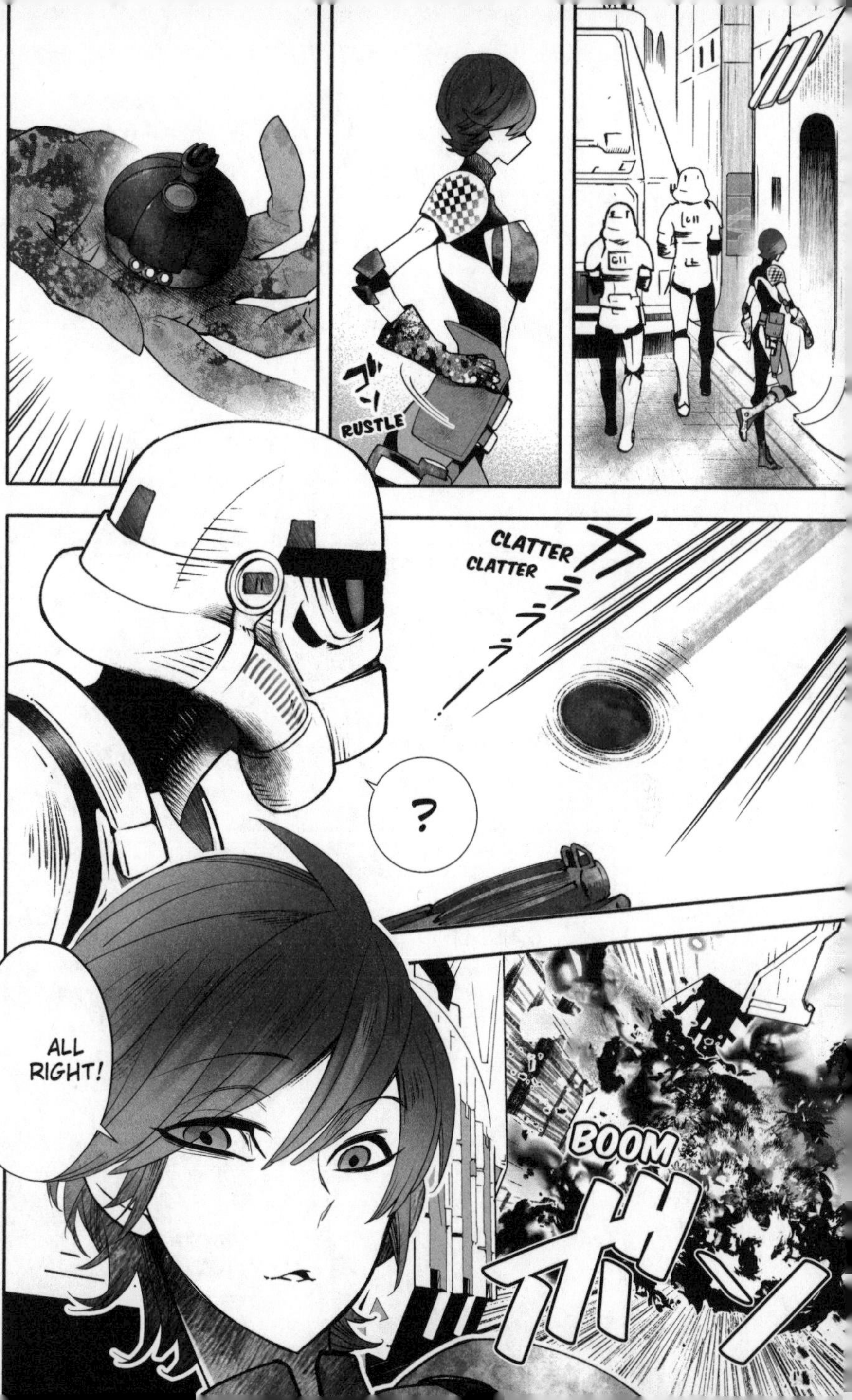
RUSTLE
CLATTER CLATTER
?
BOOM
ALL RIGHT!

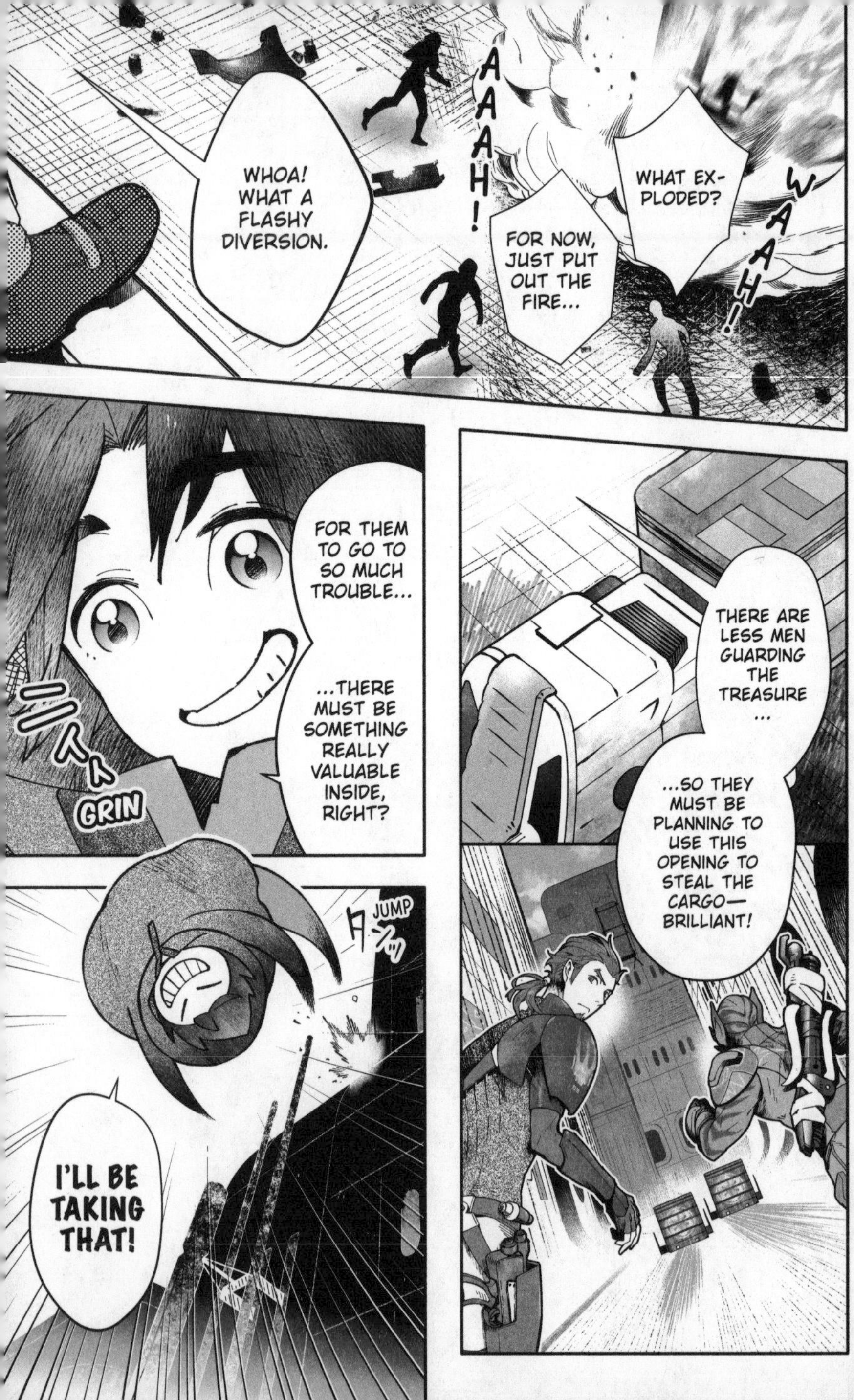
WAAAH!
WHAT EX-PLODED?
AAAAH!
FOR NOW, JUST PUT OUT THE FIRE...
WHOA! WHAT A FLASHY DIVERSION.
THERE ARE LESS MEN GUARDING THE TREASURE...
...SO THEY MUST BE PLANNING TO USE THIS OPENING TO STEAL THE CARGO— BRILLIANT!
FOR THEM TO GO TO SO MUCH TROUBLE...
...THERE MUST BE SOMETHING REALLY VALUABLE INSIDE, RIGHT?
GRIN
JUMP
I'LL BE TAKING THAT!

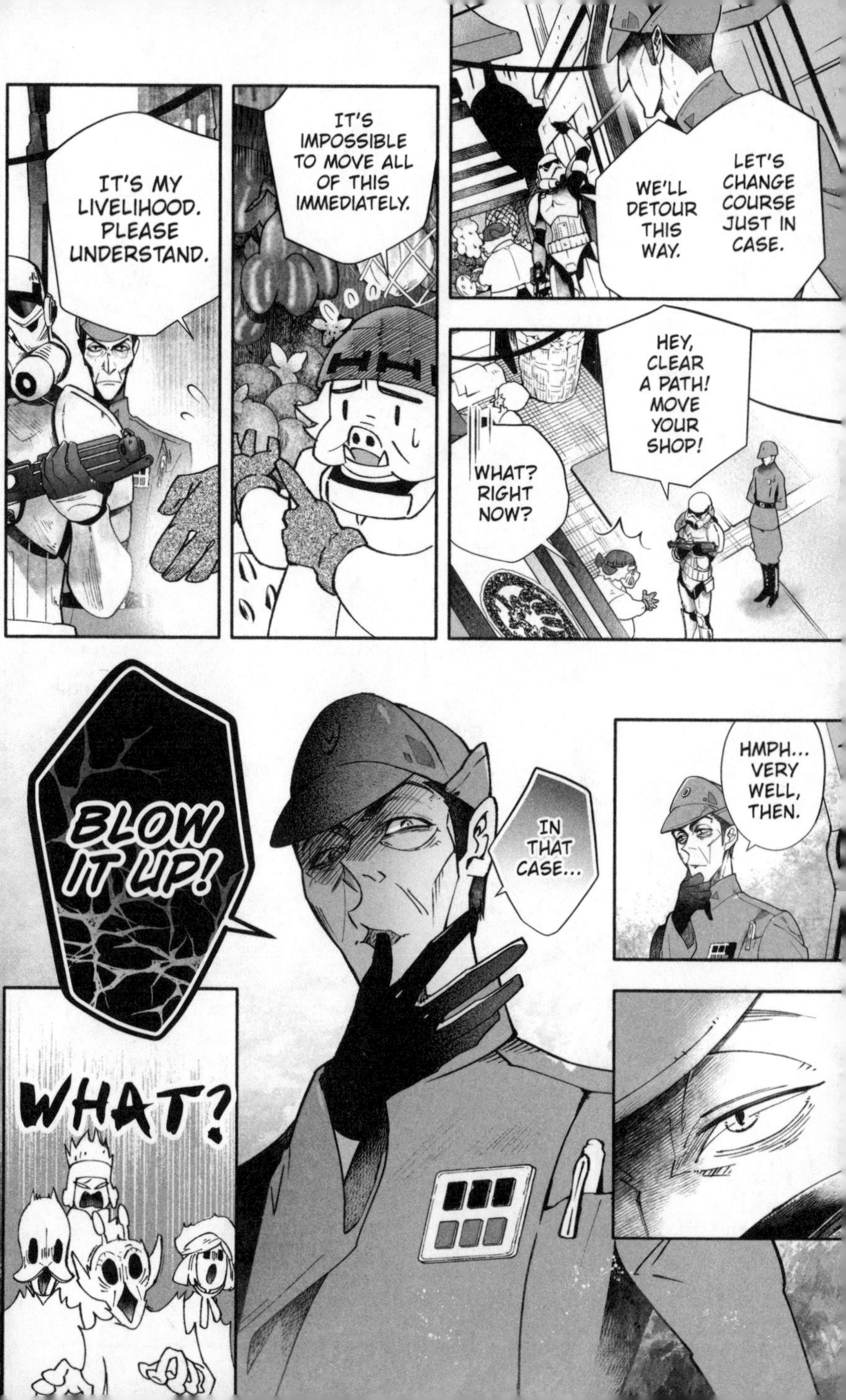
LET'S CHANGE COURSE JUST IN CASE.
WE'LL DETOUR THIS WAY.
HEY, CLEAR A PATH! MOVE YOUR SHOP!
WHAT? RIGHT NOW?
IT'S IMPOSSIBLE TO MOVE ALL OF THIS IMMEDIATELY.
IT'S MY LIVELIHOOD. PLEASE UNDERSTAND.
HMPH... VERY WELL, THEN.
IN THAT CASE...
BLOW IT UP!
WHAT?

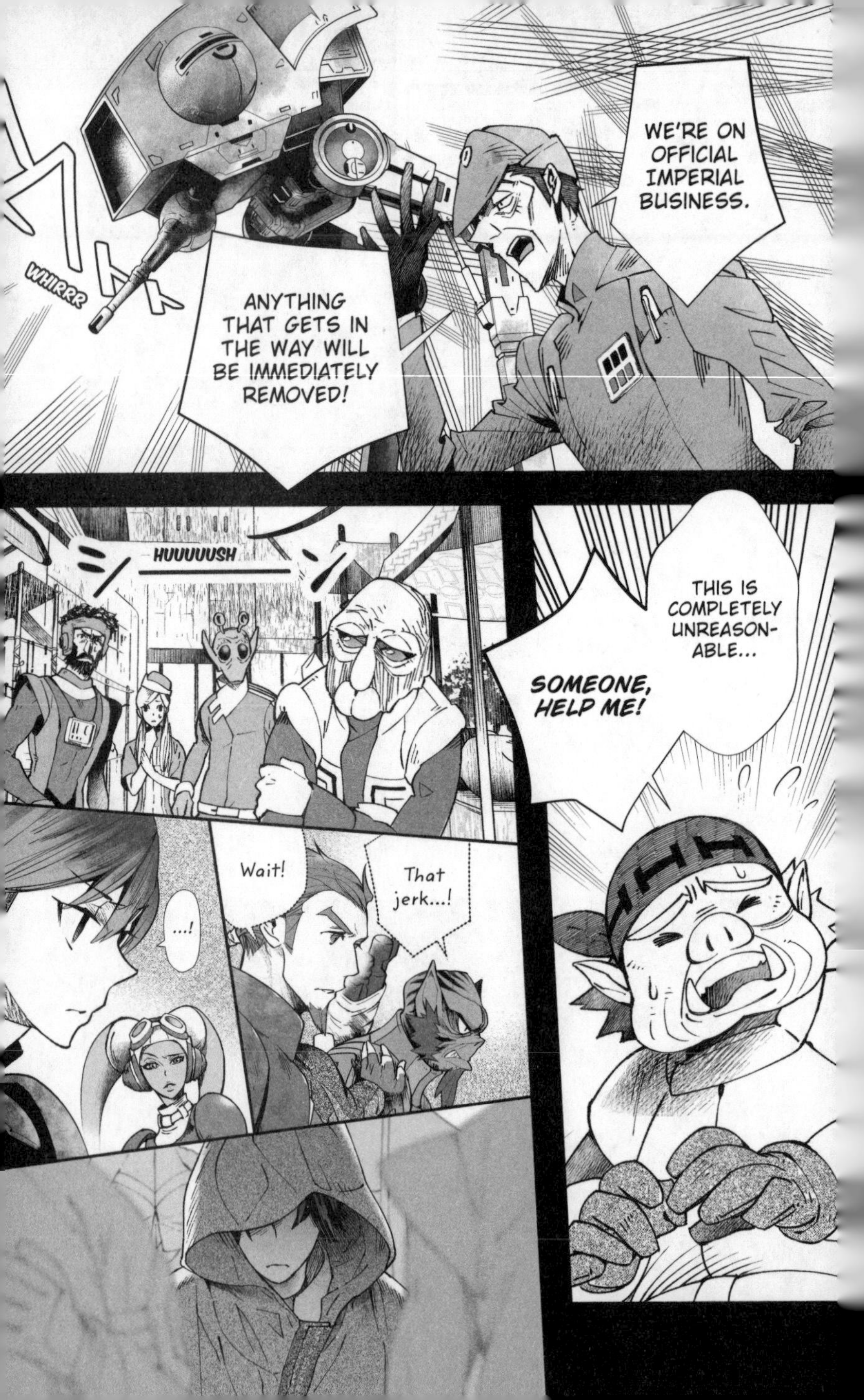
WE'RE ON OFFICIAL IMPERIAL BUSINESS.
ANYTHING THAT GETS IN THE WAY WILL BE IMMEDIATELY REMOVED!
WHIRRR
THIS IS COMPLETELY UNREASON-ABLE...
SOMEONE, HELP ME!
HUUUUUSH
That jerk...!
Wait!
...!

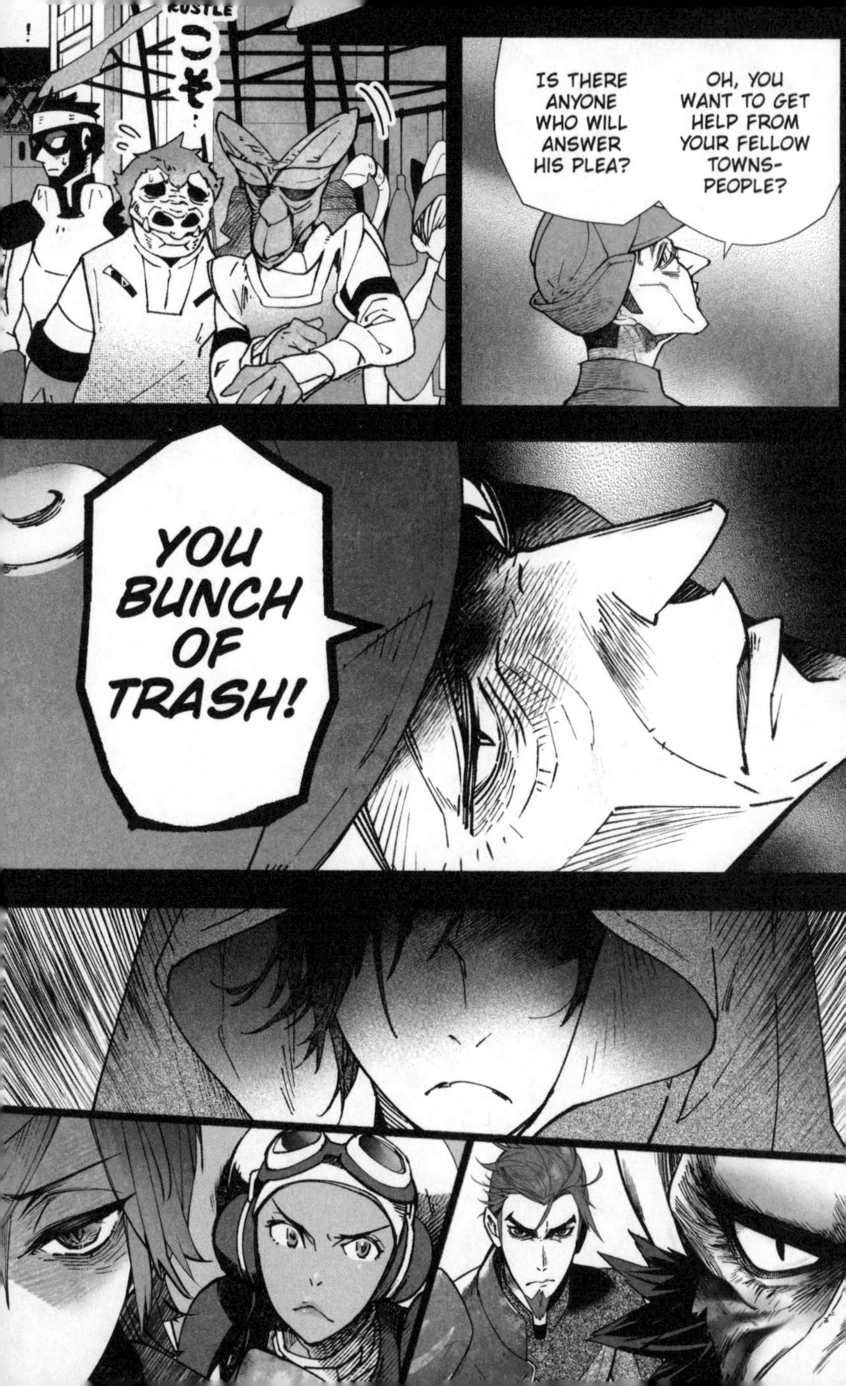
OH, YOU WANT TO GET HELP FROM YOUR FELLOW TOWNS-PEOPLE?
IS THERE ANYONE WHO WILL ANSWER HIS PLEA?
RUSTLE
こそ
!
YOU BUNCH OF TRASH!

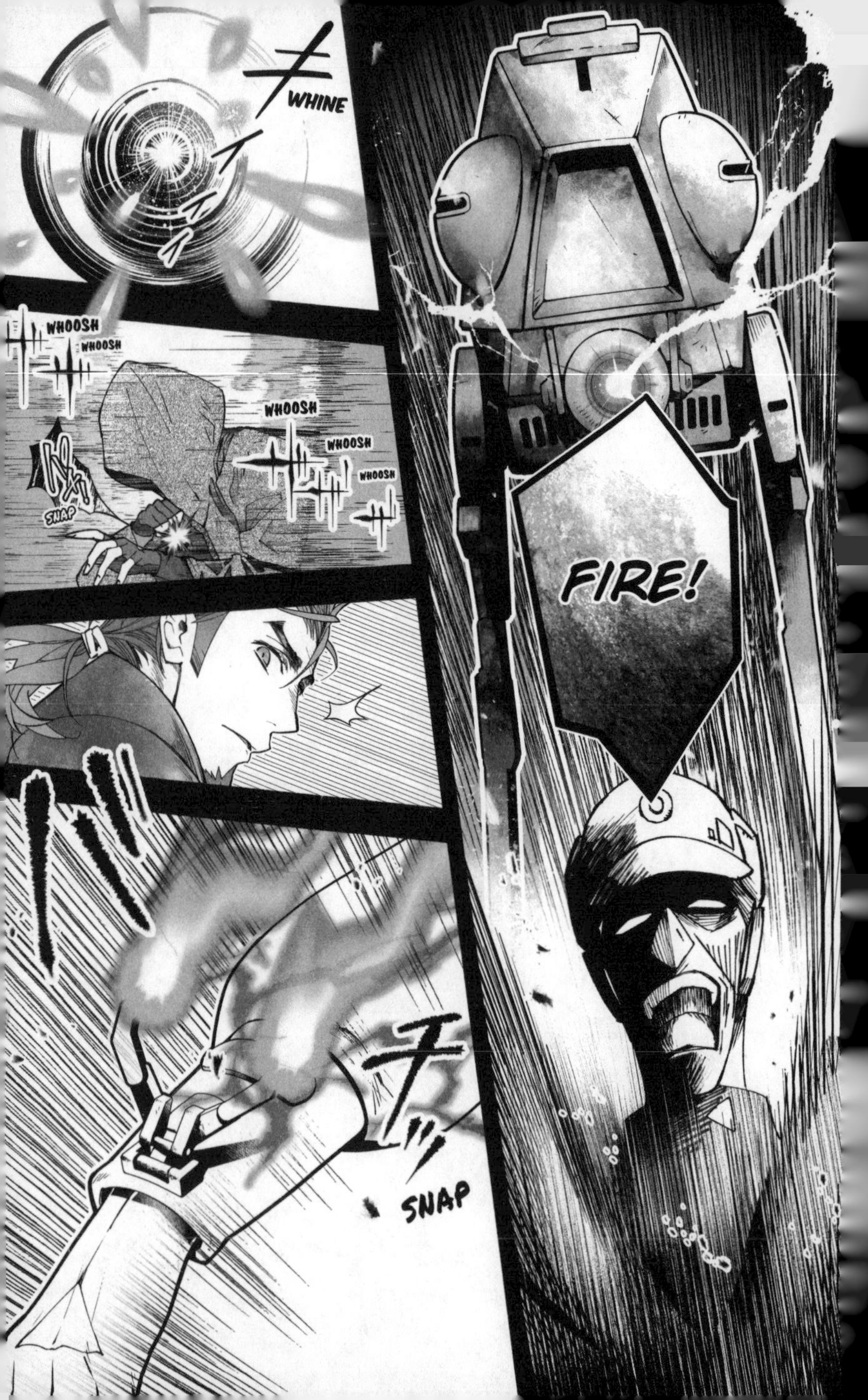
FIRE!
WHINE
WHOOSH
WHOOSH
WHOOSH
WHOOSH
WHOOSH
SNAP
SNAP

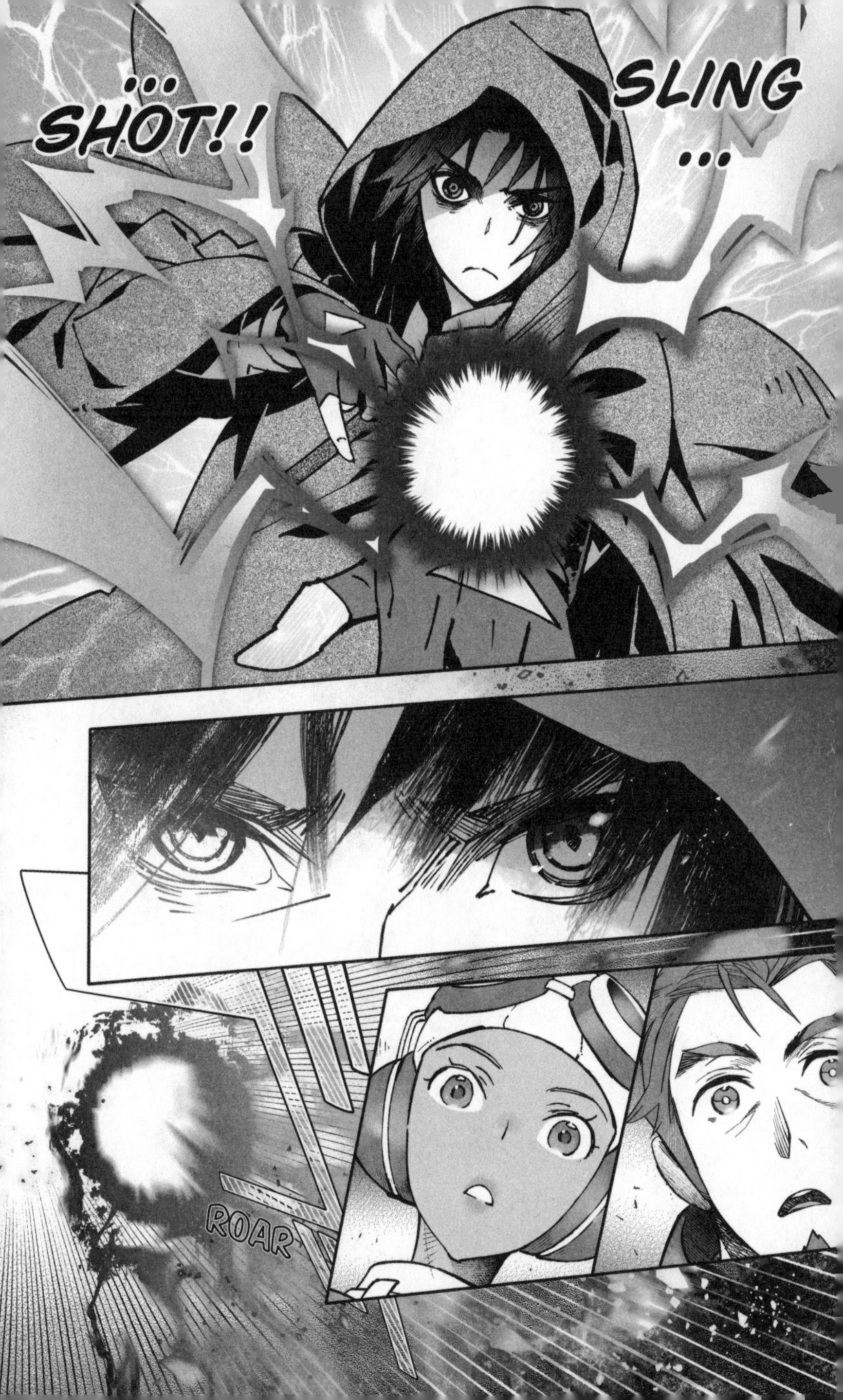
SLING
...
...
SHOT!!
ROAR

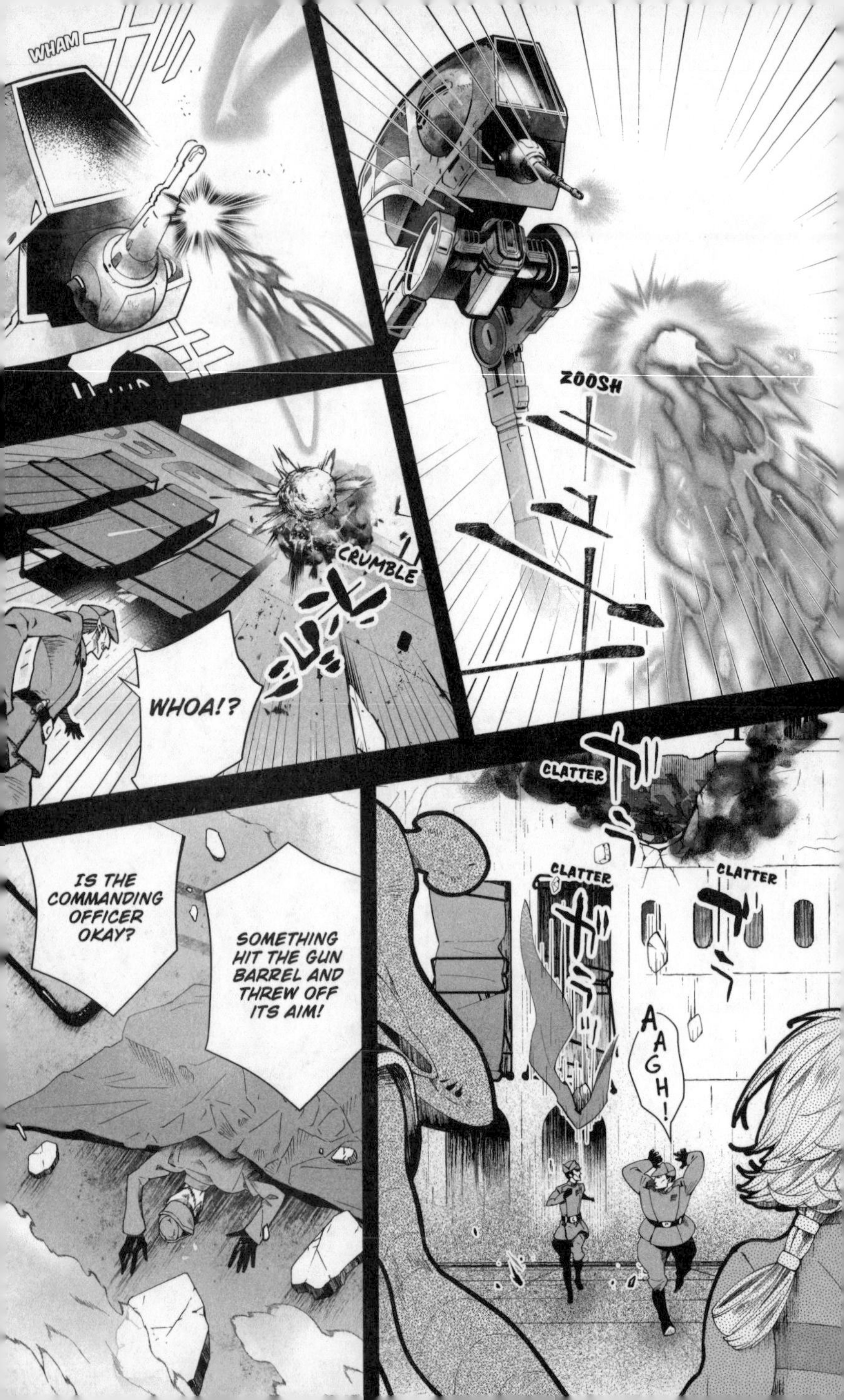
ZOOSH
WHAM
CRUMBLE
WHOA!?
CLATTER
CLATTER
CLATTER
AAGH!
IS THE COMMANDING OFFICER OKAY?
SOMETHING HIT THE GUN BARREL AND THREW OFF ITS AIM!

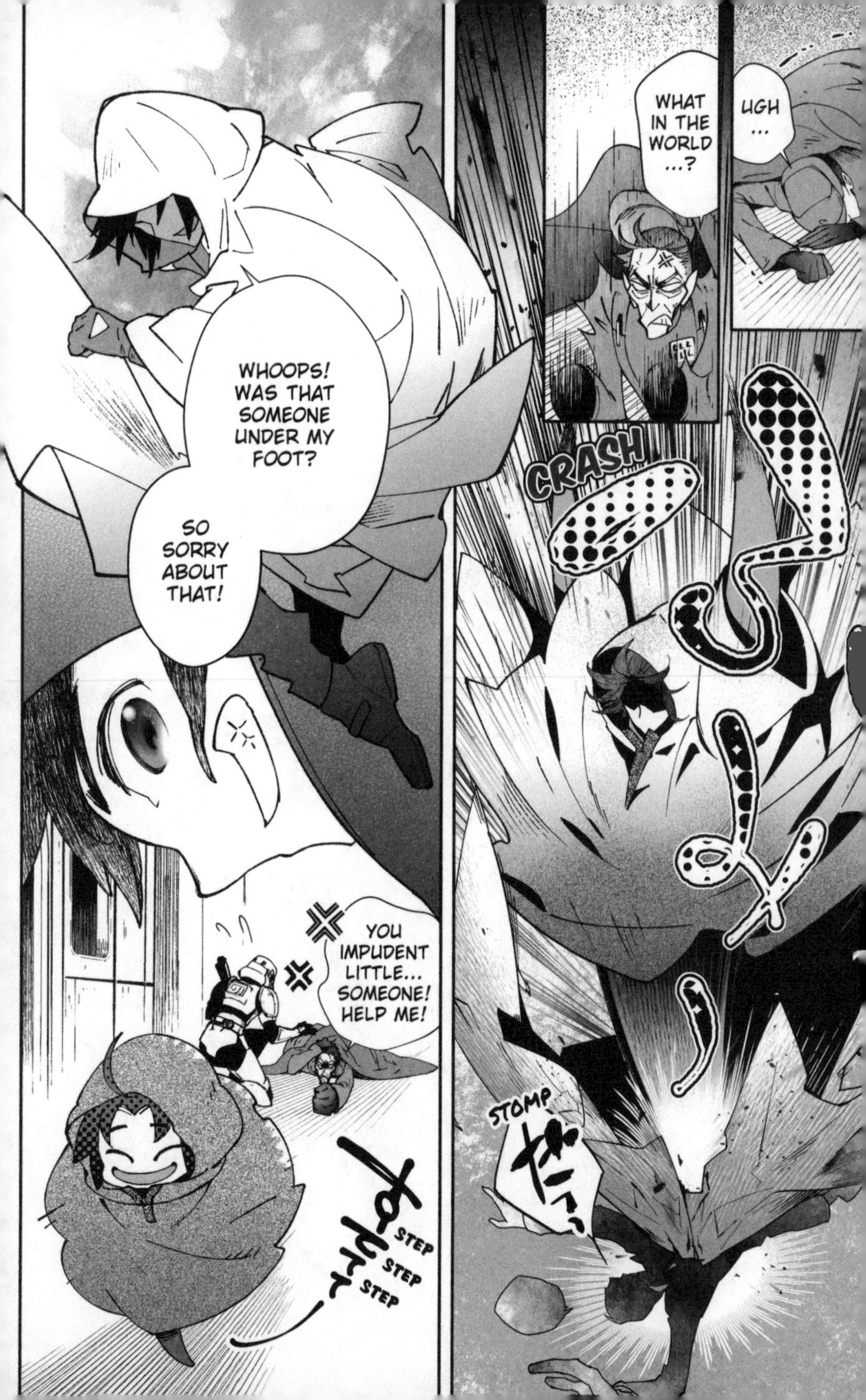
UGH ...
WHAT IN THE WORLD ...?
CRASH
STOMP
WHOOPS! WAS THAT SOMEONE UNDER MY FOOT?
SO SORRY ABOUT THAT!
YOU IMPUDENT LITTLE... SOMEONE! HELP ME!
STEP STEP STEP

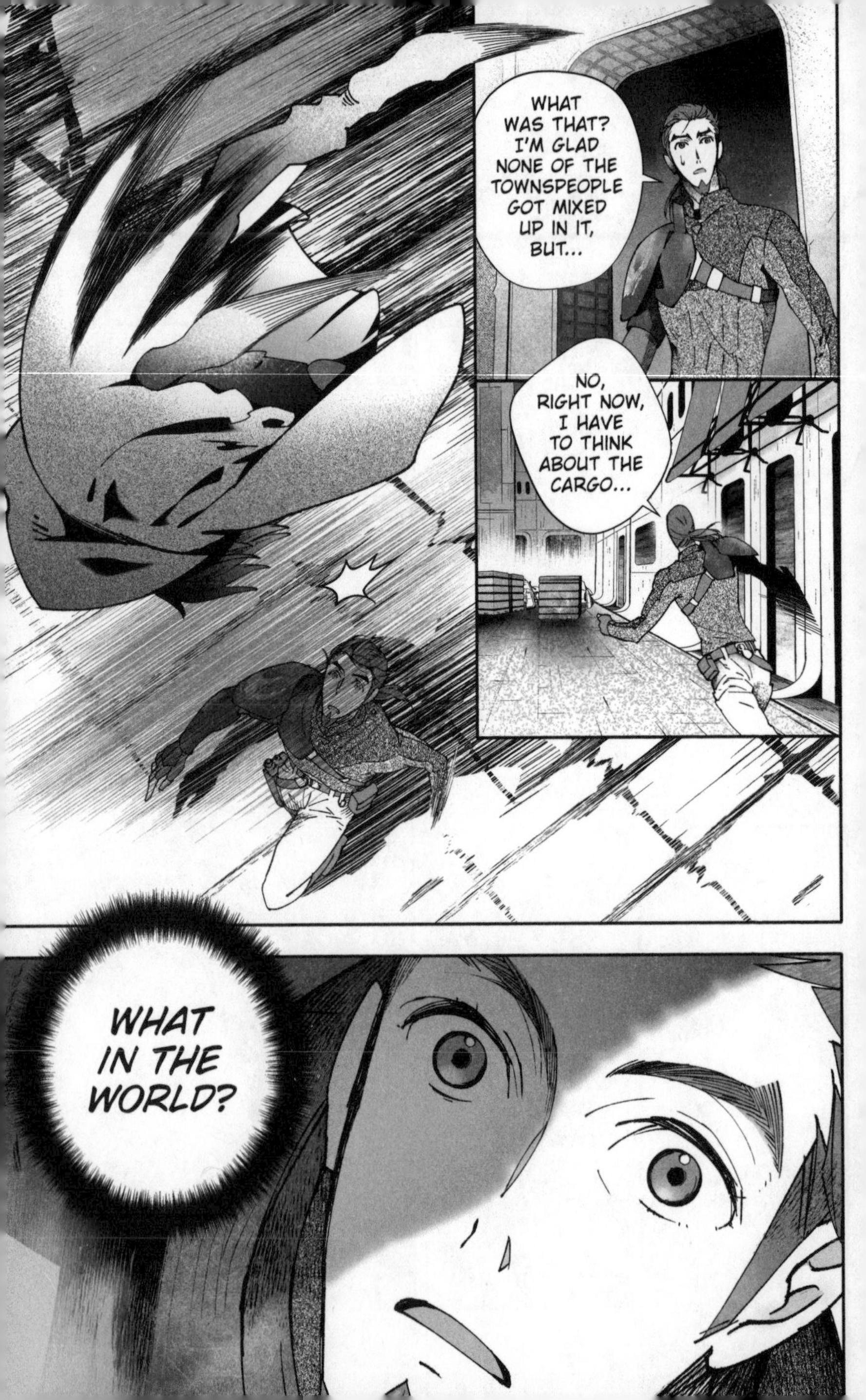
WHAT WAS THAT? I'M GLAD NONE OF THE TOWNSPEOPLE GOT MIXED UP IN IT, BUT...
NO, RIGHT NOW, I HAVE TO THINK ABOUT THE CARGO...
WHAT IN THE WORLD?

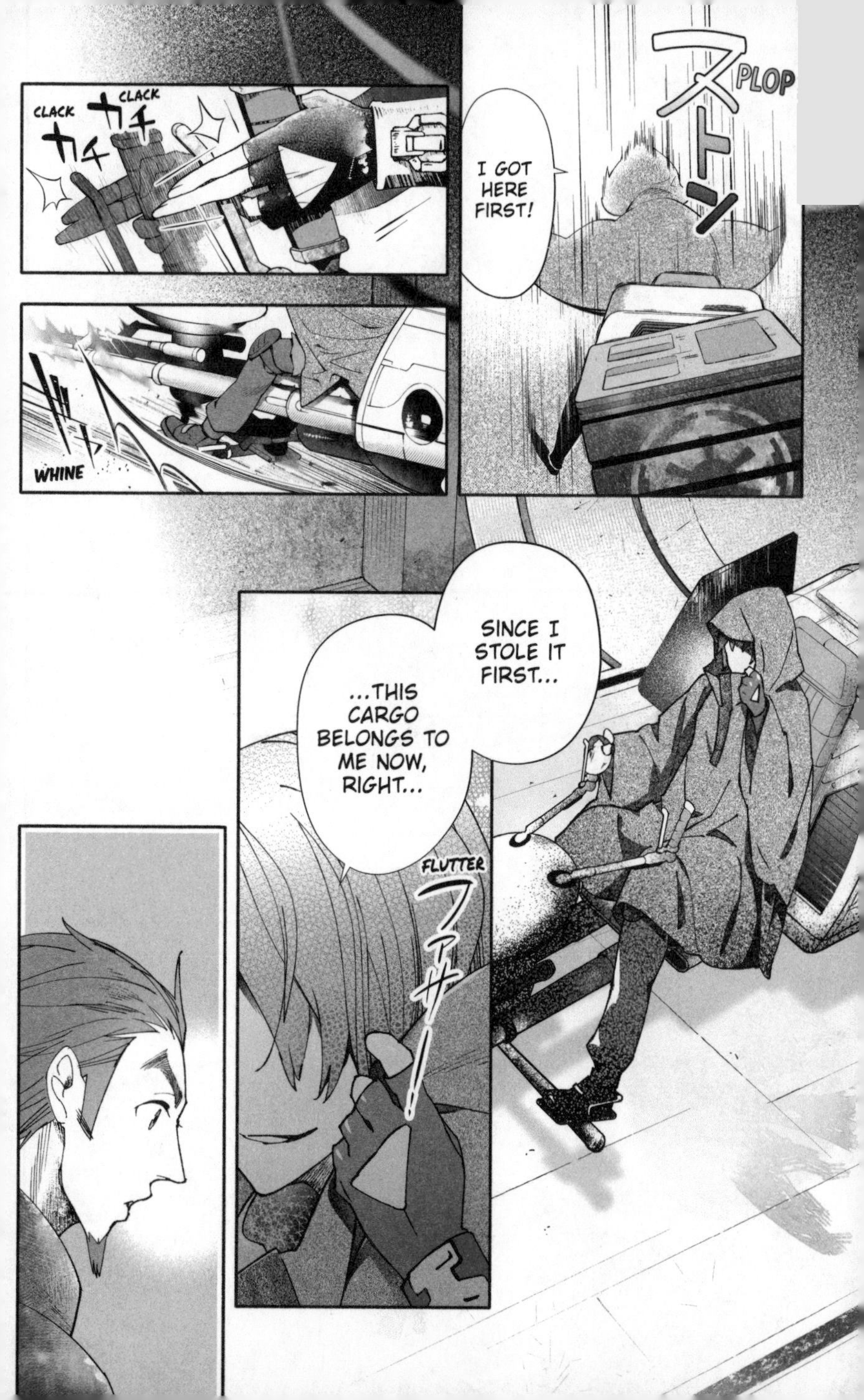
PLOP
I GOT HERE FIRST!
CLACK
CLACK
WHINE
SINCE I STOLE IT FIRST...
...THIS CARGO BELONGS TO ME NOW, RIGHT...
FLUTTER

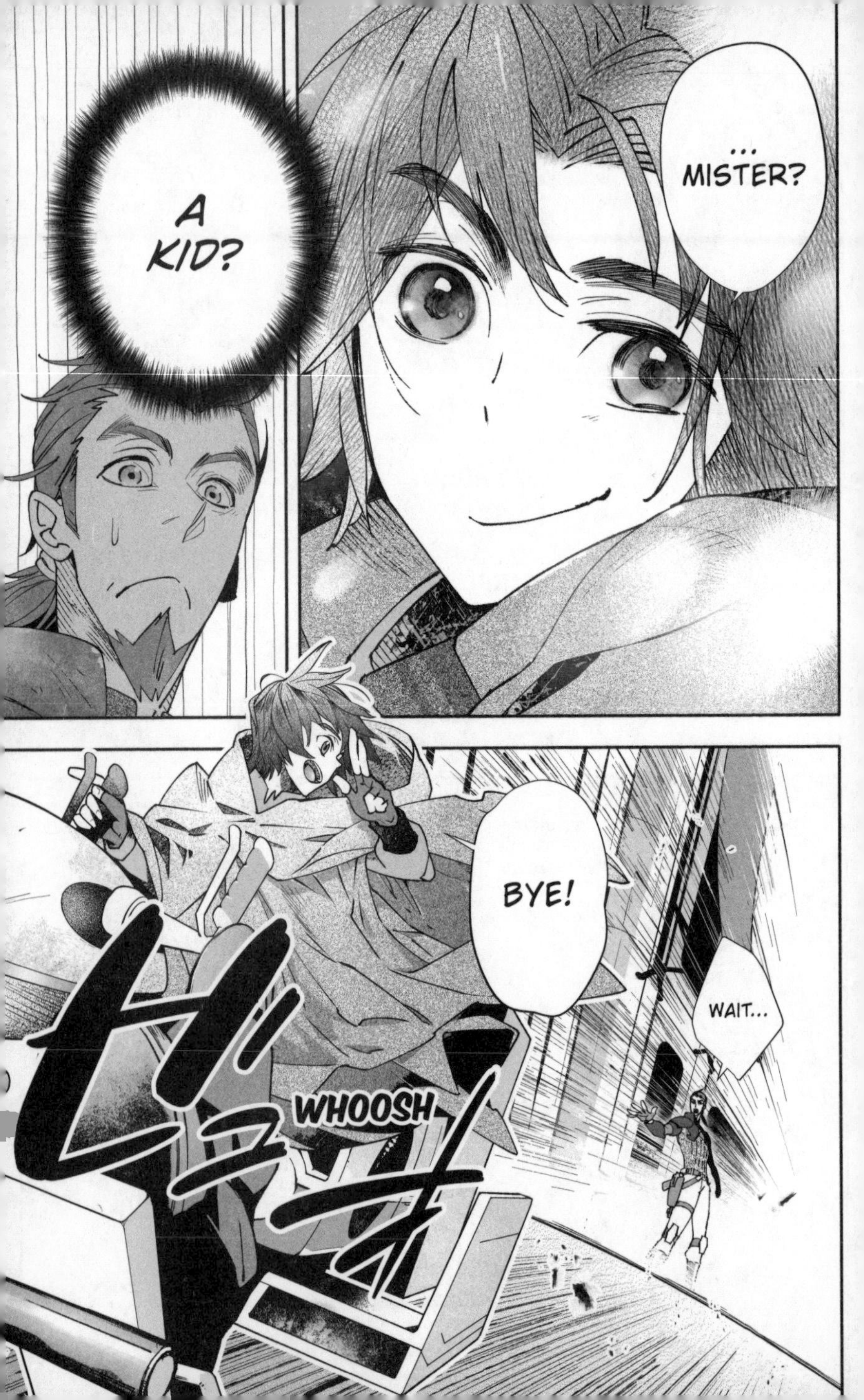

... MISTER?
A KID?
BYE!
WAIT...
WHOOSH

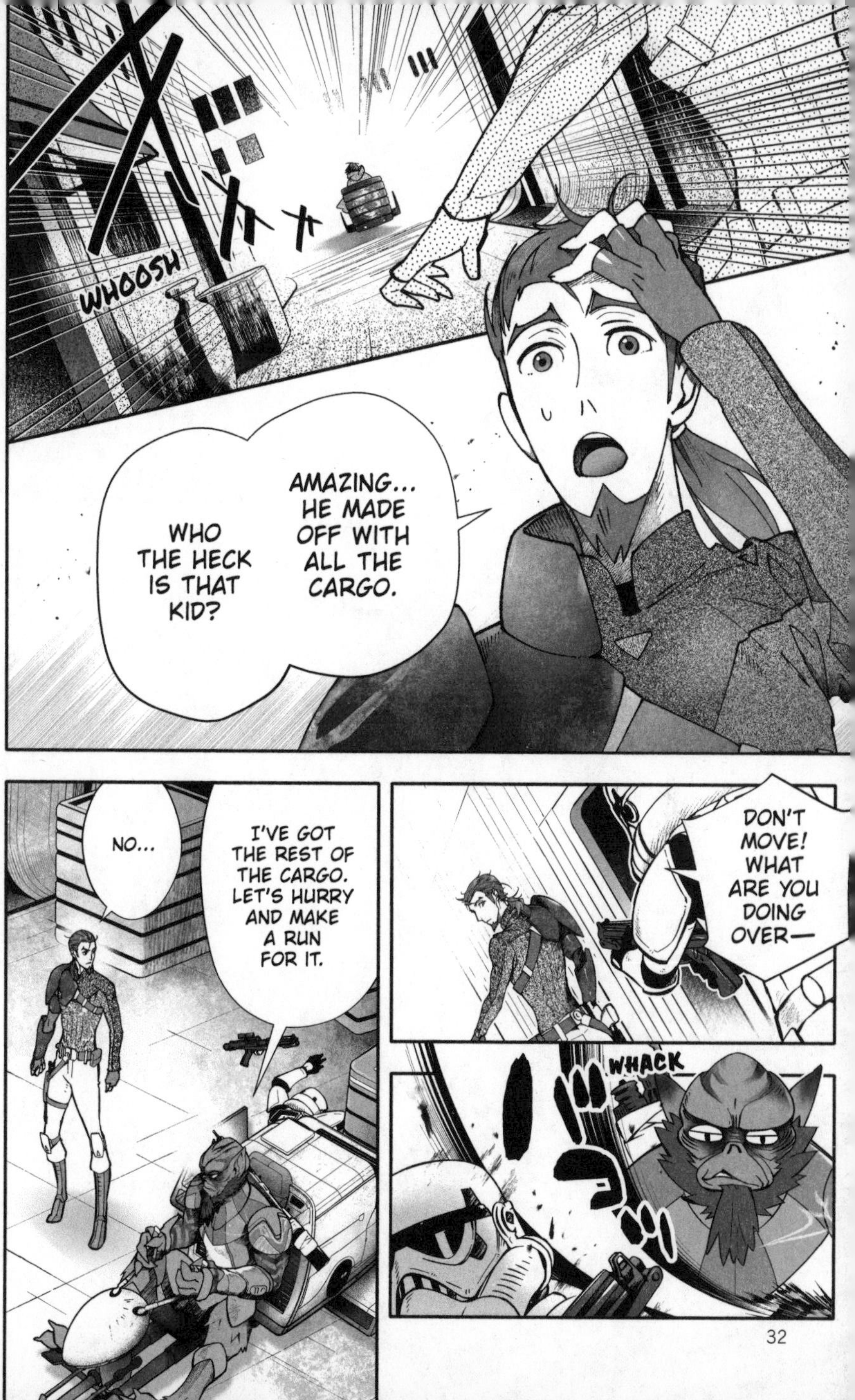
WHOOSH
AMAZING... HE MADE OFF WITH ALL THE CARGO.
WHO THE HECK IS THAT KID?
DON'T MOVE! WHAT ARE YOU DOING OVER—
WHACK
I'VE GOT THE REST OF THE CARGO. LET'S HURRY AND MAKE A RUN FOR IT.
NO...

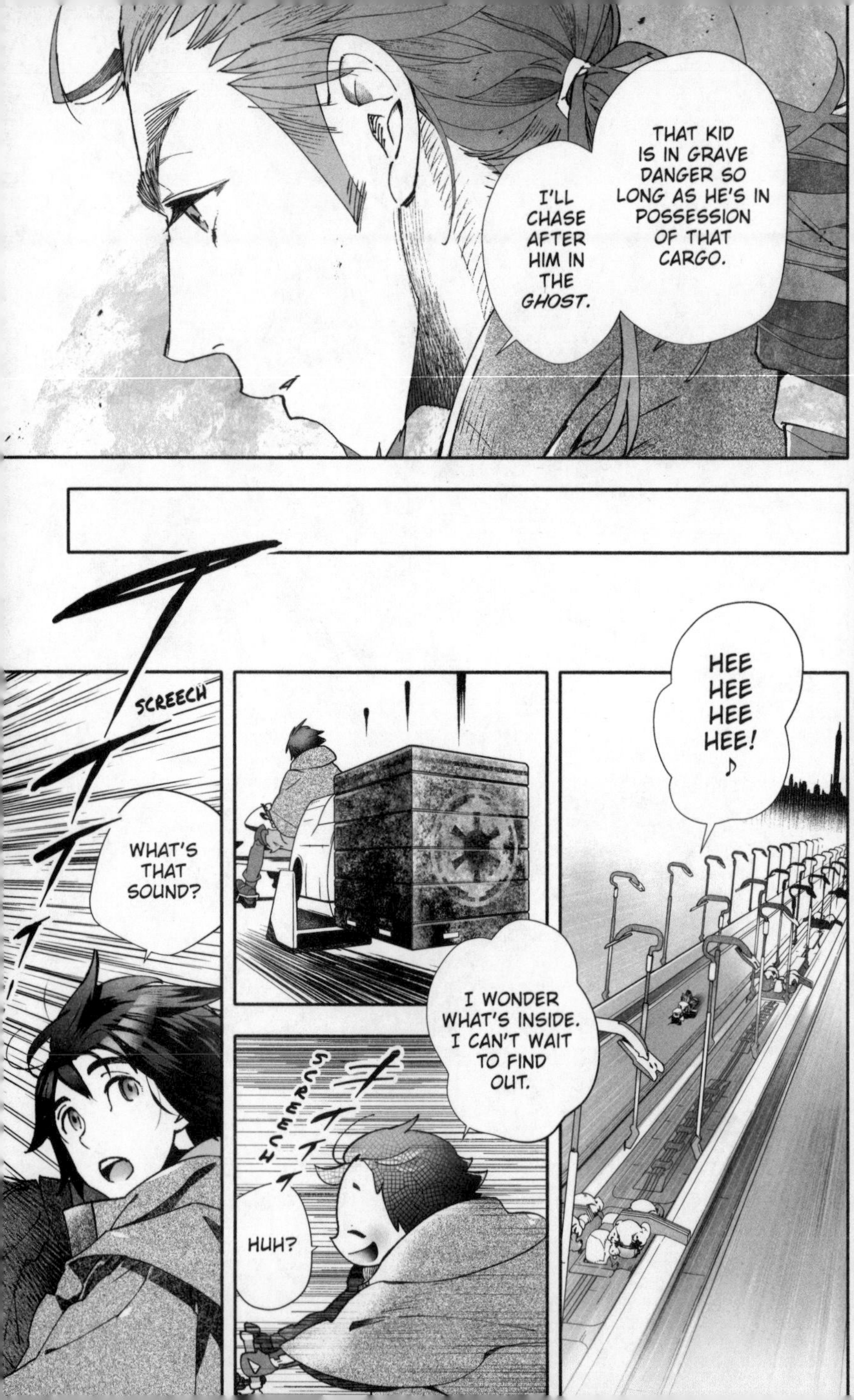
THAT KID IS IN GRAVE DANGER SO LONG AS HE'S IN POSSESSION OF THAT CARGO.
I'LL CHASE AFTER HIM IN THE *GHOST*.
HEE HEE HEE HEE! ♪
I WONDER WHAT'S INSIDE. I CAN'T WAIT TO FIND OUT.
SCREECH
HUH?
SCREECH
WHAT'S THAT SOUND?

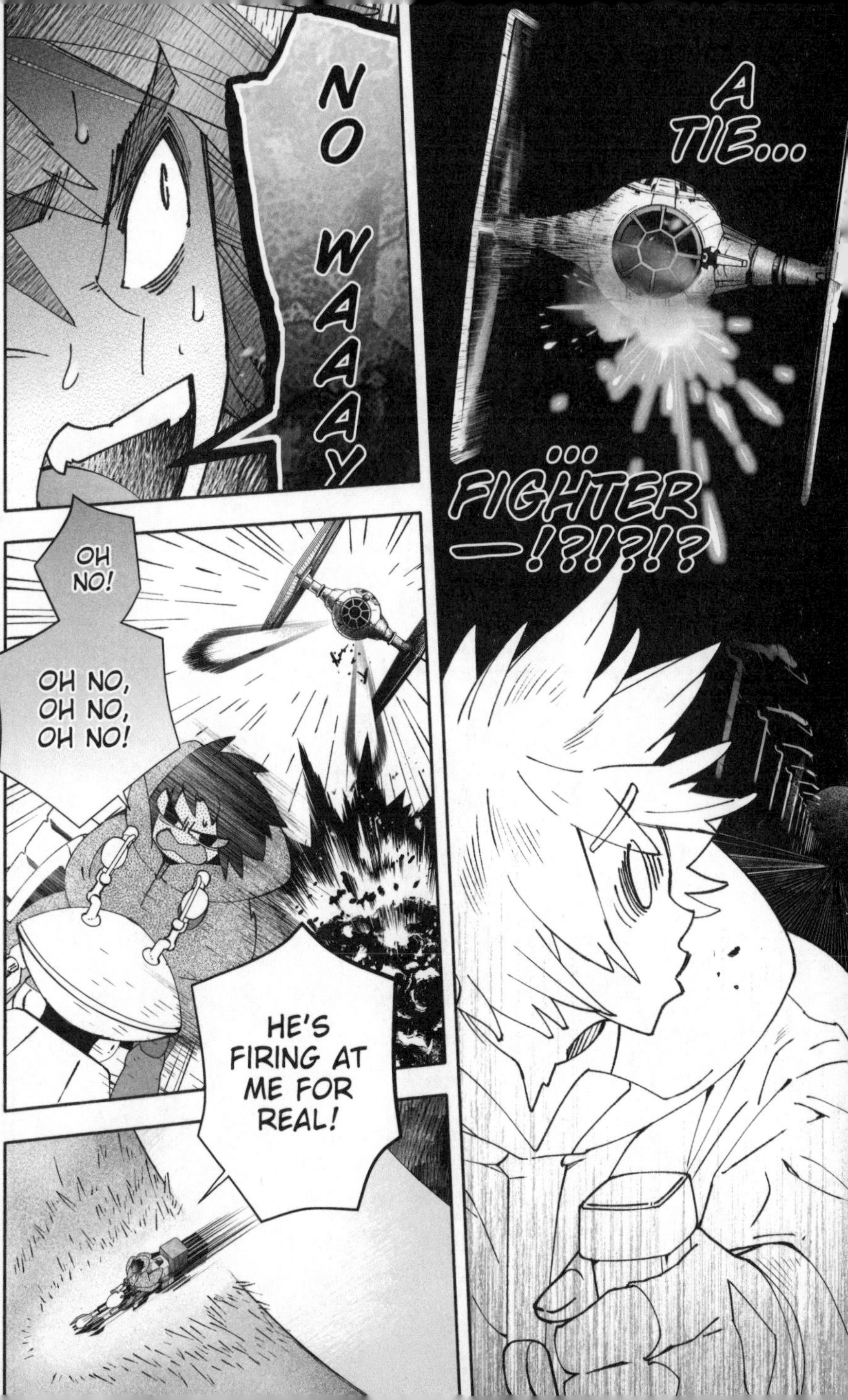
A TIE...
...FIGHTER—!?!?!?
NO WAAAAY
OH NO!
OH NO, OH NO, OH NO!
HE'S FIRING AT ME FOR REAL!

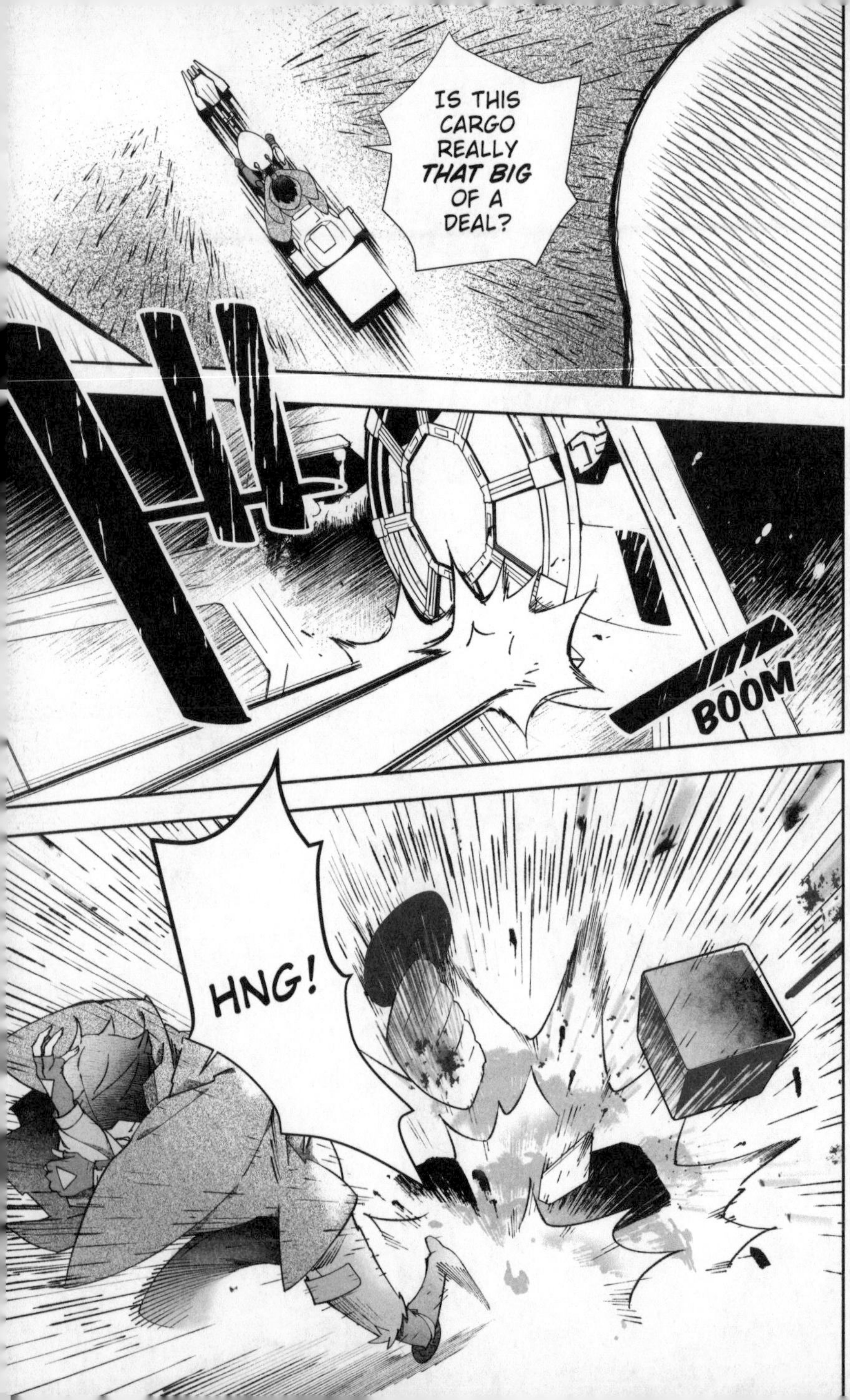
IS THIS CARGO REALLY THAT BIG OF A DEAL?
BOOM
HNG!

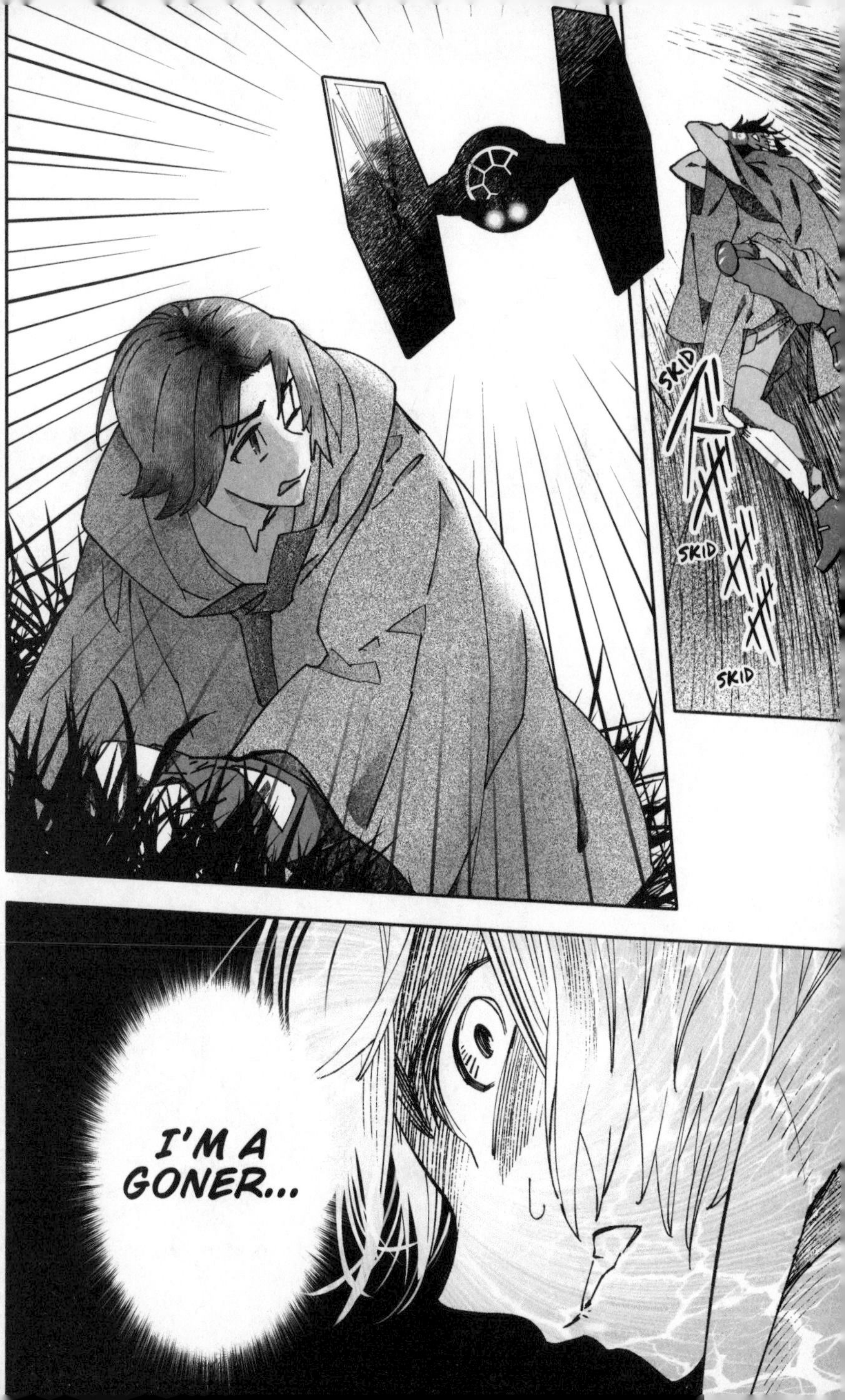
SKID
SKID
SKID
I'M A GONER...

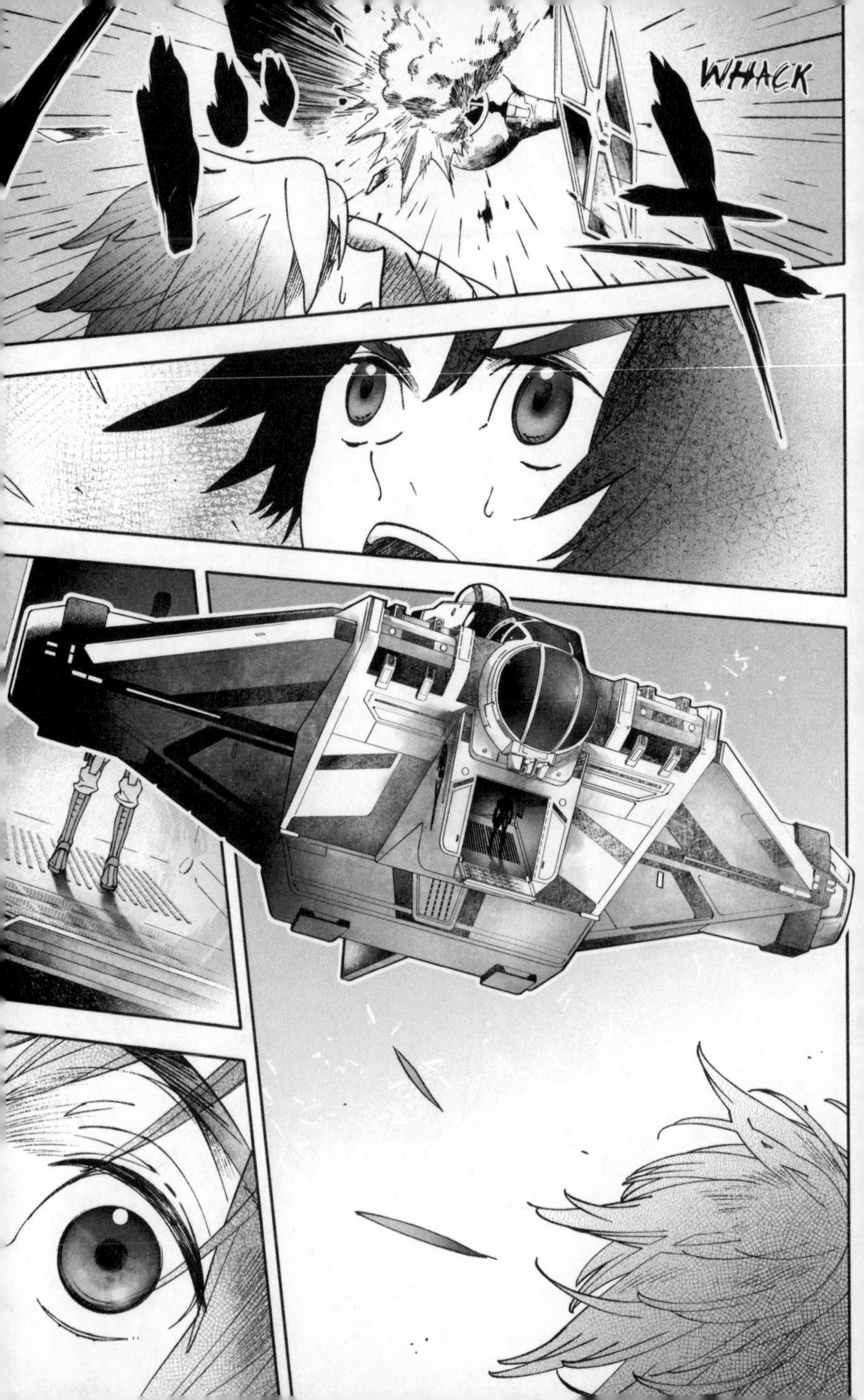
WHACK

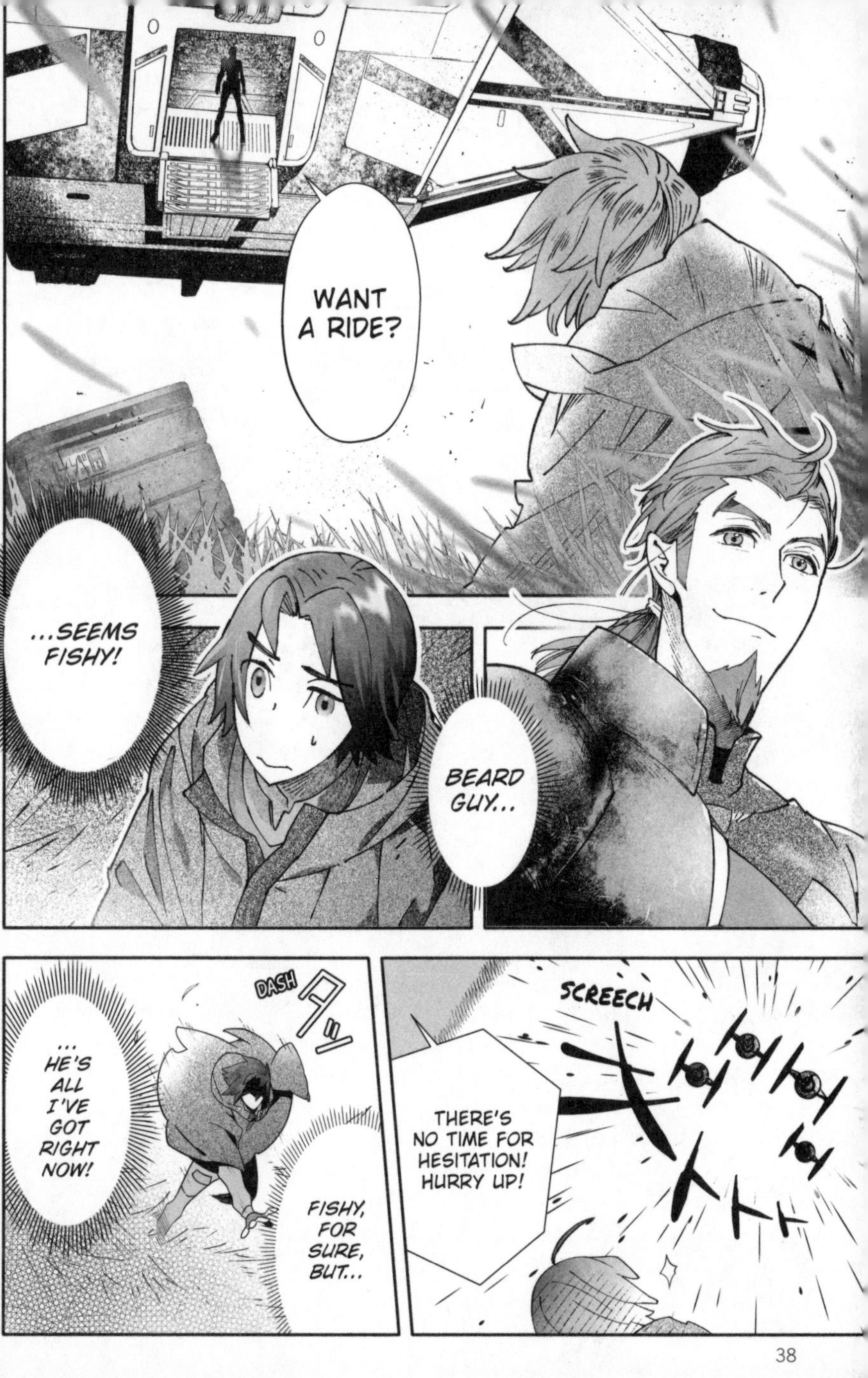
WANT A RIDE?
BEARD GUY...
...SEEMS FISHY!
SCREECH
THERE'S NO TIME FOR HESITATION! HURRY UP!
DASH
FISHY, FOR SURE, BUT...
... HE'S ALL I'VE GOT RIGHT NOW!

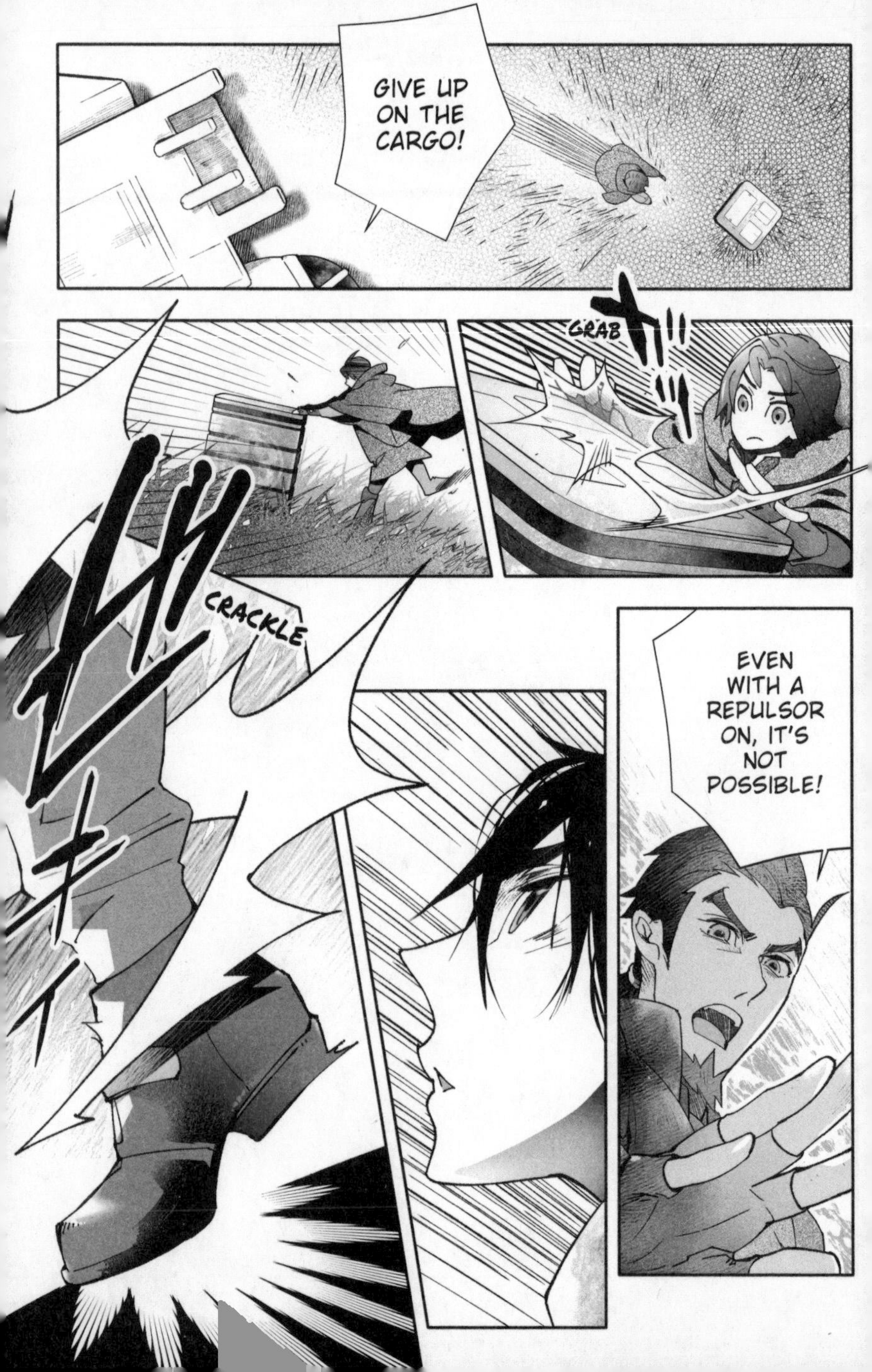
GIVE UP ON THE CARGO!
GRAB
CRACKLE
EVEN WITH A REPULSOR ON, IT'S NOT POSSIBLE!

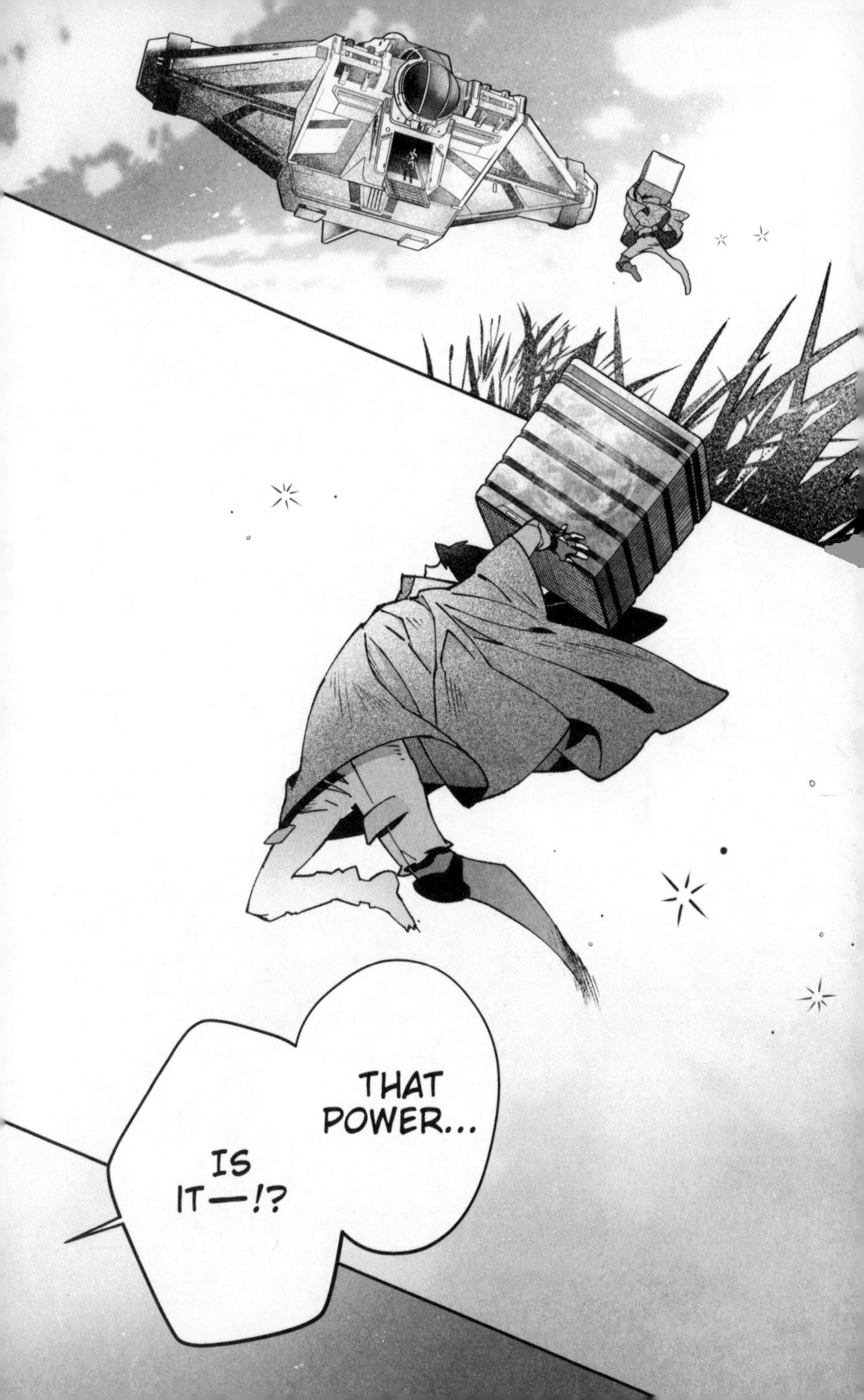
THAT POWER...
IS IT—!?

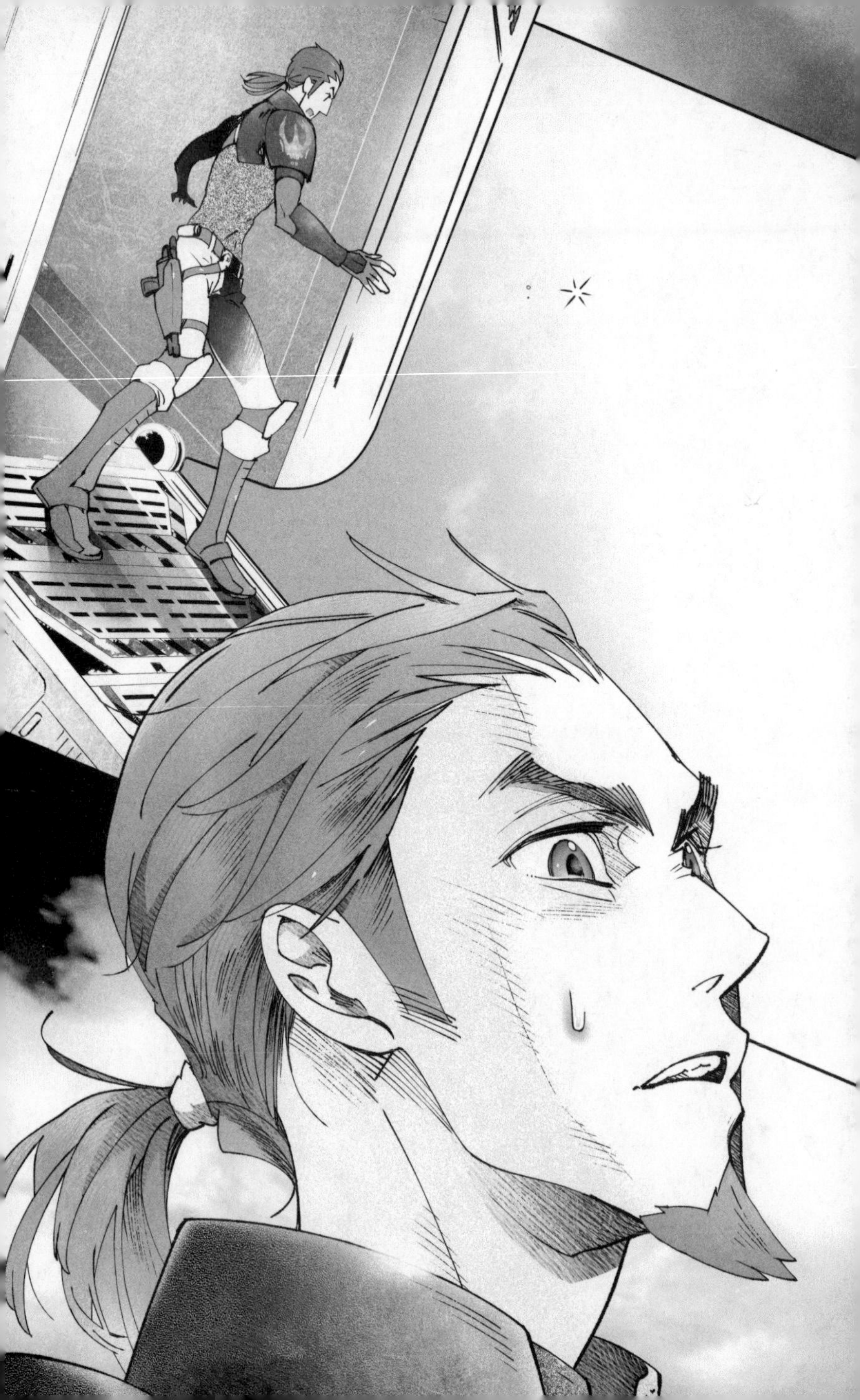

STAR WARS
REBELS

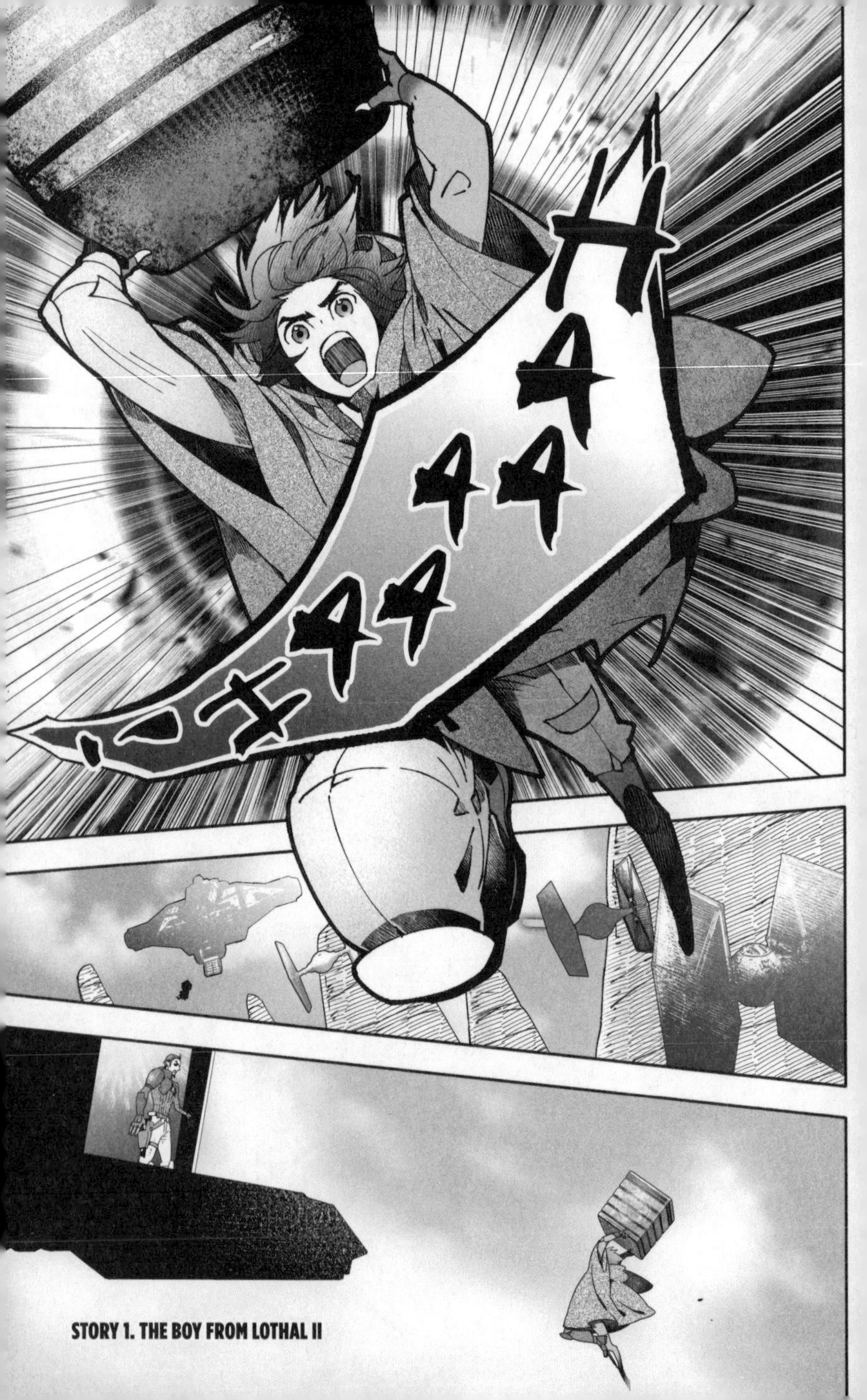
HAAAAAH!
STORY 1. THE BOY FROM LOTHAL II

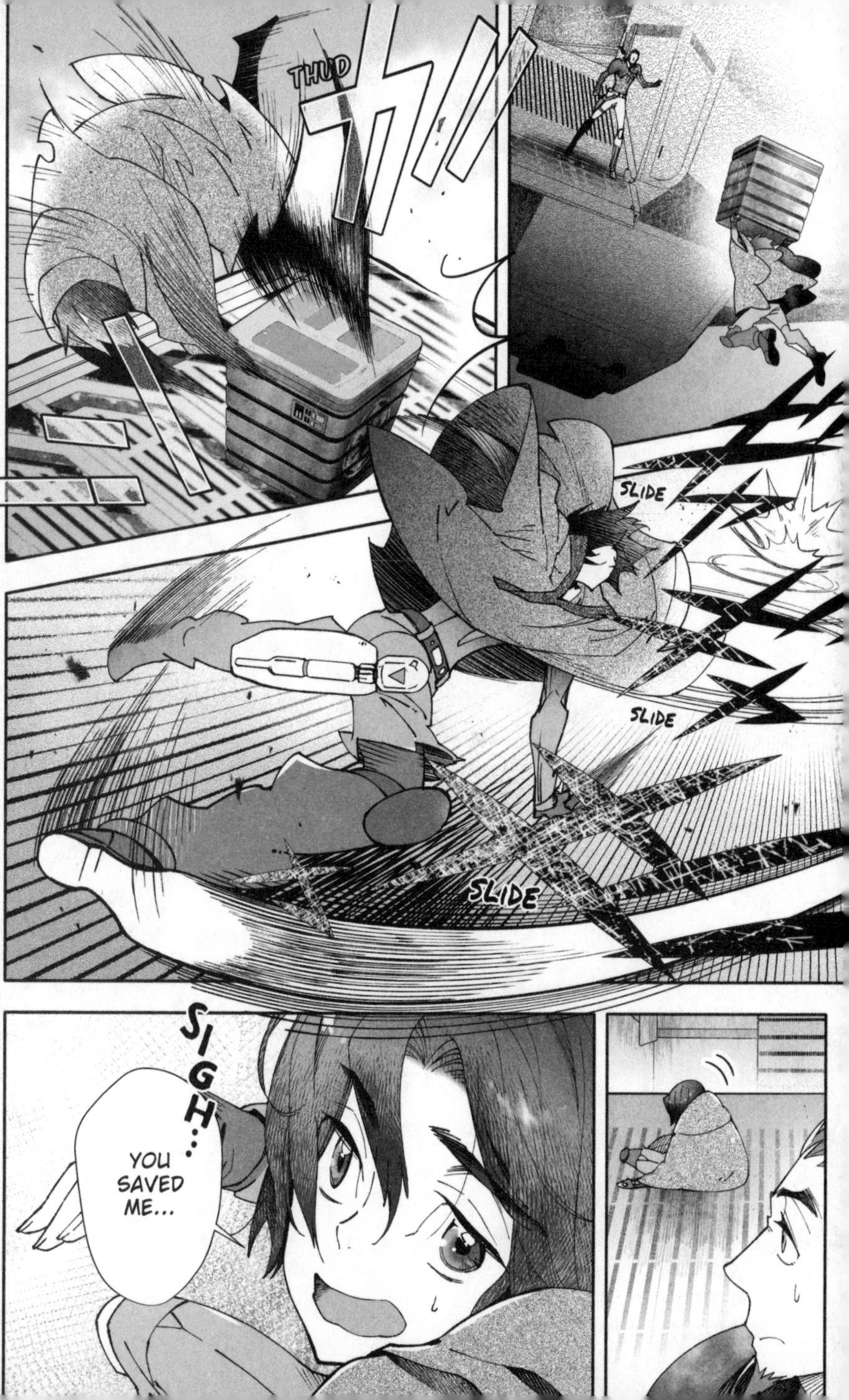
THUD
SLIDE
SLIDE
SLIDE
SIGH...
YOU SAVED ME...

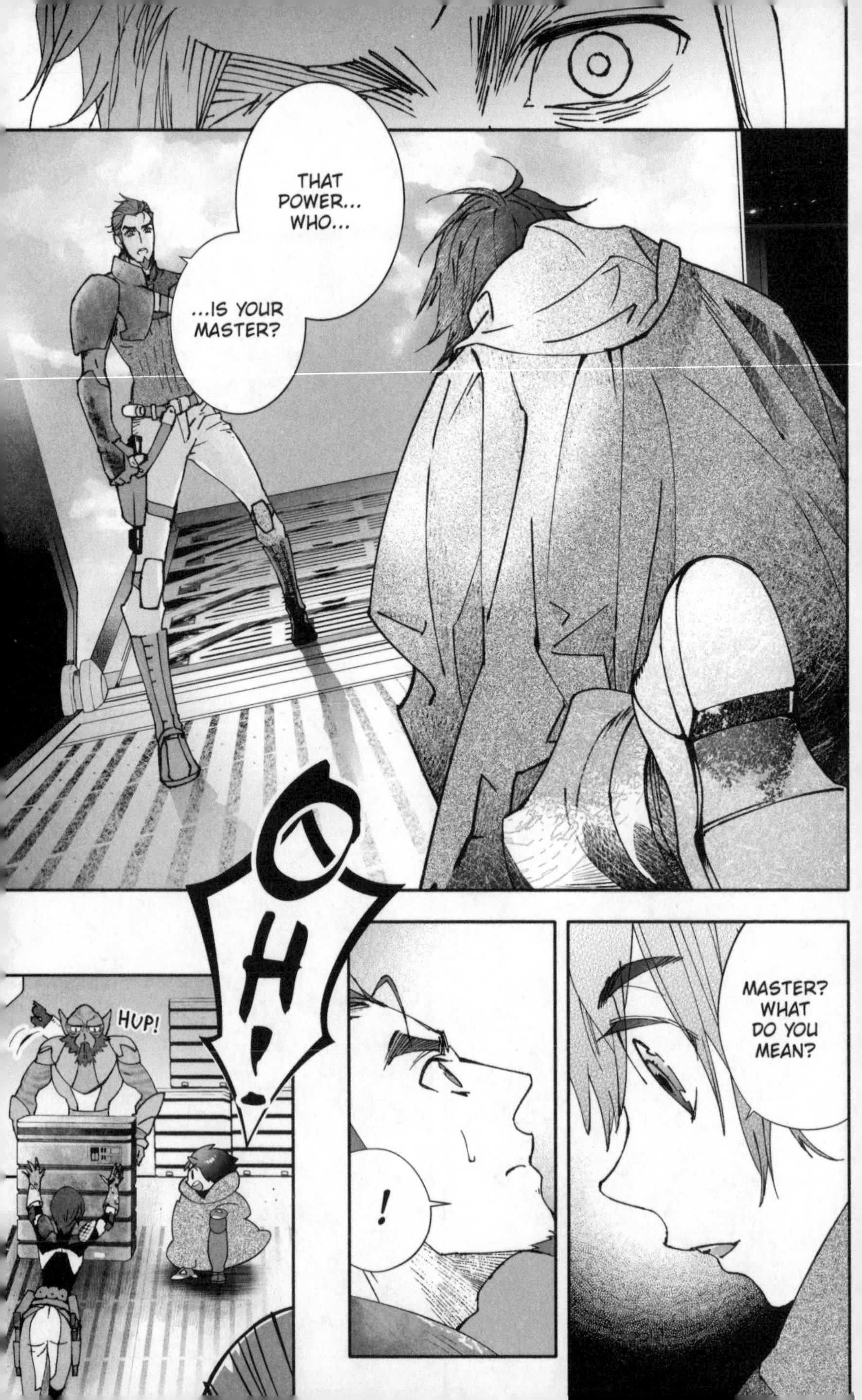
THAT POWER... WHO...
...IS YOUR MASTER?
MASTER? WHAT DO YOU MEAN?
!
OH!
HUP!

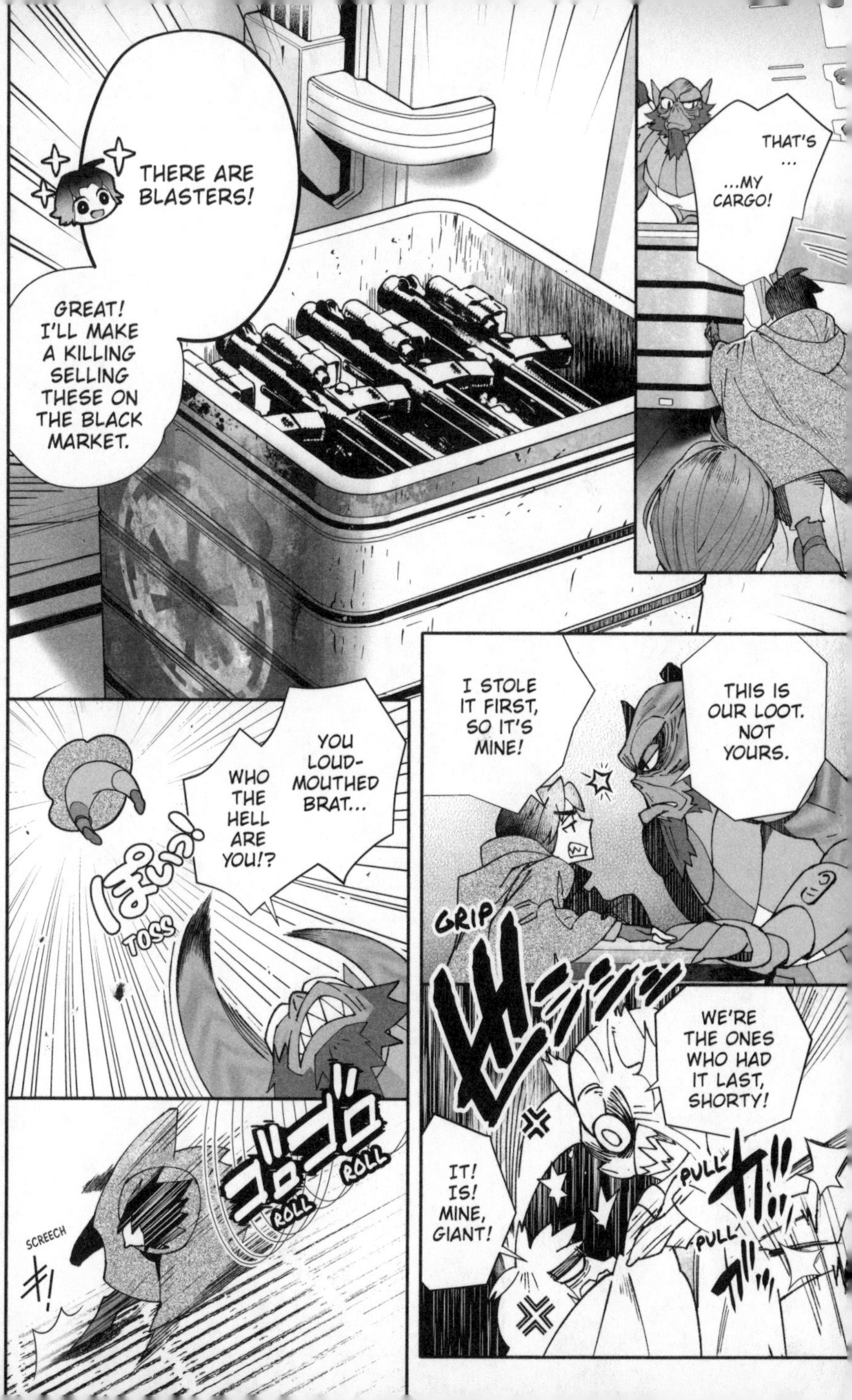

THAT'S ...
...MY CARGO!
THERE ARE BLASTERS!
GREAT! I'LL MAKE A KILLING SELLING THESE ON THE BLACK MARKET.
THIS IS OUR LOOT. NOT YOURS.
I STOLE IT FIRST, SO IT'S MINE!
GRIP
YOU LOUD-MOUTHED BRAT...
WHO THE HELL ARE YOU!?
ぽいっ
TOSS
WE'RE THE ONES WHO HAD IT LAST, SHORTY!
IT! IS! MINE, GIANT!
PULL
PULL
ゴロゴロ
ROLL
ROLL
SCREECH

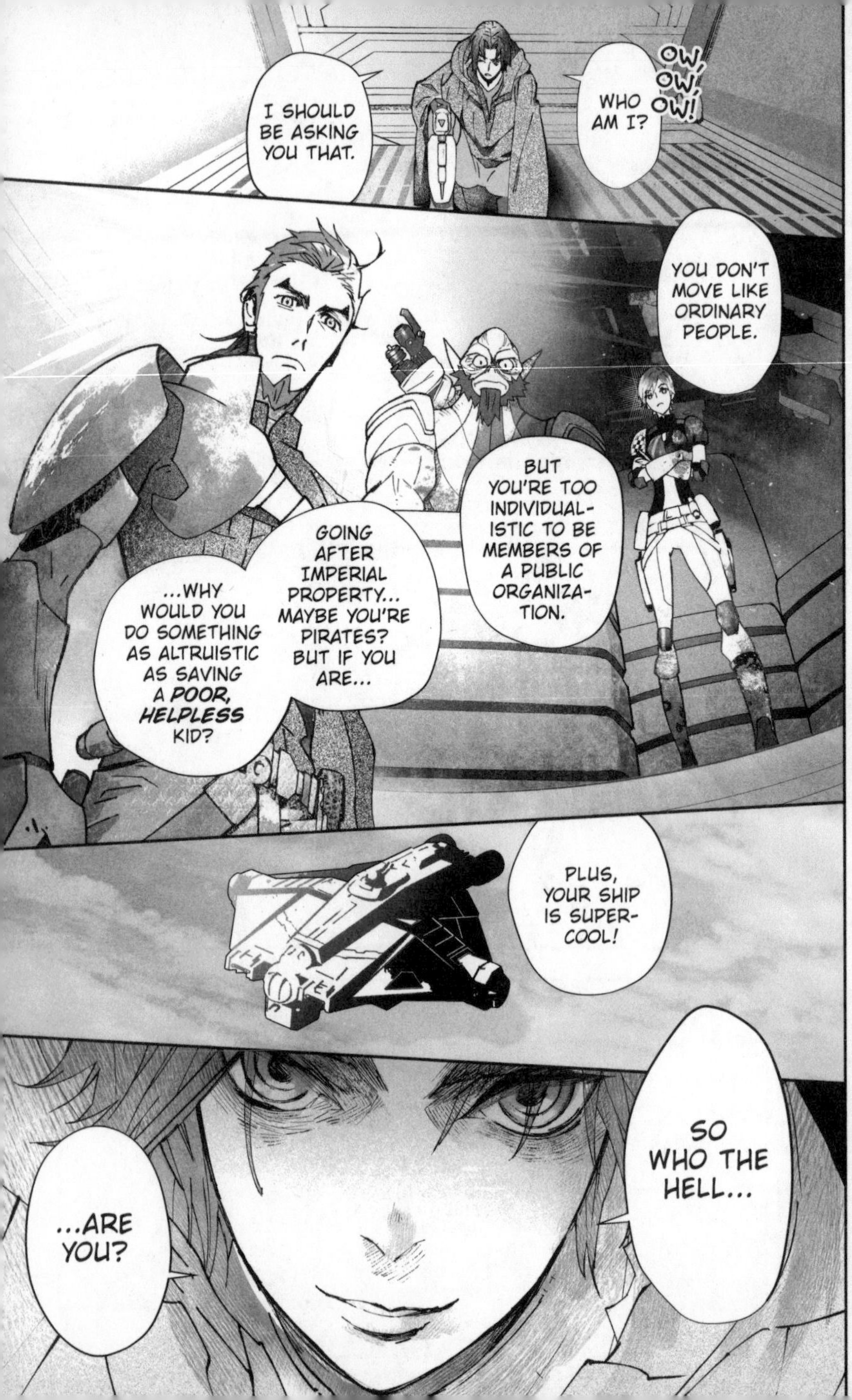
OW, OW, OW!
WHO AM I?
I SHOULD BE ASKING YOU THAT.
YOU DON'T MOVE LIKE ORDINARY PEOPLE.
BUT YOU'RE TOO INDIVIDUALISTIC TO BE MEMBERS OF A PUBLIC ORGANIZATION.
GOING AFTER IMPERIAL PROPERTY... MAYBE YOU'RE PIRATES? BUT IF YOU ARE...
...WHY WOULD YOU DO SOMETHING AS ALTRUISTIC AS SAVING A *POOR, HELPLESS* KID?
PLUS, YOUR SHIP IS SUPER-COOL!
SO WHO THE HELL...
...ARE YOU?

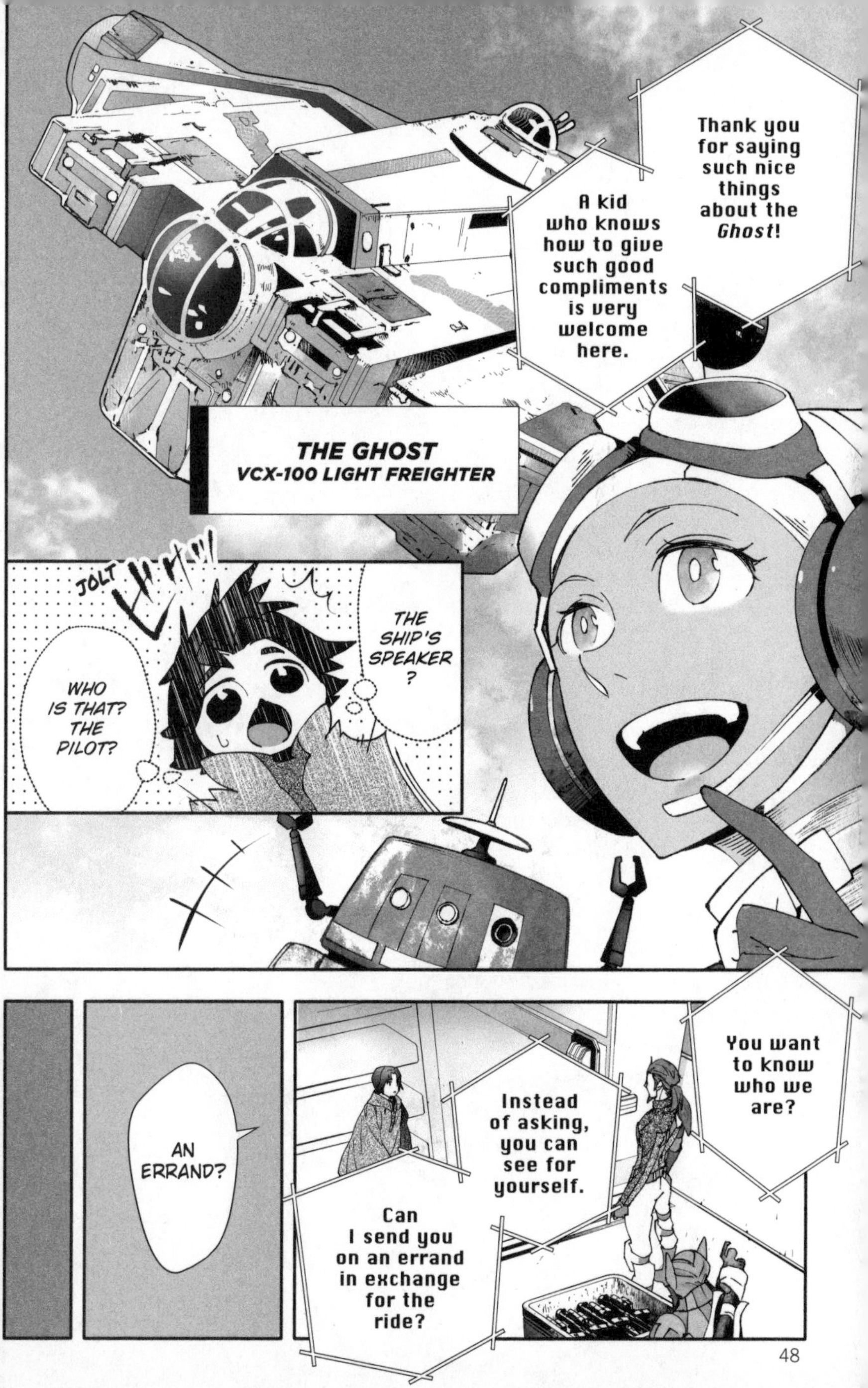
Thank you for saying such nice things about the *Ghost*!
A kid who knows how to give such good compliments is very welcome here.
THE GHOST
VCX-100 LIGHT FREIGHTER
JOLT
THE SHIP'S SPEAKER?
WHO IS THAT? THE PILOT?
You want to know who we are?
Instead of asking, you can see for yourself.
Can I send you on an errand in exchange for the ride?
AN ERRAND?

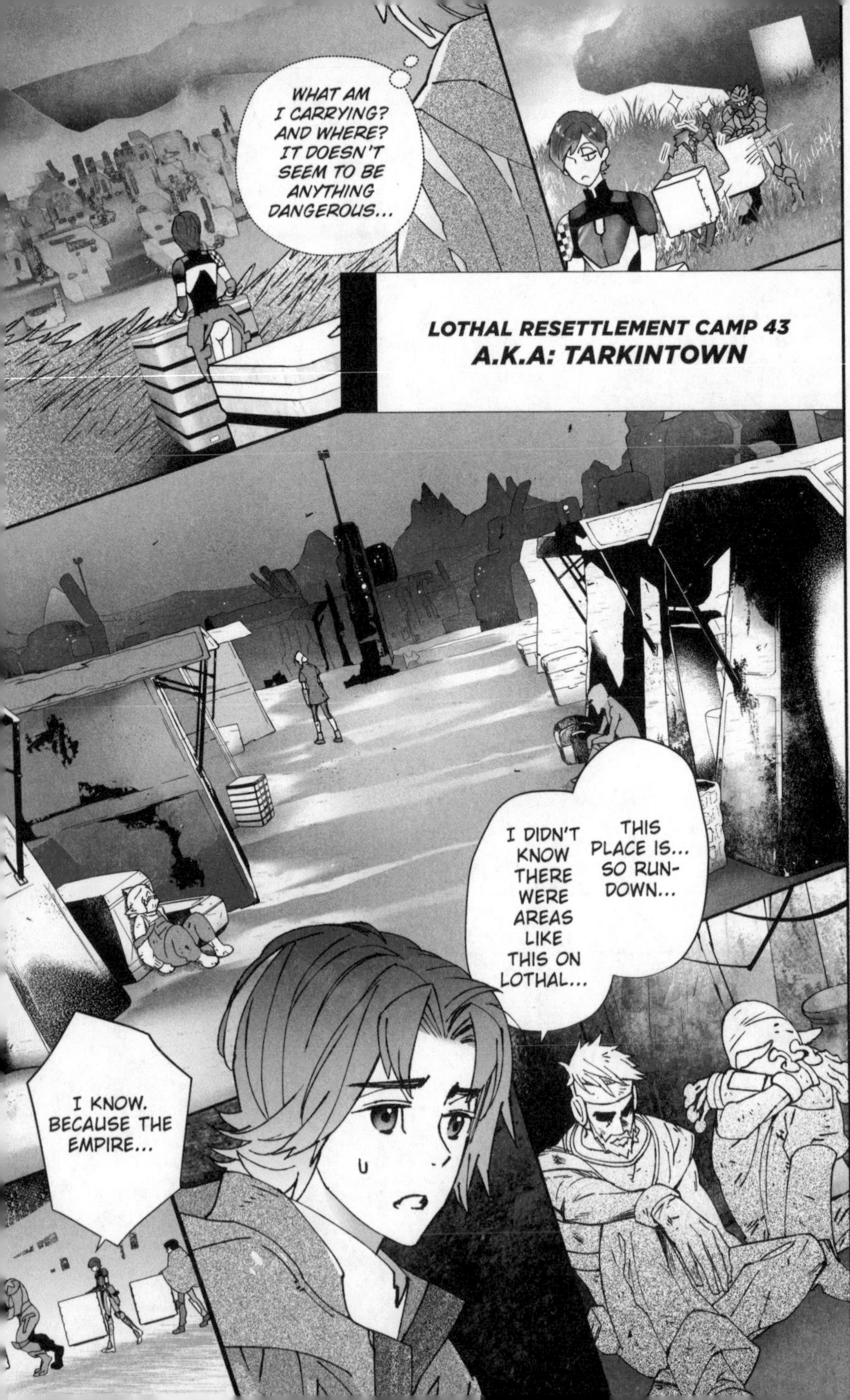
WHAT AM I CARRYING? AND WHERE? IT DOESN'T SEEM TO BE ANYTHING DANGEROUS...
LOTHAL RESETTLEMENT CAMP 43
A.K.A: TARKINTOWN
THIS PLACE IS... SO RUN-DOWN...
I DIDN'T KNOW THERE WERE AREAS LIKE THIS ON LOTHAL...
I KNOW. BECAUSE THE EMPIRE...

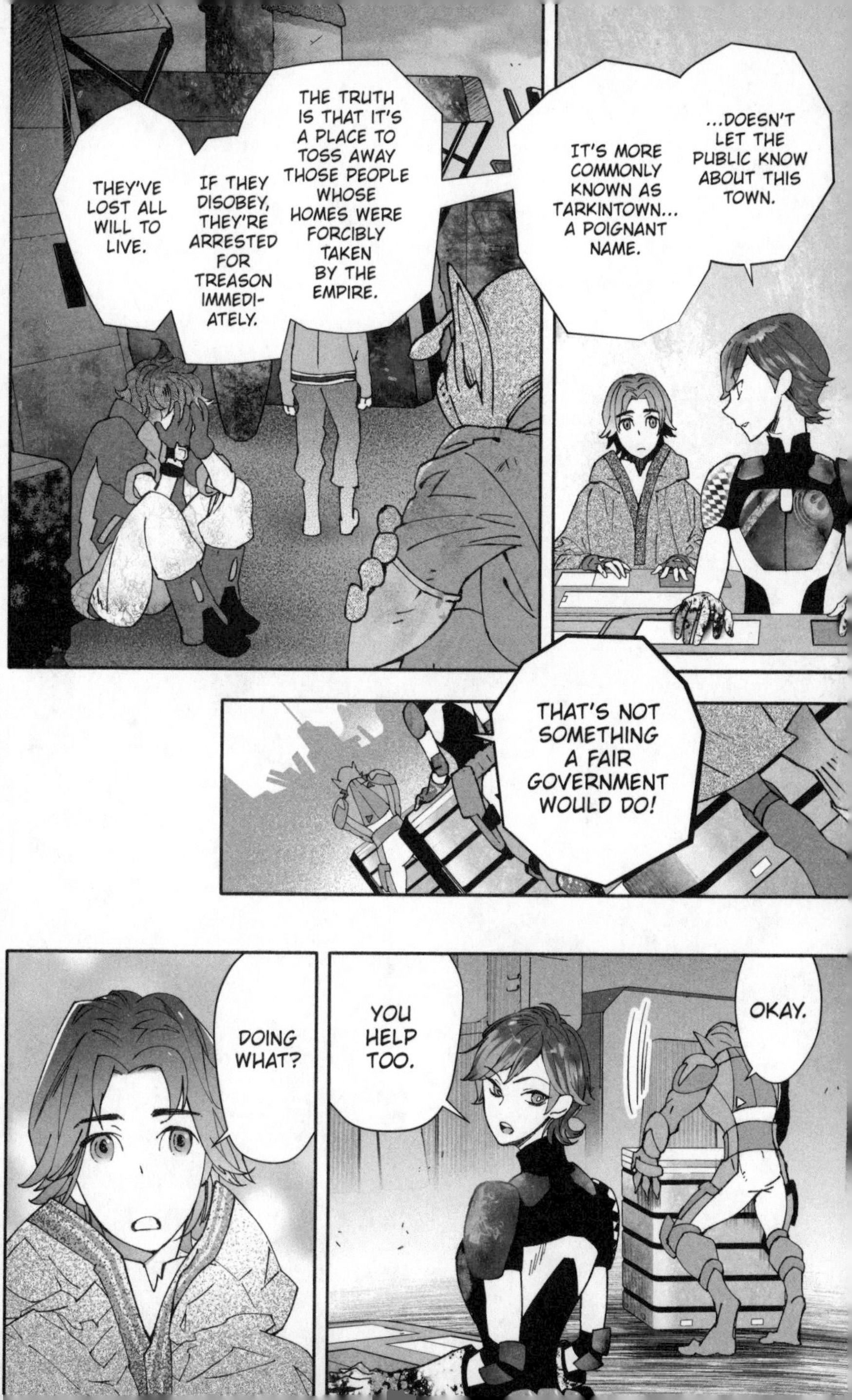
...DOESN'T LET THE PUBLIC KNOW ABOUT THIS TOWN.
IT'S MORE COMMONLY KNOWN AS TARKINTOWN... A POIGNANT NAME.
THE TRUTH IS THAT IT'S A PLACE TO TOSS AWAY THOSE PEOPLE WHOSE HOMES WERE FORCIBLY TAKEN BY THE EMPIRE.
IF THEY DISOBEY, THEY'RE ARRESTED FOR TREASON IMMEDI-ATELY.
THEY'VE LOST ALL WILL TO LIVE.
THAT'S NOT SOMETHING A FAIR GOVERNMENT WOULD DO!
OKAY.
YOU HELP TOO.
DOING WHAT?

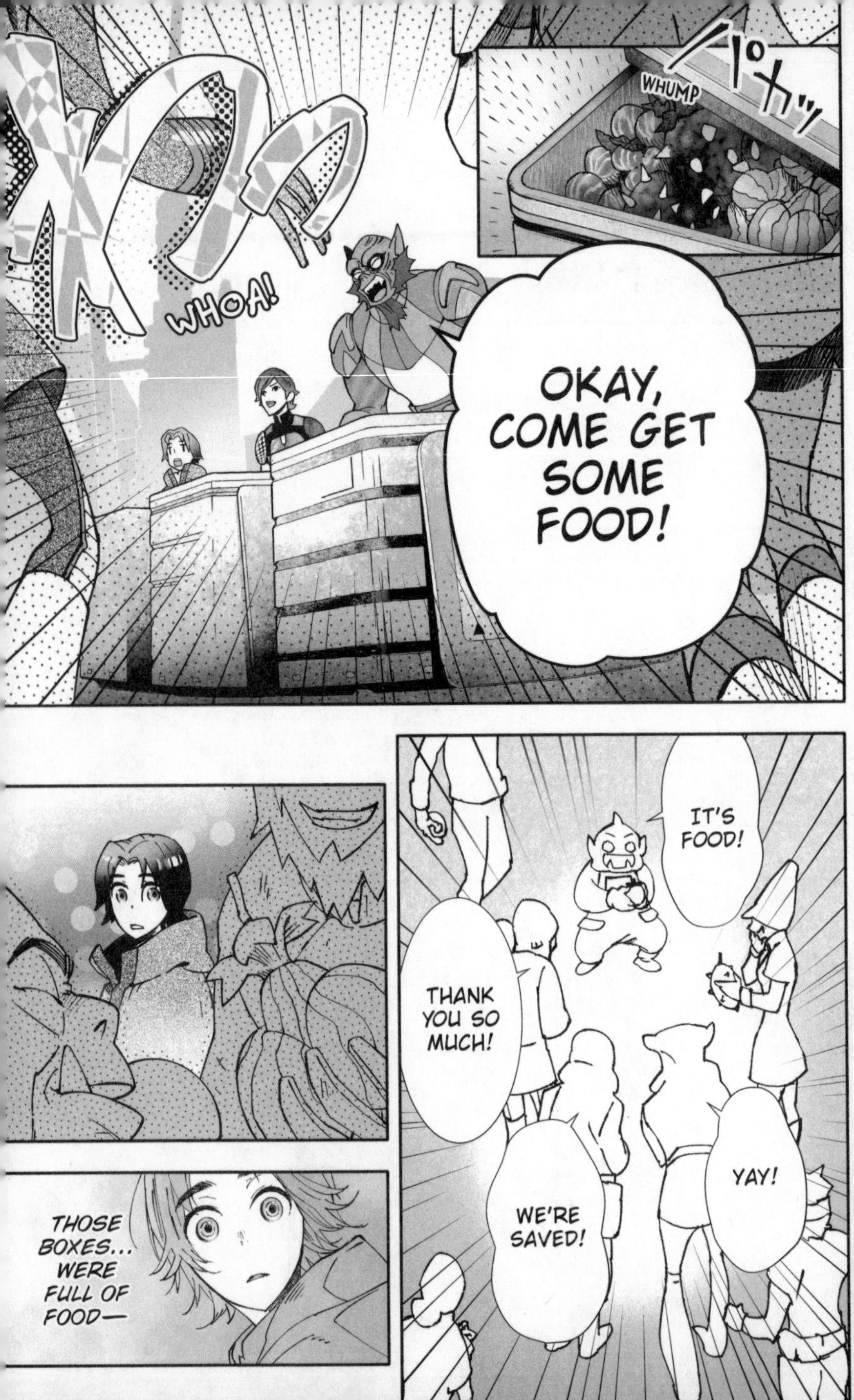
WHUMP
パカッ
OKAY, COME GET SOME FOOD!
WHOA!
IT'S FOOD!
THANK YOU SO MUCH!
YAY!
WE'RE SAVED!
THOSE BOXES... WERE FULL OF FOOD—

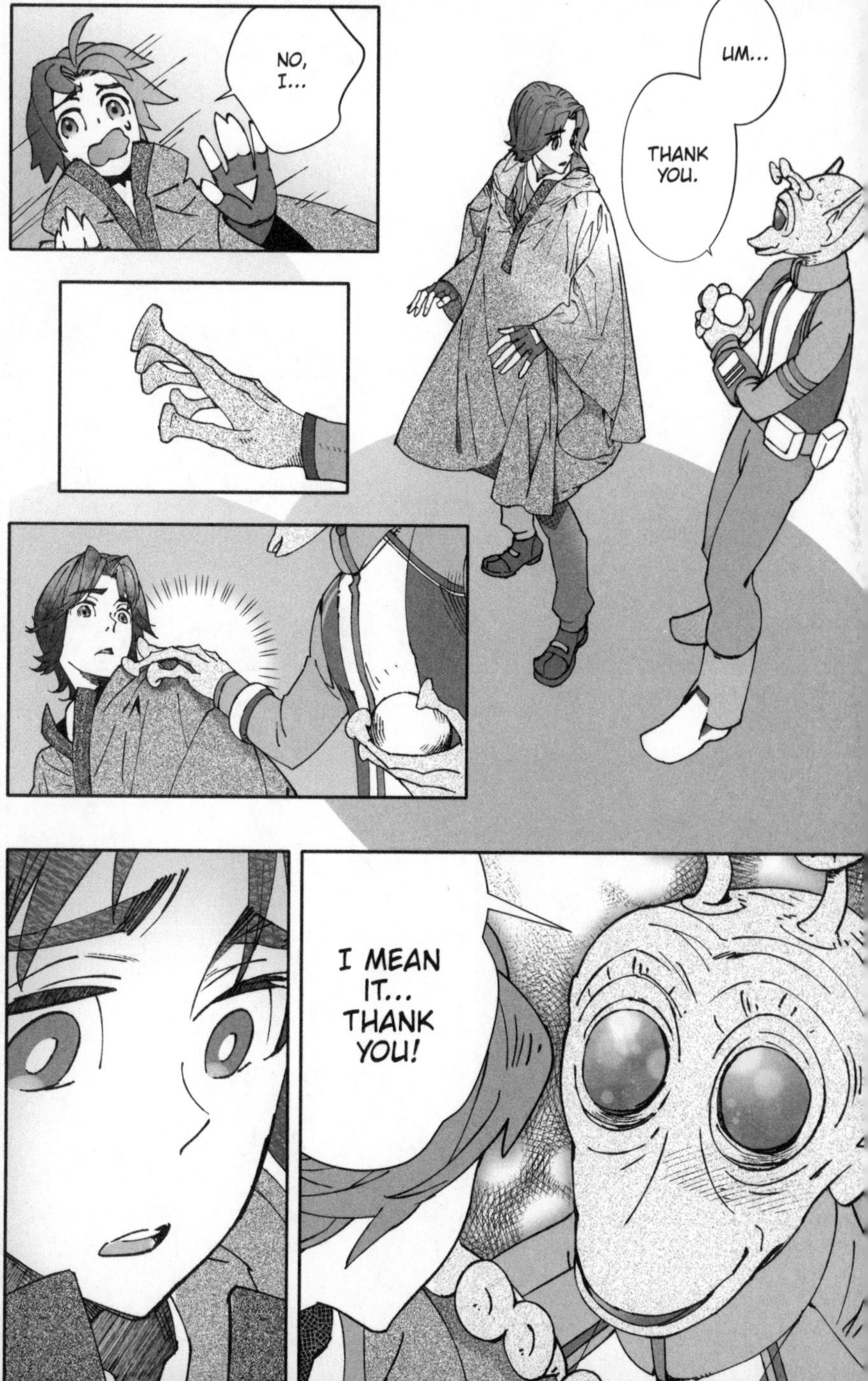
UM...
THANK YOU.
NO, I...
I MEAN IT... THANK YOU!

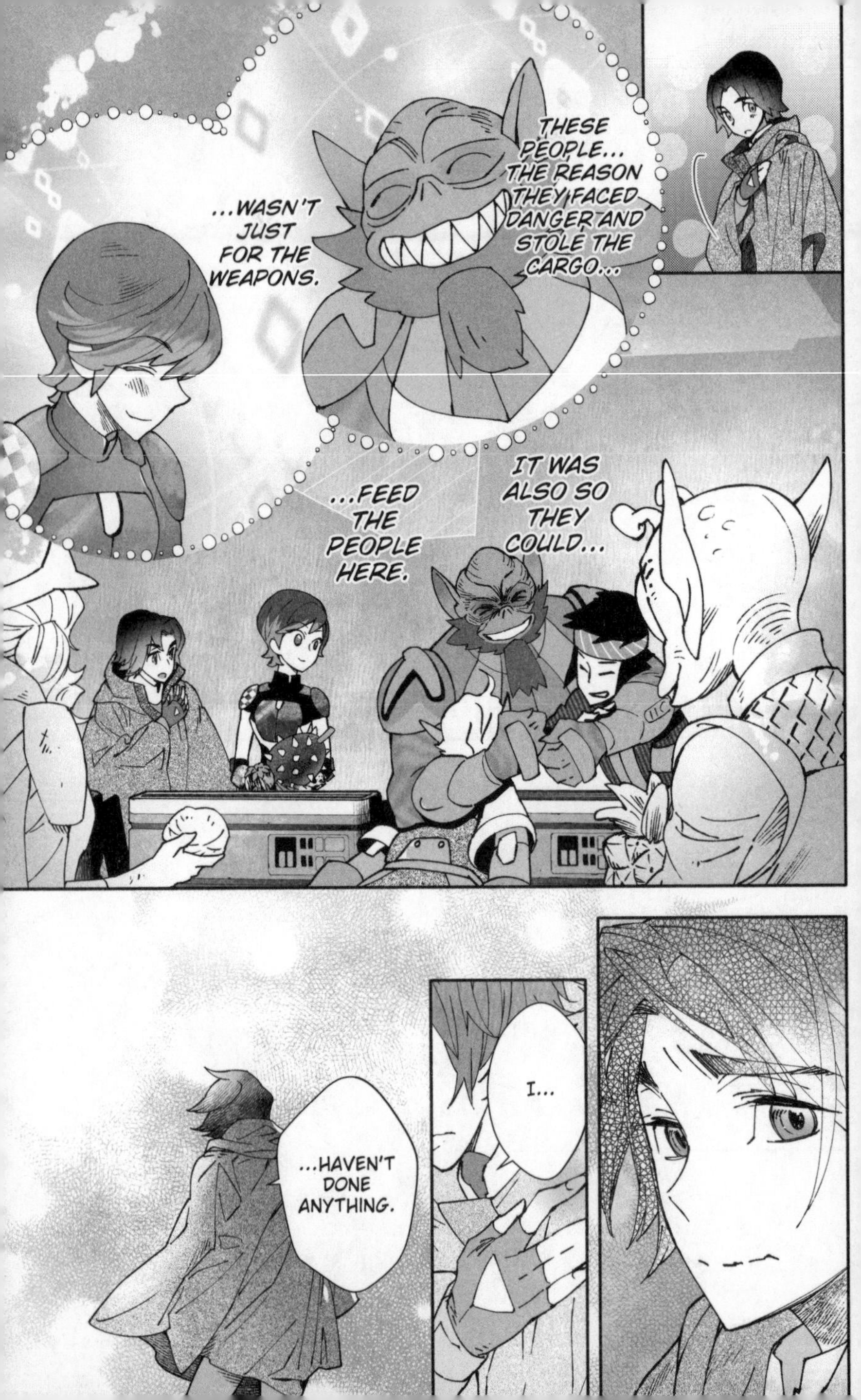
THESE PEOPLE... THE REASON THEY FACED DANGER AND STOLE THE CARGO...
...WASN'T JUST FOR THE WEAPONS.
IT WAS ALSO SO THEY COULD...
...FEED THE PEOPLE HERE.
I...
...HAVEN'T DONE ANYTHING.

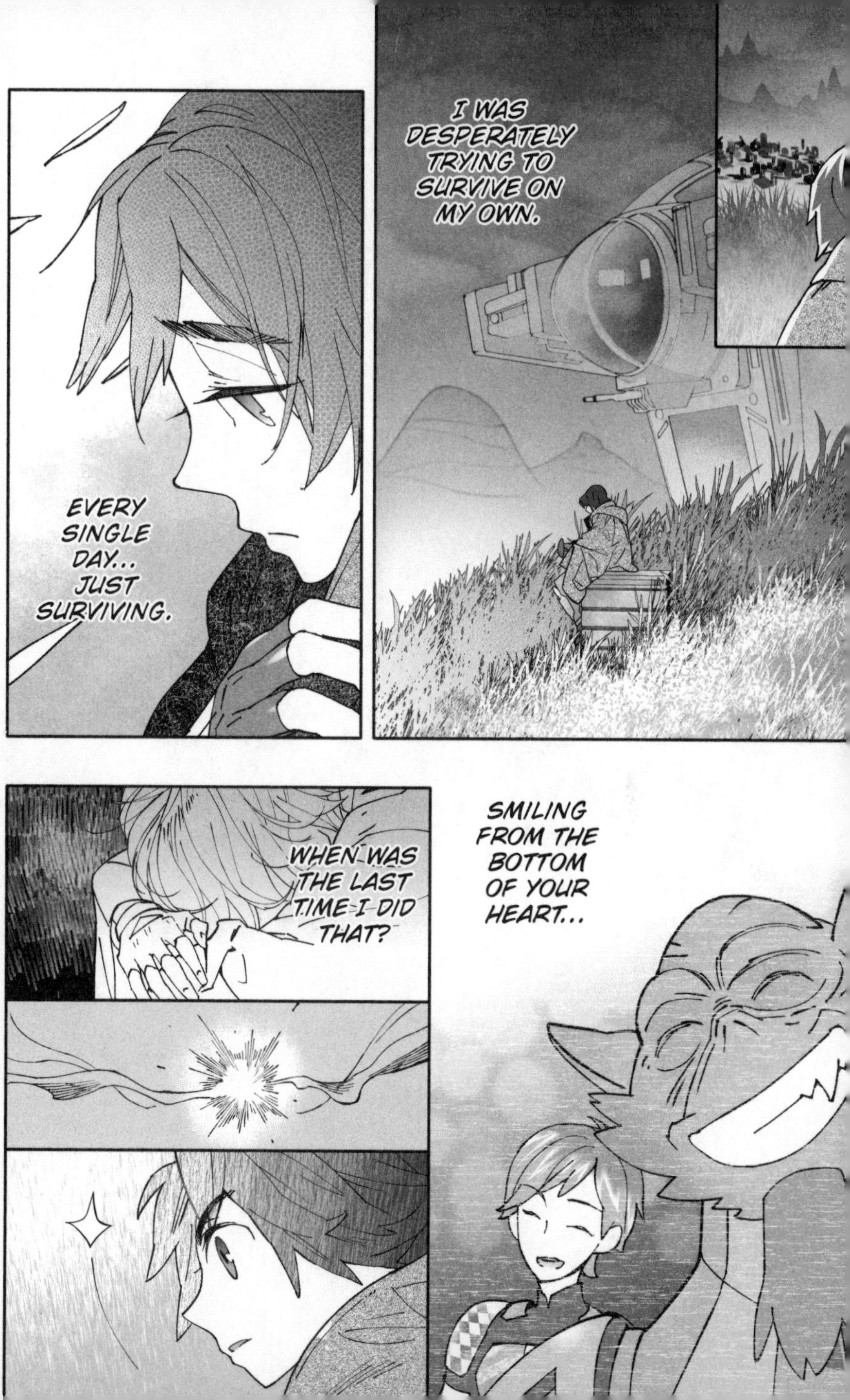
I WAS DESPERATELY TRYING TO SURVIVE ON MY OWN.
EVERY SINGLE DAY... JUST SURVIVING.
SMILING FROM THE BOTTOM OF YOUR HEART...
WHEN WAS THE LAST TIME I DID THAT?

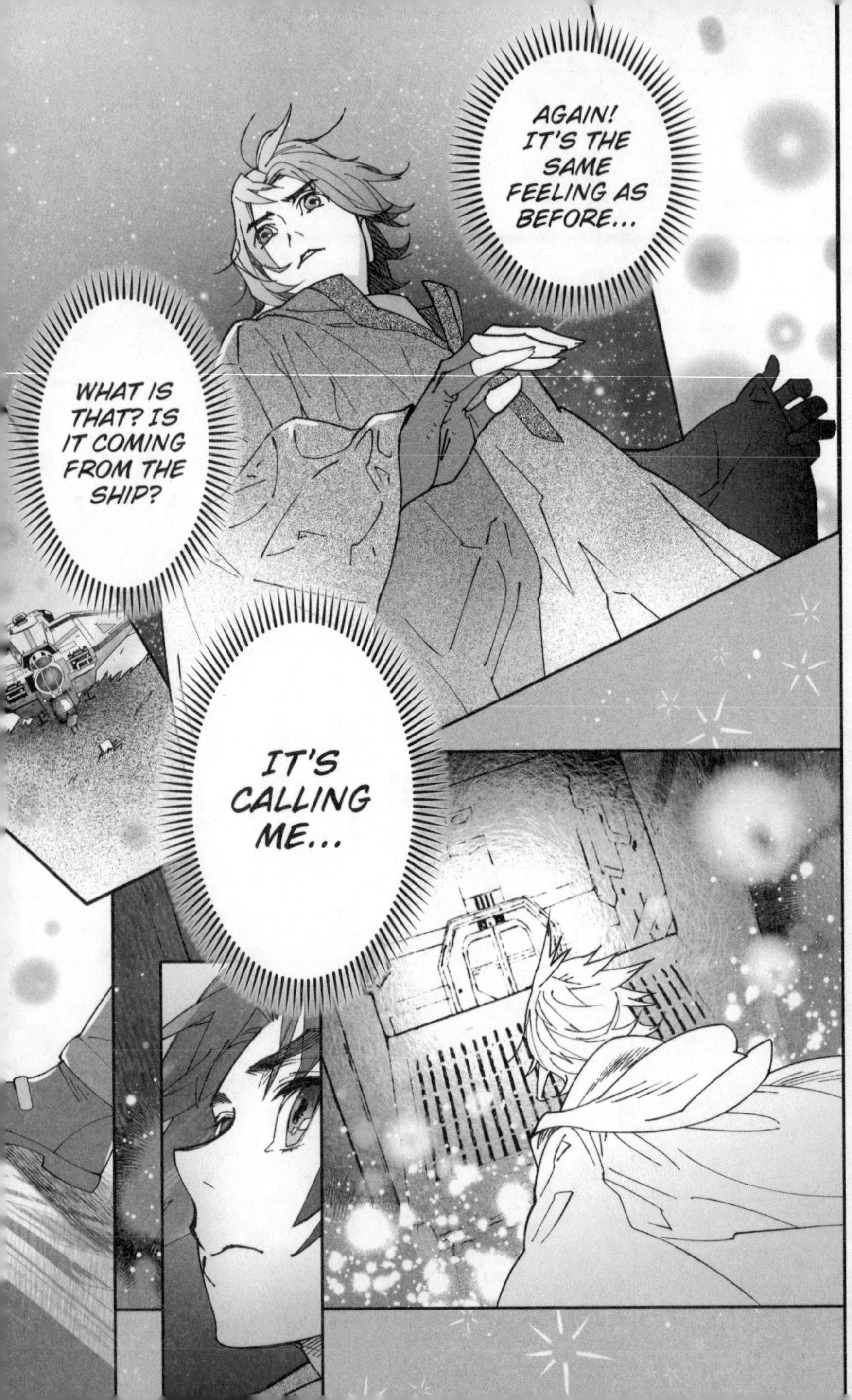
AGAIN! IT'S THE SAME FEELING AS BEFORE...
WHAT IS THAT? IS IT COMING FROM THE SHIP?
IT'S CALLING ME...

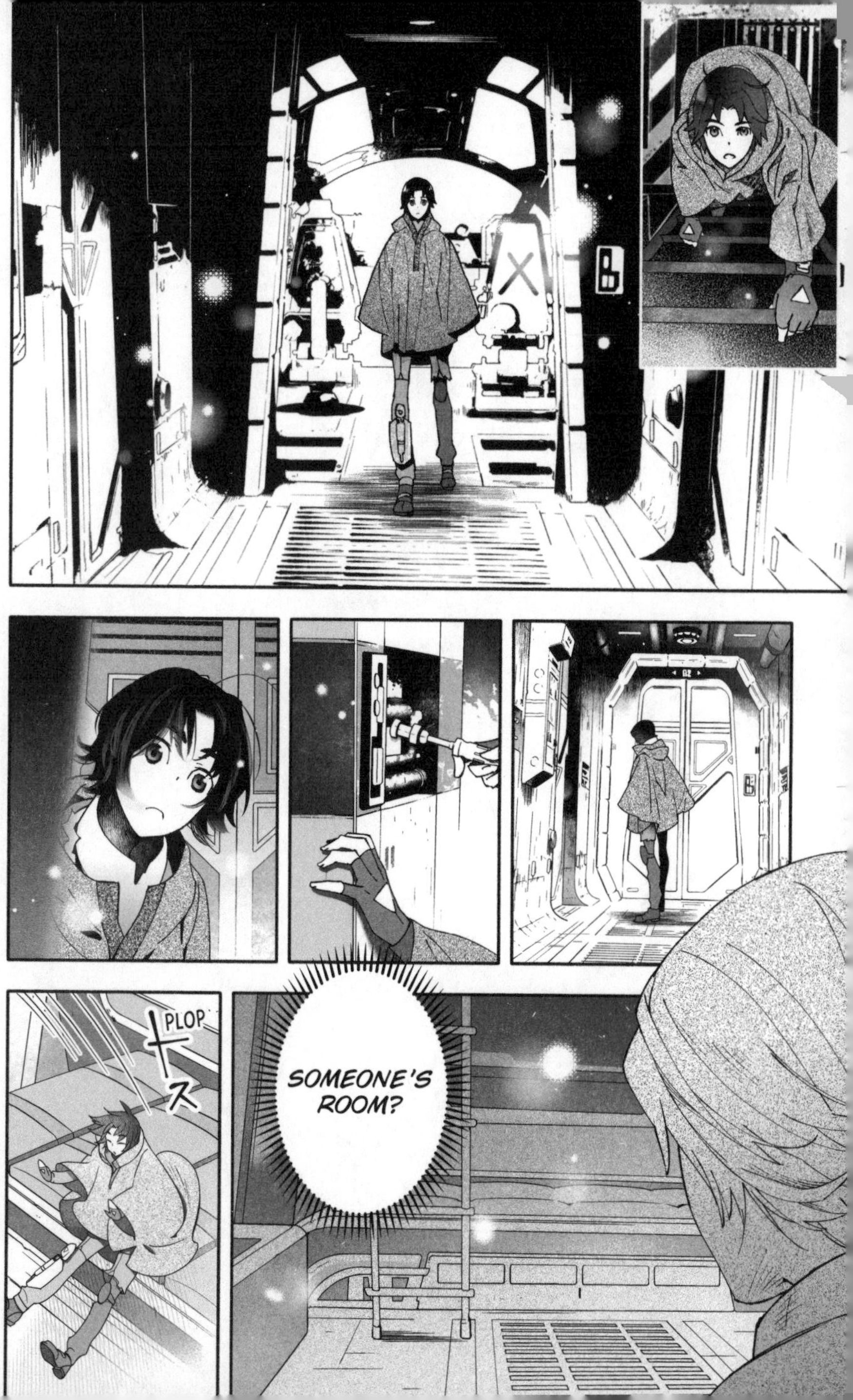
SOMEONE'S ROOM?
PLOP
トス

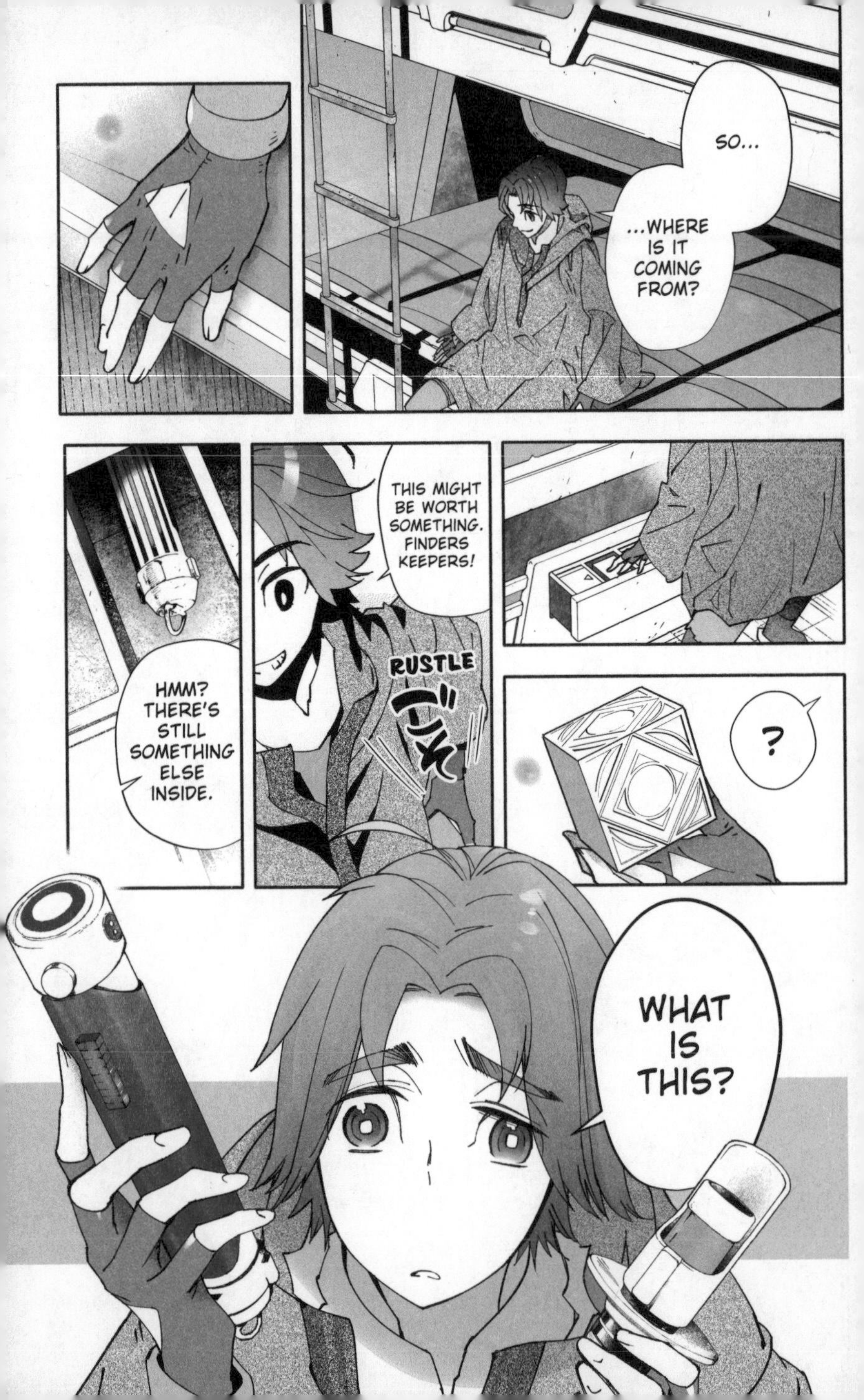
SO...
...WHERE IS IT COMING FROM?
?
THIS MIGHT BE WORTH SOMETHING. FINDERS KEEPERS!
RUSTLE
HMM? THERE'S STILL SOMETHING ELSE INSIDE.
WHAT IS THIS?

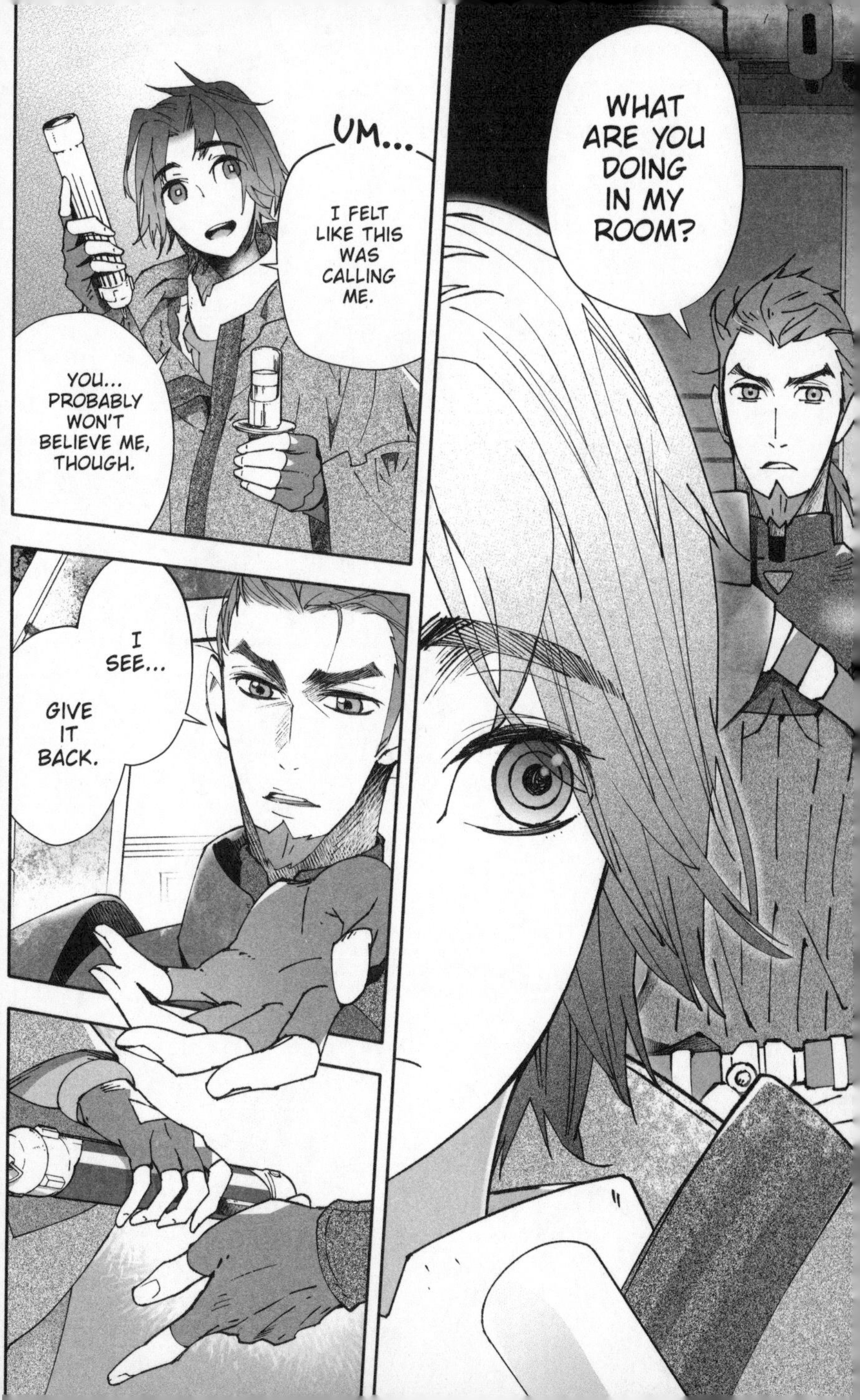
WHAT ARE YOU DOING IN MY ROOM?
UM...
I FELT LIKE THIS WAS CALLING ME.
YOU... PROBABLY WON'T BELIEVE ME, THOUGH.
I SEE...
GIVE IT BACK.

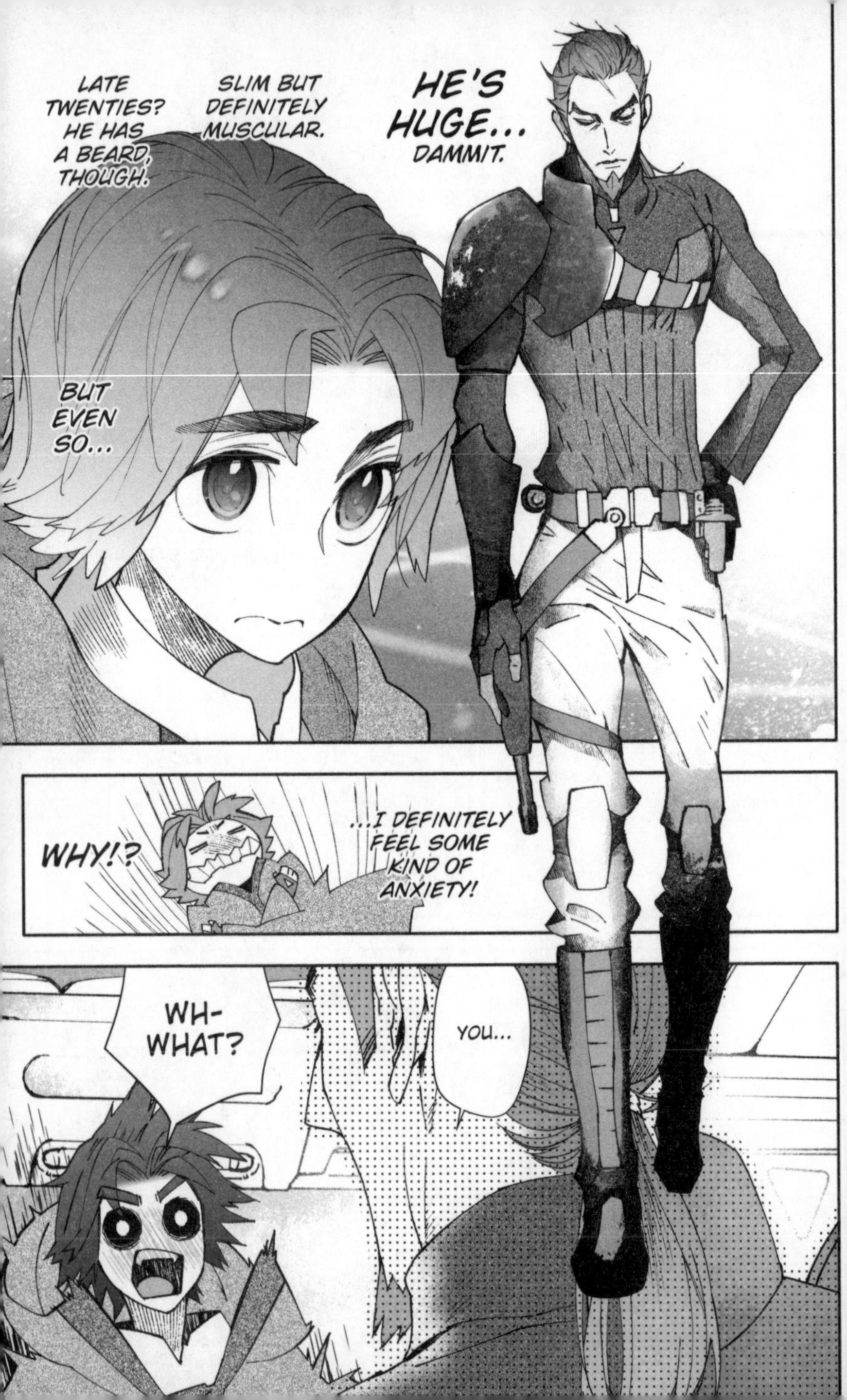
HE'S HUGE... DAMMIT.
SLIM BUT DEFINITELY MUSCULAR.
LATE TWENTIES? HE HAS A BEARD, THOUGH.
BUT EVEN SO...
...I DEFINITELY FEEL SOME KIND OF ANXIETY!
WHY!?
YOU...
WH-WHAT?

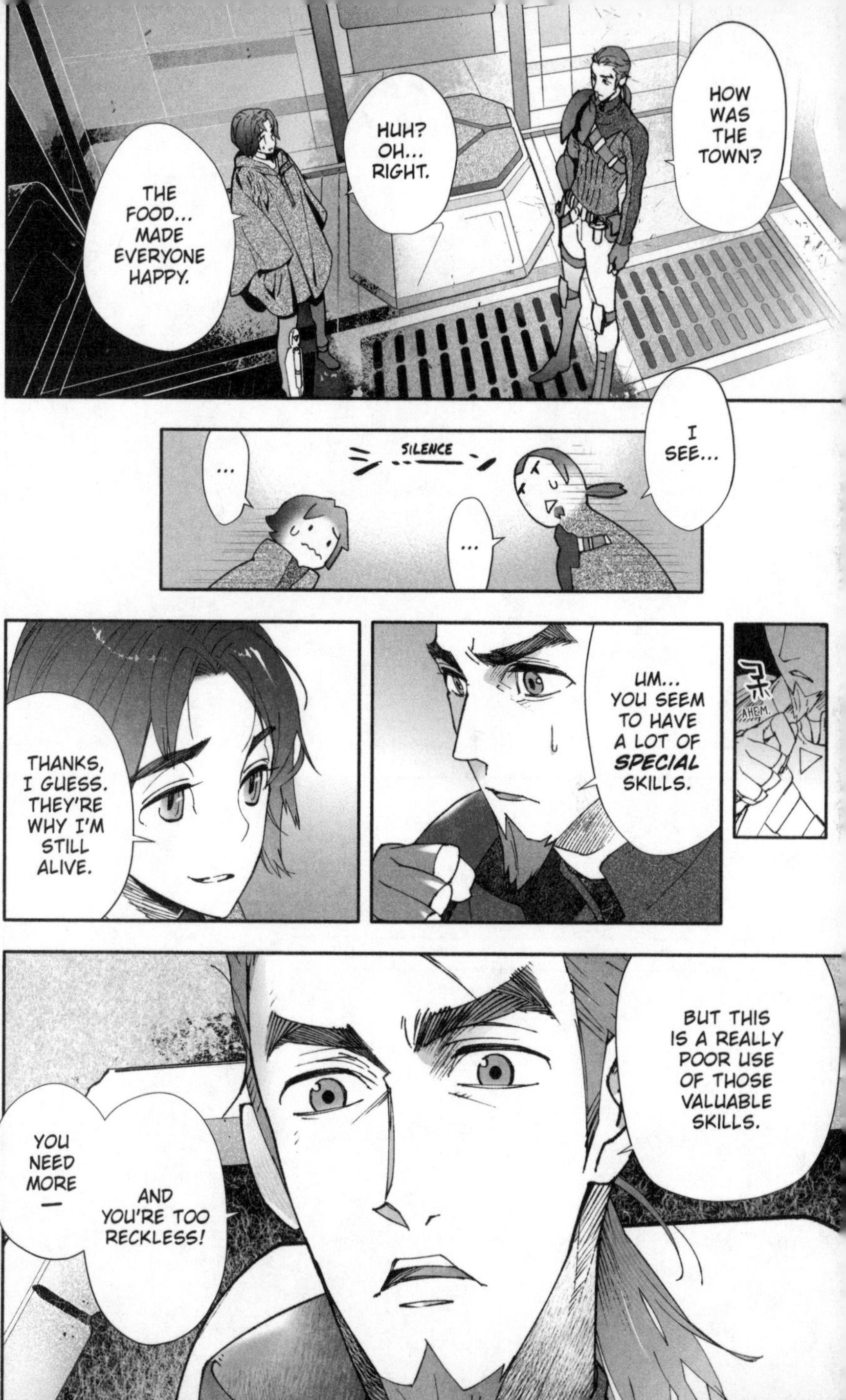
HOW WAS THE TOWN?
HUH? OH... RIGHT.
THE FOOD... MADE EVERYONE HAPPY.
I SEE...
SILENCE
...
...
AHEM.
UM... YOU SEEM TO HAVE A LOT OF SPECIAL SKILLS.
THANKS, I GUESS. THEY'RE WHY I'M STILL ALIVE.
BUT THIS IS A REALLY POOR USE OF THOSE VALUABLE SKILLS.
YOU NEED MORE —
AND YOU'RE TOO RECKLESS!

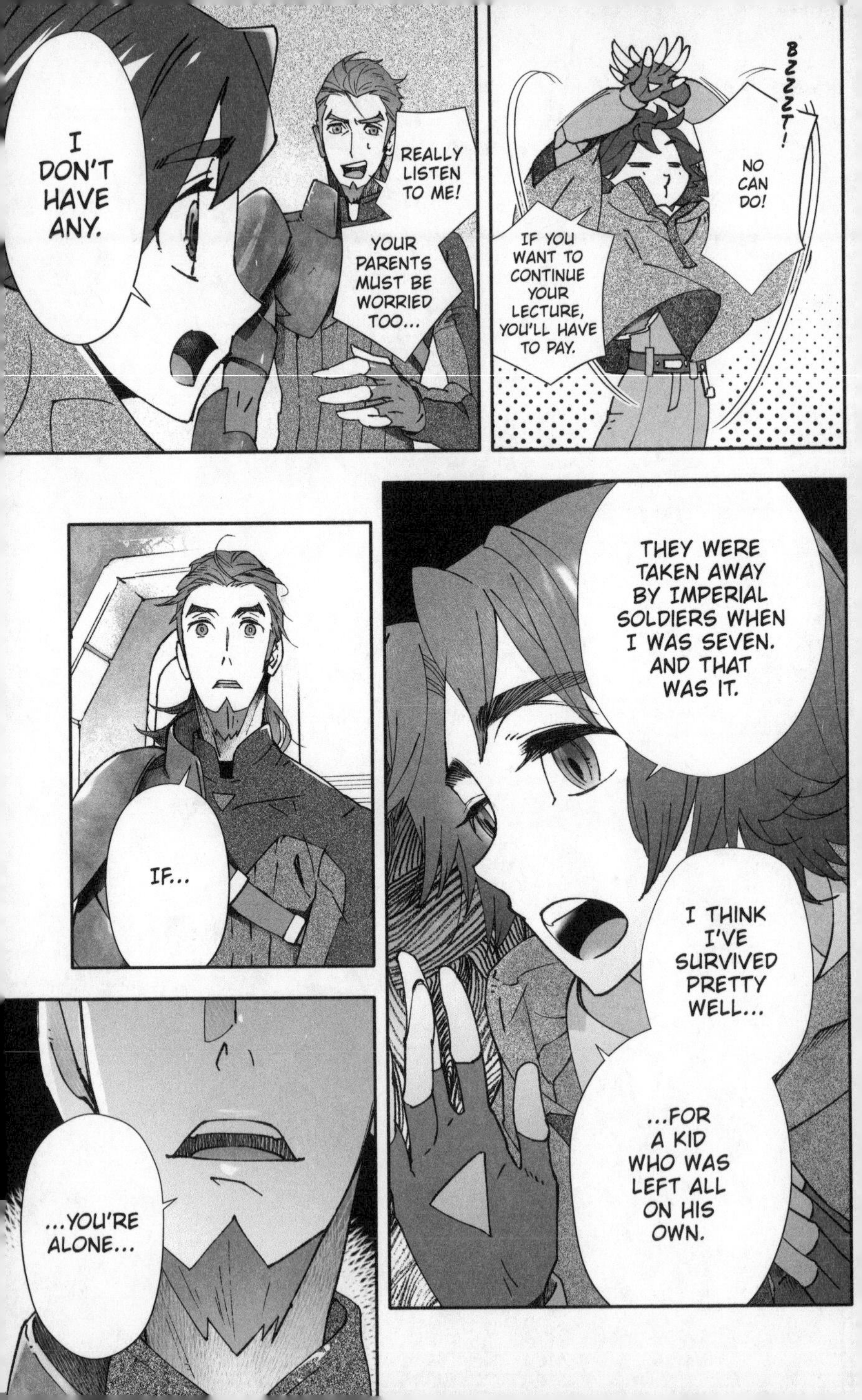
BZZZT!
NO CAN DO!
IF YOU WANT TO CONTINUE YOUR LECTURE, YOU'LL HAVE TO PAY.
REALLY LISTEN TO ME!
YOUR PARENTS MUST BE WORRIED TOO...
I DON'T HAVE ANY.
THEY WERE TAKEN AWAY BY IMPERIAL SOLDIERS WHEN I WAS SEVEN. AND THAT WAS IT.
I THINK I'VE SURVIVED PRETTY WELL...
...FOR A KID WHO WAS LEFT ALL ON HIS OWN.
IF...
...YOU'RE ALONE...

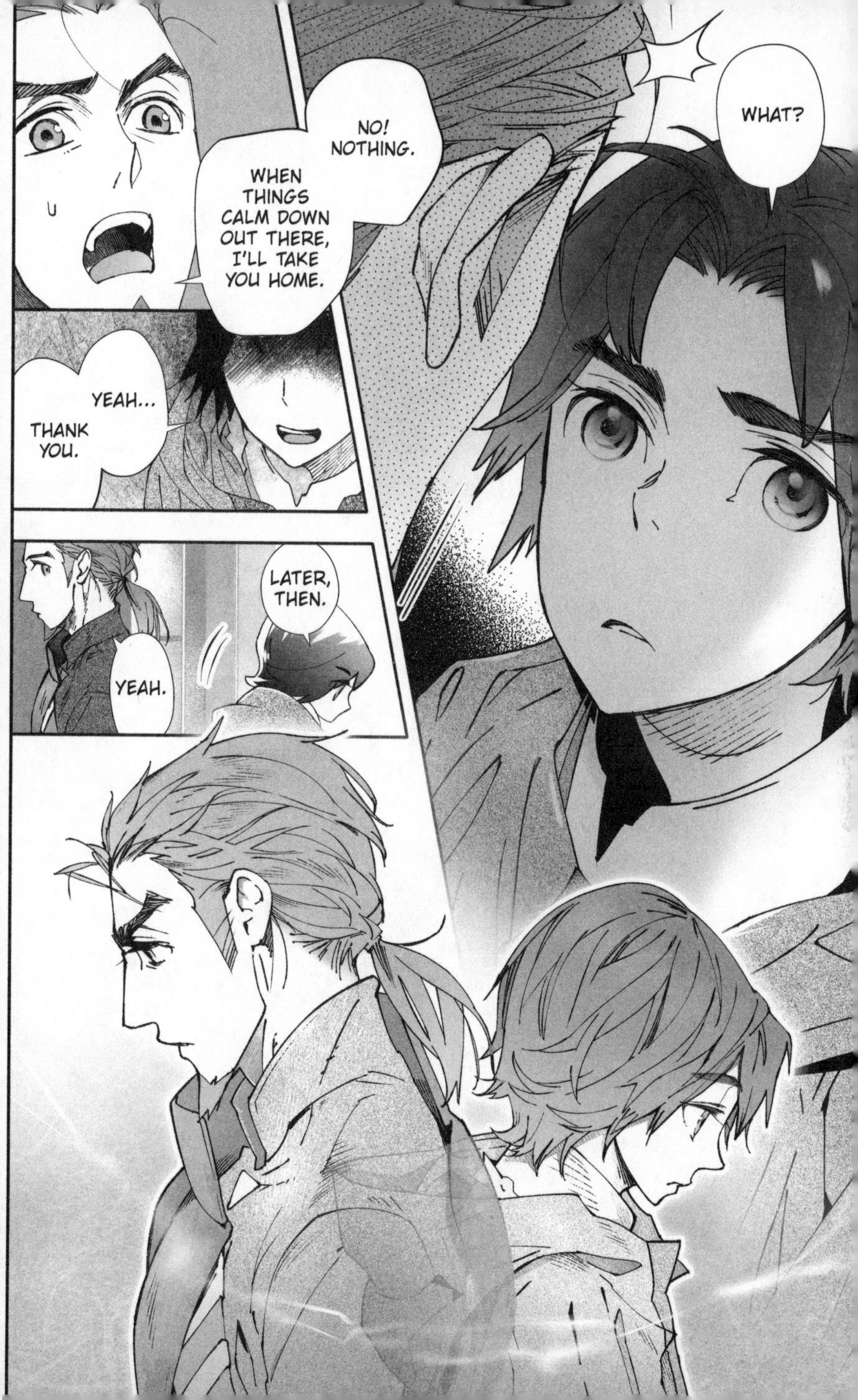
WHAT?
NO! NOTHING.
WHEN THINGS CALM DOWN OUT THERE, I'LL TAKE YOU HOME.
YEAH...
THANK YOU.
LATER, THEN.
YEAH.

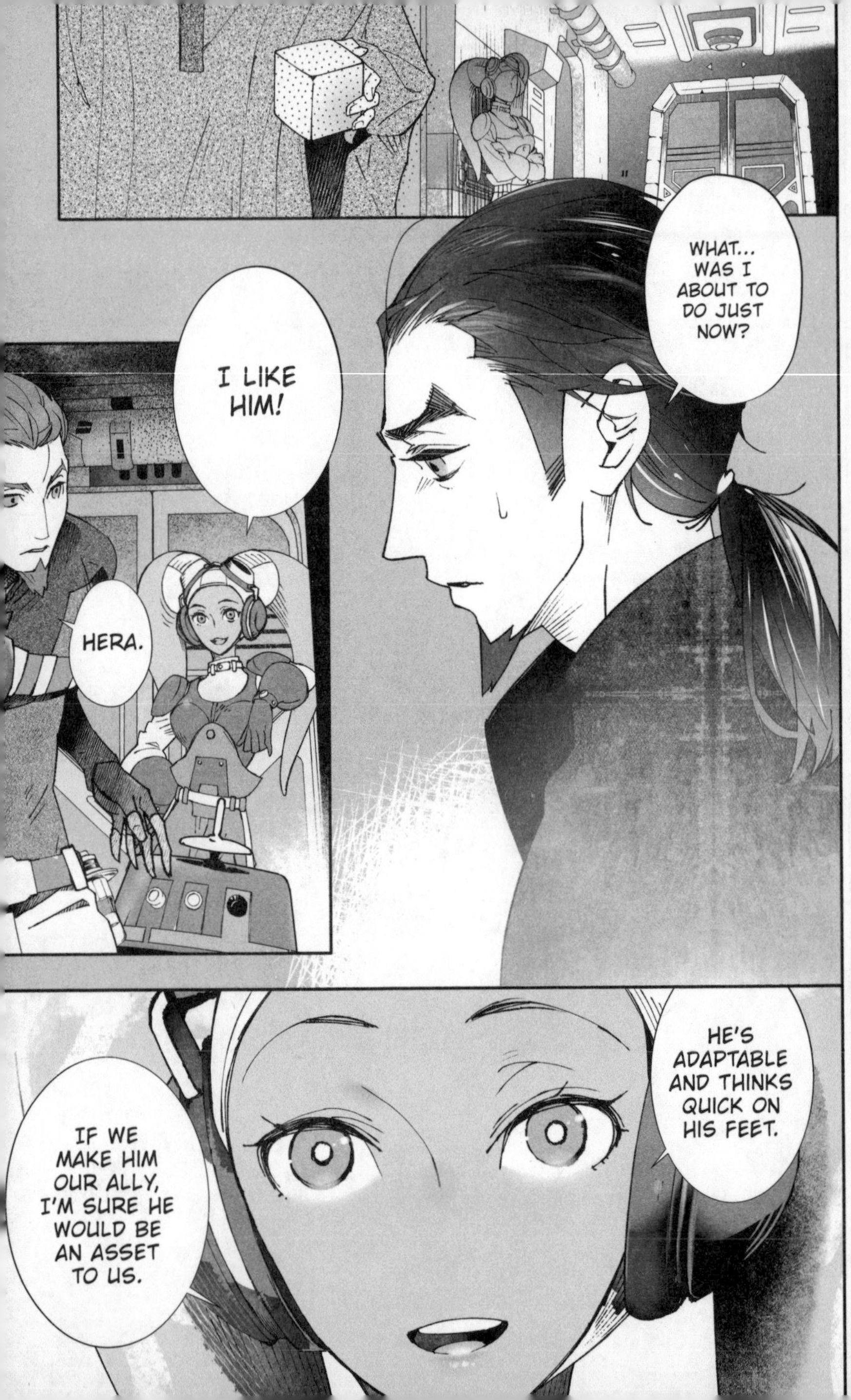
WHAT... WAS I ABOUT TO DO JUST NOW?
I LIKE HIM!
HERA.
HE'S ADAPTABLE AND THINKS QUICK ON HIS FEET.
IF WE MAKE HIM OUR ALLY, I'M SURE HE WOULD BE AN ASSET TO US.

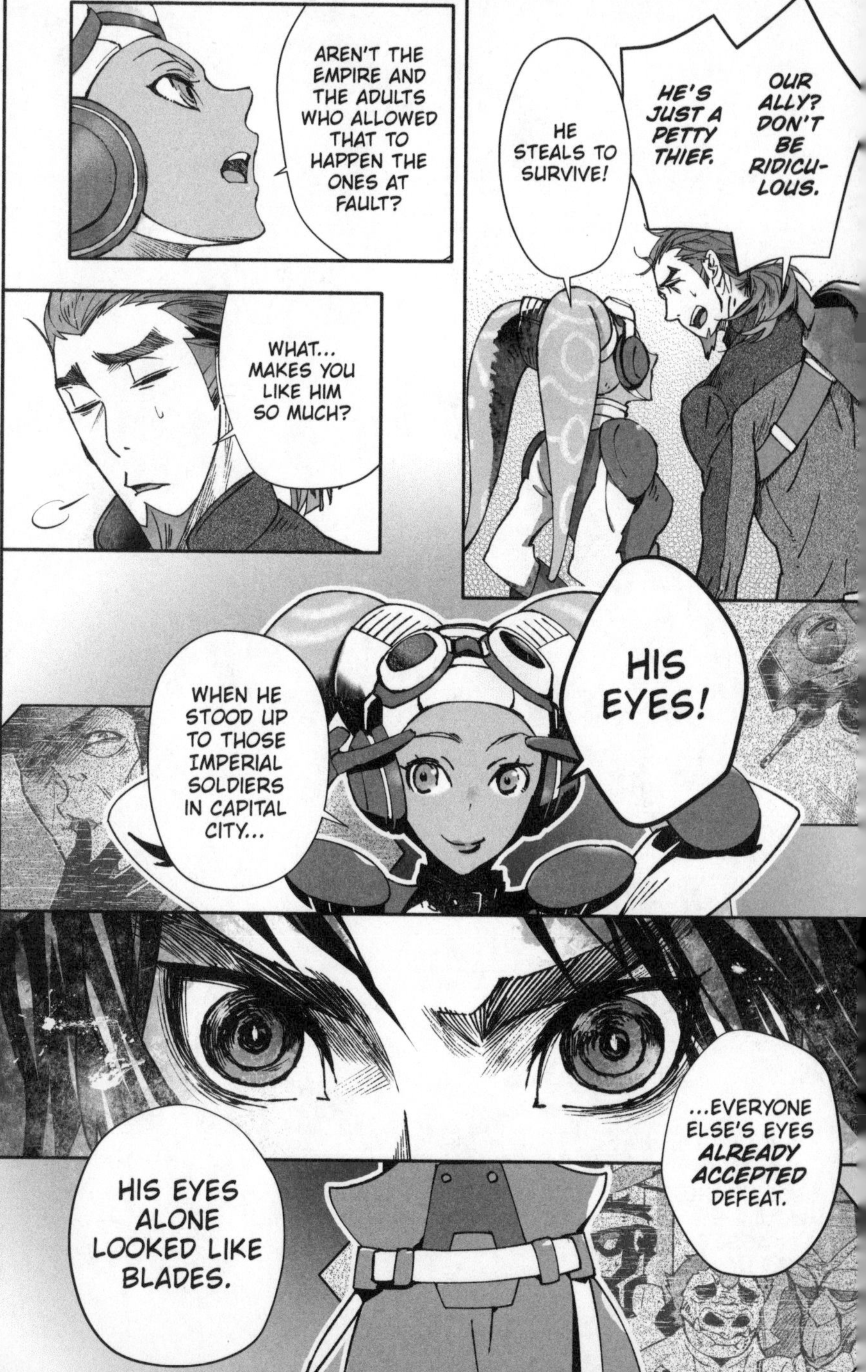
OUR ALLY? DON'T BE RIDICULOUS.
HE'S JUST A PETTY THIEF.
HE STEALS TO SURVIVE!
AREN'T THE EMPIRE AND THE ADULTS WHO ALLOWED THAT TO HAPPEN THE ONES AT FAULT?
WHAT... MAKES YOU LIKE HIM SO MUCH?
HIS EYES!
WHEN HE STOOD UP TO THOSE IMPERIAL SOLDIERS IN CAPITAL CITY...
...EVERYONE ELSE'S EYES ALREADY ACCEPTED DEFEAT.
HIS EYES ALONE LOOKED LIKE BLADES.

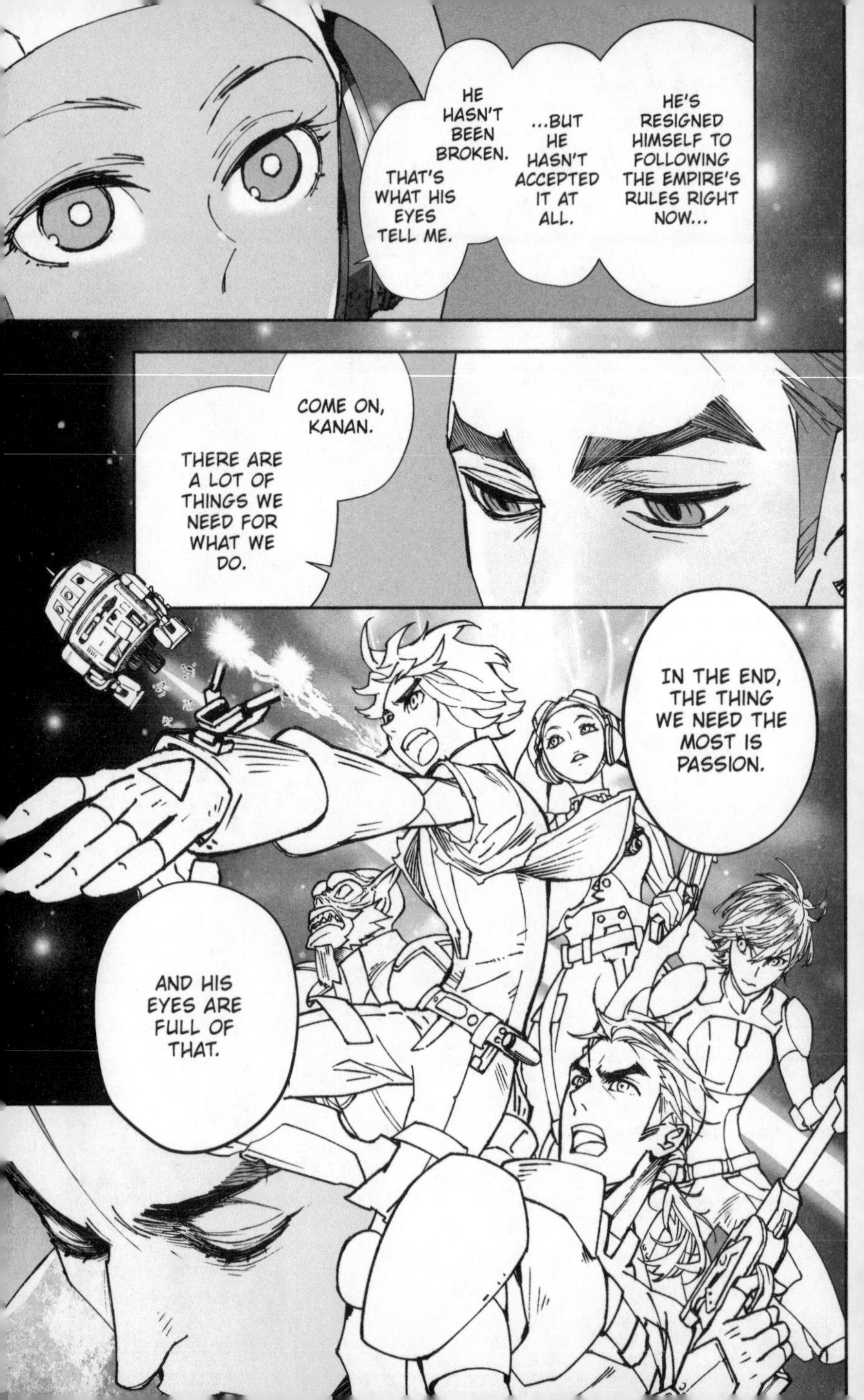
HE'S RESIGNED HIMSELF TO FOLLOWING THE EMPIRE'S RULES RIGHT NOW...
...BUT HE HASN'T ACCEPTED IT AT ALL.
HE HASN'T BEEN BROKEN.
THAT'S WHAT HIS EYES TELL ME.
COME ON, KANAN.
THERE ARE A LOT OF THINGS WE NEED FOR WHAT WE DO.
IN THE END, THE THING WE NEED THE MOST IS PASSION.
AND HIS EYES ARE FULL OF THAT.

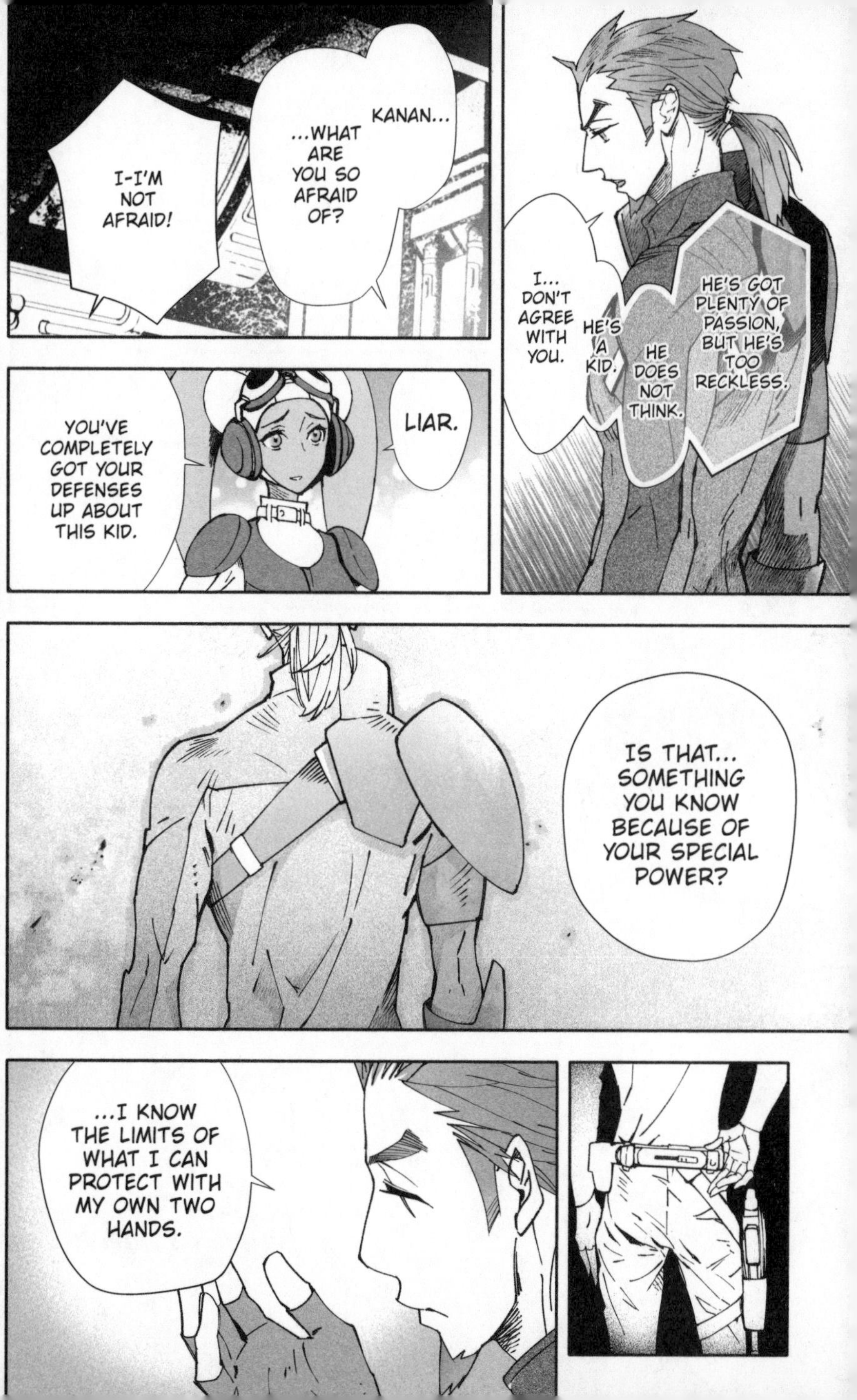
HE'S GOT PLENTY OF PASSION, BUT HE'S TOO RECKLESS.
HE DOES NOT THINK.
HE'S A KID.
I... DON'T AGREE WITH YOU.
KANAN...
...WHAT ARE YOU SO AFRAID OF?
I-I'M NOT AFRAID!
LIAR.
YOU'VE COMPLETELY GOT YOUR DEFENSES UP ABOUT THIS KID.
IS THAT... SOMETHING YOU KNOW BECAUSE OF YOUR SPECIAL POWER?
...I KNOW THE LIMITS OF WHAT I CAN PROTECT WITH MY OWN TWO HANDS.

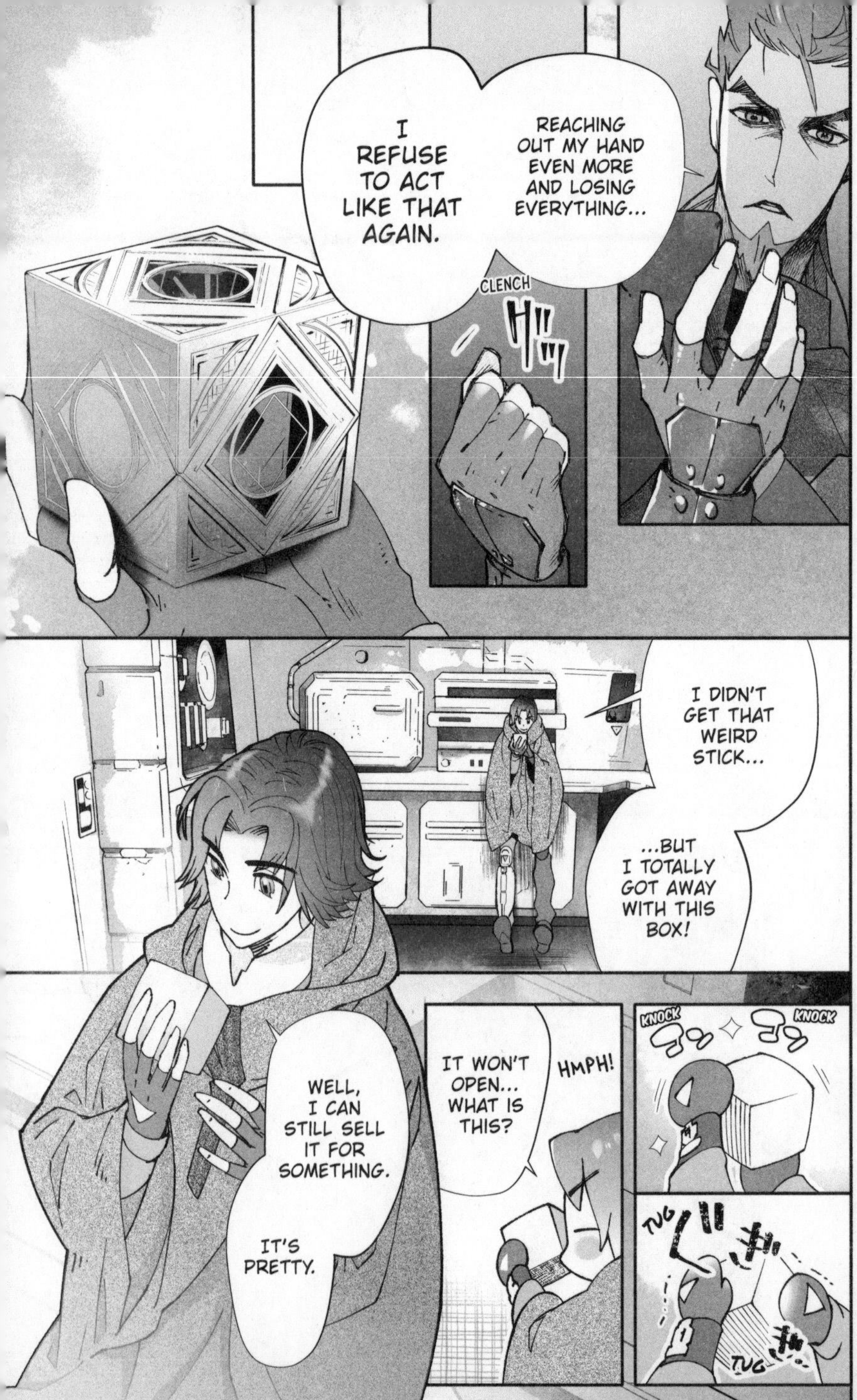
REACHING OUT MY HAND EVEN MORE AND LOSING EVERYTHING...
I REFUSE TO ACT LIKE THAT AGAIN.
CLENCH
I DIDN'T GET THAT WEIRD STICK...
...BUT I TOTALLY GOT AWAY WITH THIS BOX!
KNOCK
KNOCK
TUG
TUG
HMPH!
IT WON'T OPEN... WHAT IS THIS?
WELL, I CAN STILL SELL IT FOR SOMETHING.
IT'S PRETTY.

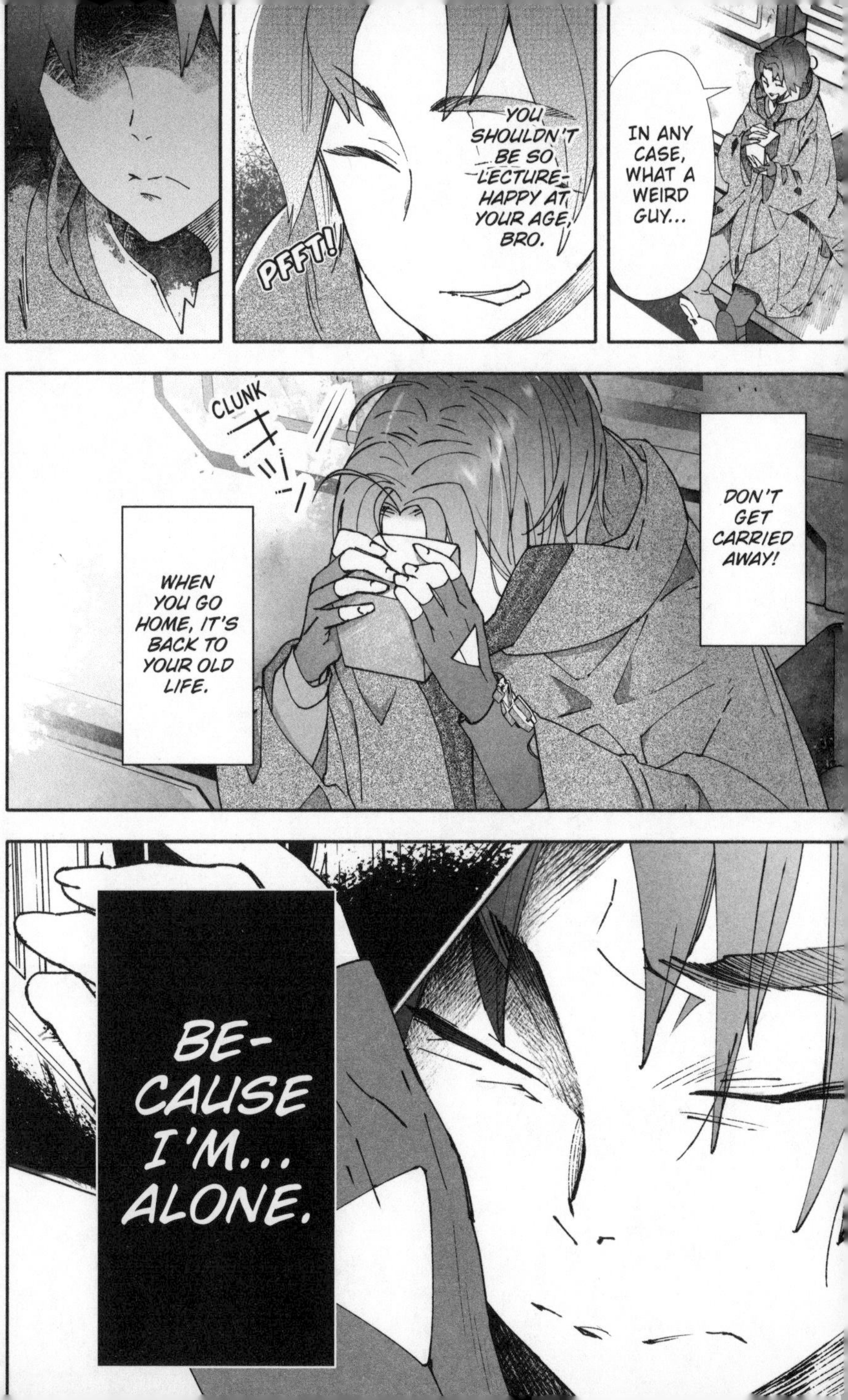
IN ANY CASE, WHAT A WEIRD GUY...
YOU SHOULDN'T BE SO LECTURE-HAPPY AT YOUR AGE, BRO.
PFFT!
CLUNK
DON'T GET CARRIED AWAY!
WHEN YOU GO HOME, IT'S BACK TO YOUR OLD LIFE.
BE-CAUSE I'M... ALONE.

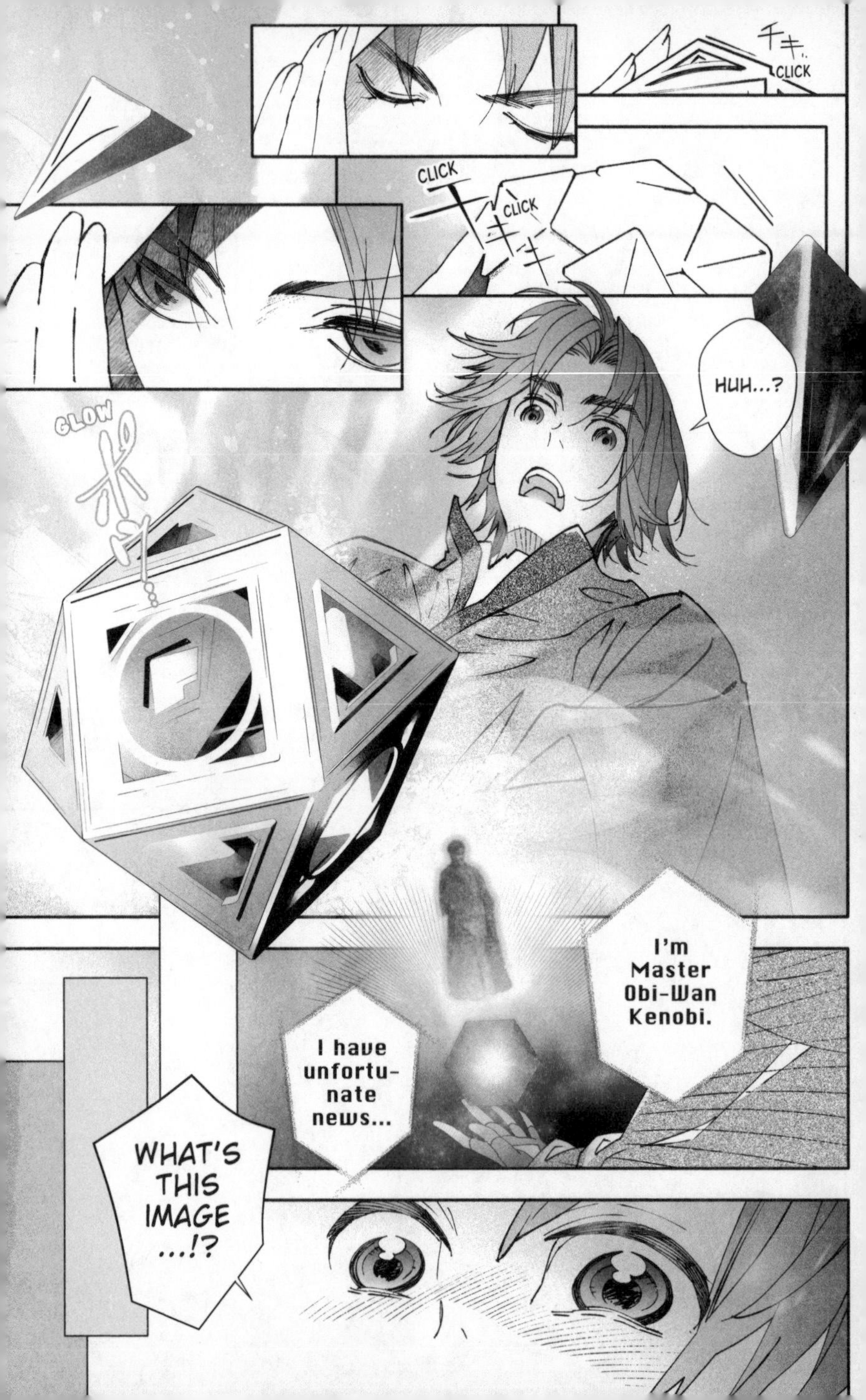
チキ.. CLICK
CLICK
CLICK
HUH...?
GLOW
I'm Master Obi-Wan Kenobi.
I have unfortunate news...
WHAT'S THIS IMAGE ...!?

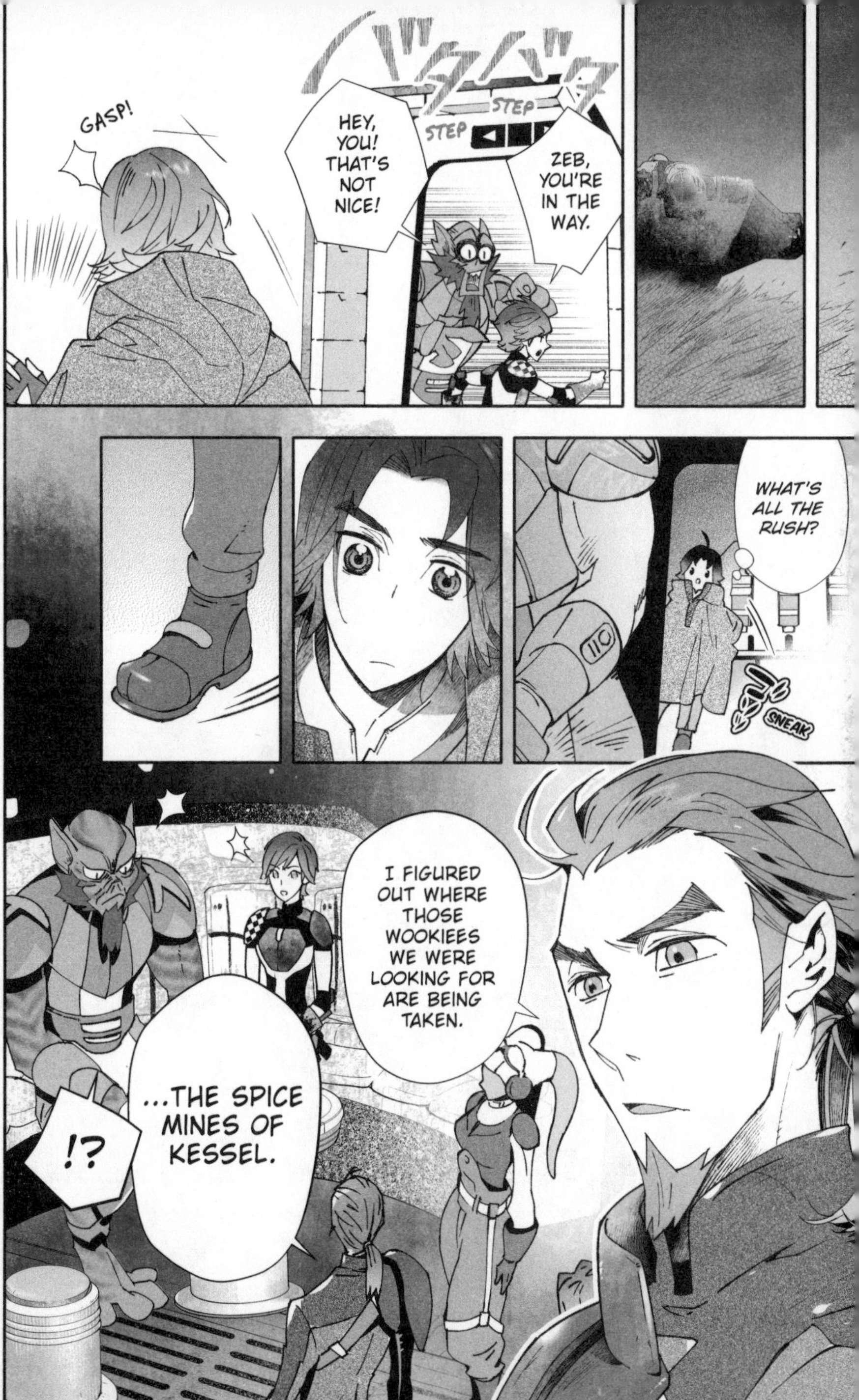

バタバタ
STEP
STEP
ZEB, YOU'RE IN THE WAY.
HEY, YOU! THAT'S NOT NICE!
GASP!
WHAT'S ALL THE RUSH?
SNEAK
I FIGURED OUT WHERE THOSE WOOKIEES WE WERE LOOKING FOR ARE BEING TAKEN.
...THE SPICE MINES OF KESSEL.
!?

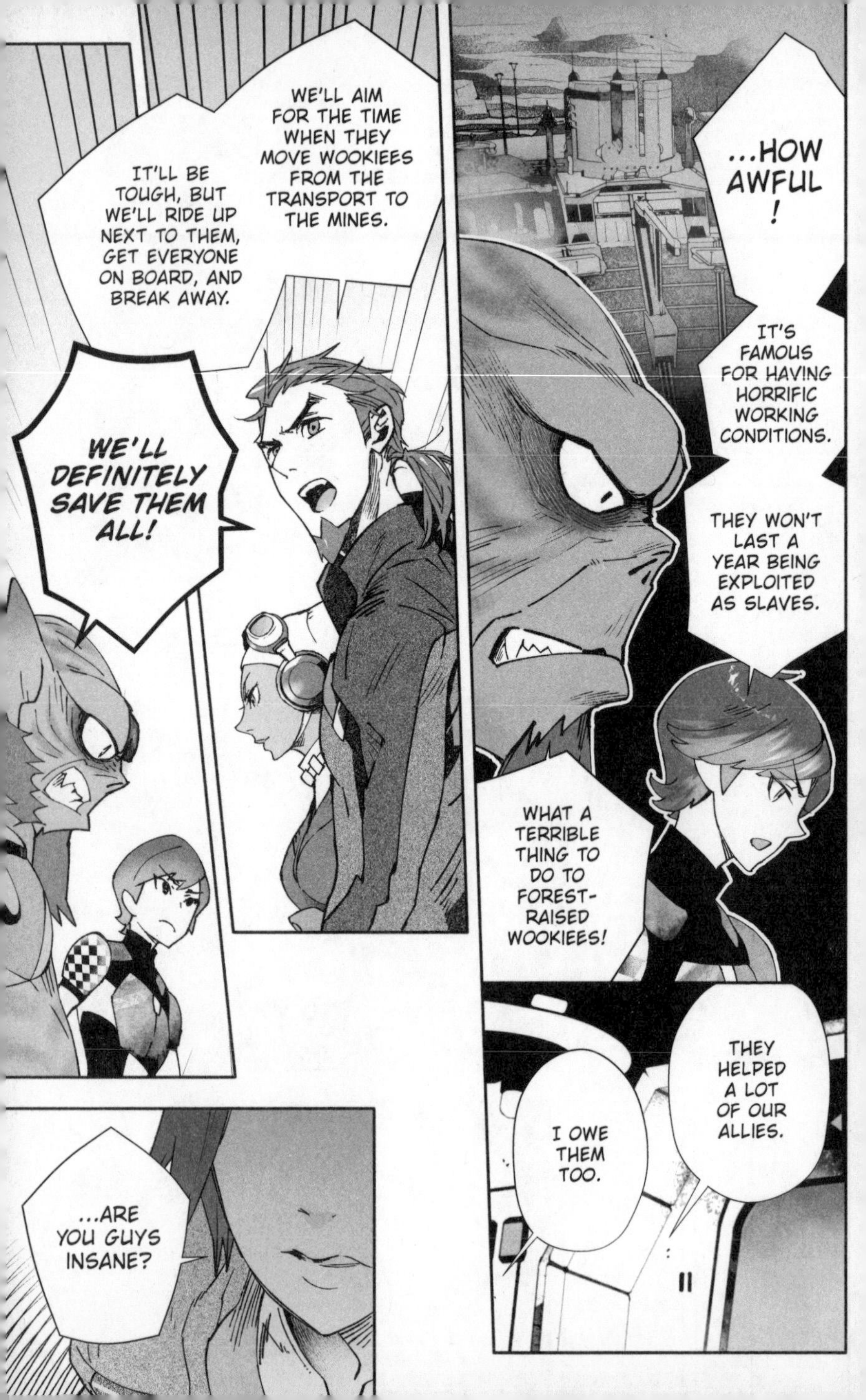

...HOW AWFUL!
IT'S FAMOUS FOR HAVING HORRIFIC WORKING CONDITIONS.
THEY WON'T LAST A YEAR BEING EXPLOITED AS SLAVES.
WHAT A TERRIBLE THING TO DO TO FOREST-RAISED WOOKIEES!
WE'LL AIM FOR THE TIME WHEN THEY MOVE WOOKIEES FROM THE TRANSPORT TO THE MINES.
IT'LL BE TOUGH, BUT WE'LL RIDE UP NEXT TO THEM, GET EVERYONE ON BOARD, AND BREAK AWAY.
WE'LL DEFINITELY SAVE THEM ALL!
THEY HELPED A LOT OF OUR ALLIES.
I OWE THEM TOO.
...ARE YOU GUYS INSANE?

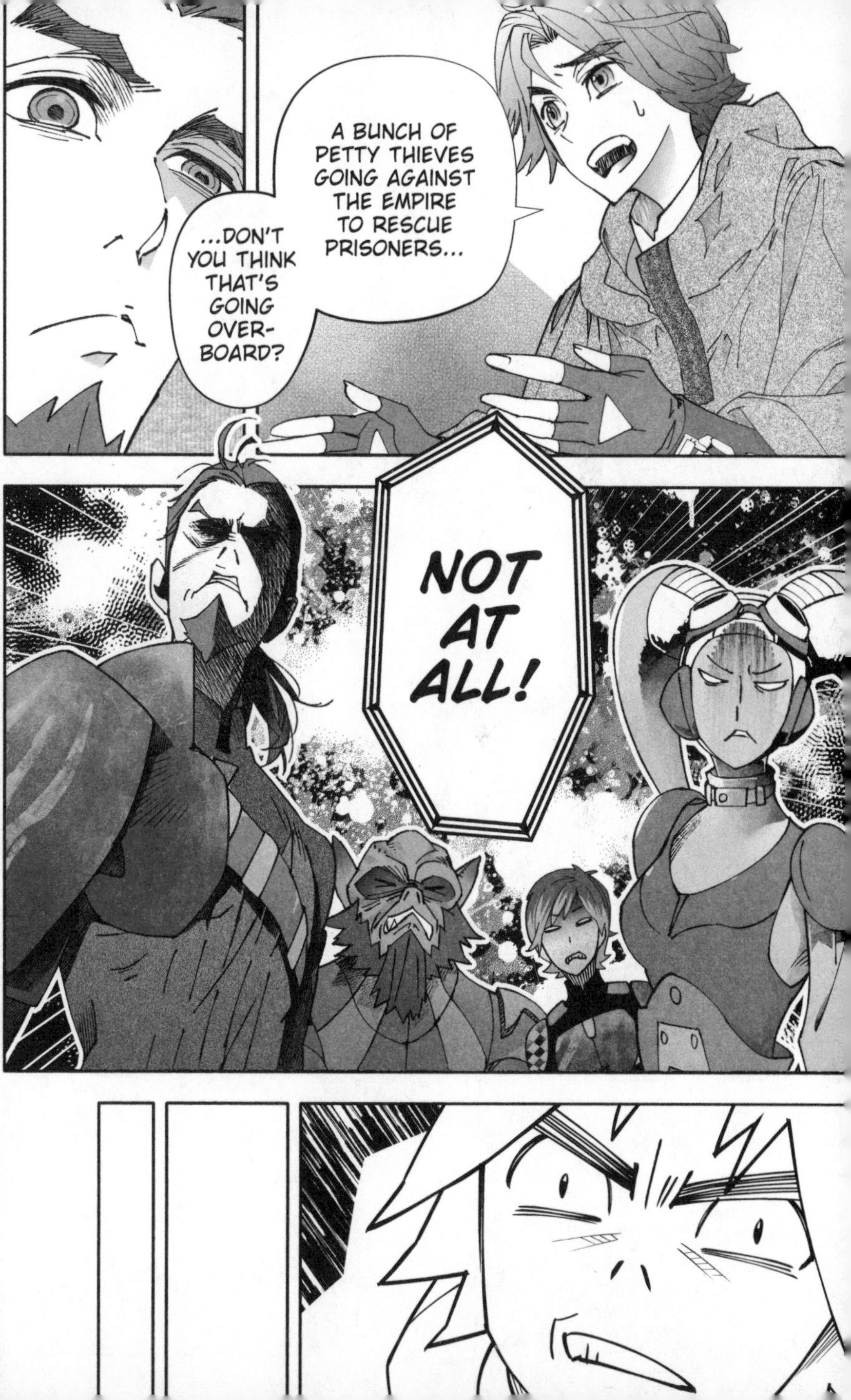
A BUNCH OF PETTY THIEVES GOING AGAINST THE EMPIRE TO RESCUE PRISONERS...
...DON'T YOU THINK THAT'S GOING OVER-BOARD?
NOT AT ALL!

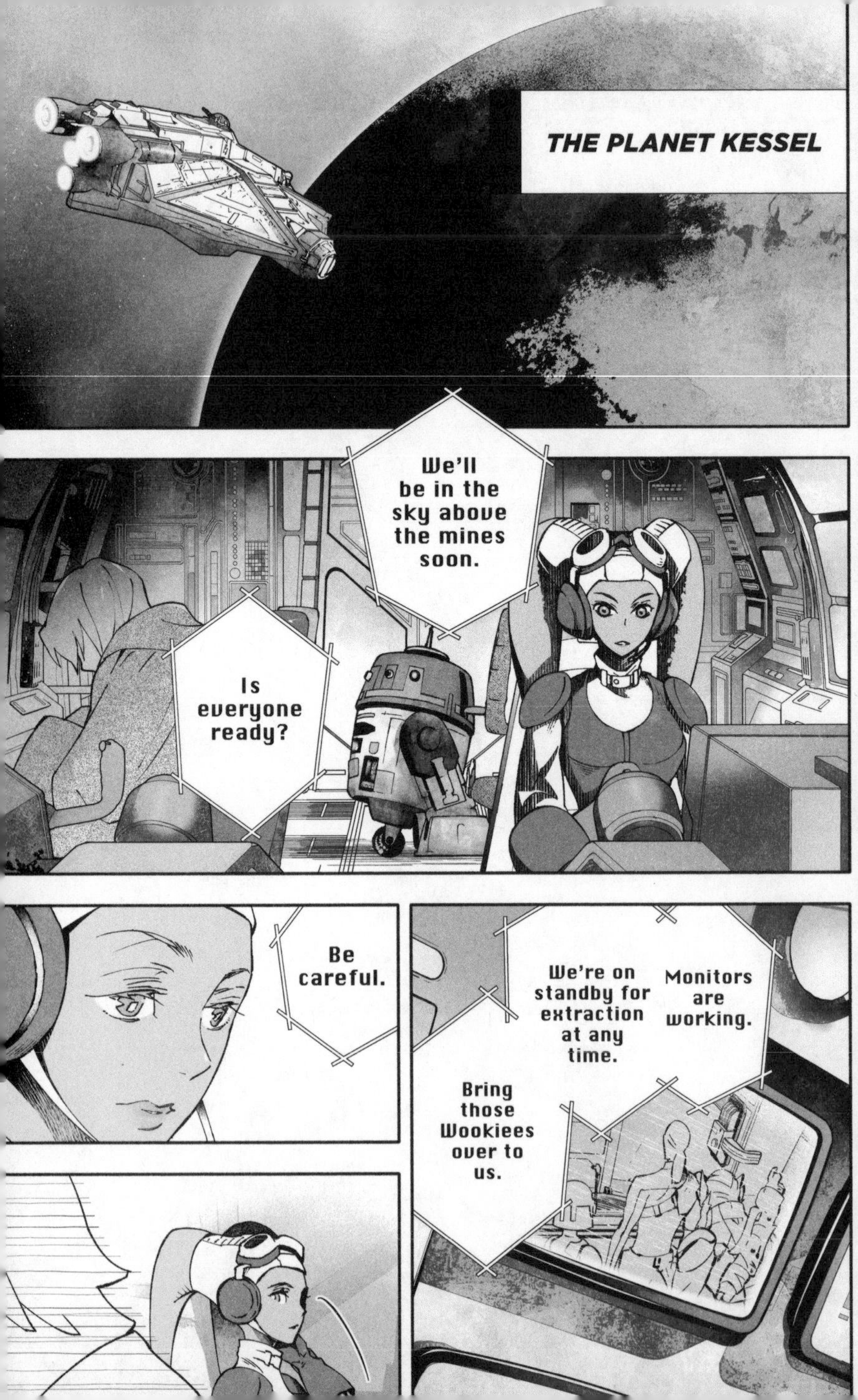
THE PLANET KESSEL
We'll be in the sky above the mines soon.
Is everyone ready?
Monitors are working.
We're on standby for extraction at any time.
Bring those Wookiees over to us.
Be careful.

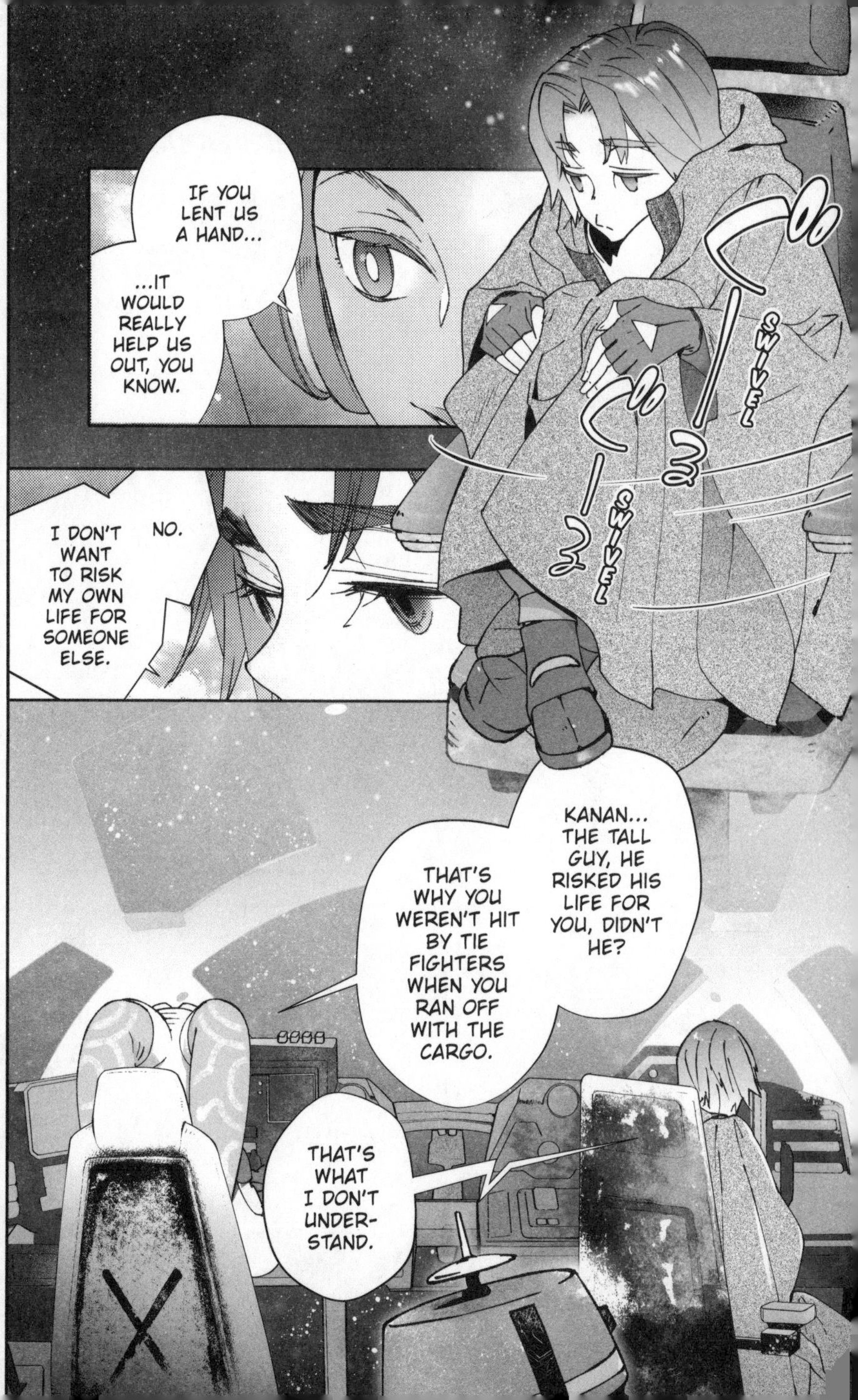
SWIVEL
SWIVEL
IF YOU LENT US A HAND...
...IT WOULD REALLY HELP US OUT, YOU KNOW.
NO.
I DON'T WANT TO RISK MY OWN LIFE FOR SOMEONE ELSE.
KANAN... THE TALL GUY, HE RISKED HIS LIFE FOR YOU, DIDN'T HE?
THAT'S WHY YOU WEREN'T HIT BY TIE FIGHTERS WHEN YOU RAN OFF WITH THE CARGO.
THAT'S WHAT I DON'T UNDER-STAND.

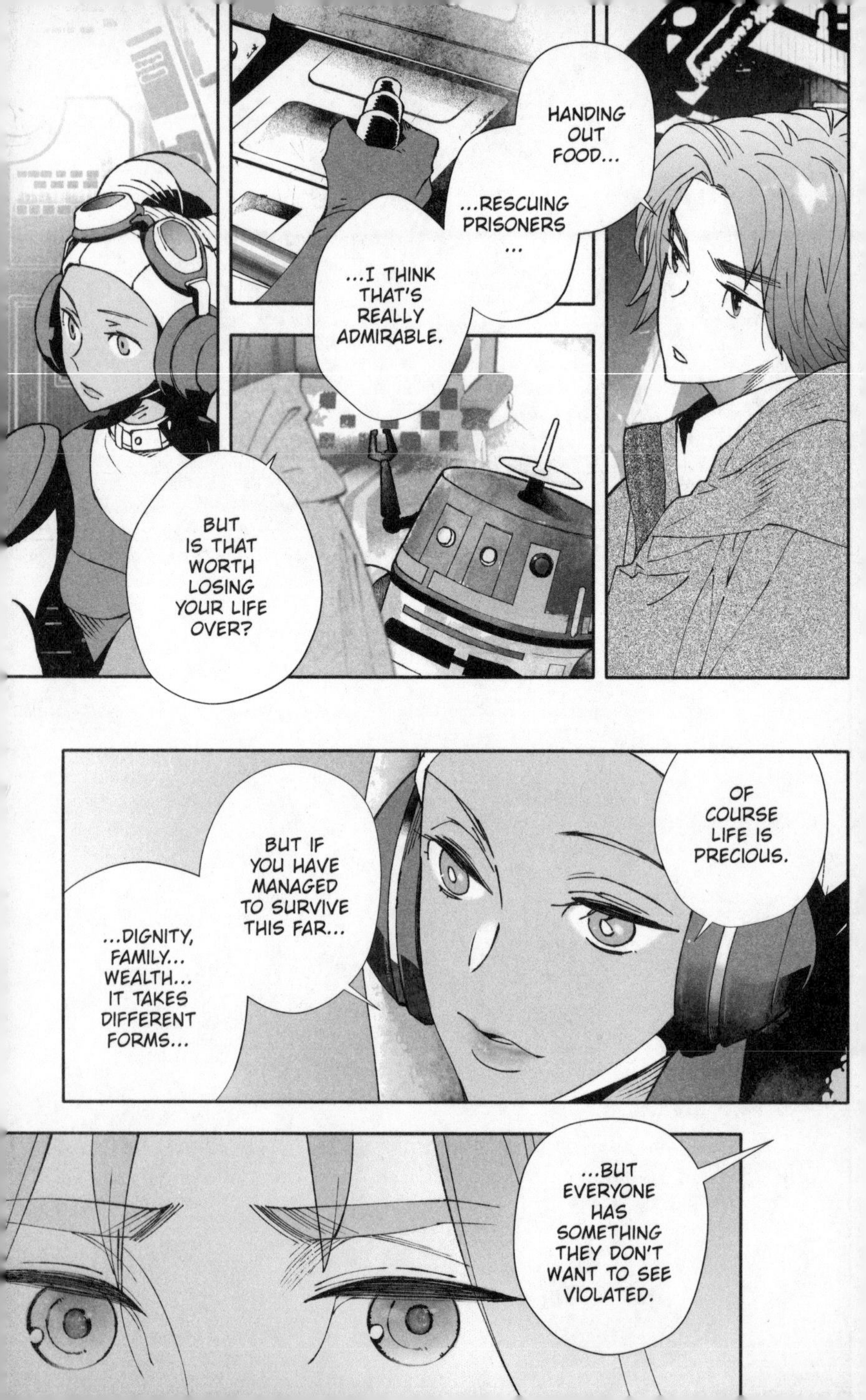
HANDING OUT FOOD...
...RESCUING PRISONERS ...
...I THINK THAT'S REALLY ADMIRABLE.
BUT IS THAT WORTH LOSING YOUR LIFE OVER?
OF COURSE LIFE IS PRECIOUS.
BUT IF YOU HAVE MANAGED TO SURVIVE THIS FAR...
...DIGNITY, FAMILY... WEALTH... IT TAKES DIFFERENT FORMS...
...BUT EVERYONE HAS SOMETHING THEY DON'T WANT TO SEE VIOLATED.

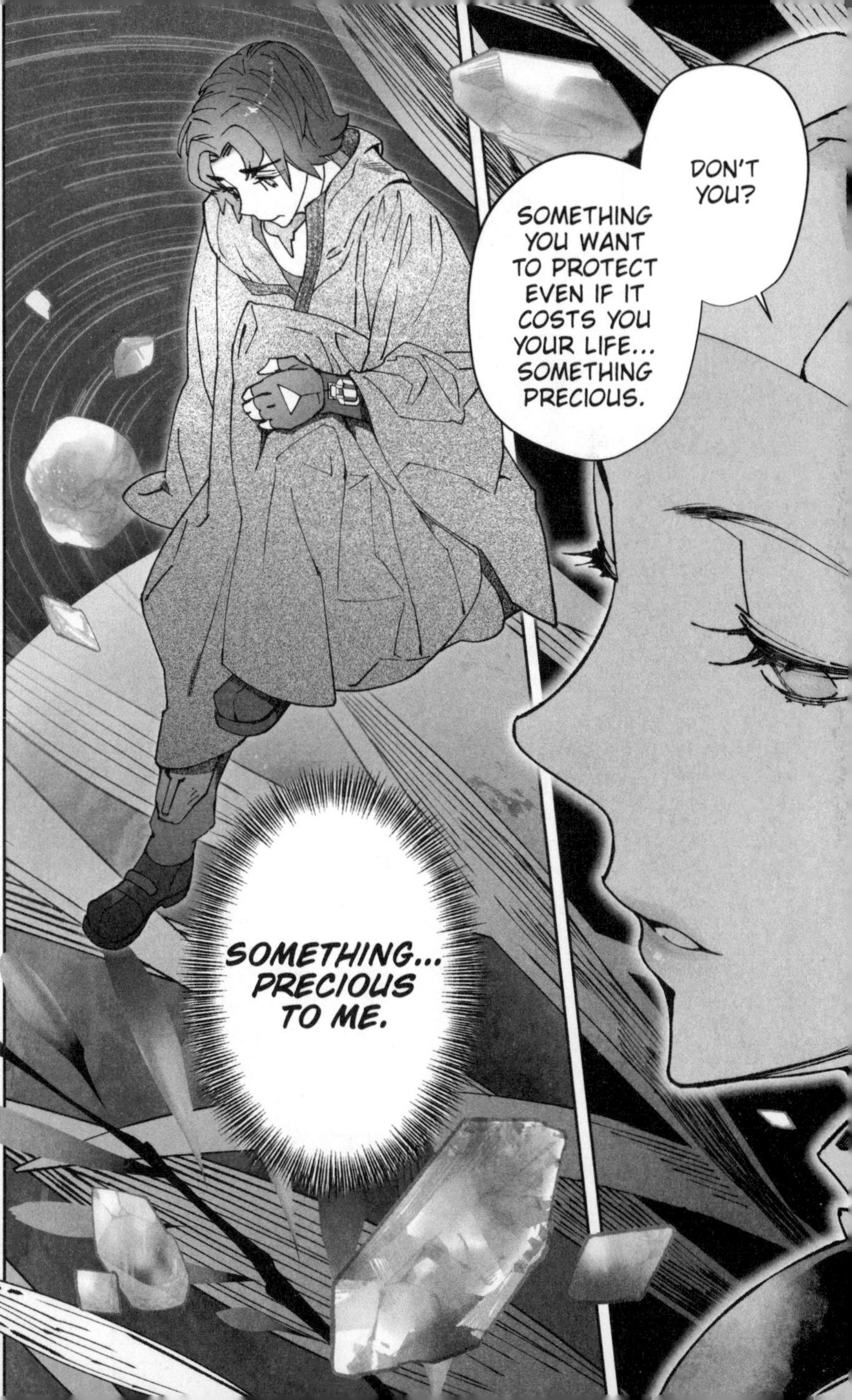
DON'T YOU?
SOMETHING YOU WANT TO PROTECT EVEN IF IT COSTS YOU YOUR LIFE... SOMETHING PRECIOUS.
SOMETHING... PRECIOUS TO ME.

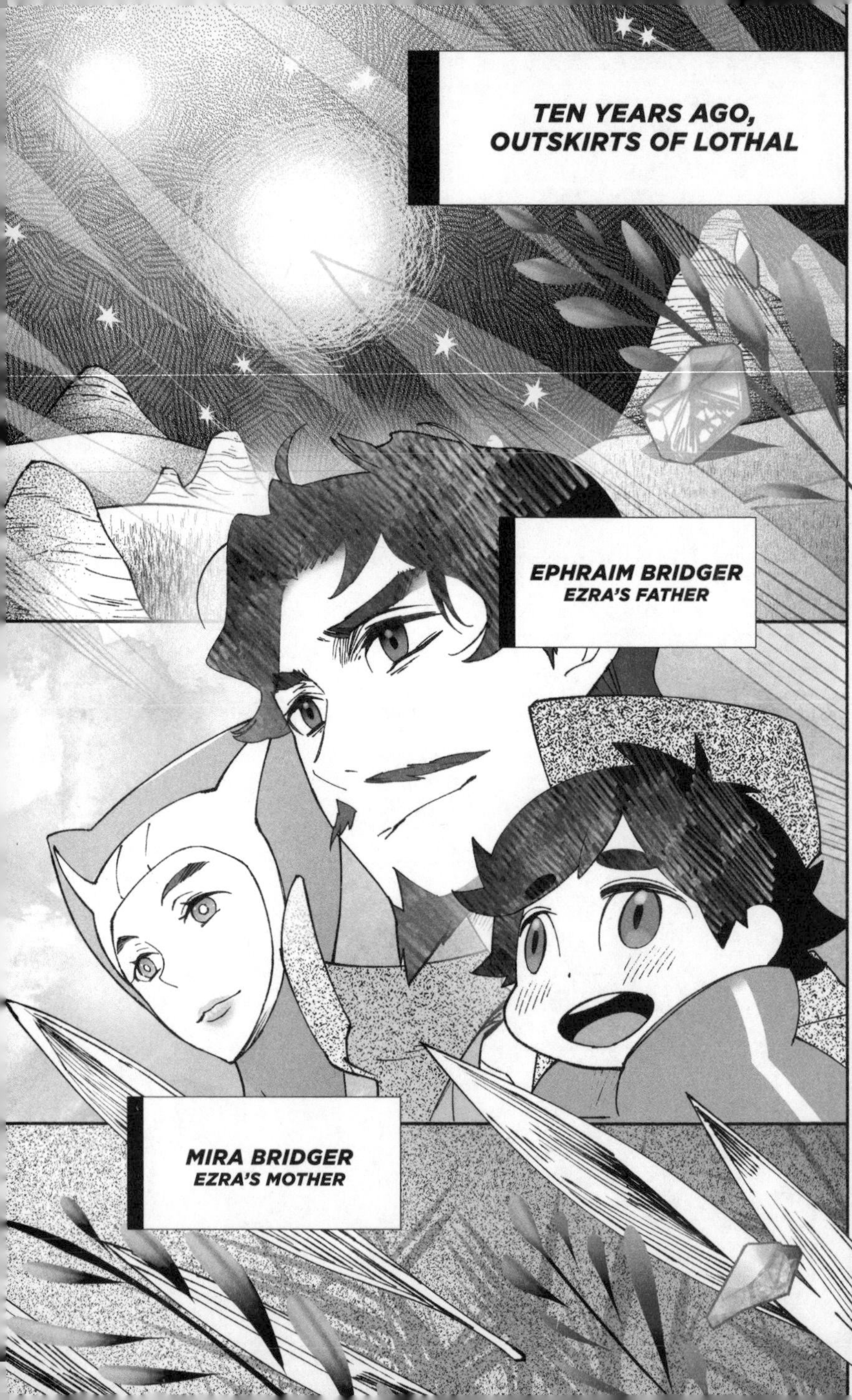
TEN YEARS AGO, OUTSKIRTS OF LOTHAL
EPHRAIM BRIDGER
EZRA'S FATHER
MIRA BRIDGER
EZRA'S MOTHER

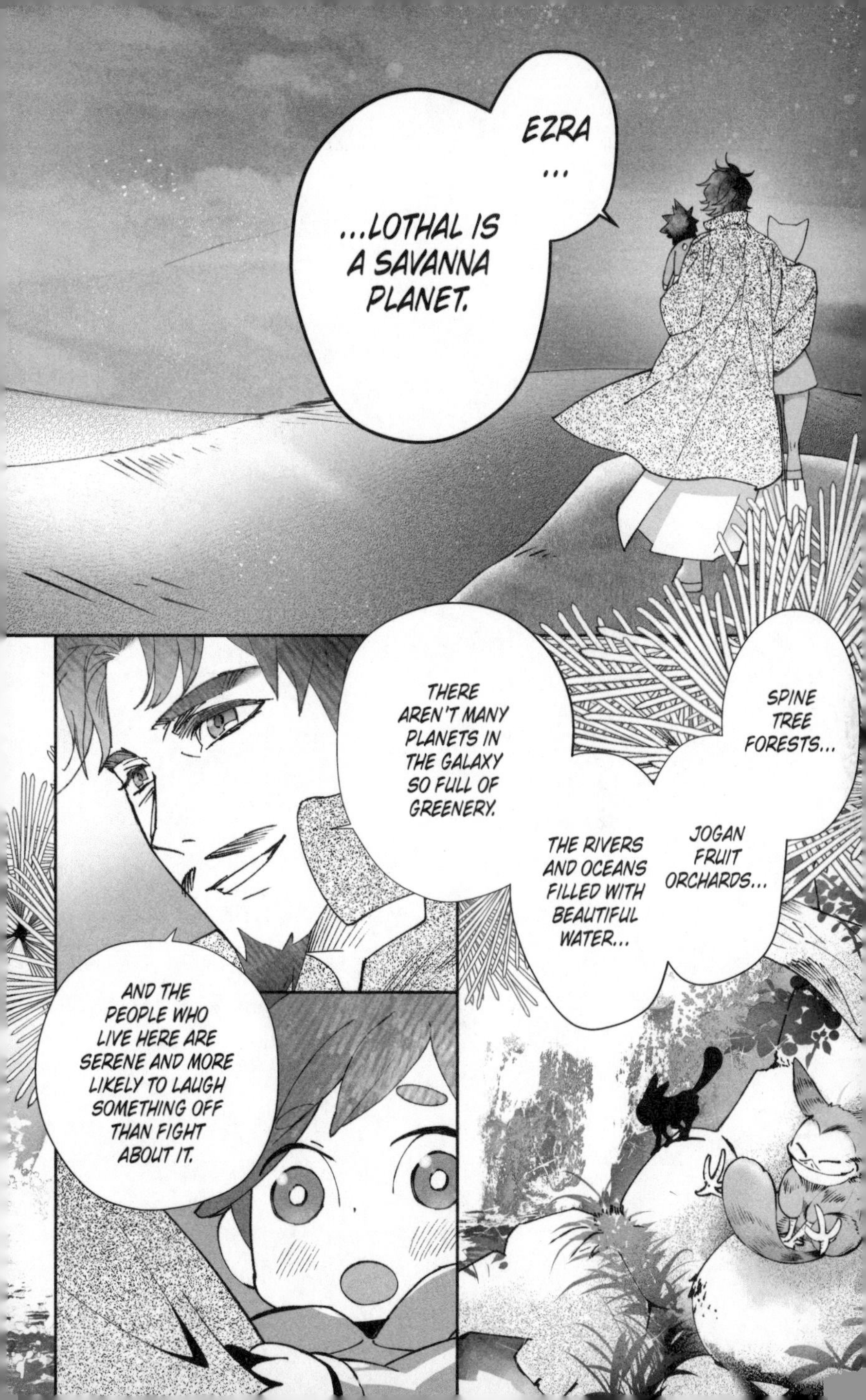
EZRA
...
...LOTHAL IS A SAVANNA PLANET.
THERE AREN'T MANY PLANETS IN THE GALAXY SO FULL OF GREENERY.
SPINE TREE FORESTS...
JOGAN FRUIT ORCHARDS...
THE RIVERS AND OCEANS FILLED WITH BEAUTIFUL WATER...
AND THE PEOPLE WHO LIVE HERE ARE SERENE AND MORE LIKELY TO LAUGH SOMETHING OFF THAN FIGHT ABOUT IT.

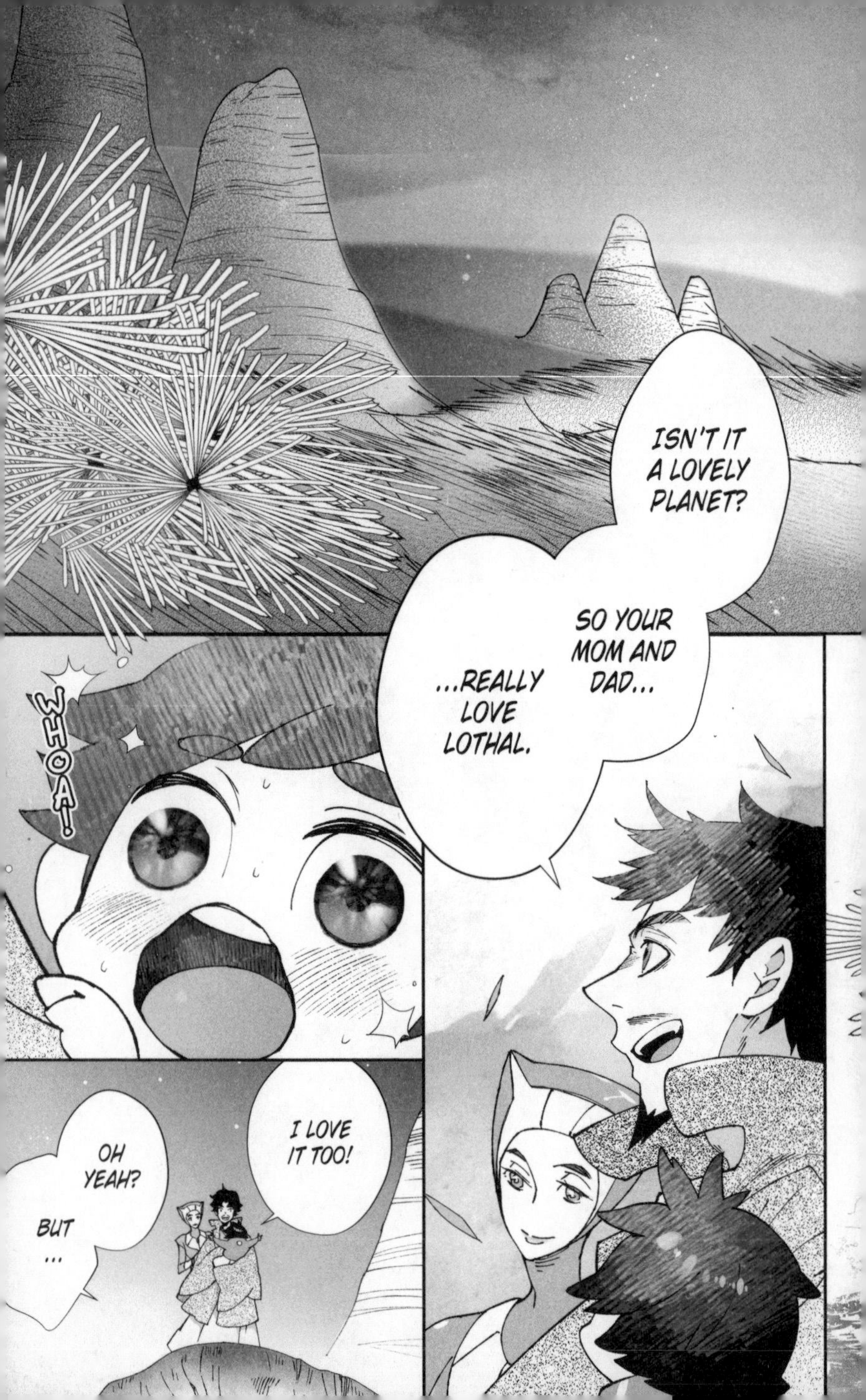
ISN'T IT A LOVELY PLANET?
SO YOUR MOM AND DAD... ...REALLY LOVE LOTHAL.
WHOA!
I LOVE IT TOO!
OH YEAH? BUT ...

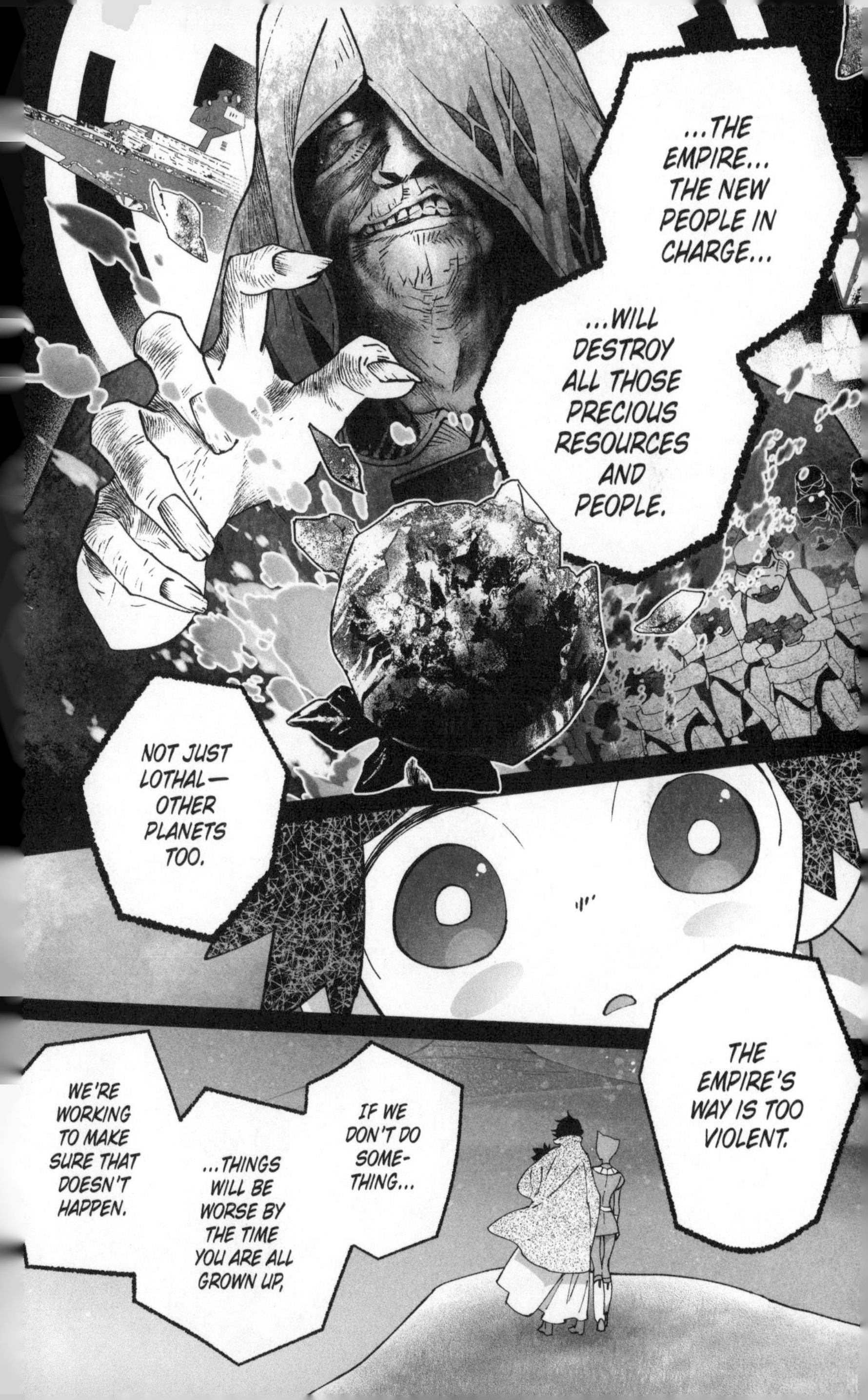
...THE EMPIRE... THE NEW PEOPLE IN CHARGE...
...WILL DESTROY ALL THOSE PRECIOUS RESOURCES AND PEOPLE.
NOT JUST LOTHAL— OTHER PLANETS TOO.
THE EMPIRE'S WAY IS TOO VIOLENT.
IF WE DON'T DO SOME-THING...
...THINGS WILL BE WORSE BY THE TIME YOU ARE ALL GROWN UP,
WE'RE WORKING TO MAKE SURE THAT DOESN'T HAPPEN.

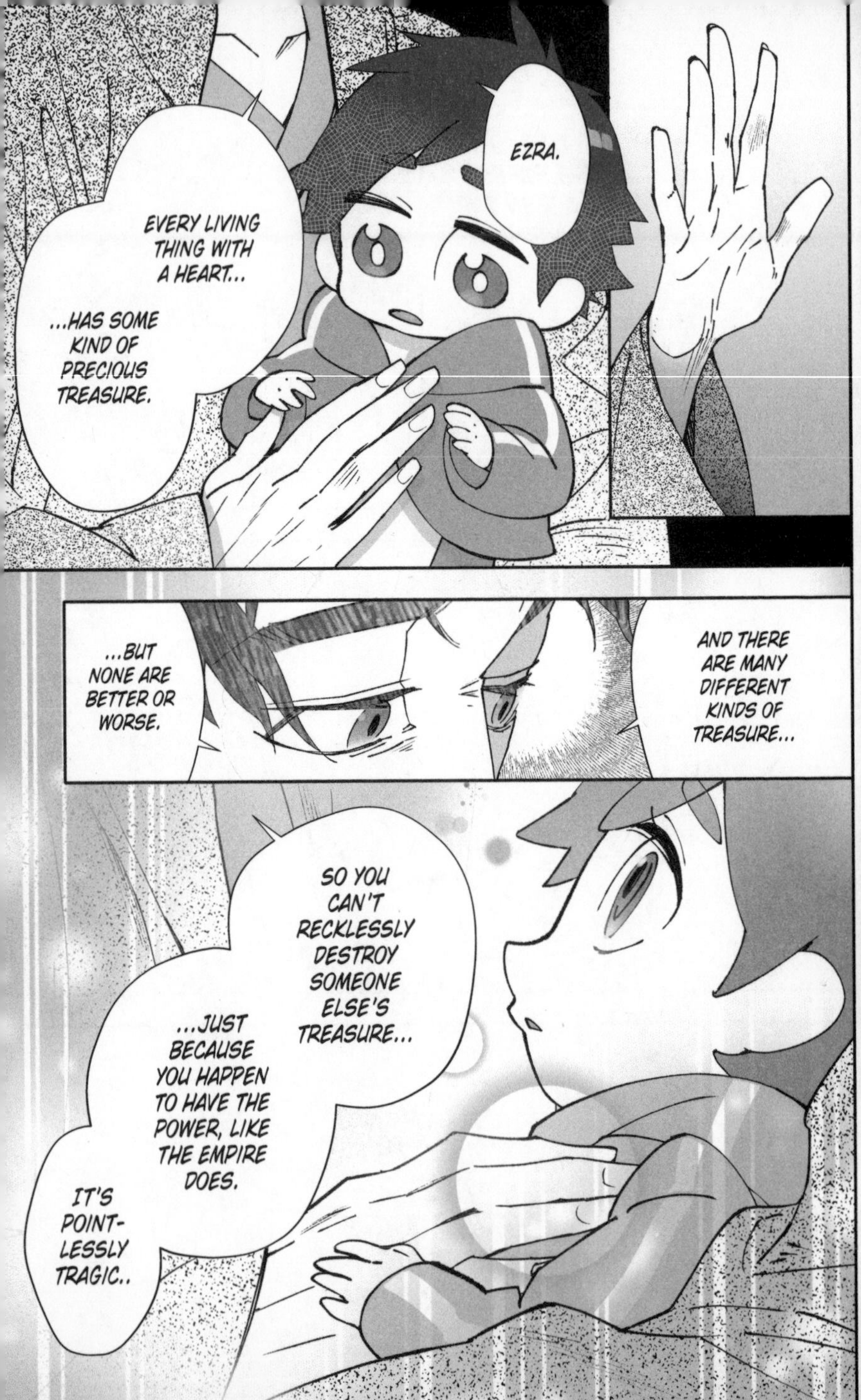
EZRA.
EVERY LIVING THING WITH A HEART...
...HAS SOME KIND OF PRECIOUS TREASURE.
AND THERE ARE MANY DIFFERENT KINDS OF TREASURE...
...BUT NONE ARE BETTER OR WORSE.
SO YOU CAN'T RECKLESSLY DESTROY SOMEONE ELSE'S TREASURE...
...JUST BECAUSE YOU HAPPEN TO HAVE THE POWER, LIKE THE EMPIRE DOES.
IT'S POINTLESSLY TRAGIC..

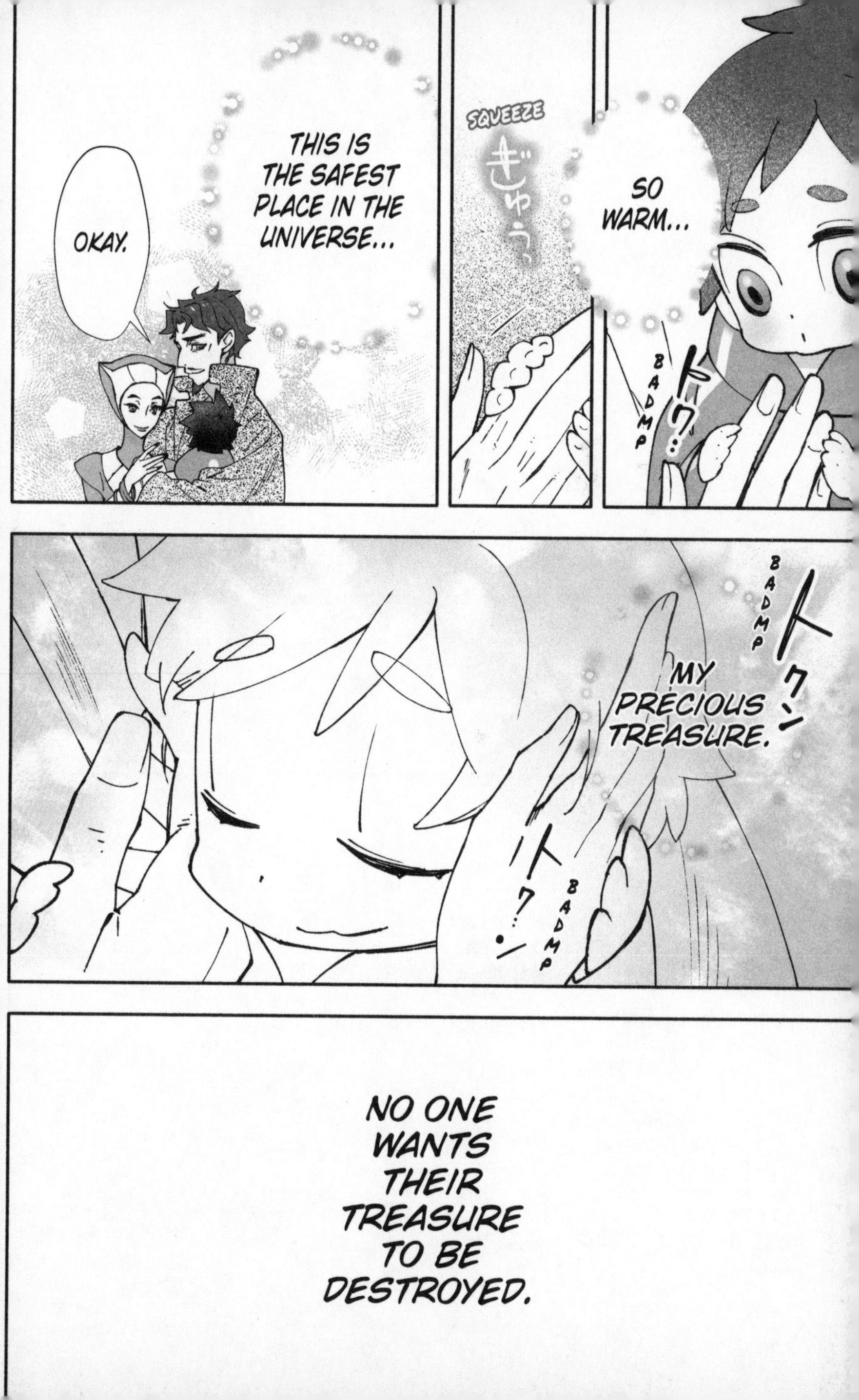
SO WARM...
BADMP
SQUEEZE
ぎゅうっ
THIS IS THE SAFEST PLACE IN THE UNIVERSE...
OKAY.
BADMP
MY PRECIOUS TREASURE.
BADMP
NO ONE WANTS THEIR TREASURE TO BE DESTROYED.

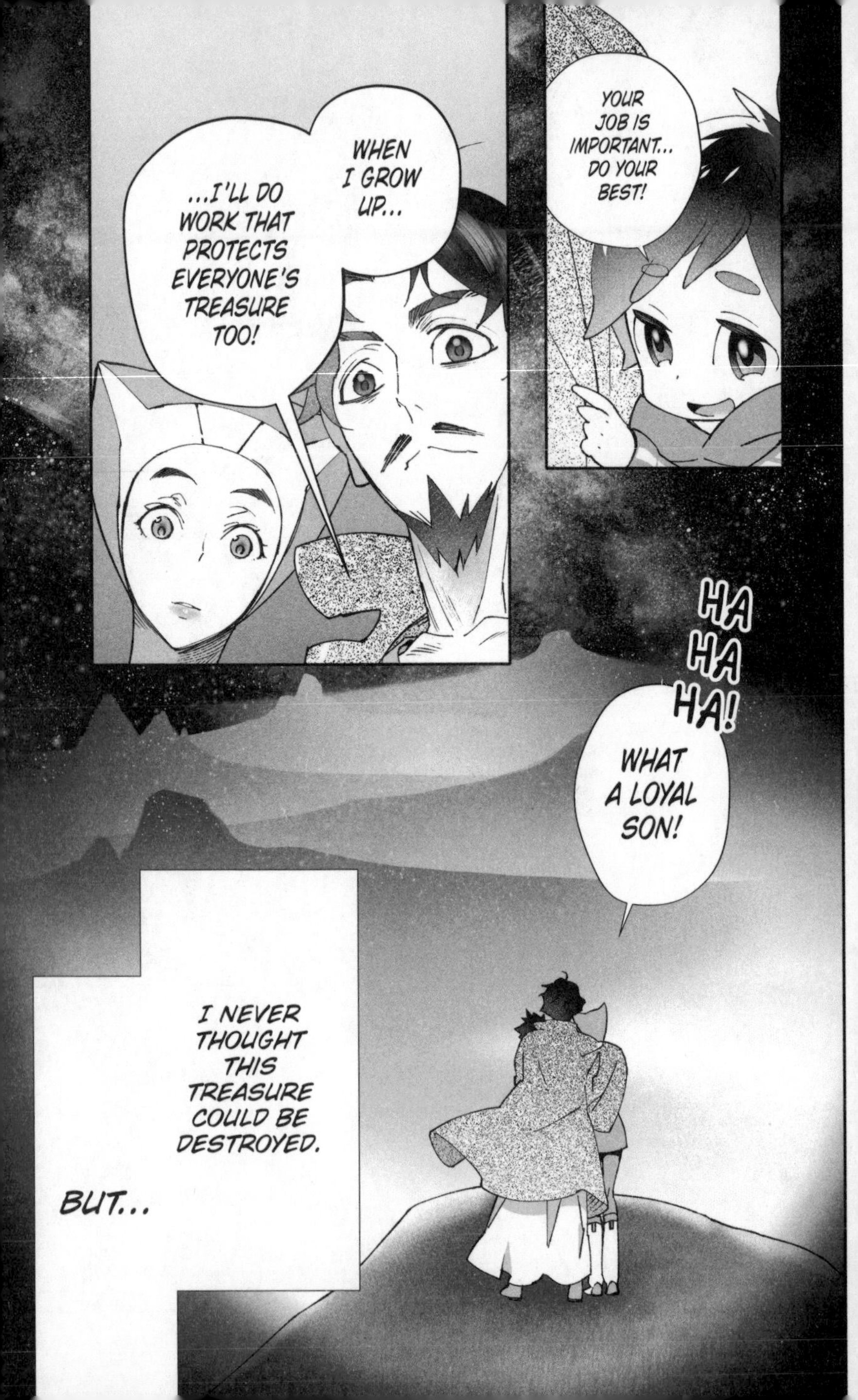
YOUR JOB IS IMPORTANT... DO YOUR BEST!
WHEN I GROW UP...
...I'LL DO WORK THAT PROTECTS EVERYONE'S TREASURE TOO!
HA HA HA!
WHAT A LOYAL SON!
I NEVER THOUGHT THIS TREASURE COULD BE DESTROYED.
BUT...

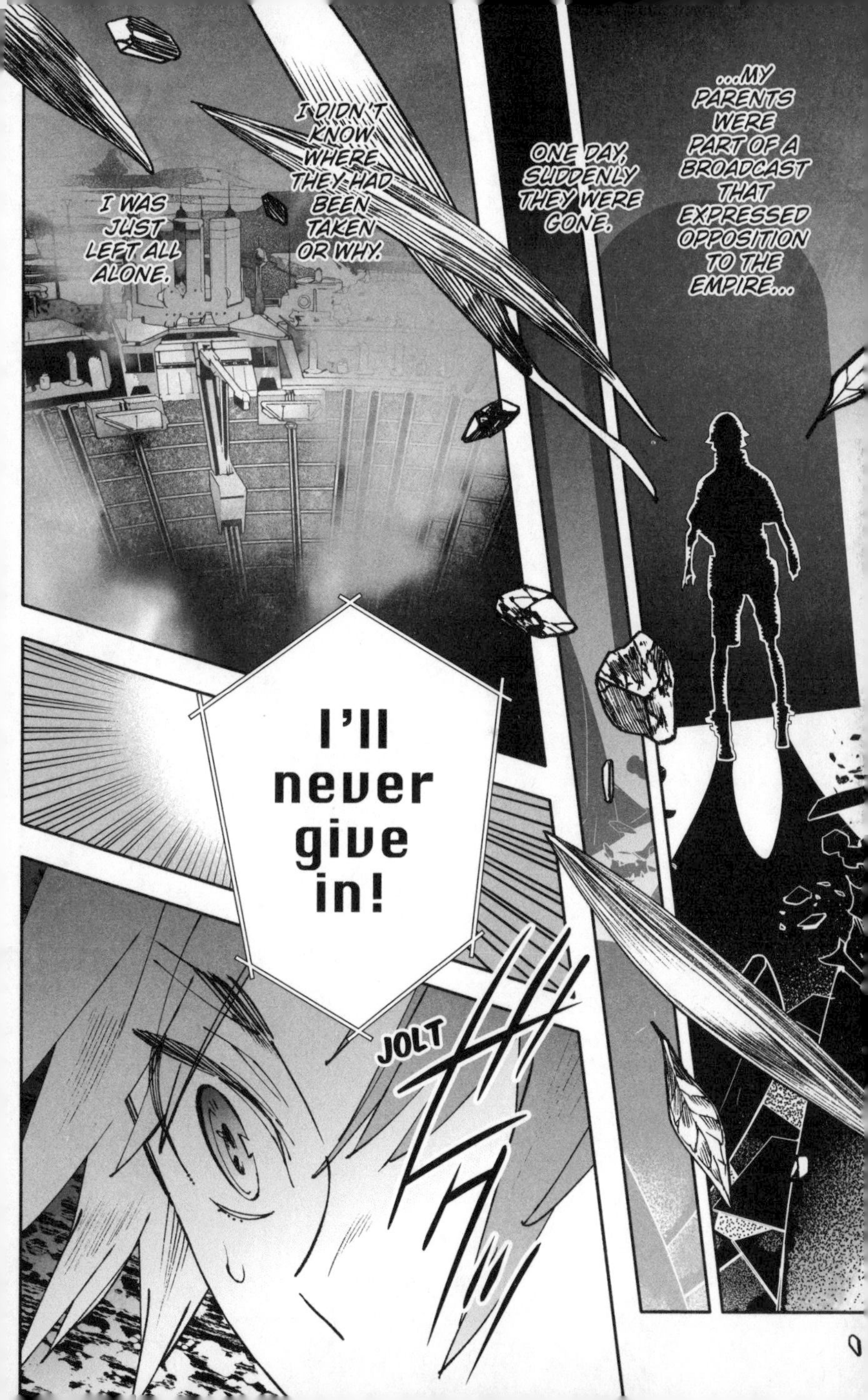
...MY PARENTS WERE PART OF A BROADCAST THAT EXPRESSED OPPOSITION TO THE EMPIRE...
ONE DAY, SUDDENLY THEY WERE GONE.
I DIDN'T KNOW WHERE THEY HAD BEEN TAKEN OR WHY.
I WAS JUST LEFT ALL ALONE.
I'll never give in!
JOLT

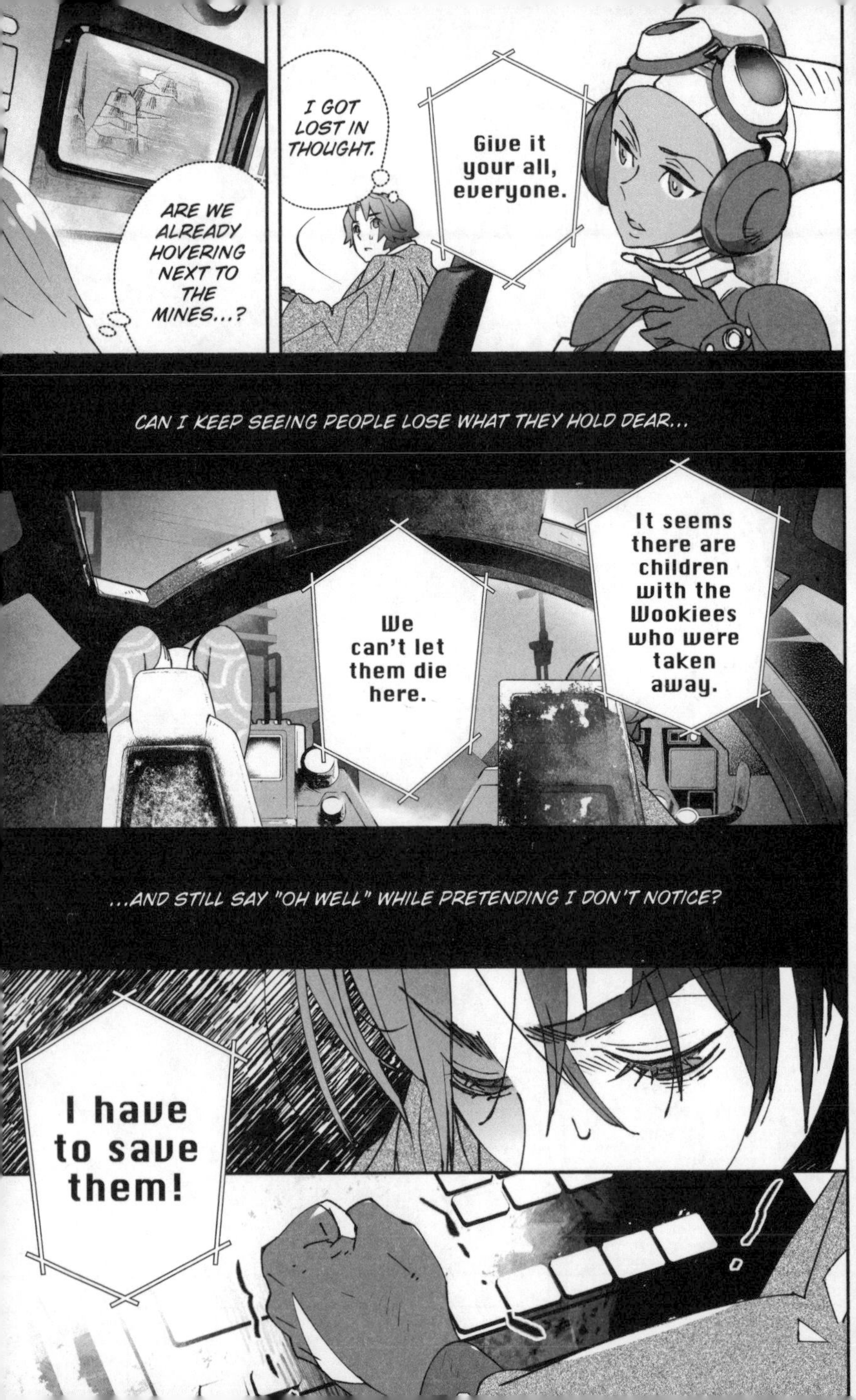
Give it your all, everyone.
I GOT LOST IN THOUGHT.
ARE WE ALREADY HOVERING NEXT TO THE MINES...?
CAN I KEEP SEEING PEOPLE LOSE WHAT THEY HOLD DEAR...
It seems there are children with the Wookiees who were taken away.
We can't let them die here.
...AND STILL SAY "OH WELL" WHILE PRETENDING I DON'T NOTICE?
I have to save them!

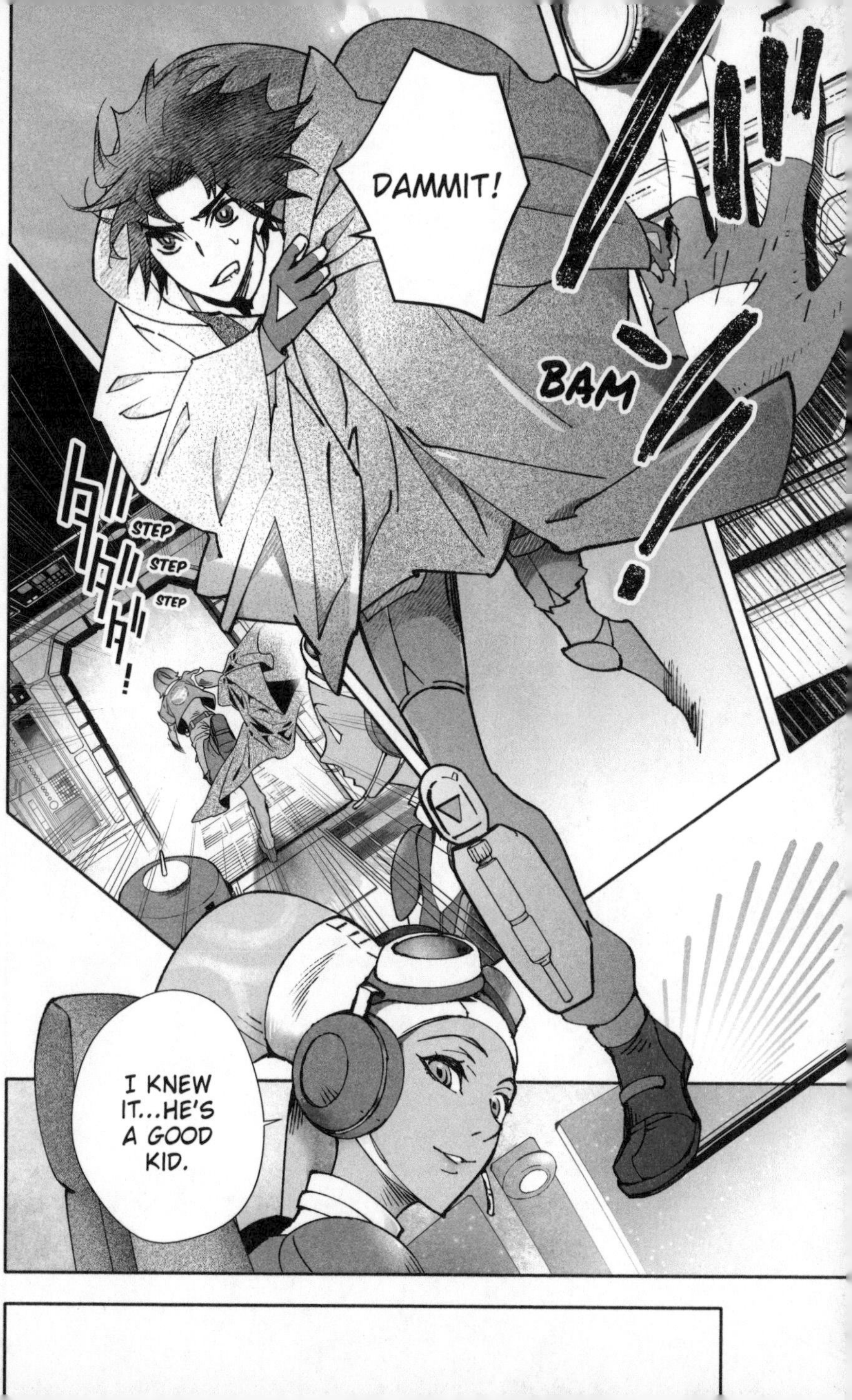
DAMMIT!
BAM
STEP
STEP
STEP
I KNEW IT...HE'S A GOOD KID.

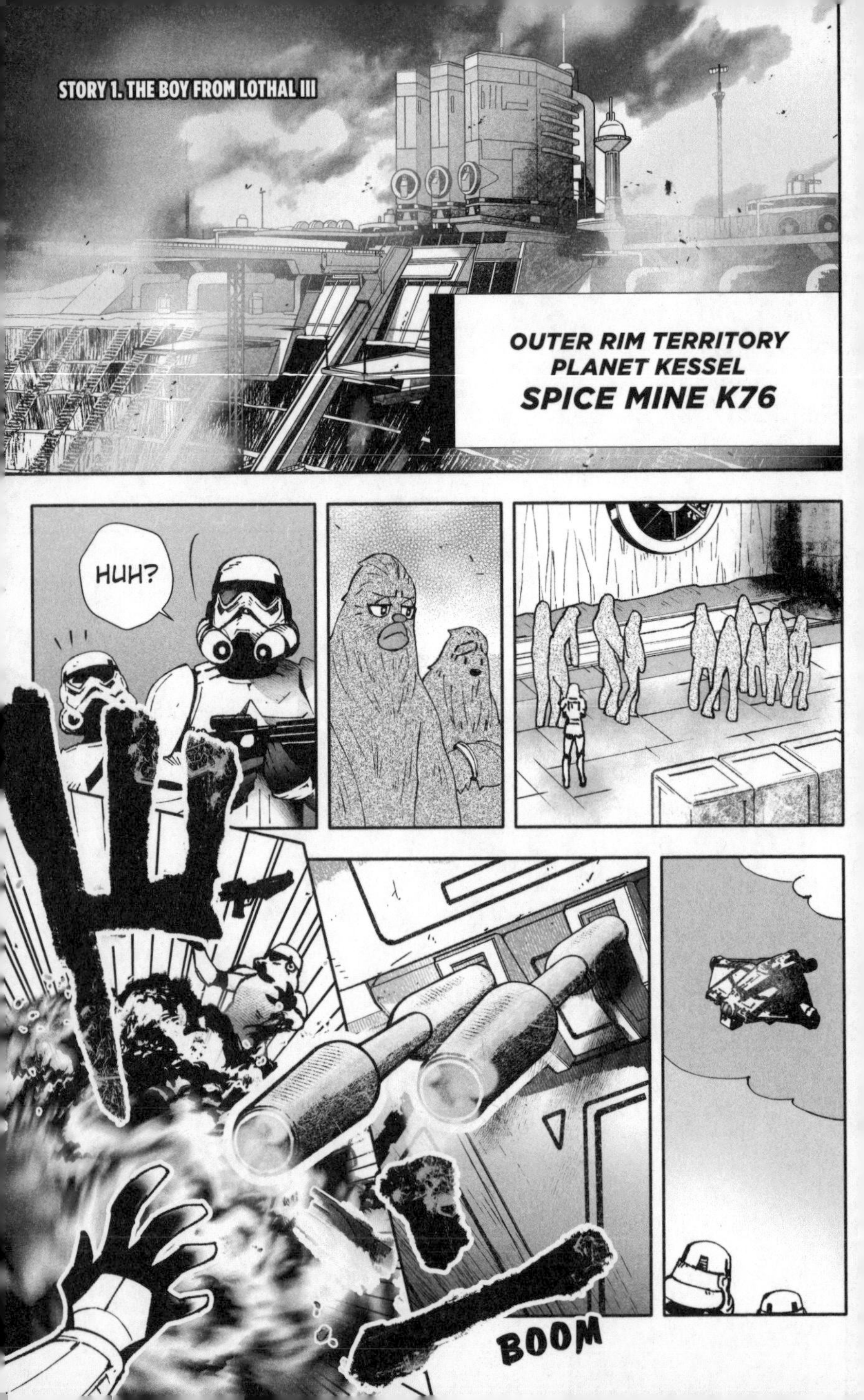
STORY 1. THE BOY FROM LOTHAL III
OUTER RIM TERRITORY
PLANET KESSEL
SPICE MINE K76
HUH?
BOOM

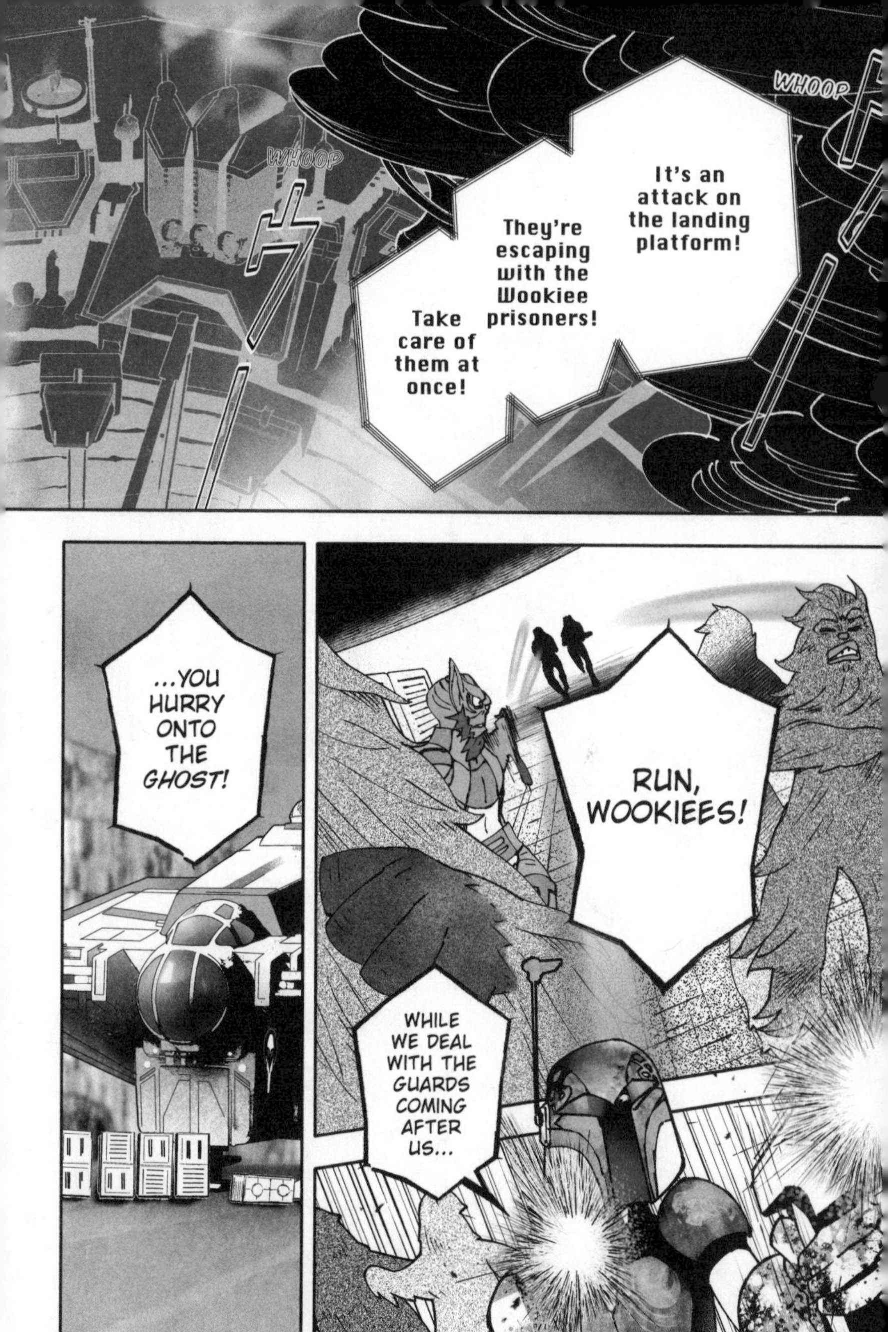
WHOOP
WHOOP
It's an attack on the landing platform!
They're escaping with the Wookiee prisoners!
Take care of them at once!
RUN, WOOKIEES!
WHILE WE DEAL WITH THE GUARDS COMING AFTER US...
...YOU HURRY ONTO THE GHOST!

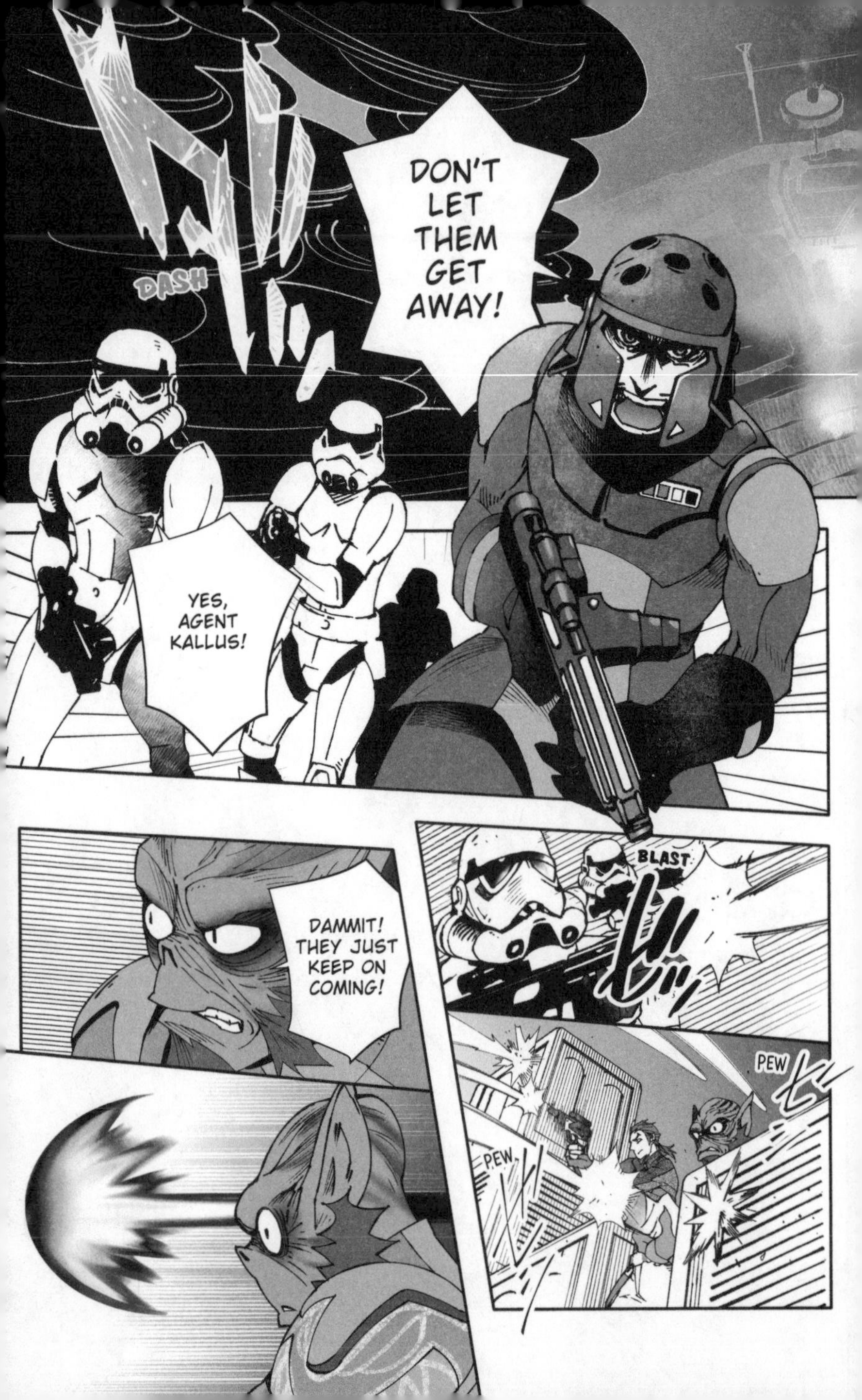
DON'T LET THEM GET AWAY!
DASH
YES, AGENT KALLUS!
BLAST
DAMMIT! THEY JUST KEEP ON COMING!
PEW
PEW

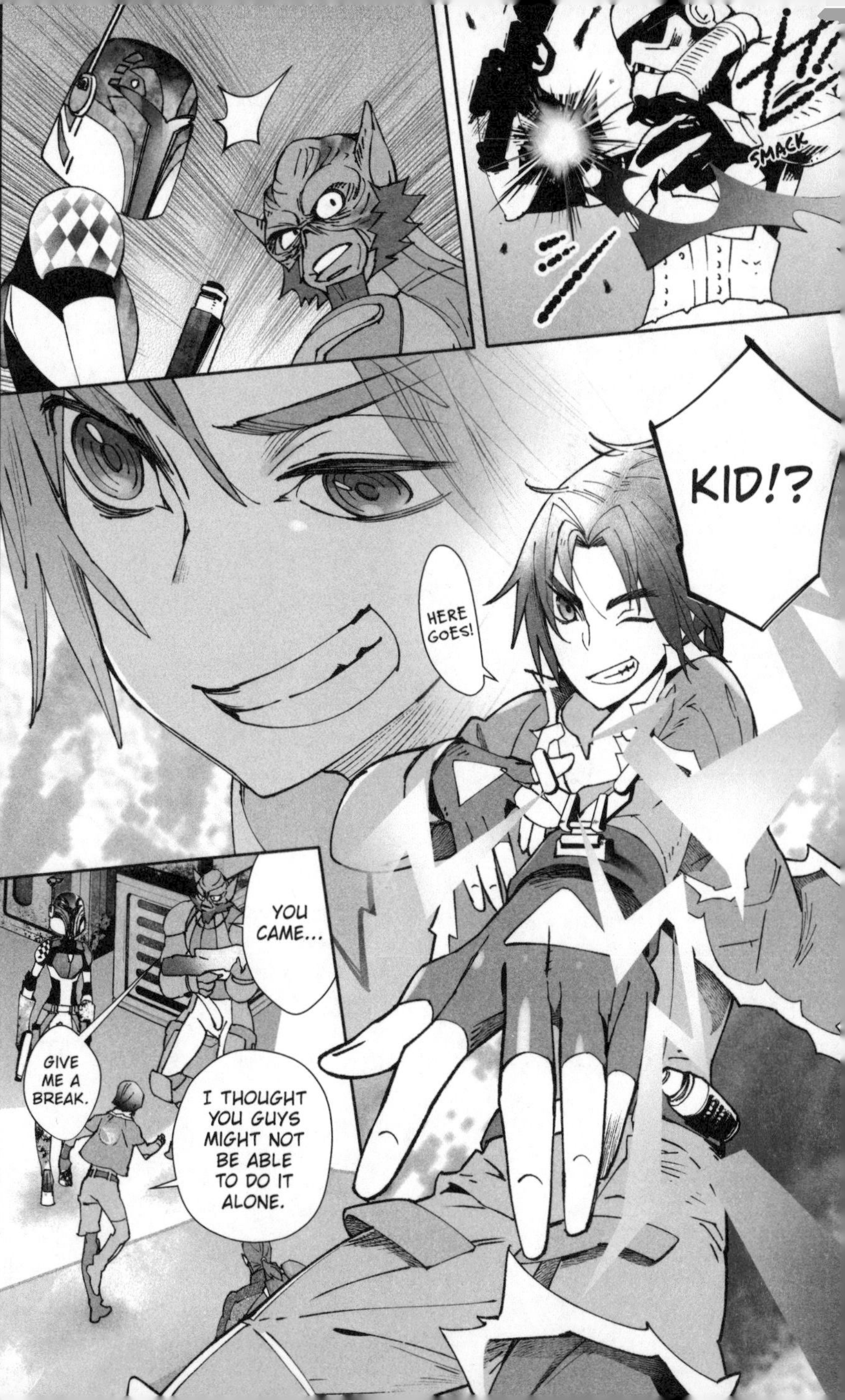
SMACK
KID!?
HERE GOES!
YOU CAME...
GIVE ME A BREAK.
I THOUGHT YOU GUYS MIGHT NOT BE ABLE TO DO IT ALONE.

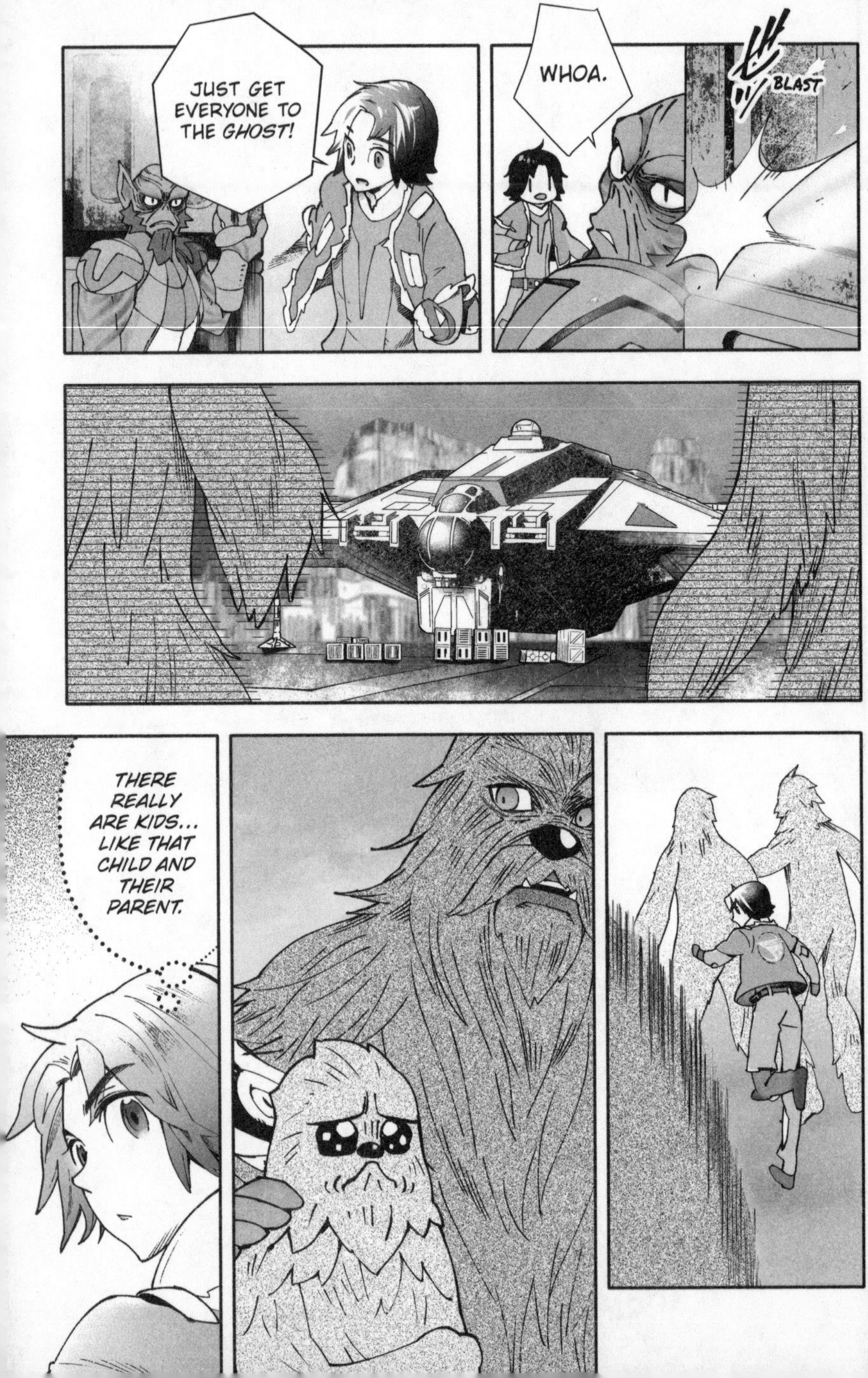
BLAST
WHOA.
JUST GET EVERYONE TO THE GHOST!
THERE REALLY ARE KIDS... LIKE THAT CHILD AND THEIR PARENT.

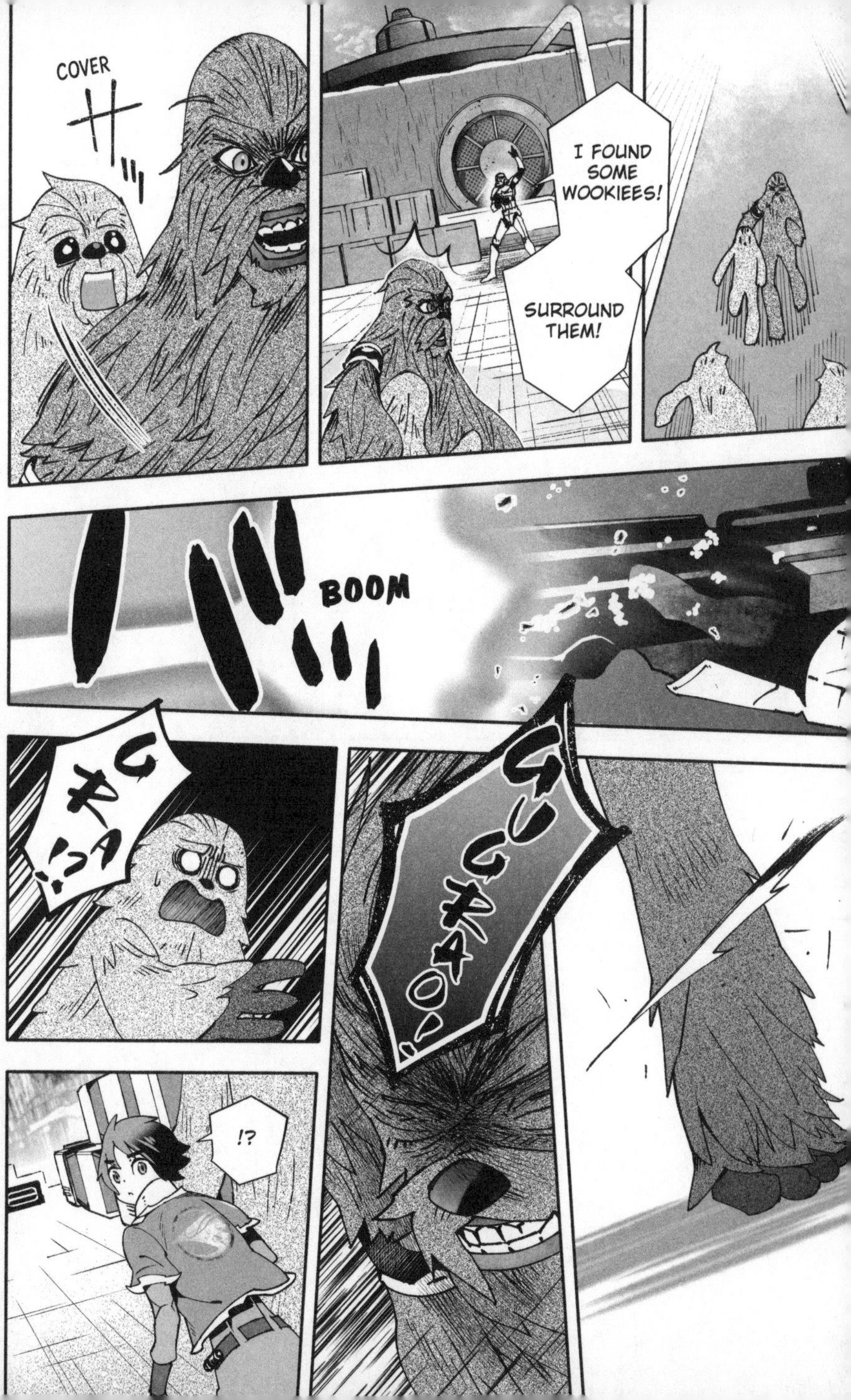
I FOUND SOME WOOKIEES!
SURROUND THEM!
COVER
BOOM
!?

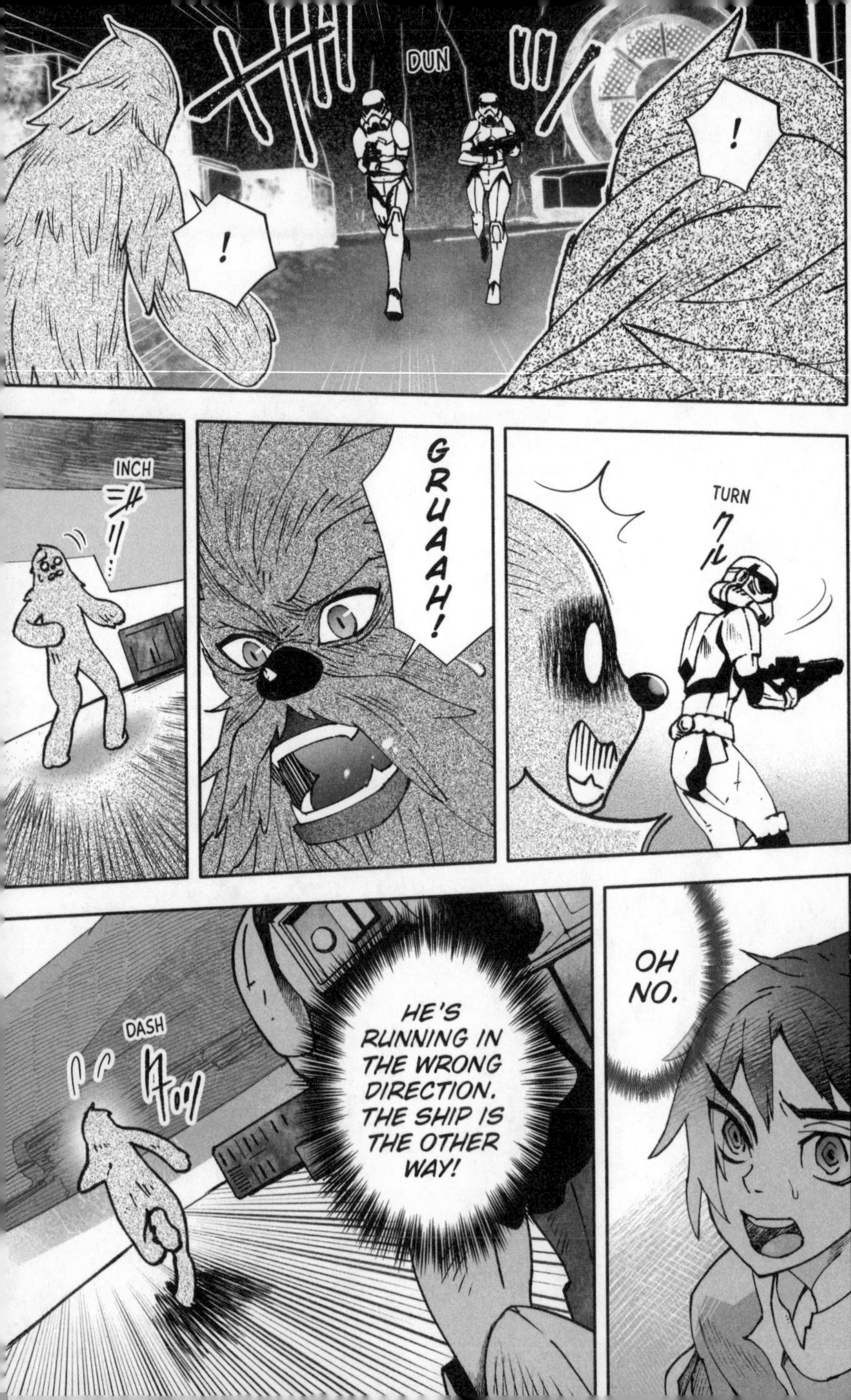
!
DUN
!
TURN
クル
GRUAAAH!
INCH
OH NO.
HE'S RUNNING IN THE WRONG DIRECTION. THE SHIP IS THE OTHER WAY!
DASH

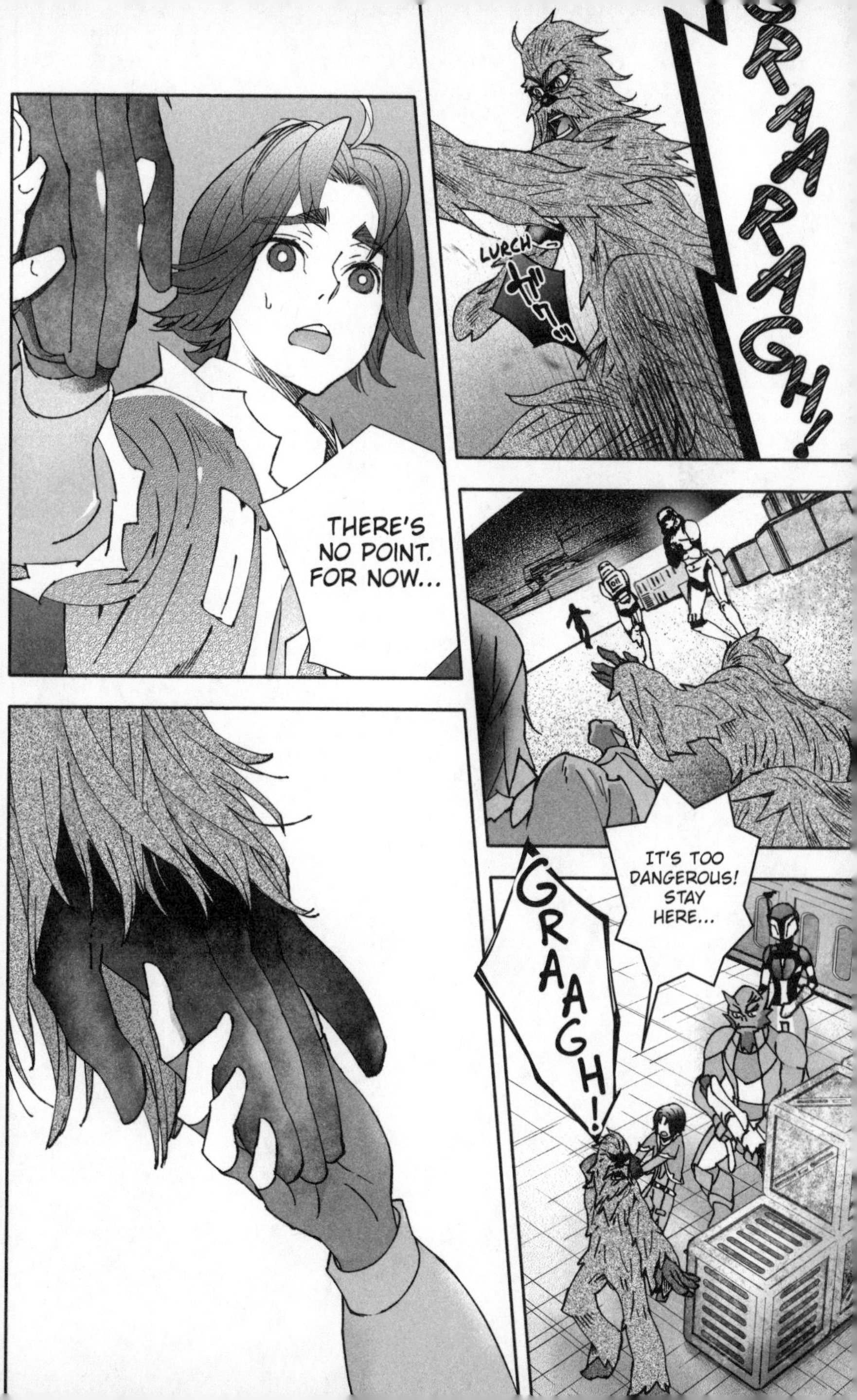
GRAARAGH!
LURCH
THERE'S NO POINT. FOR NOW...
IT'S TOO DANGEROUS! STAY HERE...
GRAAGH!

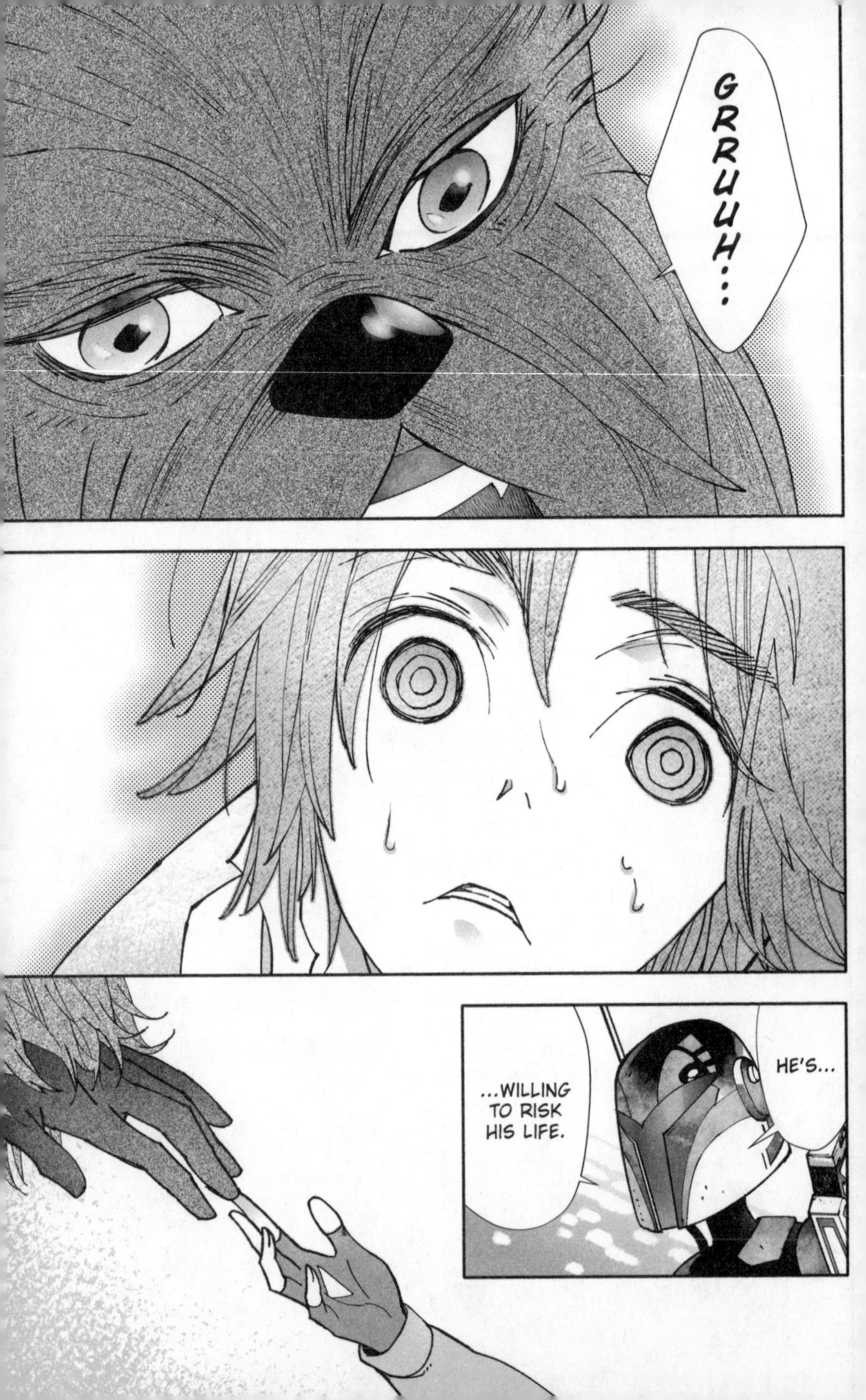
GRRUUH...
HE'S...
...WILLING TO RISK HIS LIFE.

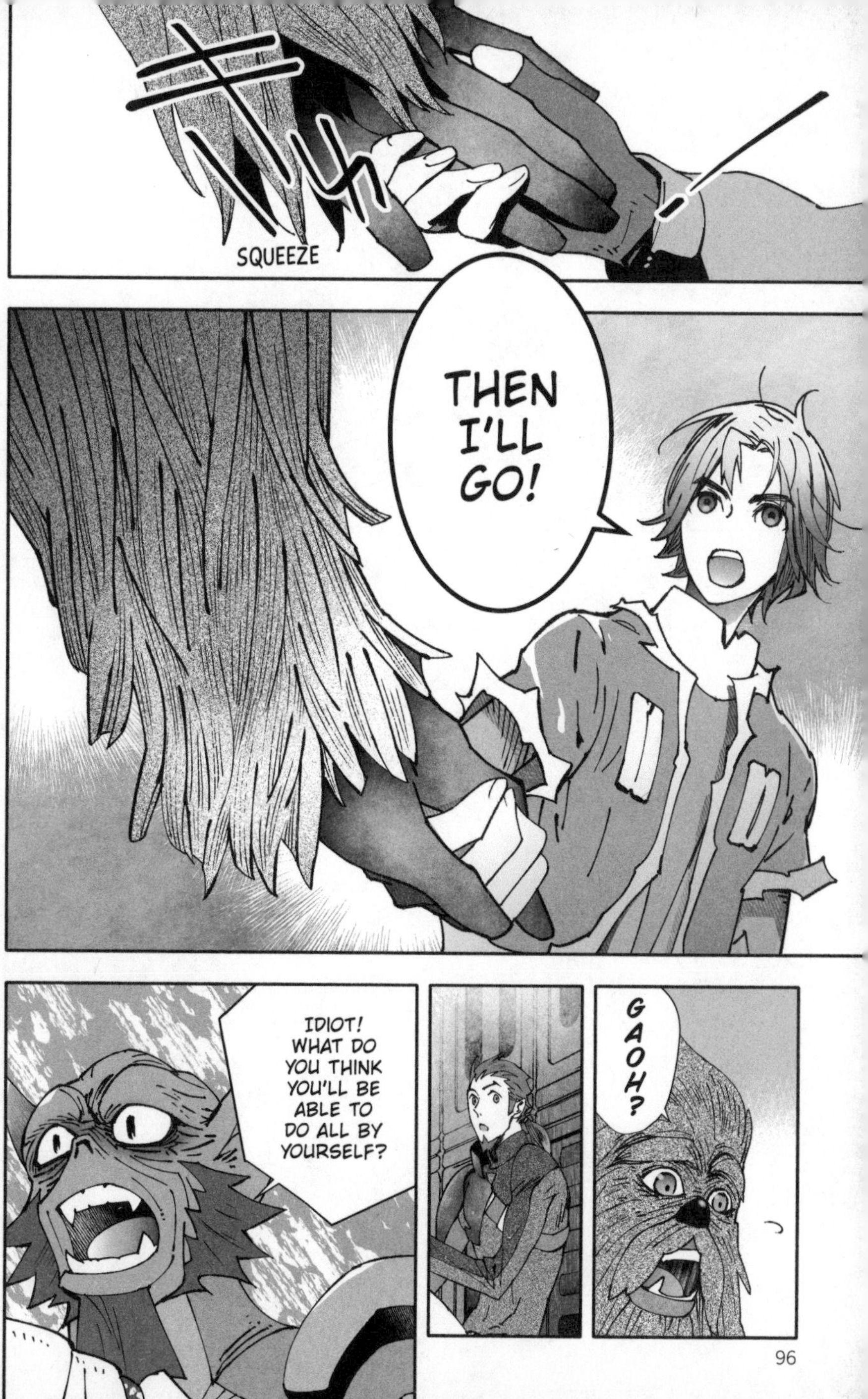
SQUEEZE
THEN I'LL GO!
GAOH?
IDIOT! WHAT DO YOU THINK YOU'LL BE ABLE TO DO ALL BY YOURSELF?

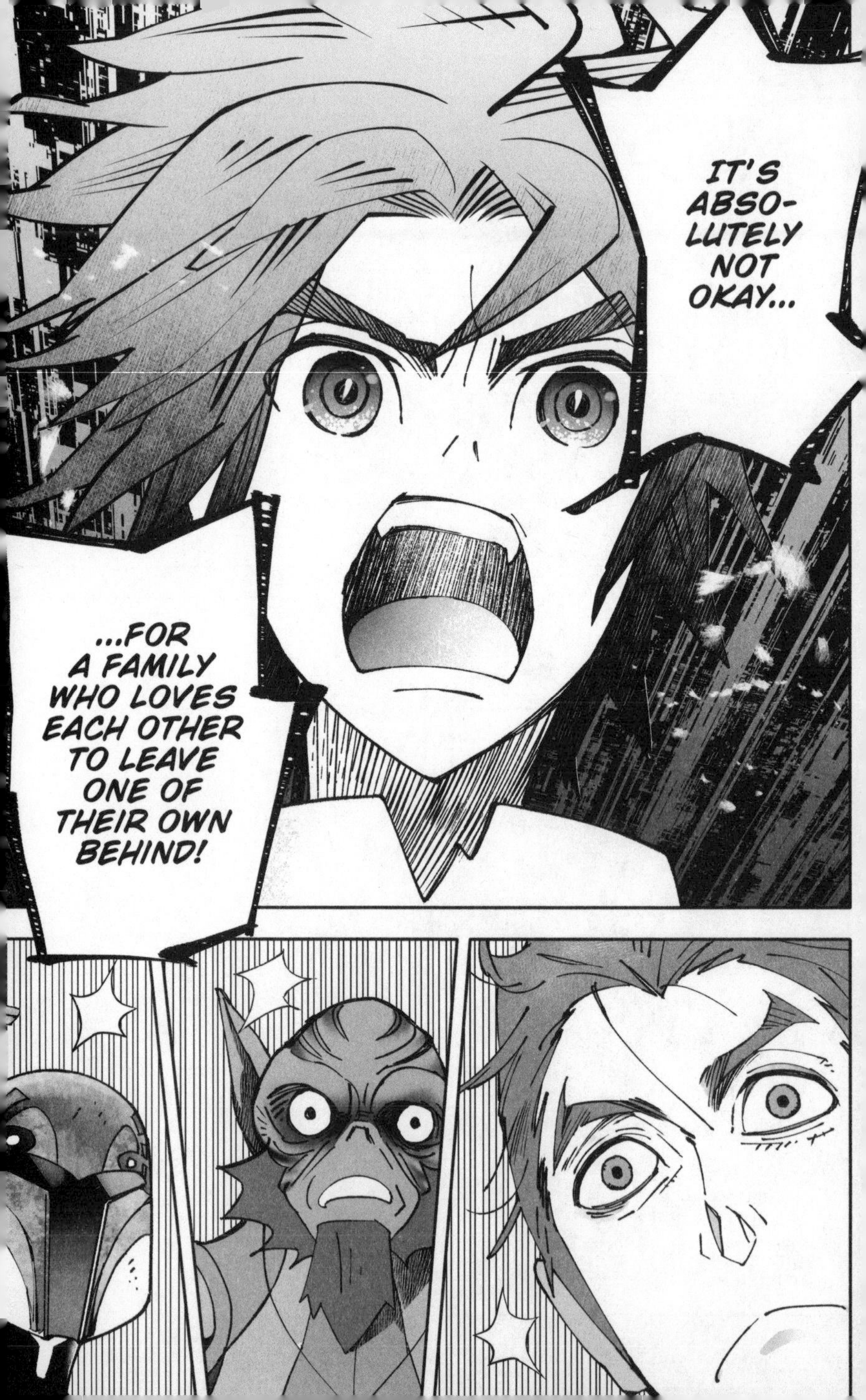
IT'S ABSO-LUTELY NOT OKAY...
...FOR A FAMILY WHO LOVES EACH OTHER TO LEAVE ONE OF THEIR OWN BEHIND!

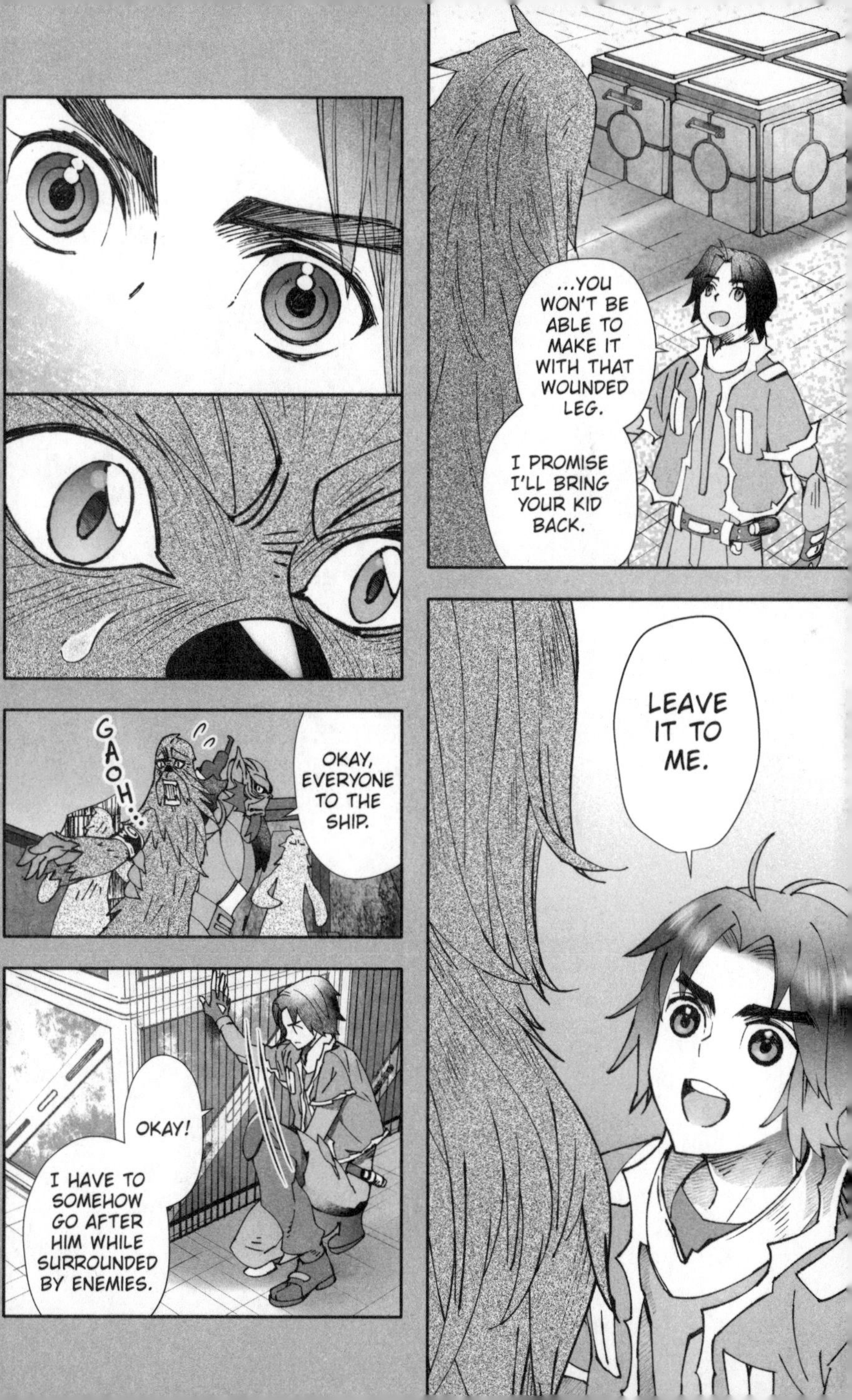
...YOU WON'T BE ABLE TO MAKE IT WITH THAT WOUNDED LEG.
I PROMISE I'LL BRING YOUR KID BACK.
LEAVE IT TO ME.
OKAY, EVERYONE TO THE SHIP.
GAOH...
OKAY!
I HAVE TO SOMEHOW GO AFTER HIM WHILE SURROUNDED BY ENEMIES.

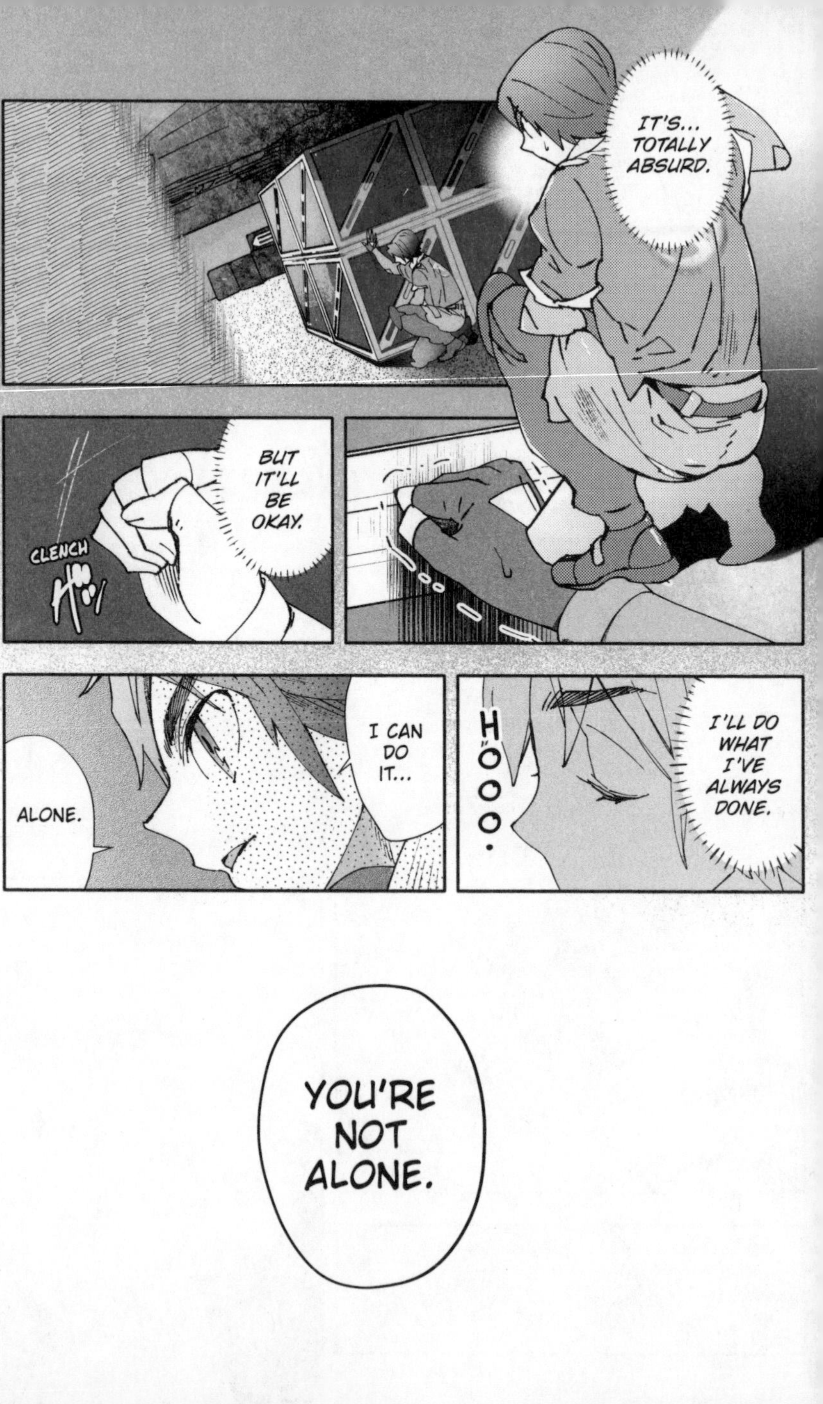
IT'S... TOTALLY ABSURD.
BUT IT'LL BE OKAY.
CLENCH
I'LL DO WHAT I'VE ALWAYS DONE.
HÖOO.
I CAN DO IT...
ALONE.
YOU'RE NOT ALONE.

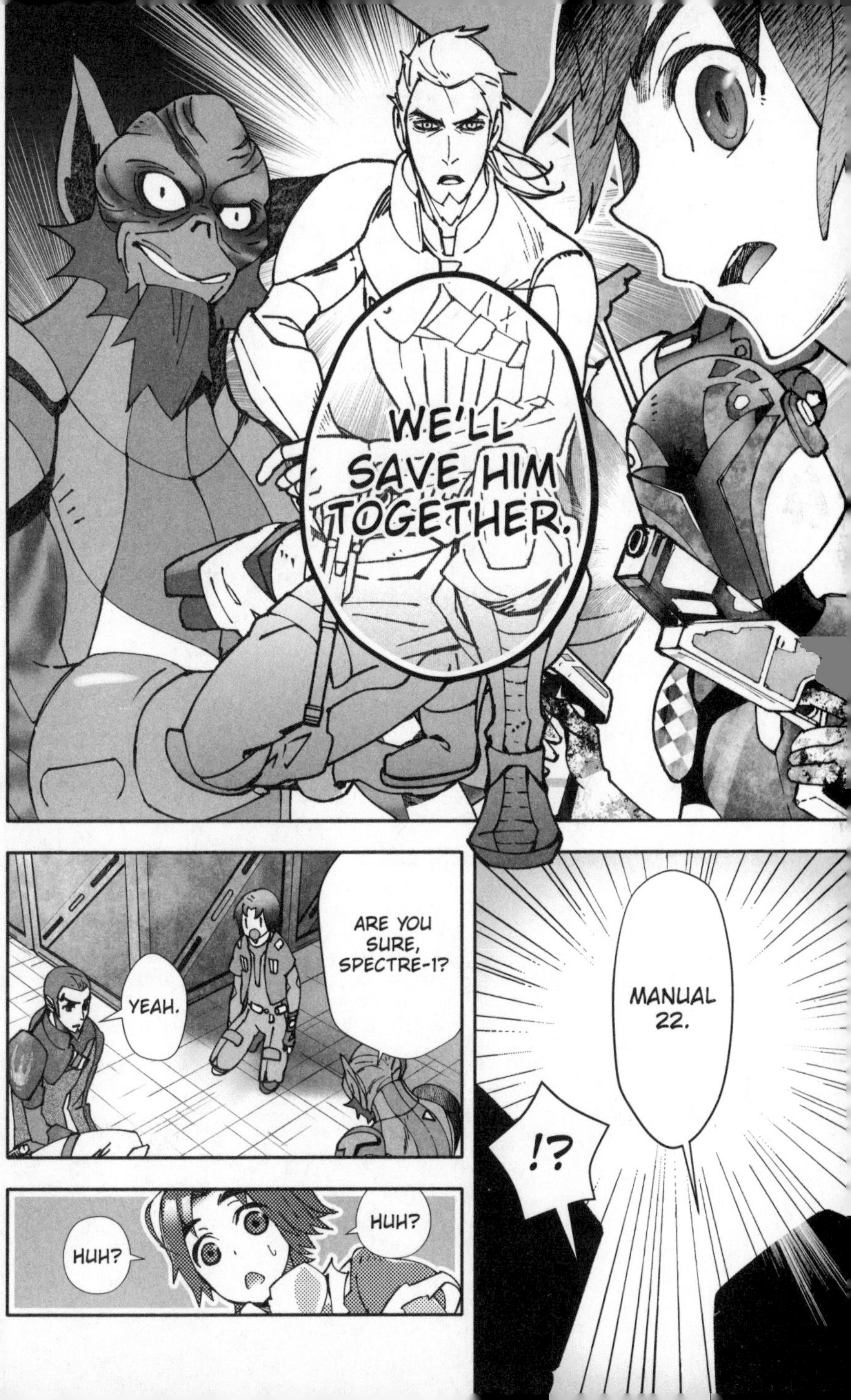
WE'LL SAVE HIM TOGETHER.
MANUAL 22.
!?
ARE YOU SURE, SPECTRE-1?
YEAH.
HUH?
HUH?

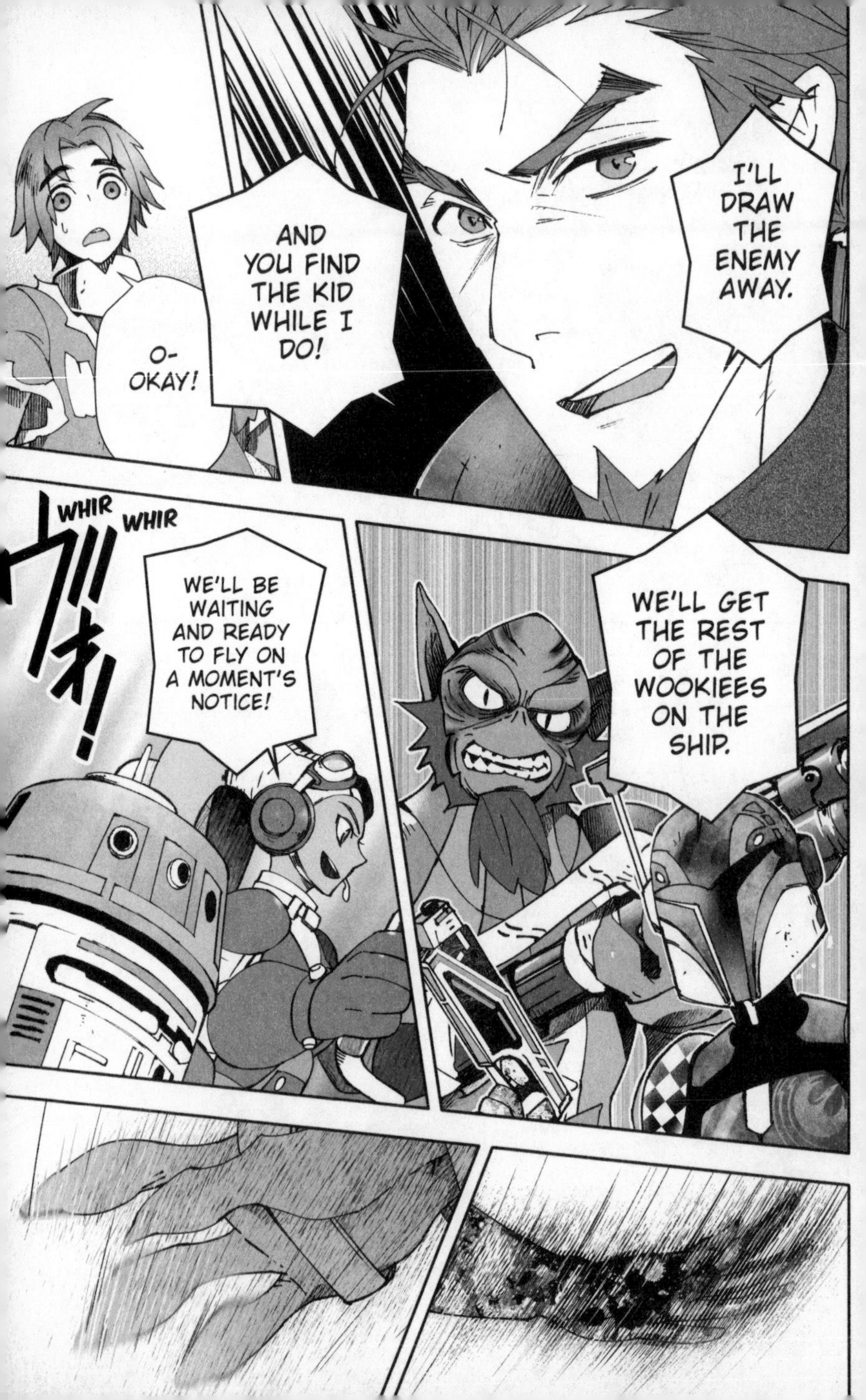
I'LL DRAW THE ENEMY AWAY.
AND YOU FIND THE KID WHILE I DO!
O-OKAY!
WE'LL GET THE REST OF THE WOOKIEES ON THE SHIP.
WHIR WHIR
WE'LL BE WAITING AND READY TO FLY ON A MOMENT'S NOTICE!

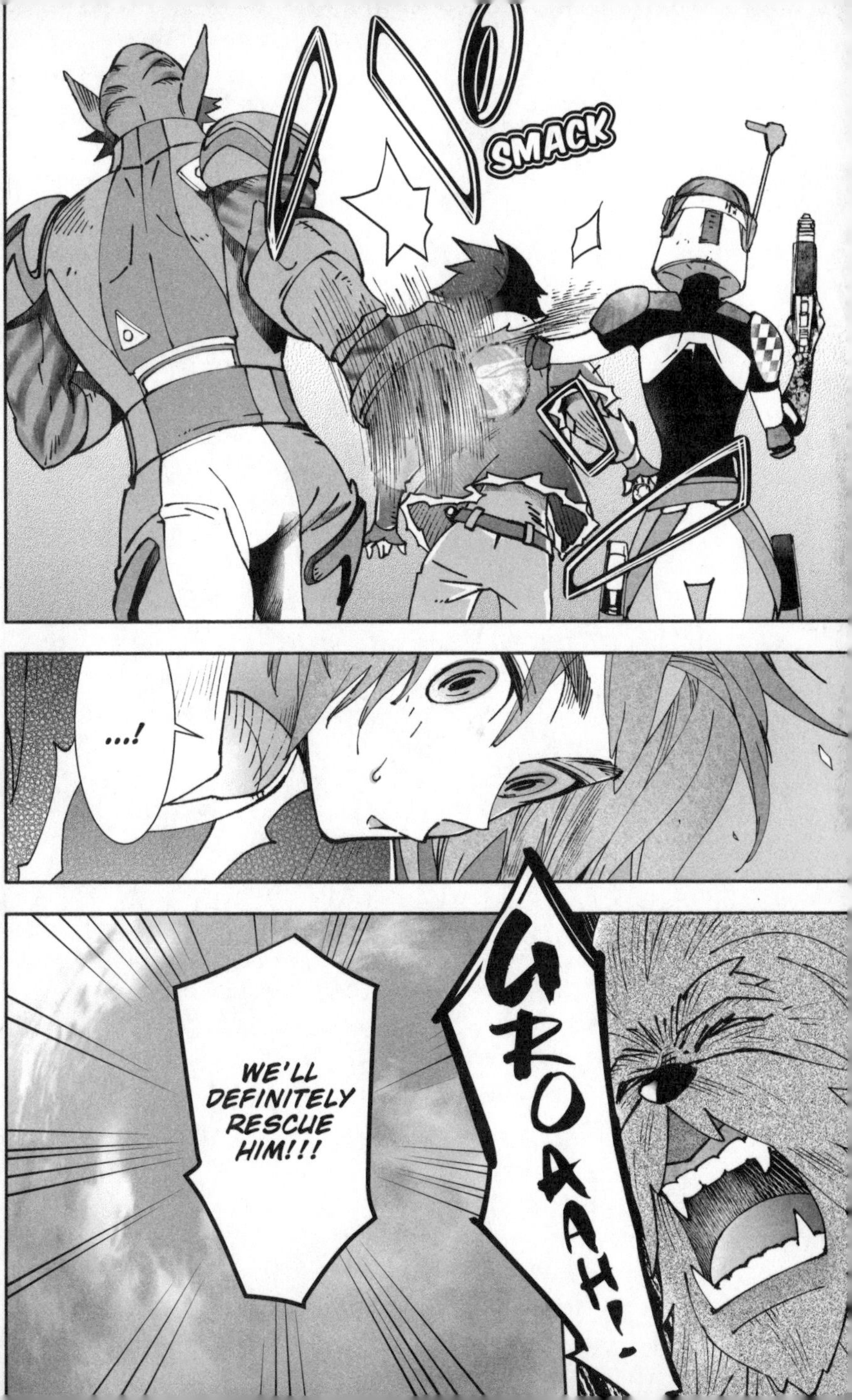
SMACK
...!
UROAAH!!
WE'LL DEFINITELY RESCUE HIM!!!

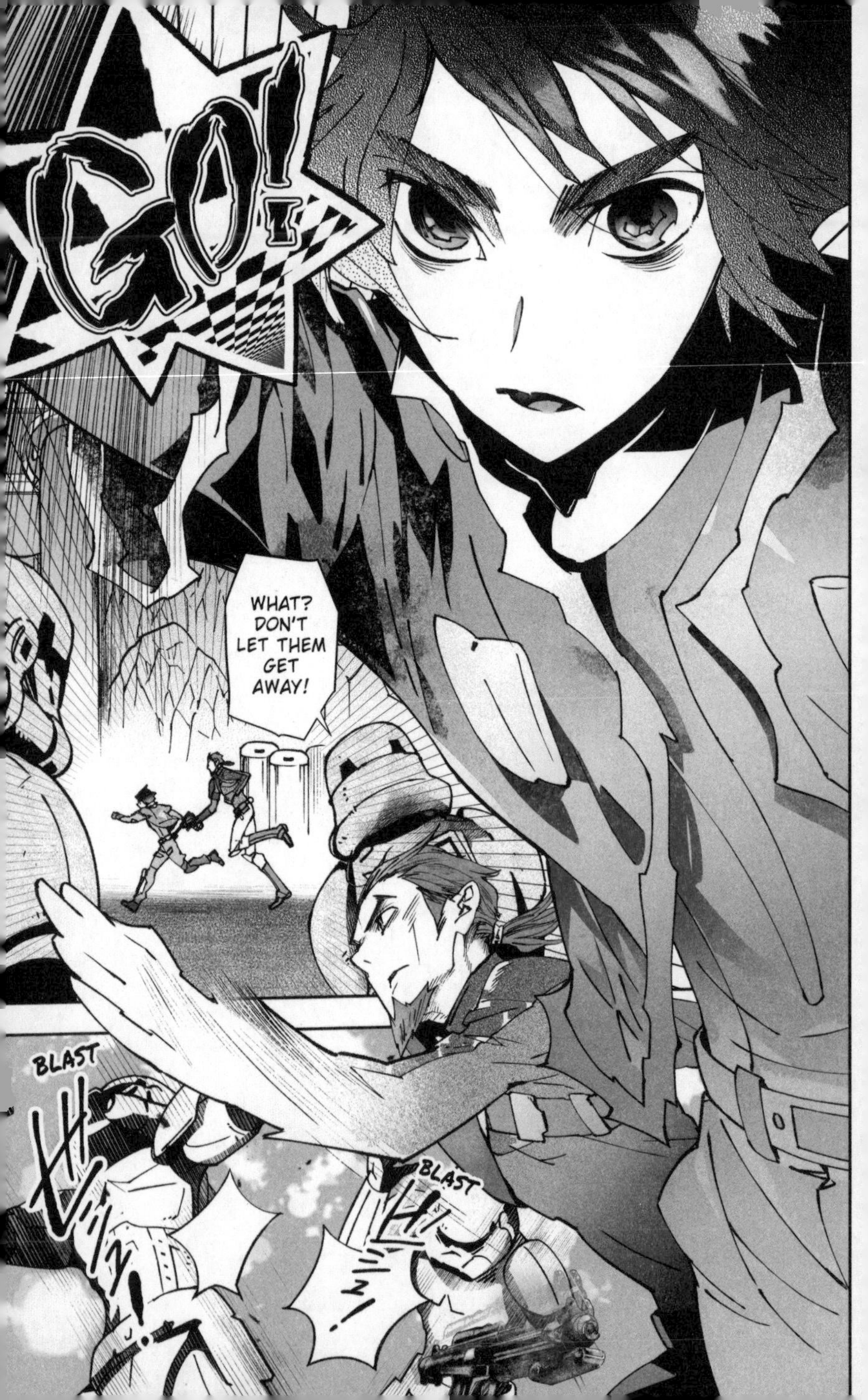
GO!
WHAT? DON'T LET THEM GET AWAY!
BLAST
BLAST

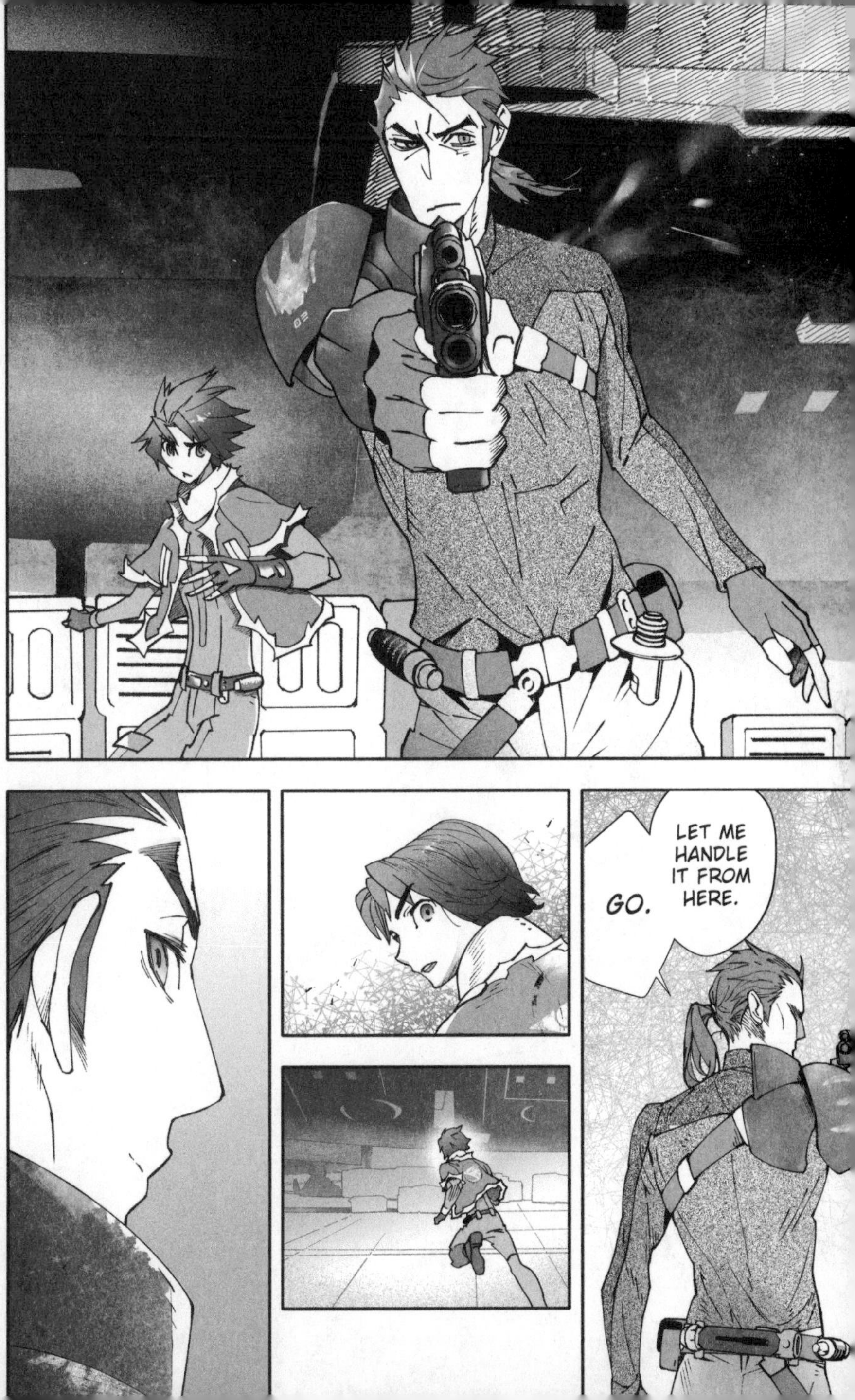
GO.
LET ME HANDLE IT FROM HERE.

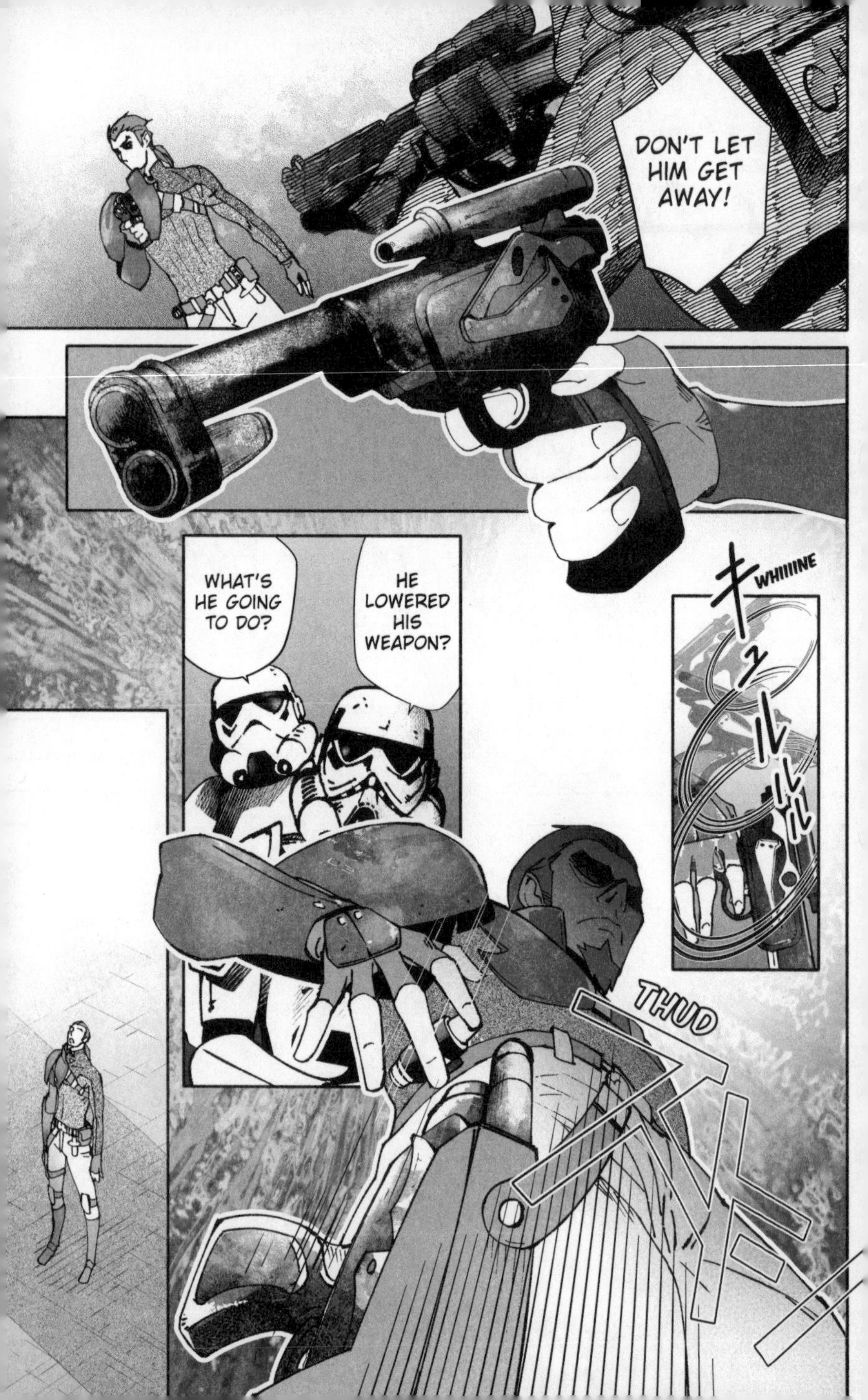
DON'T LET HIM GET AWAY!
HE LOWERED HIS WEAPON?
WHAT'S HE GOING TO DO?
WHIIIINE
THUD

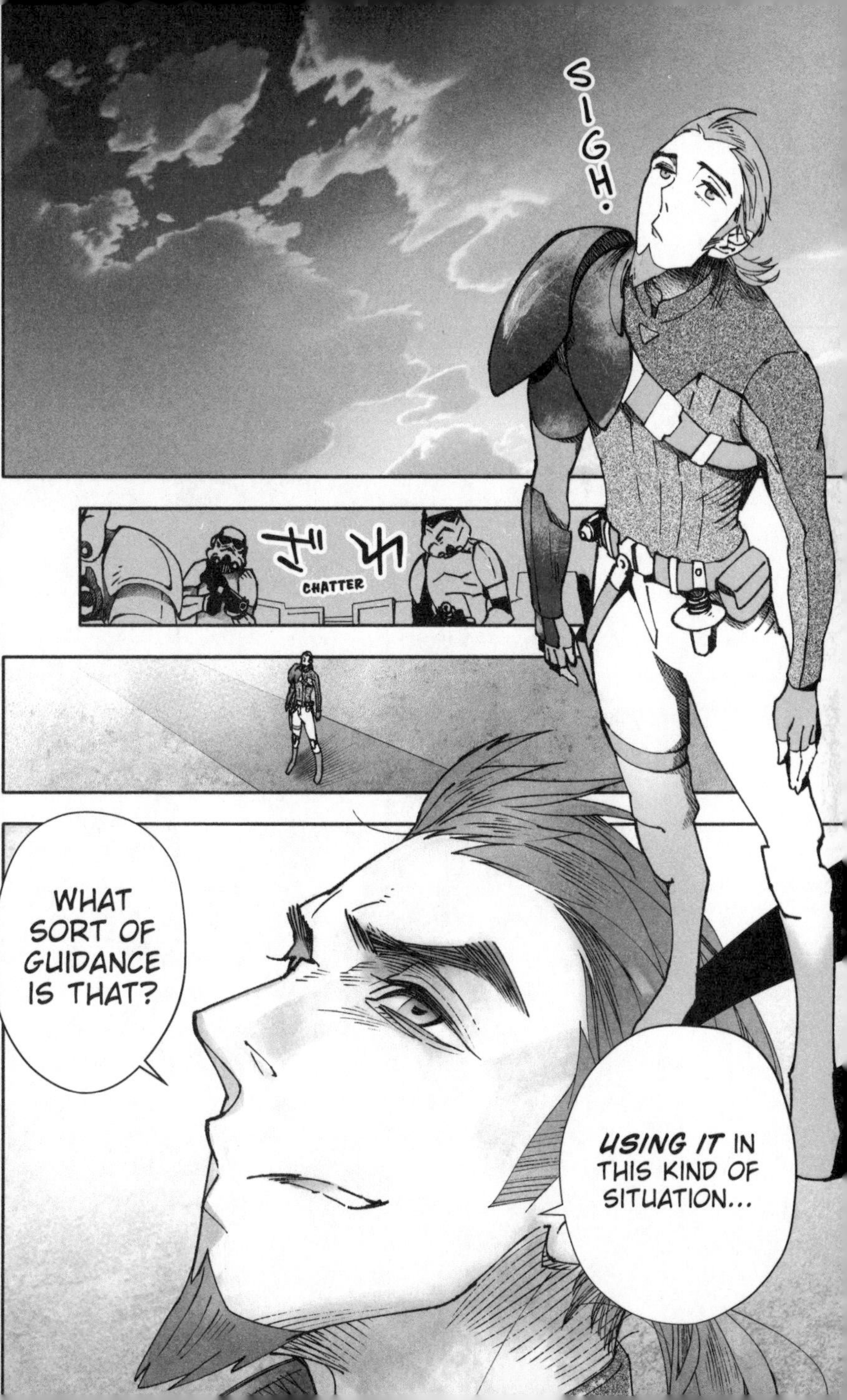
SIGH.
ざわ
CHATTER
USING IT IN THIS KIND OF SITUATION...
WHAT SORT OF GUIDANCE IS THAT?

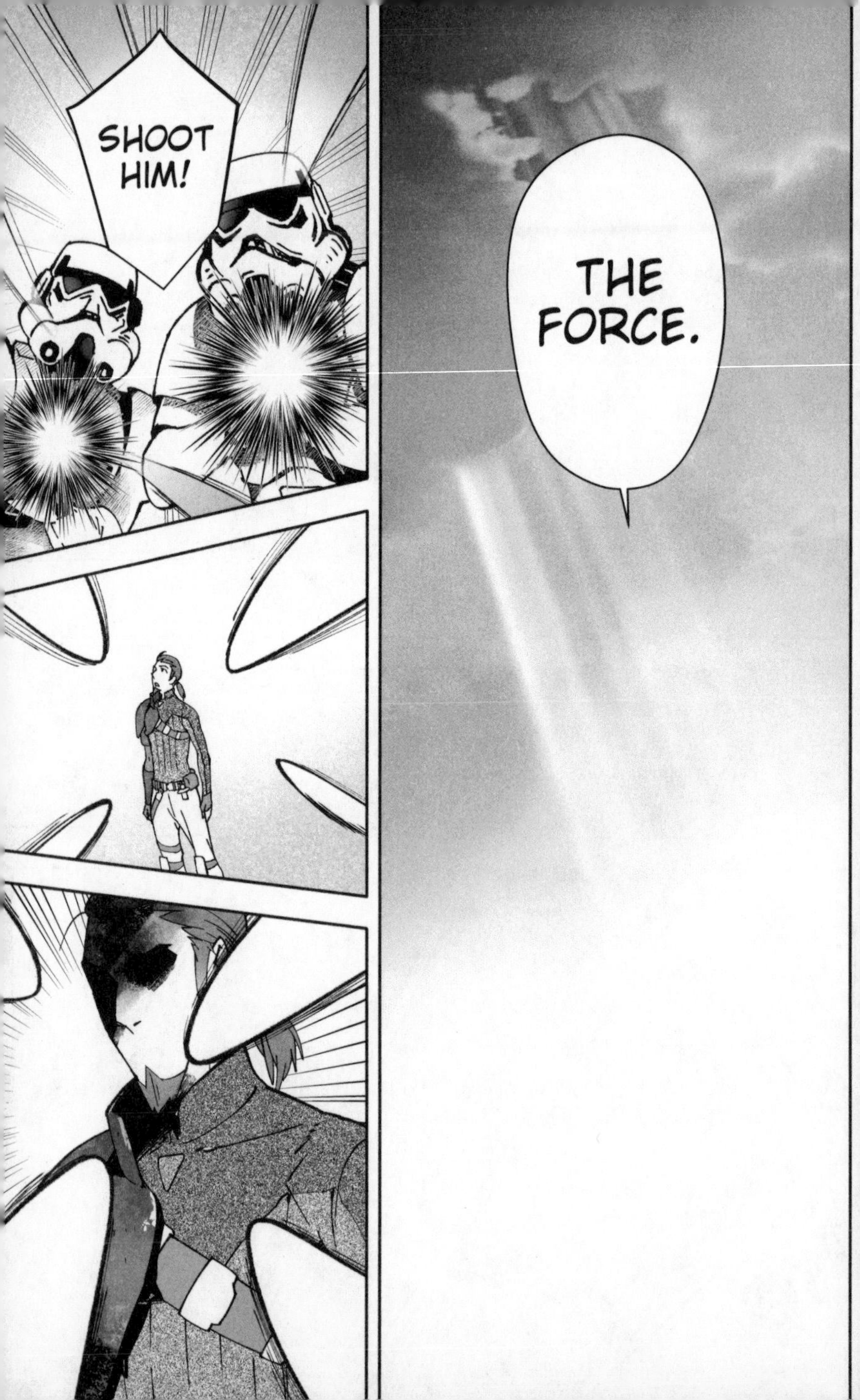
THE FORCE.
SHOOT HIM!

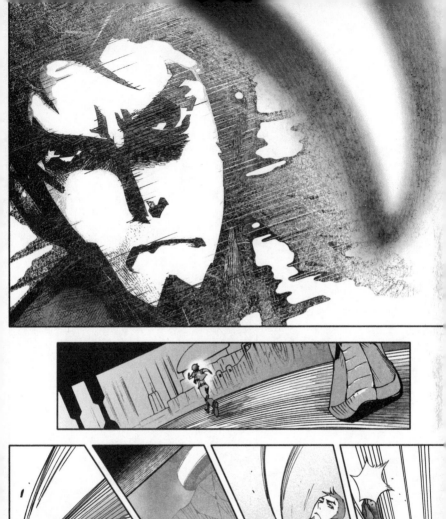

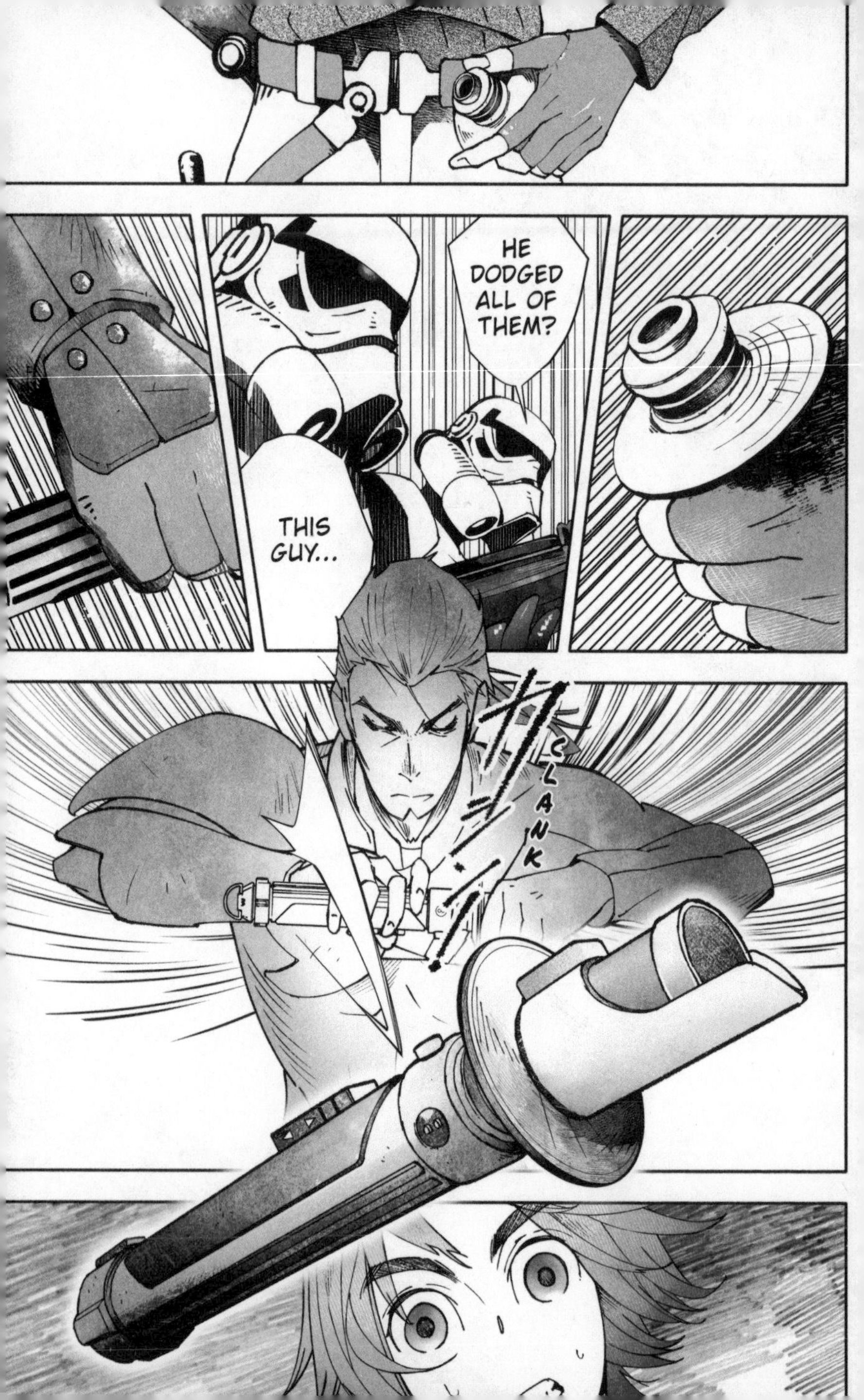
HE DODGED ALL OF THEM?
THIS GUY...
CLANK

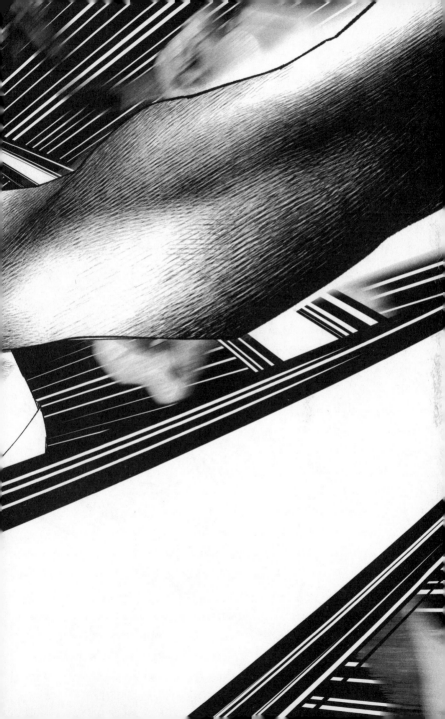

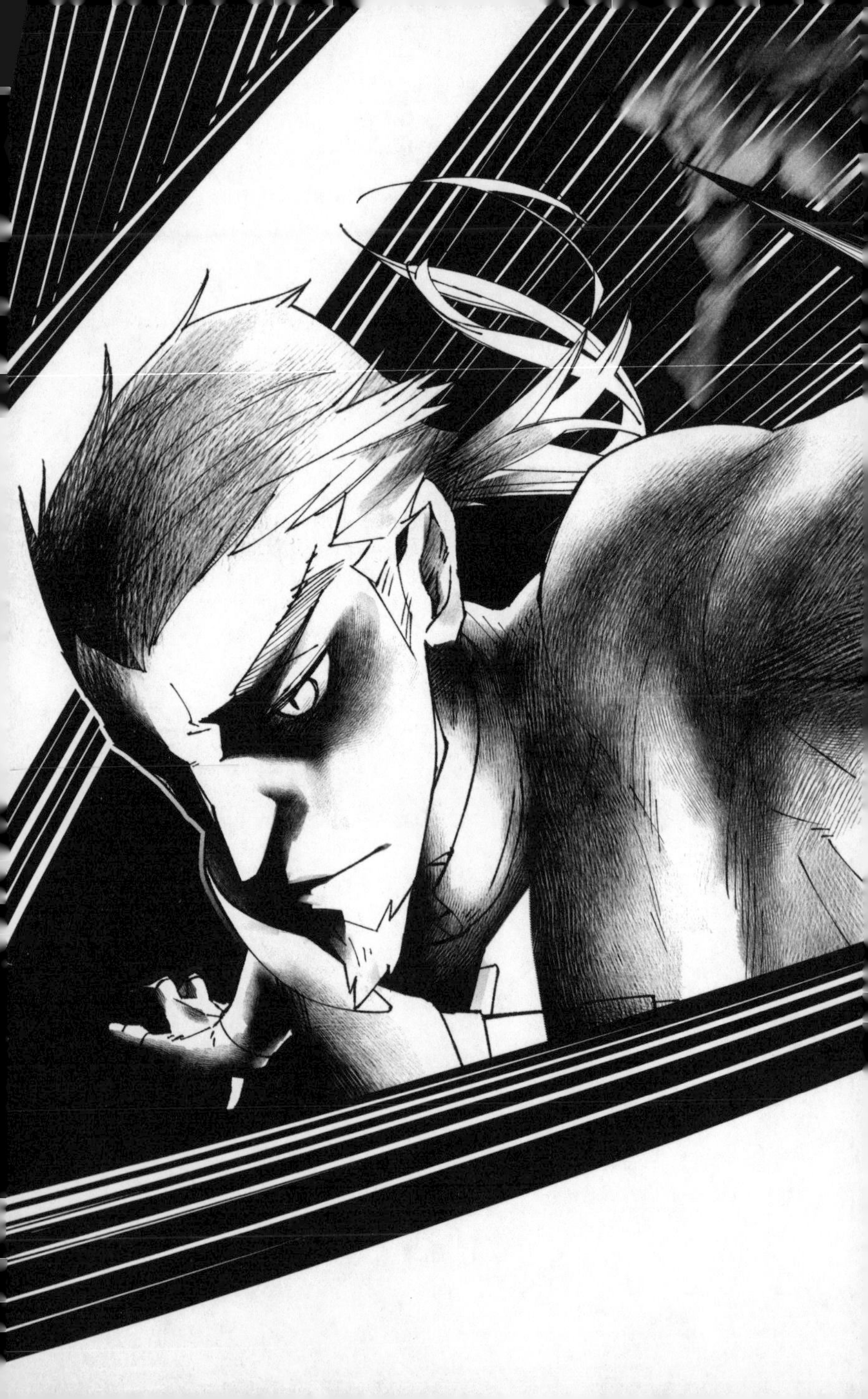

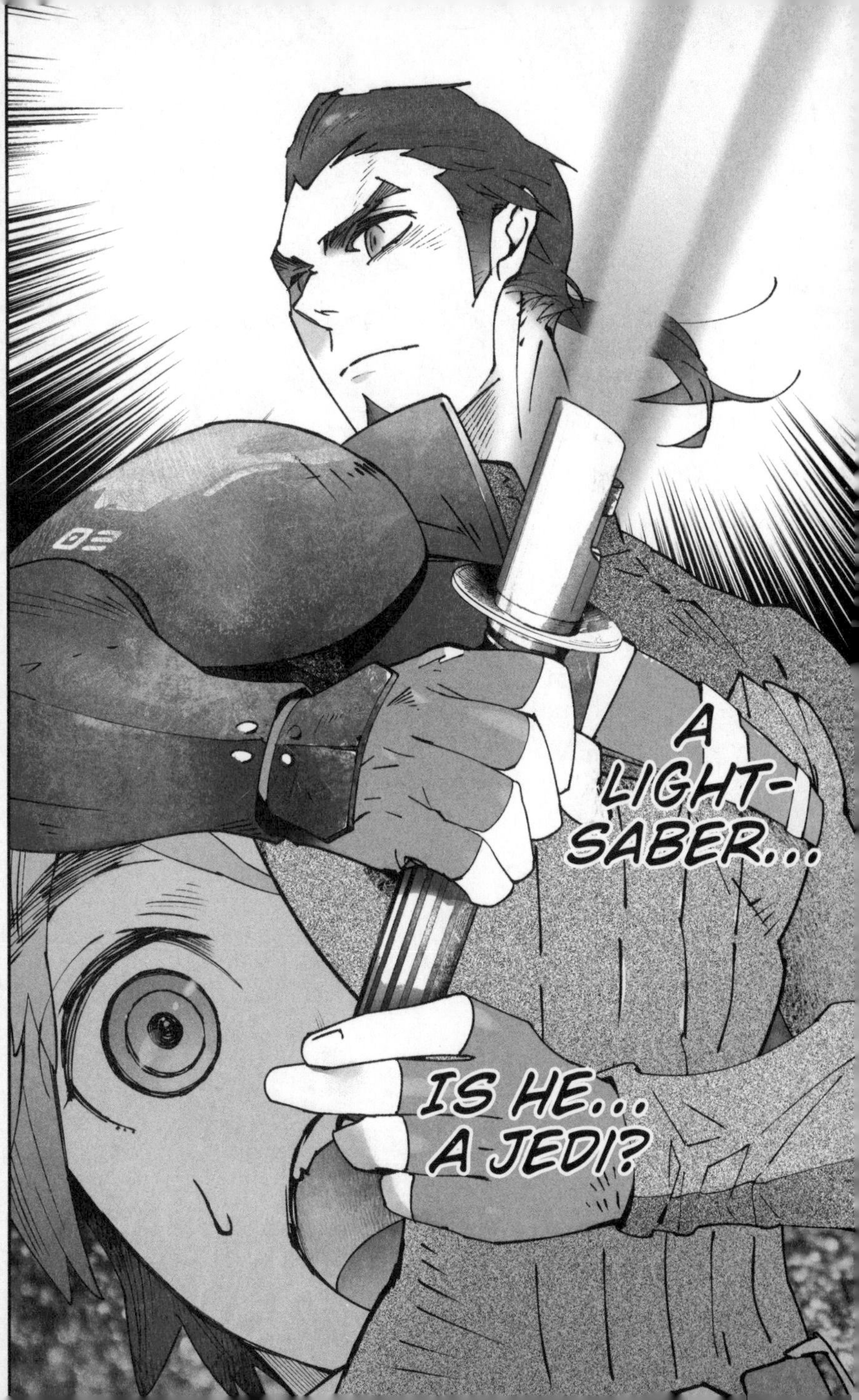
A LIGHT-SABER...
IS HE... A JEDI?

LEGENDARY WARRIORS WHO WIELD LIGHT-SABERS.

VOOM

VOOM

THE JEDI—

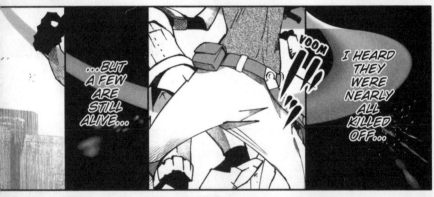

...BUT A FEW ARE STILL ALIVE...

VOOM

I HEARD THEY WERE NEARLY ALL KILLED OFF...

...BUT IS THAT REALLY TRUE? BECAUSE HE'S...

VOOM

VOOM

I HEARD THEY WERE AT FAULT FOR THE FALL OF THE FORMER REPUBLIC...

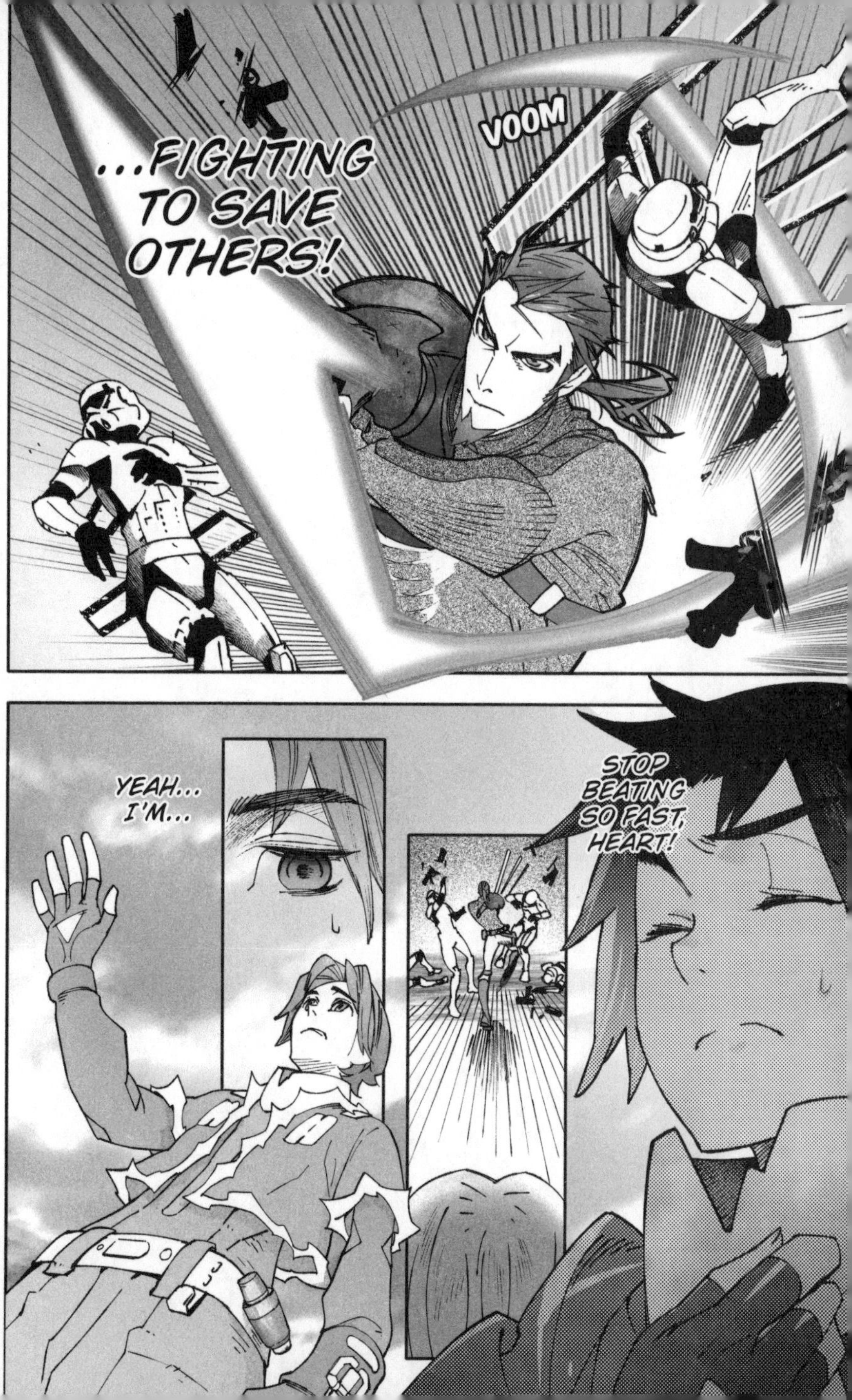
VOOM
...FIGHTING TO SAVE OTHERS!
STOP BEATING SO FAST, HEART!
YEAH... I'M...

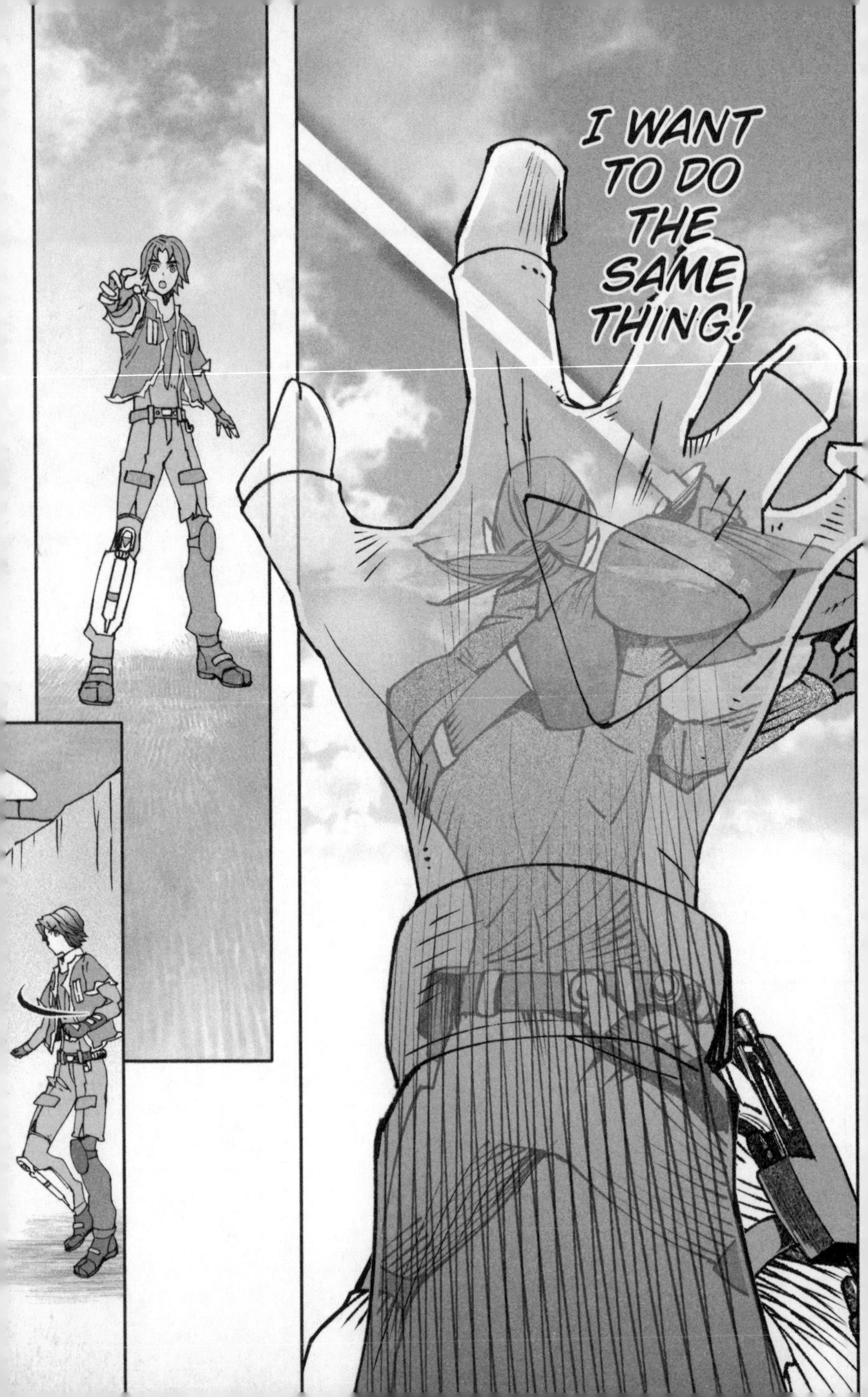
I WANT TO DO THE SAME THING!

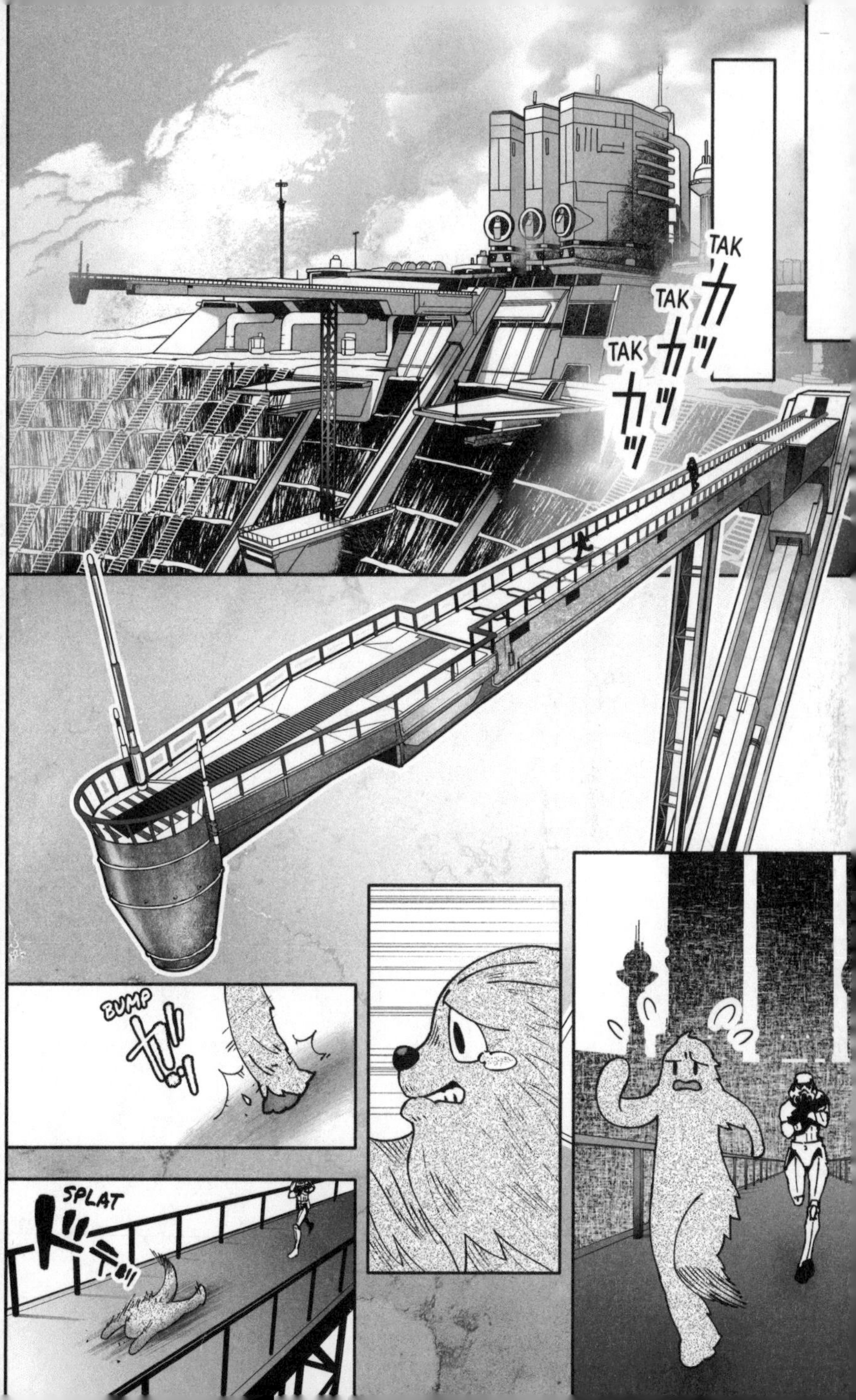
TAK カッ
TAK カッ
TAK カッ
BUMP
SPLAT

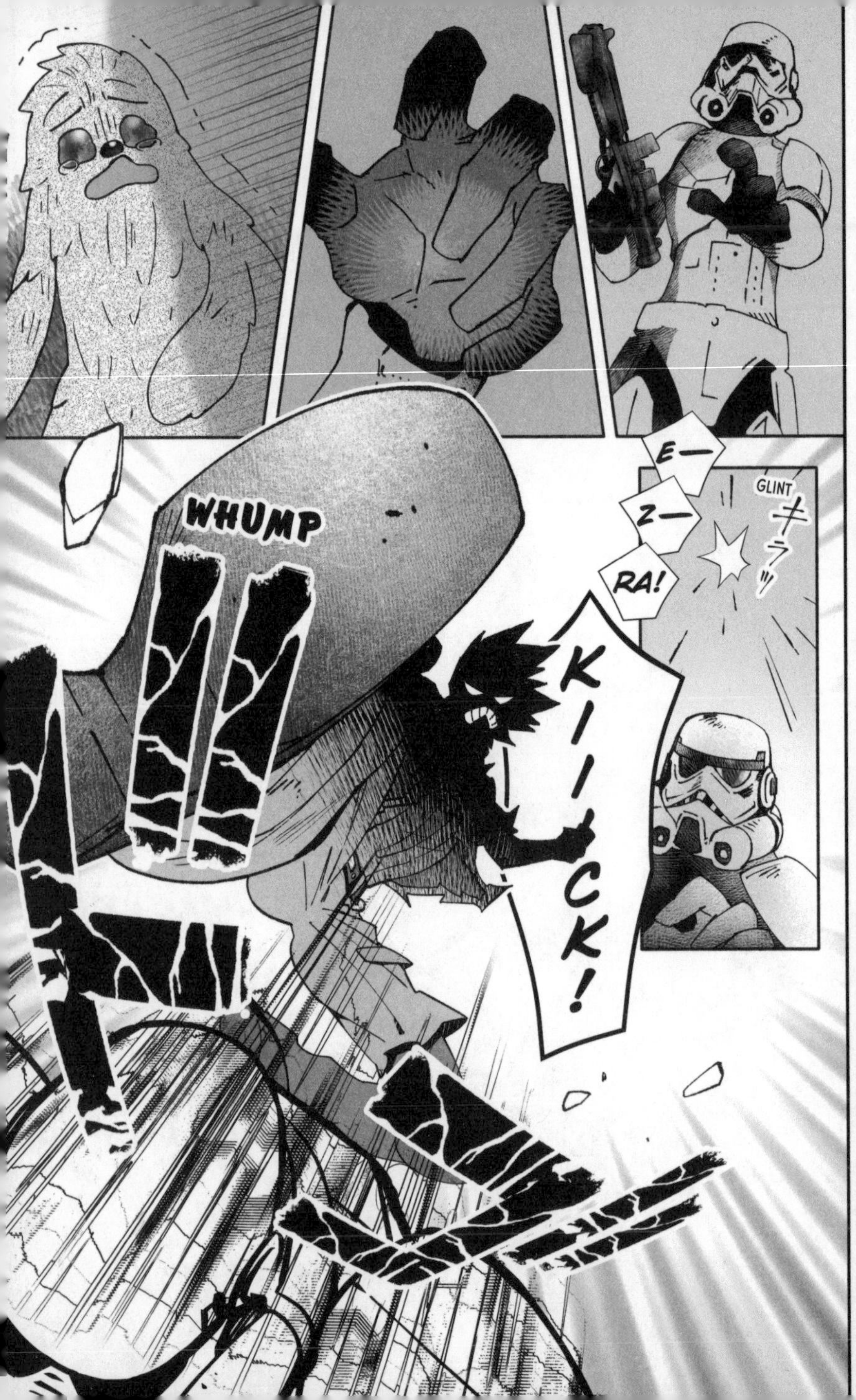
E—
Z—
RA!
GLINT
キラッ
WHUMP
KIIICK!

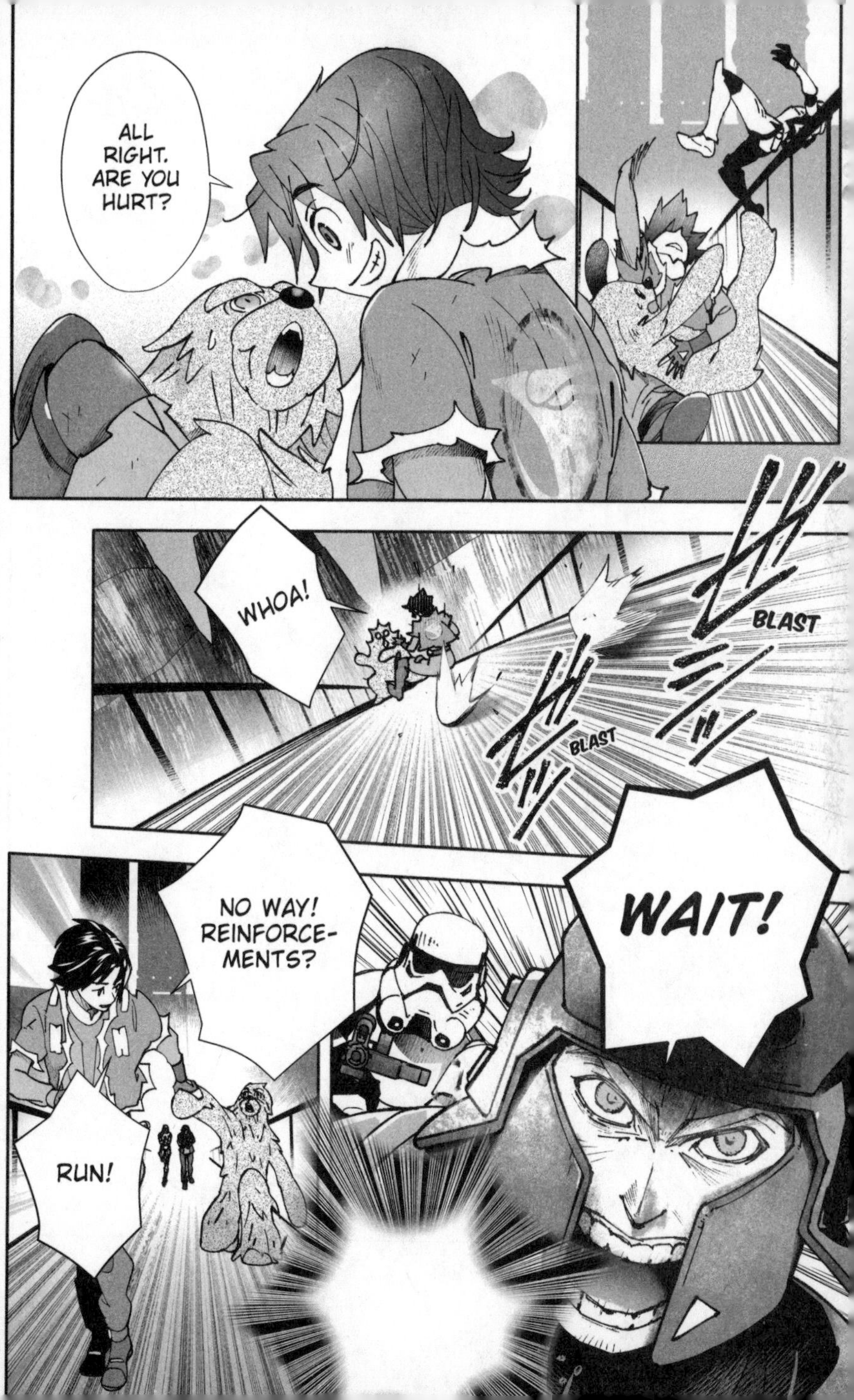
ALL RIGHT. ARE YOU HURT?
BLAST
WHOA!
BLAST
WAIT!
NO WAY! REINFORCE-MENTS?
RUN!

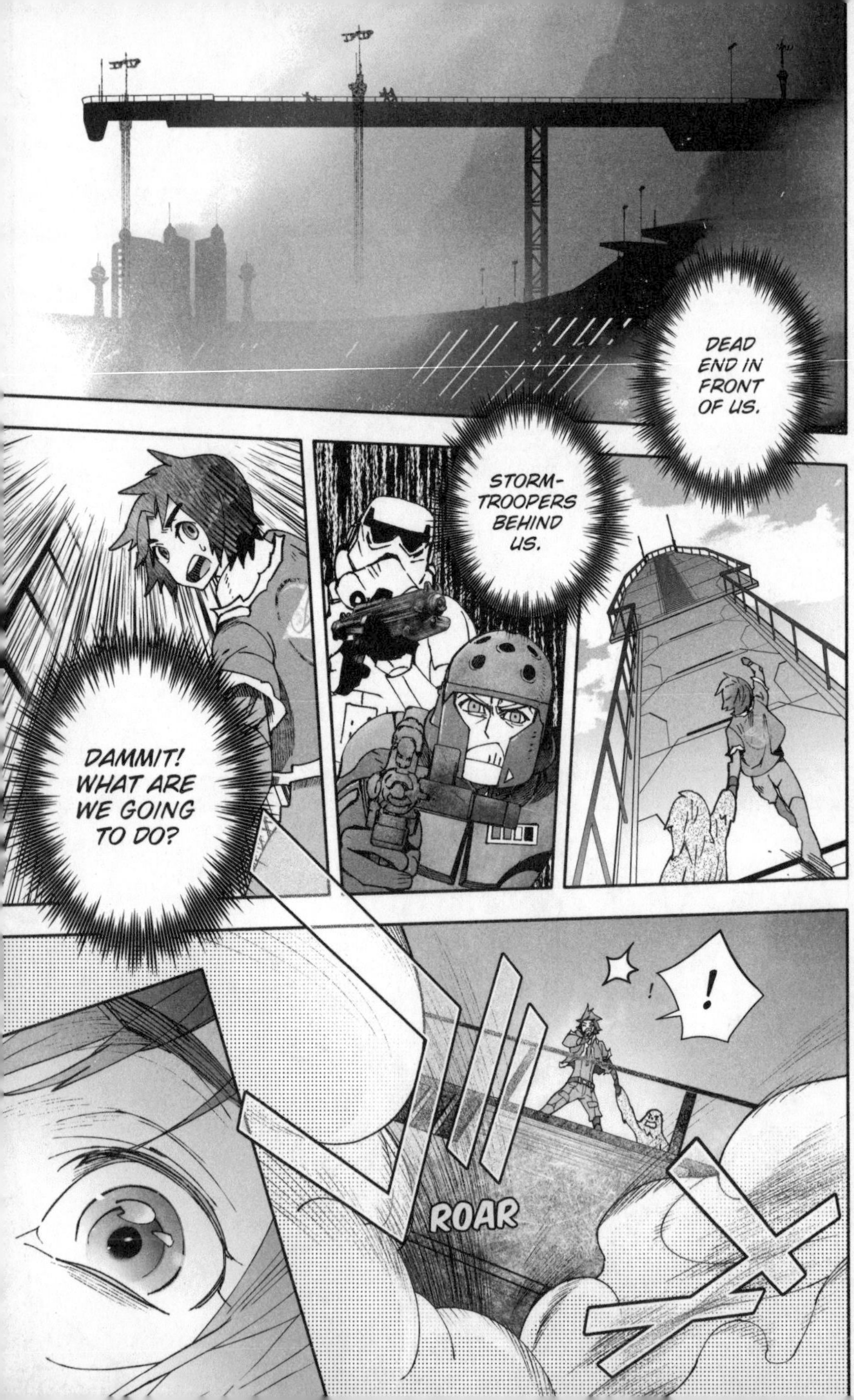

DEAD END IN FRONT OF US.
STORM-TROOPERS BEHIND US.
DAMMIT! WHAT ARE WE GOING TO DO?
!
!
ROAR

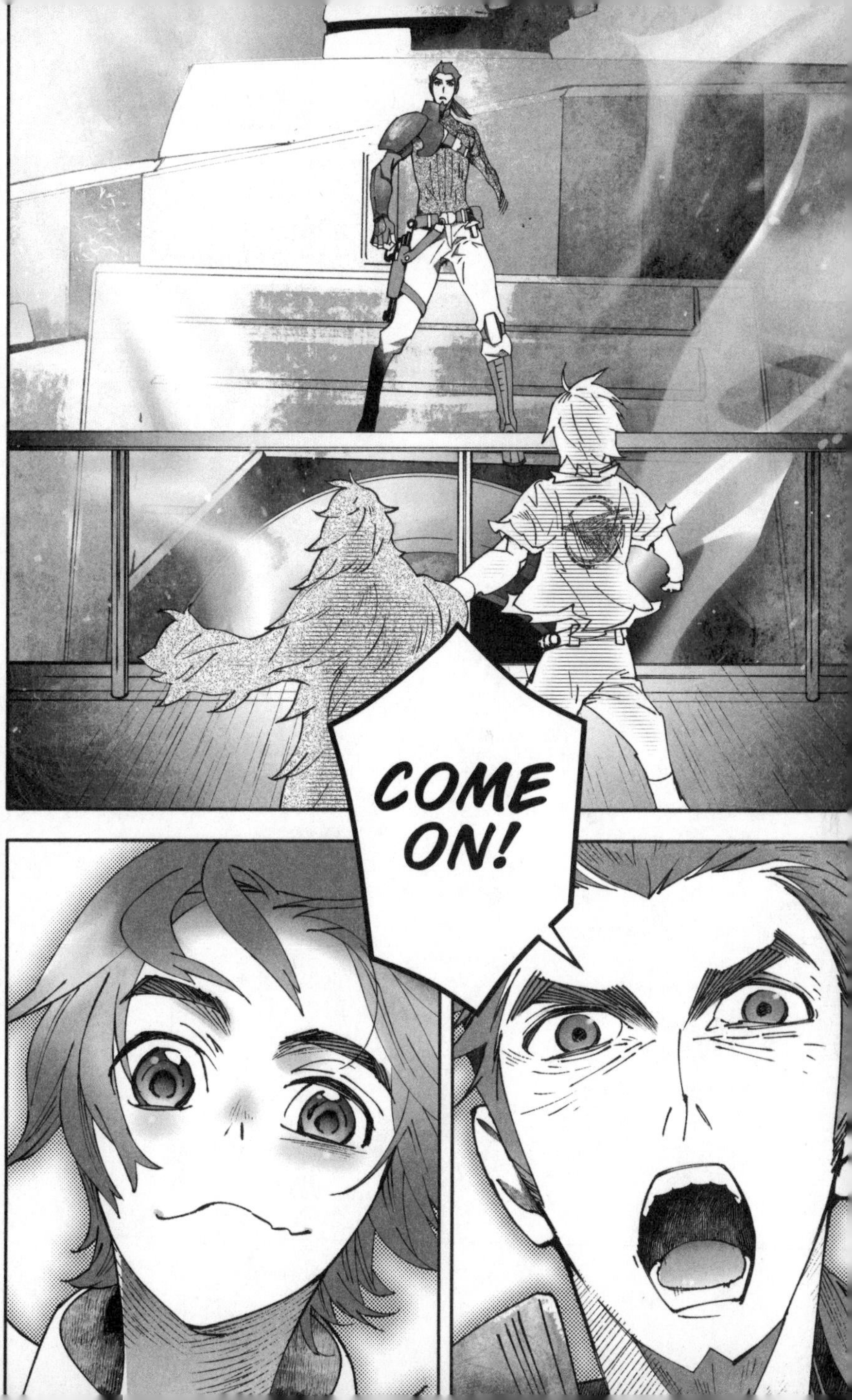
COME ON!

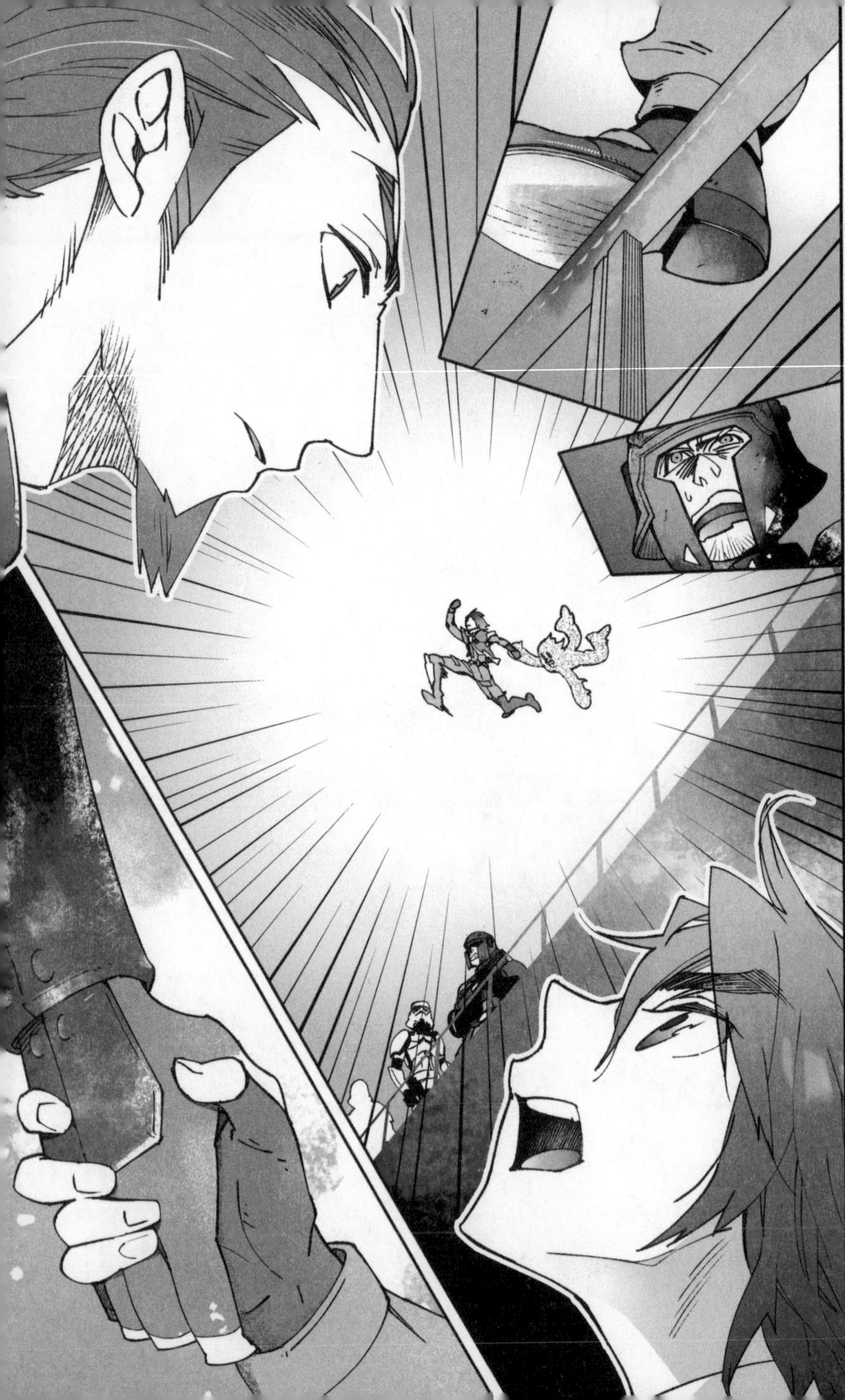

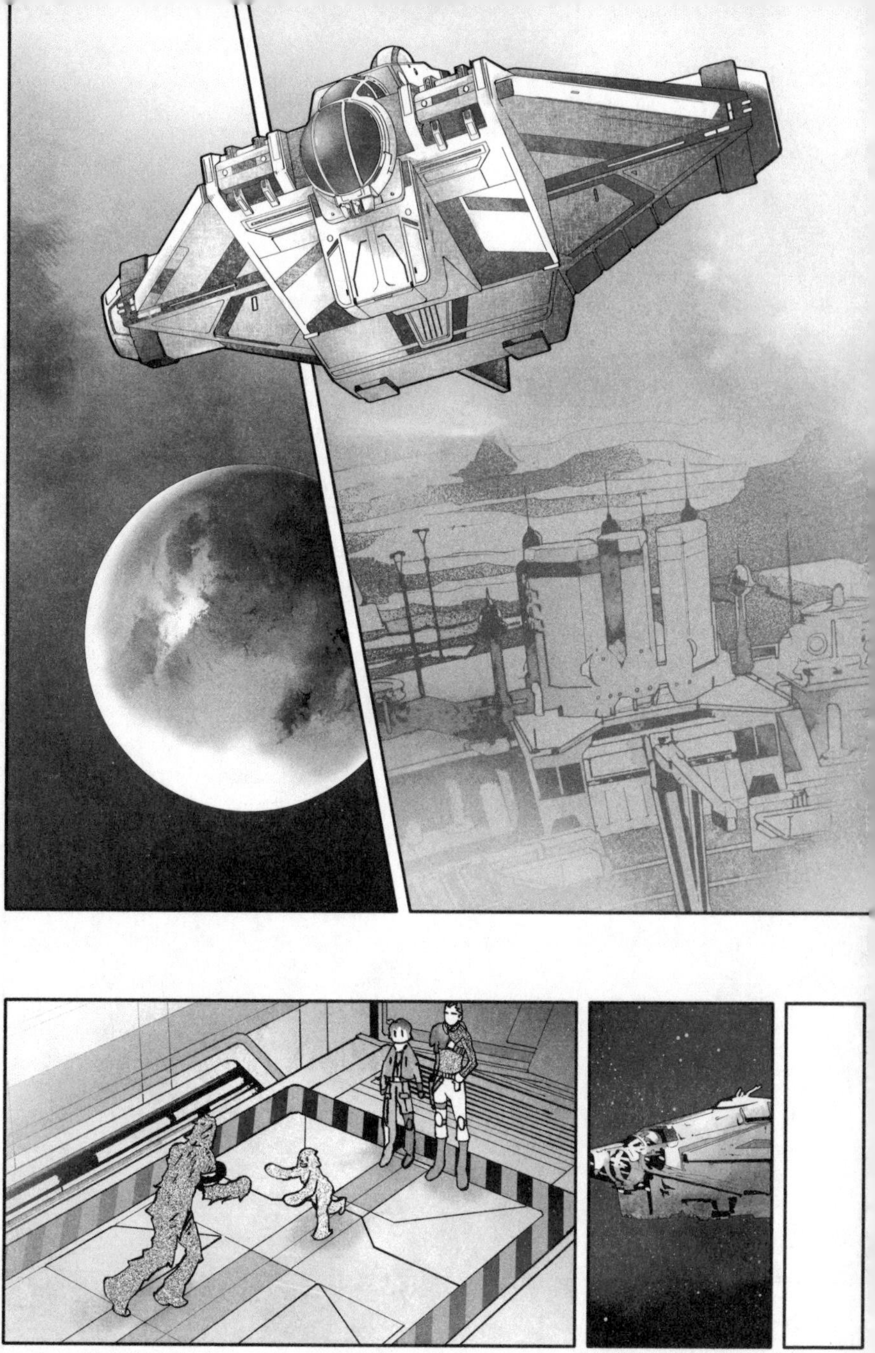

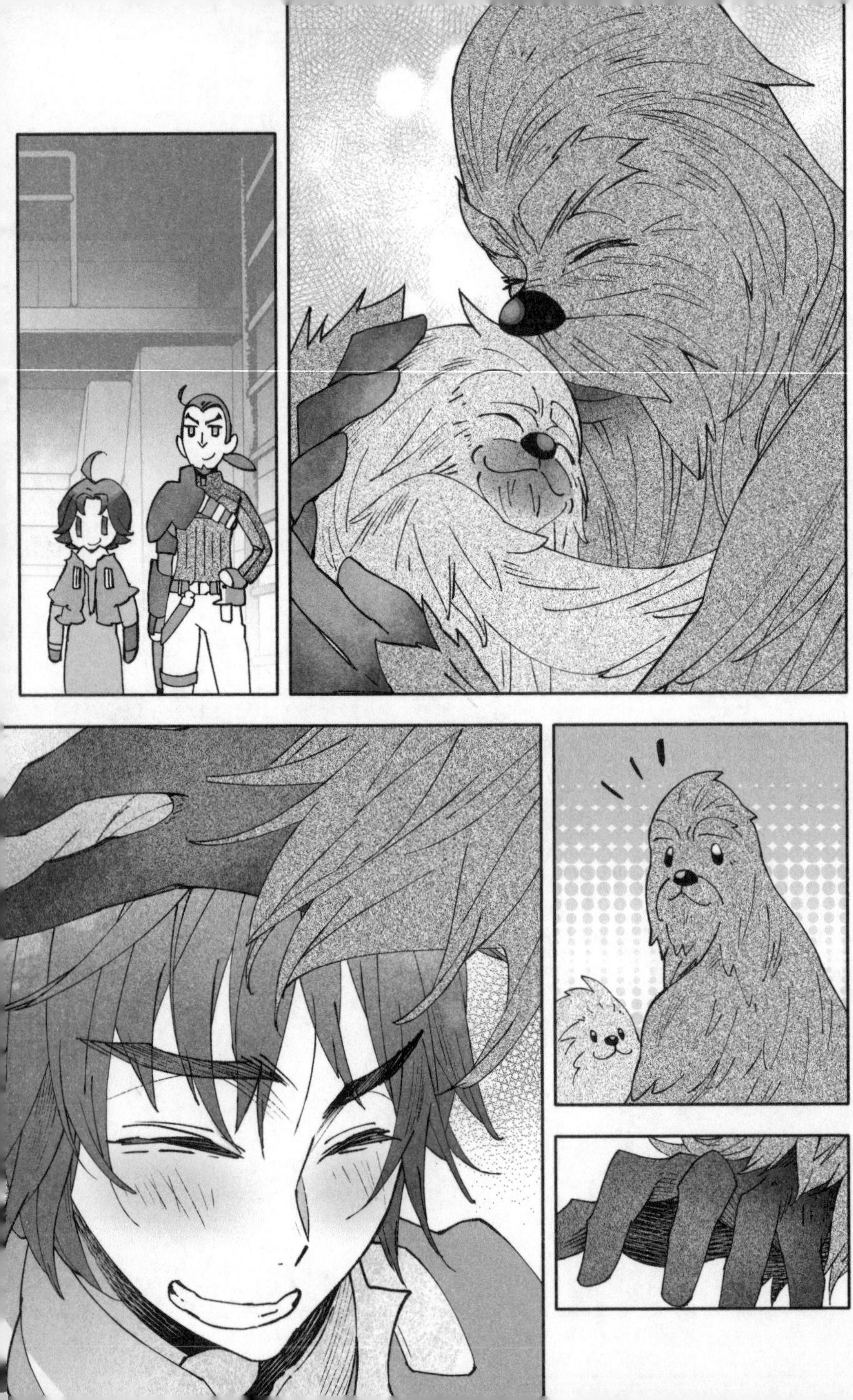

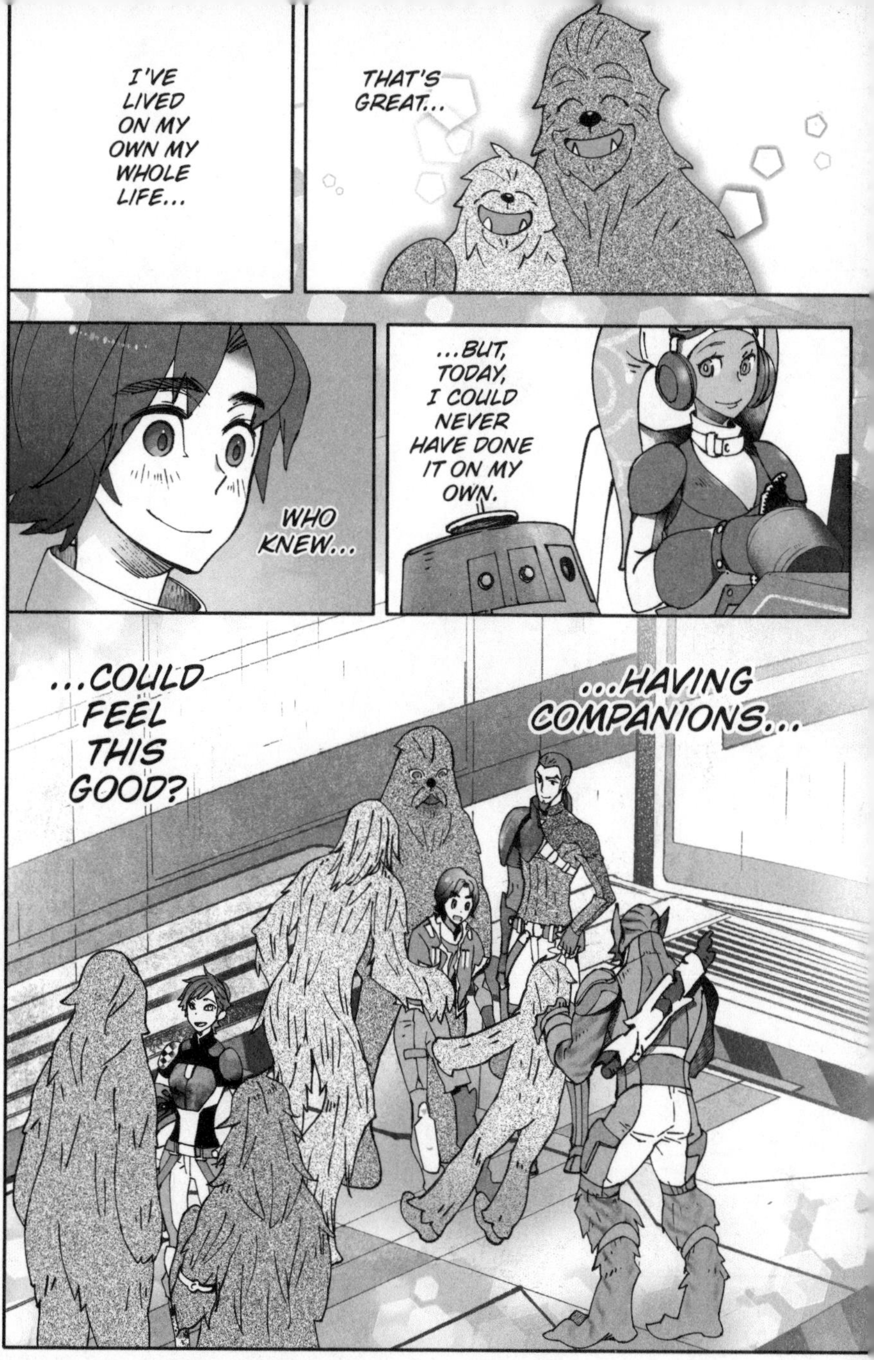
THAT'S GREAT...
I'VE LIVED ON MY OWN MY WHOLE LIFE...
...BUT, TODAY, I COULD NEVER HAVE DONE IT ON MY OWN.
WHO KNEW...
...HAVING COMPANIONS...
...COULD FEEL THIS GOOD?

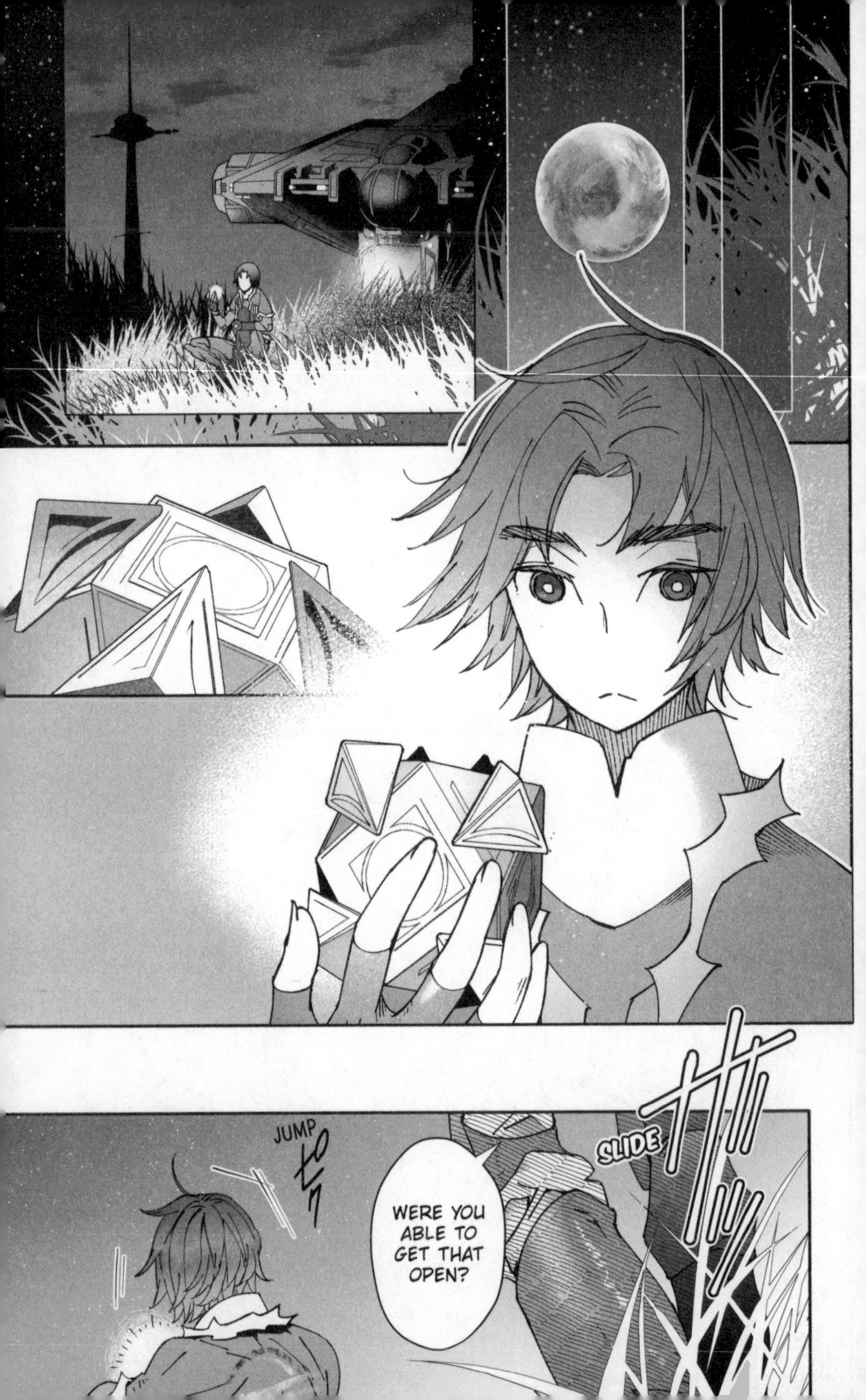
SLIDE
WERE YOU ABLE TO GET THAT OPEN?
JUMP

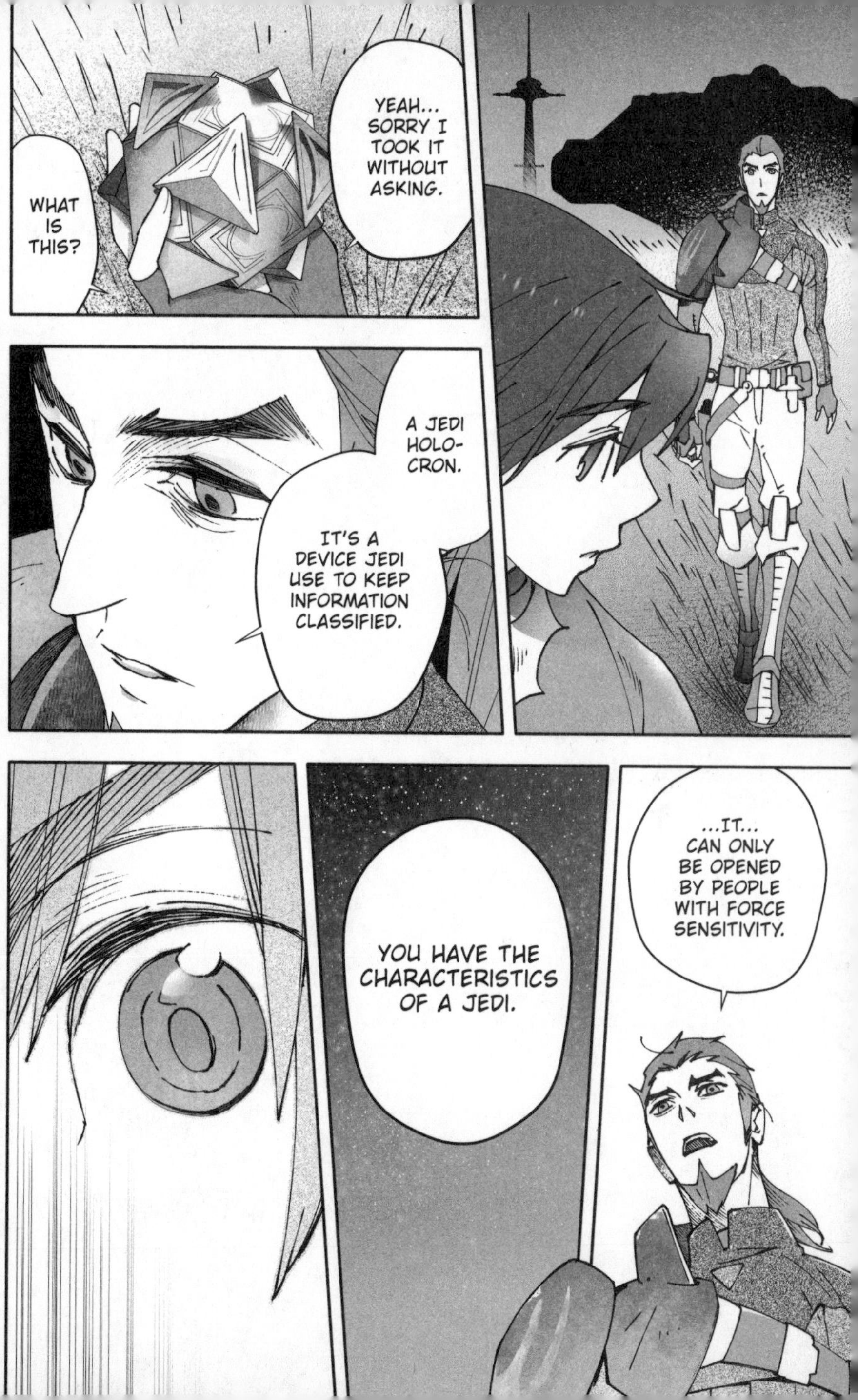
YEAH... SORRY I TOOK IT WITHOUT ASKING.
WHAT IS THIS?
A JEDI HOLOCRON.
IT'S A DEVICE JEDI USE TO KEEP INFORMATION CLASSIFIED.
...IT... CAN ONLY BE OPENED BY PEOPLE WITH FORCE SENSITIVITY.
YOU HAVE THE CHARACTERISTICS OF A JEDI.

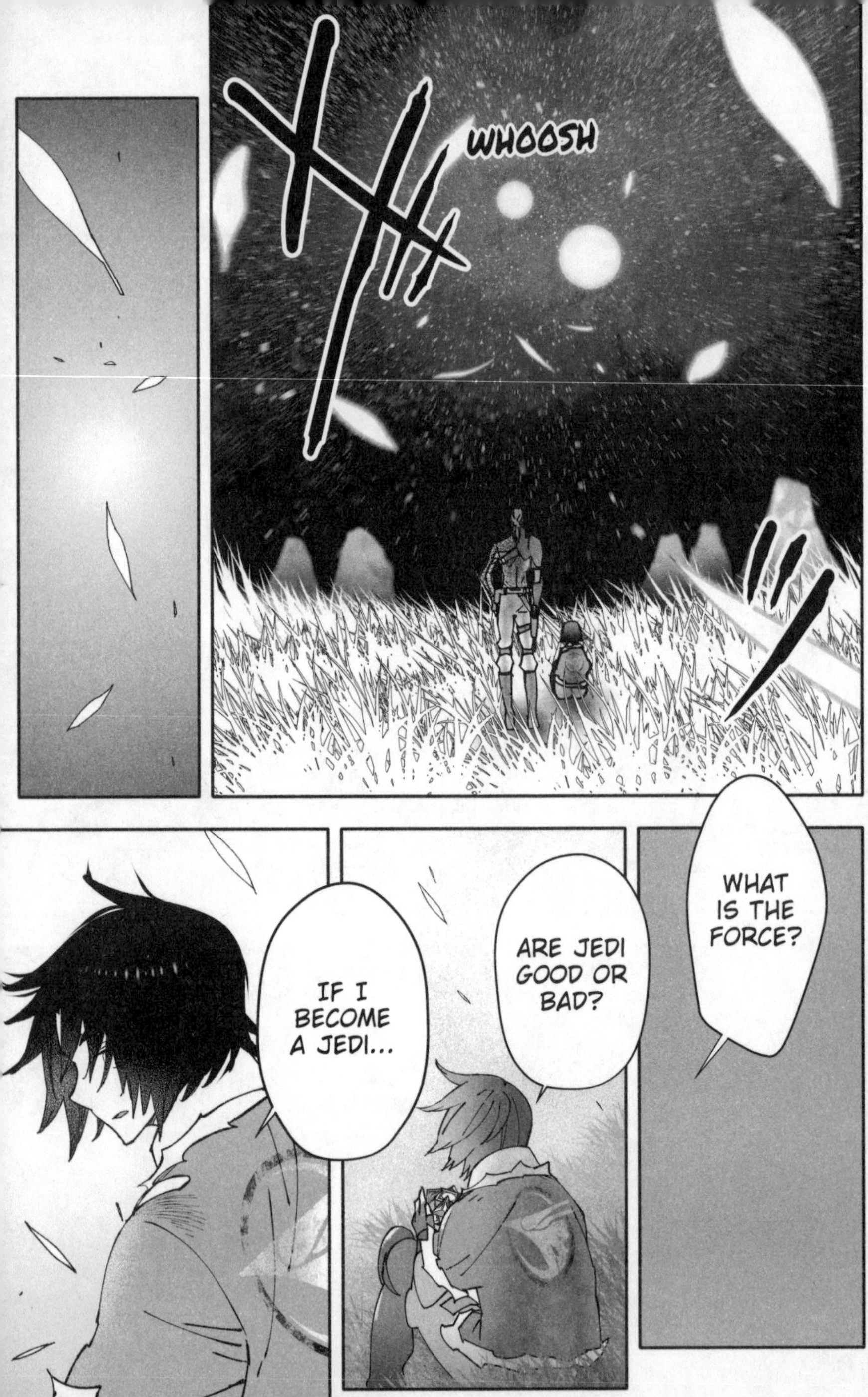
WHOOSH
WHAT IS THE FORCE?
ARE JEDI GOOD OR BAD?
IF I BECOME A JEDI...

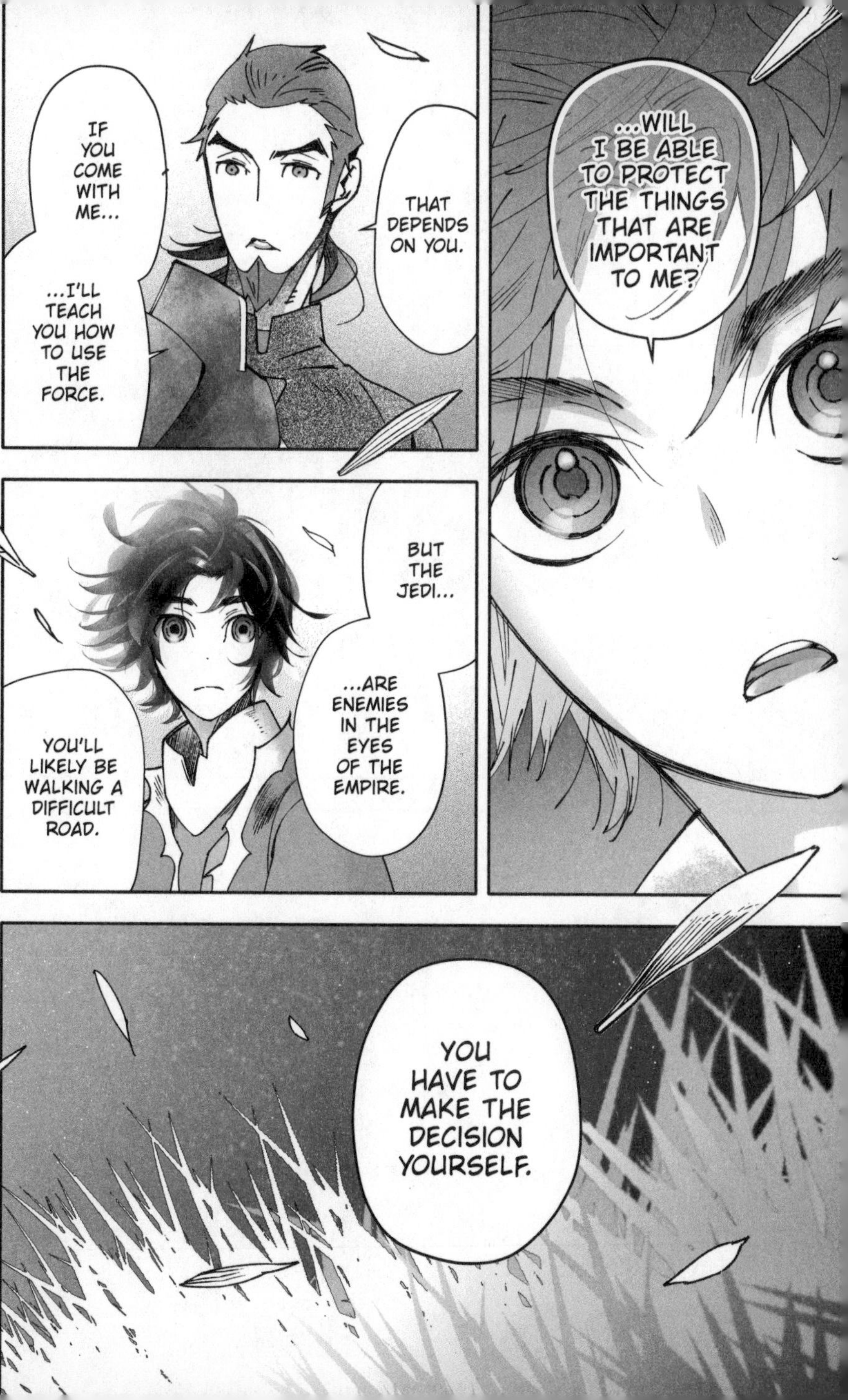
...WILL I BE ABLE TO PROTECT THE THINGS THAT ARE IMPORTANT TO ME?
THAT DEPENDS ON YOU.
IF YOU COME WITH ME...
...I'LL TEACH YOU HOW TO USE THE FORCE.
BUT THE JEDI...
...ARE ENEMIES IN THE EYES OF THE EMPIRE.
YOU'LL LIKELY BE WALKING A DIFFICULT ROAD.
YOU HAVE TO MAKE THE DECISION YOURSELF.

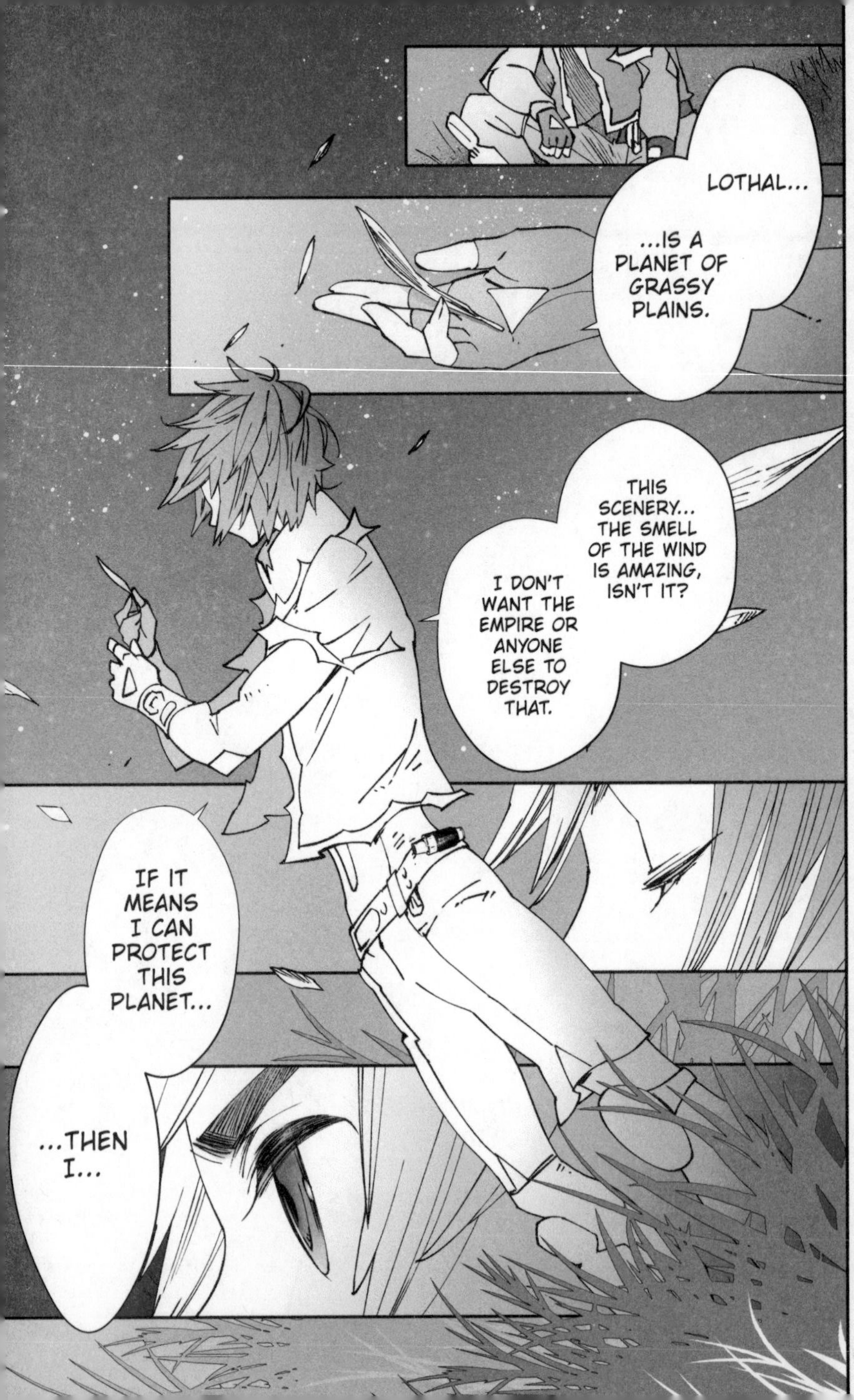
LOTHAL...
...IS A PLANET OF GRASSY PLAINS.
THIS SCENERY... THE SMELL OF THE WIND IS AMAZING, ISN'T IT?
I DON'T WANT THE EMPIRE OR ANYONE ELSE TO DESTROY THAT.
IF IT MEANS I CAN PROTECT THIS PLANET...
...THEN I...

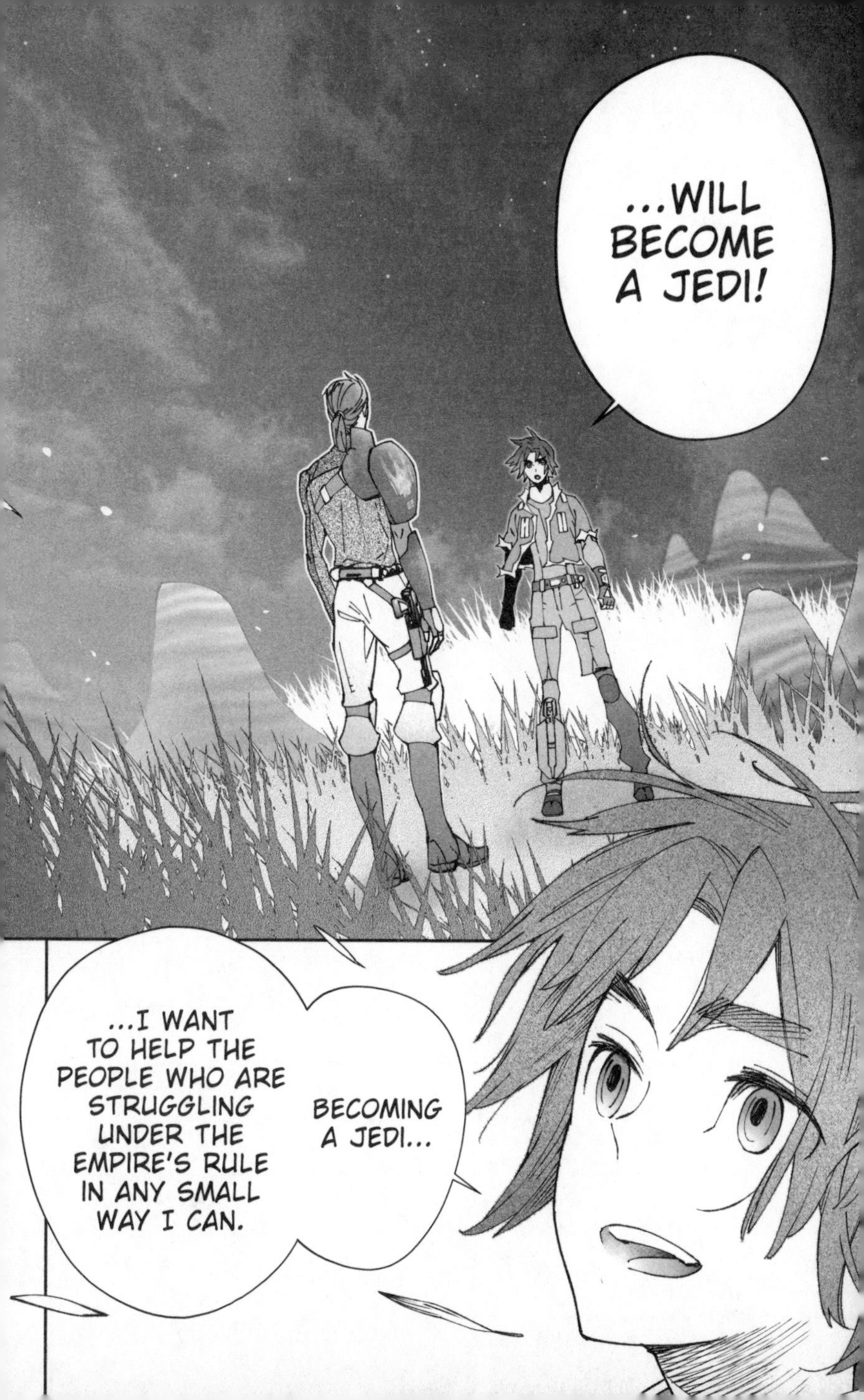
...WILL BECOME A JEDI!
BECOMING A JEDI...
...I WANT TO HELP THE PEOPLE WHO ARE STRUGGLING UNDER THE EMPIRE'S RULE IN ANY SMALL WAY I CAN.

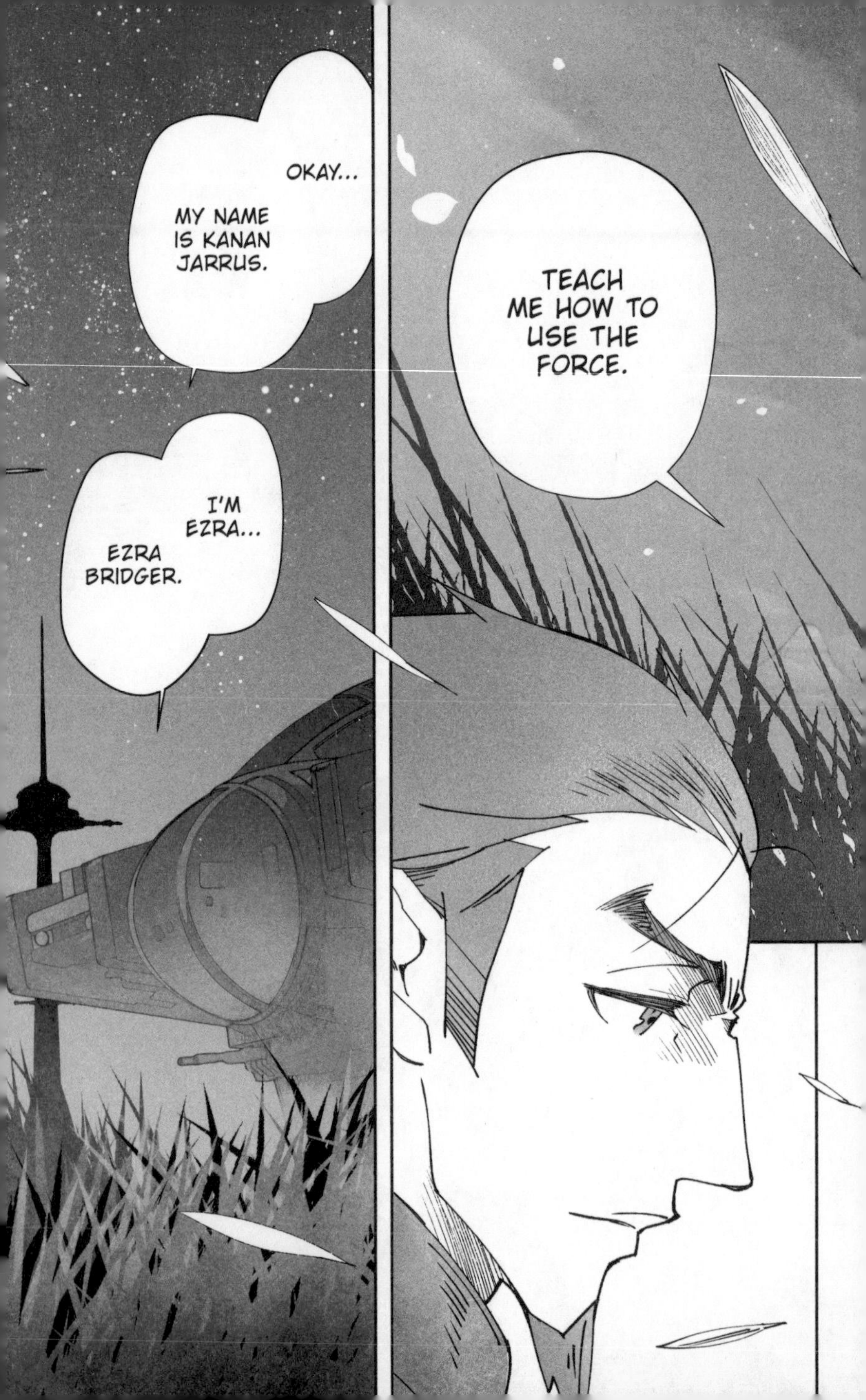
TEACH ME HOW TO USE THE FORCE.
OKAY...
MY NAME IS KANAN JARRUS.
I'M EZRA...
EZRA BRIDGER.

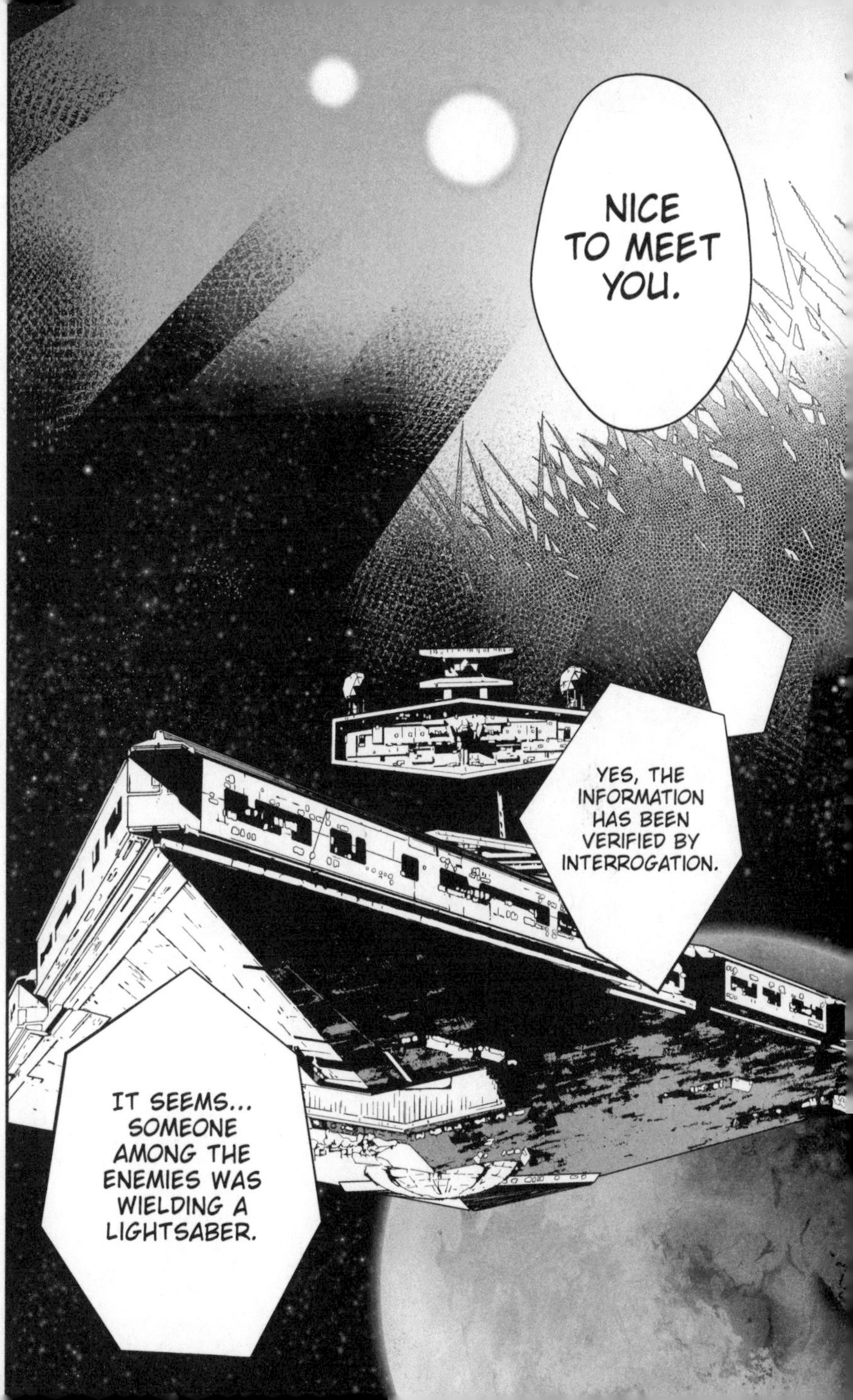
NICE TO MEET YOU.
YES, THE INFORMATION HAS BEEN VERIFIED BY INTERROGATION.
IT SEEMS... SOMEONE AMONG THE ENEMIES WAS WIELDING A LIGHTSABER.

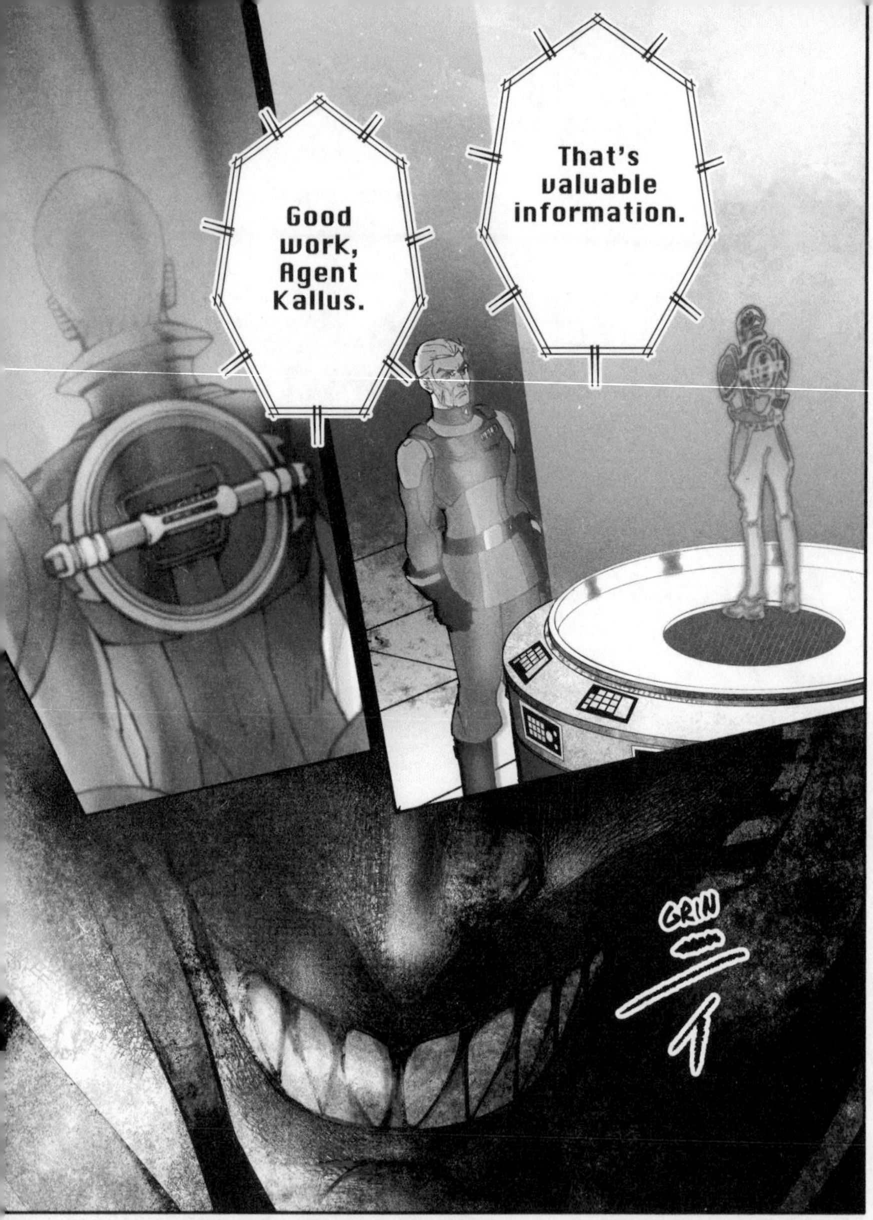
That's valuable information.
Good work, Agent Kallus.
GRIN

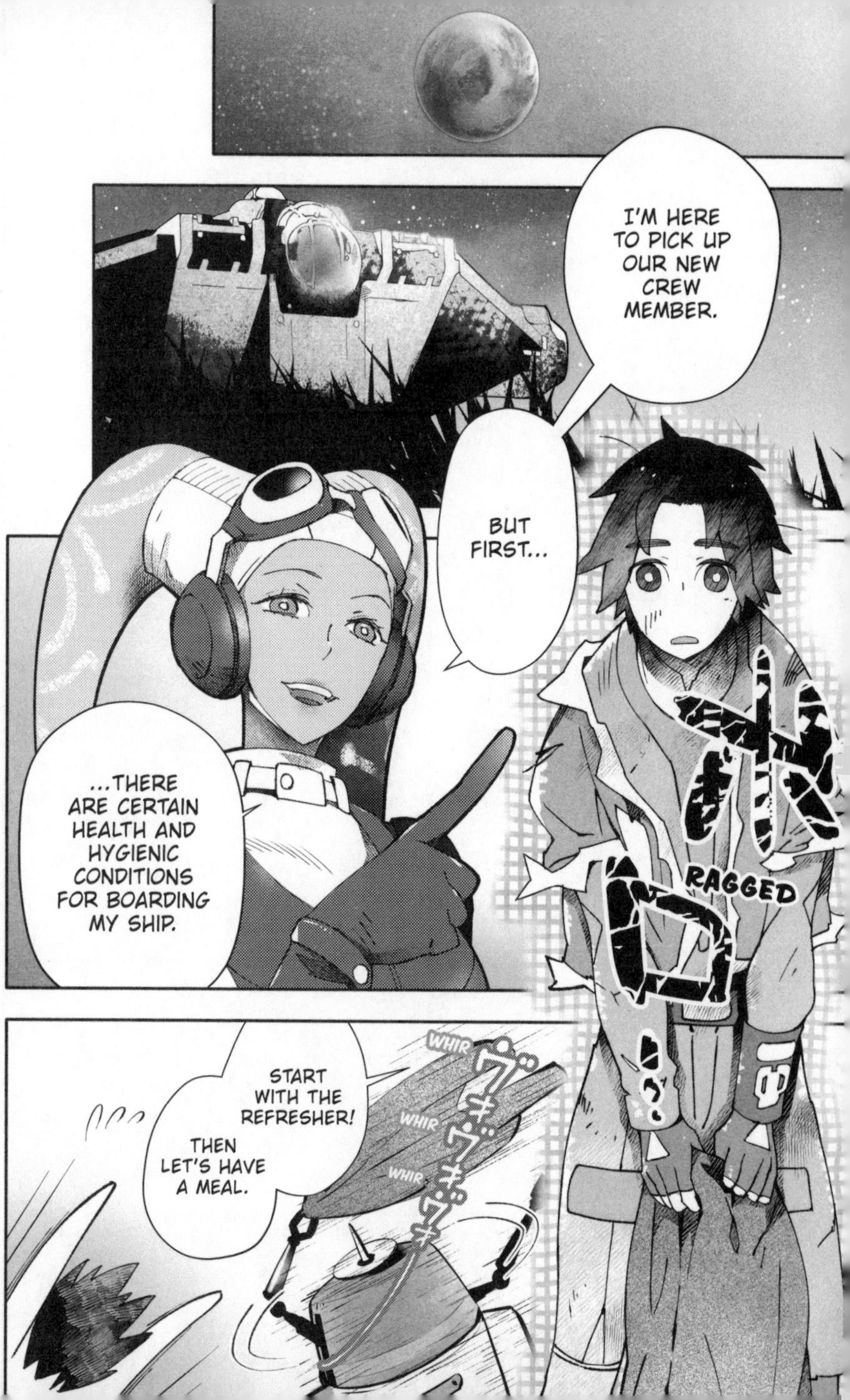

I'M HERE TO PICK UP OUR NEW CREW MEMBER.
BUT FIRST...
RAGGED
...THERE ARE CERTAIN HEALTH AND HYGIENIC CONDITIONS FOR BOARDING MY SHIP.
WHIR
WHIR
WHIR
START WITH THE REFRESHER!
THEN LET'S HAVE A MEAL.

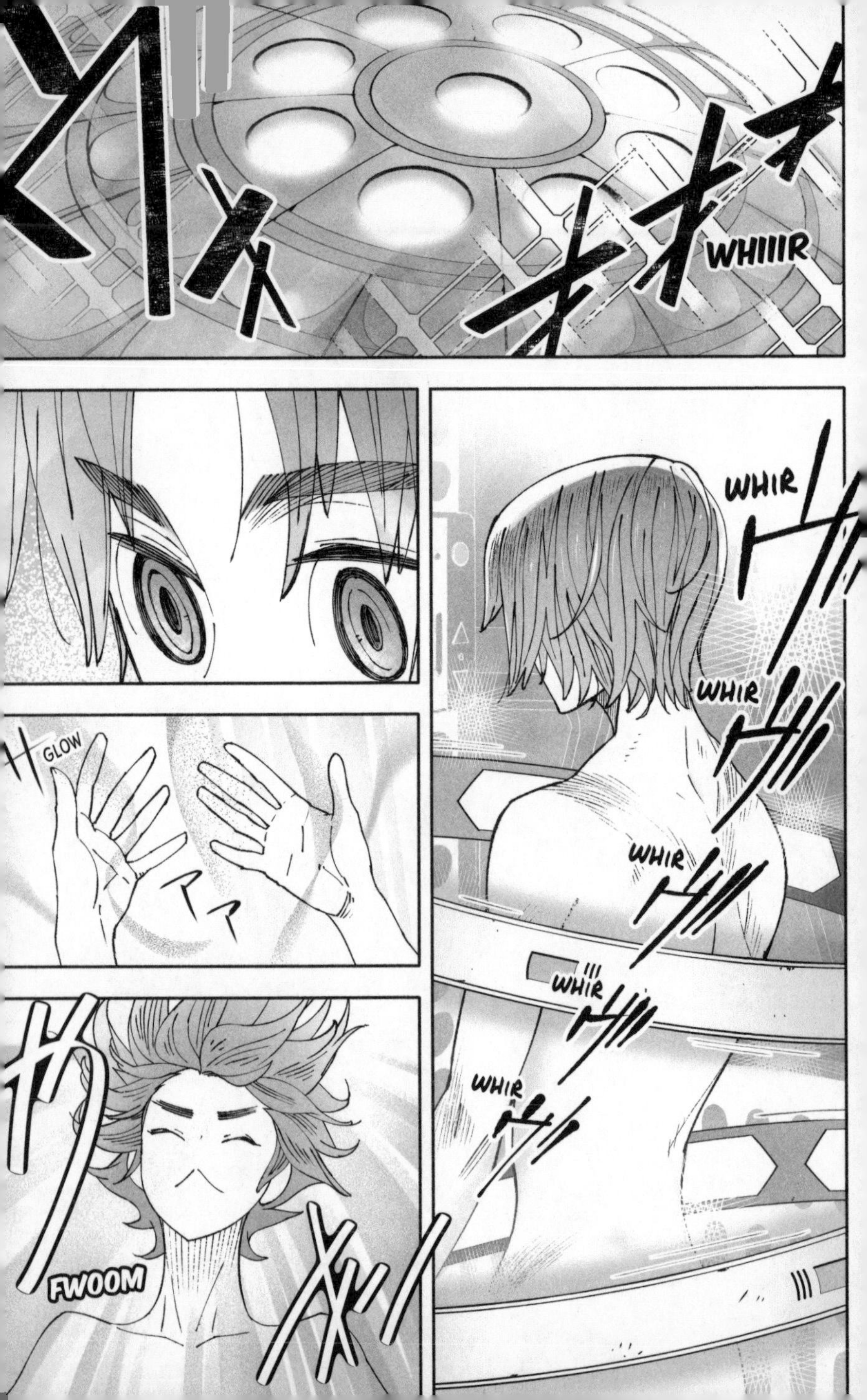
WHIIIR
WHIR
WHIR
WHIR
WHIR
WHIR
GLOW
FWOOM

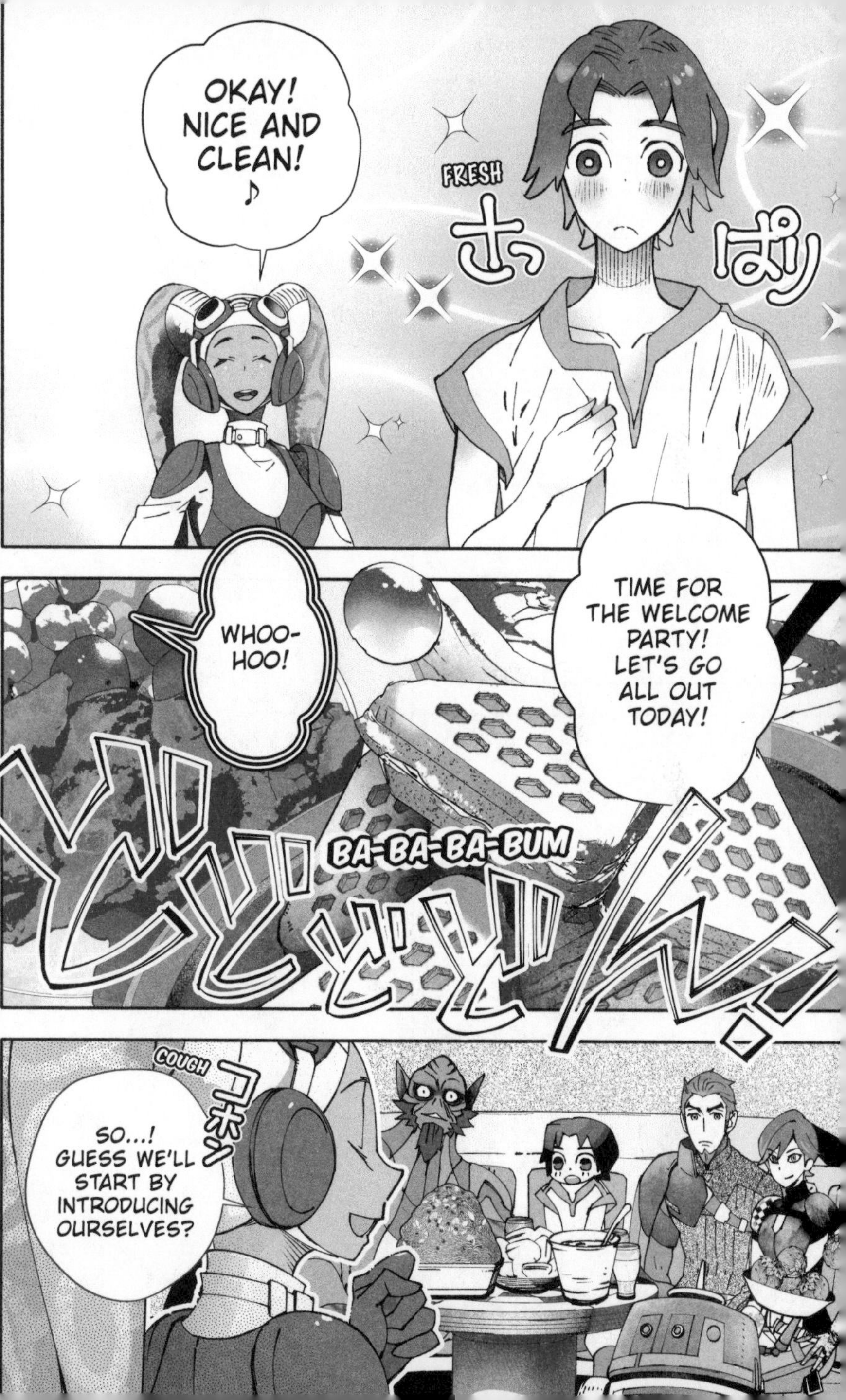
FRESH
さっぱり
OKAY! NICE AND CLEAN! ♪
TIME FOR THE WELCOME PARTY! LET'S GO ALL OUT TODAY!
WHOO-HOO!
BA-BA-BA-BUM
どどどん!
COUGH
コホン
SO...! GUESS WE'LL START BY INTRODUCING OURSELVES?

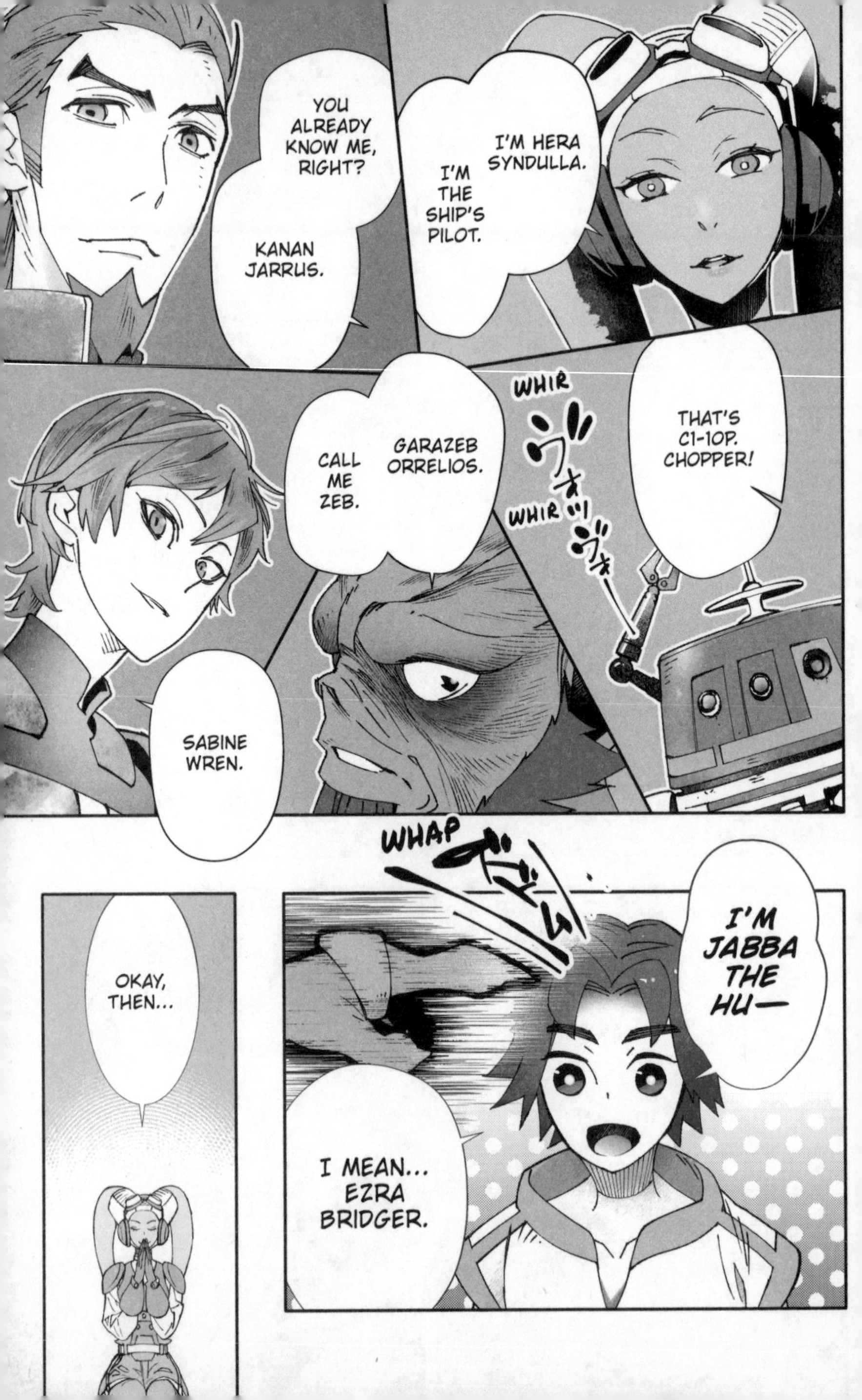
I'M HERA SYNDULLA.
I'M THE SHIP'S PILOT.
YOU ALREADY KNOW ME, RIGHT?
KANAN JARRUS.
WHIR
WHIR
THAT'S C1-10P. CHOPPER!
GARAZEB ORRELIOS.
CALL ME ZEB.
SABINE WREN.
WHAP
I'M JABBA THE HU—
I MEAN... EZRA BRIDGER.
OKAY, THEN...

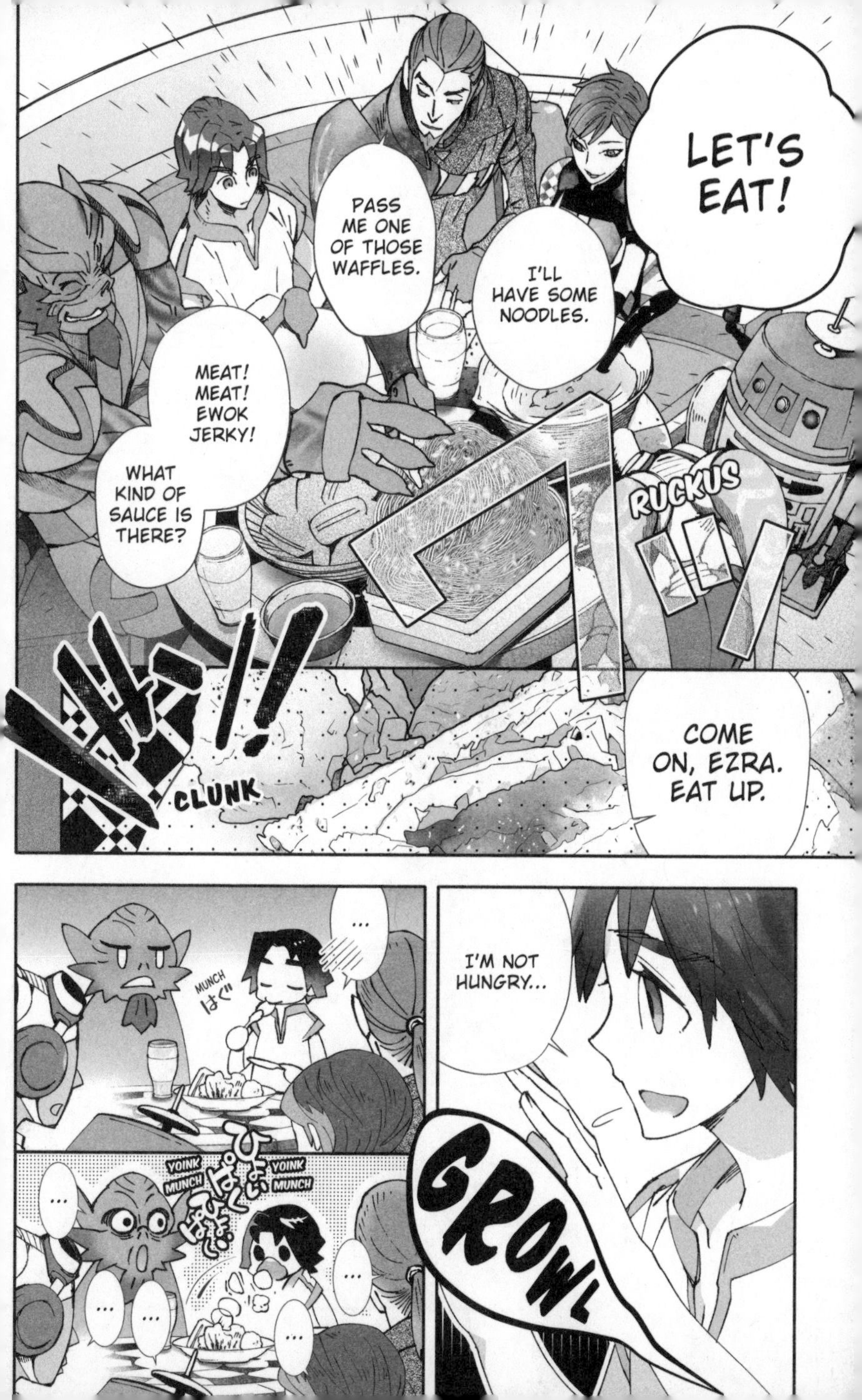
LET'S EAT!
I'LL HAVE SOME NOODLES.
PASS ME ONE OF THOSE WAFFLES.
MEAT! MEAT! EWOK JERKY!
WHAT KIND OF SAUCE IS THERE?
RUCKUS
COME ON, EZRA. EAT UP.
CLUNK
I'M NOT HUNGRY...
GROWL
...
MUNCH
はぐ
YOINK MUNCH
YOINK MUNCH
...
...
...
...
...

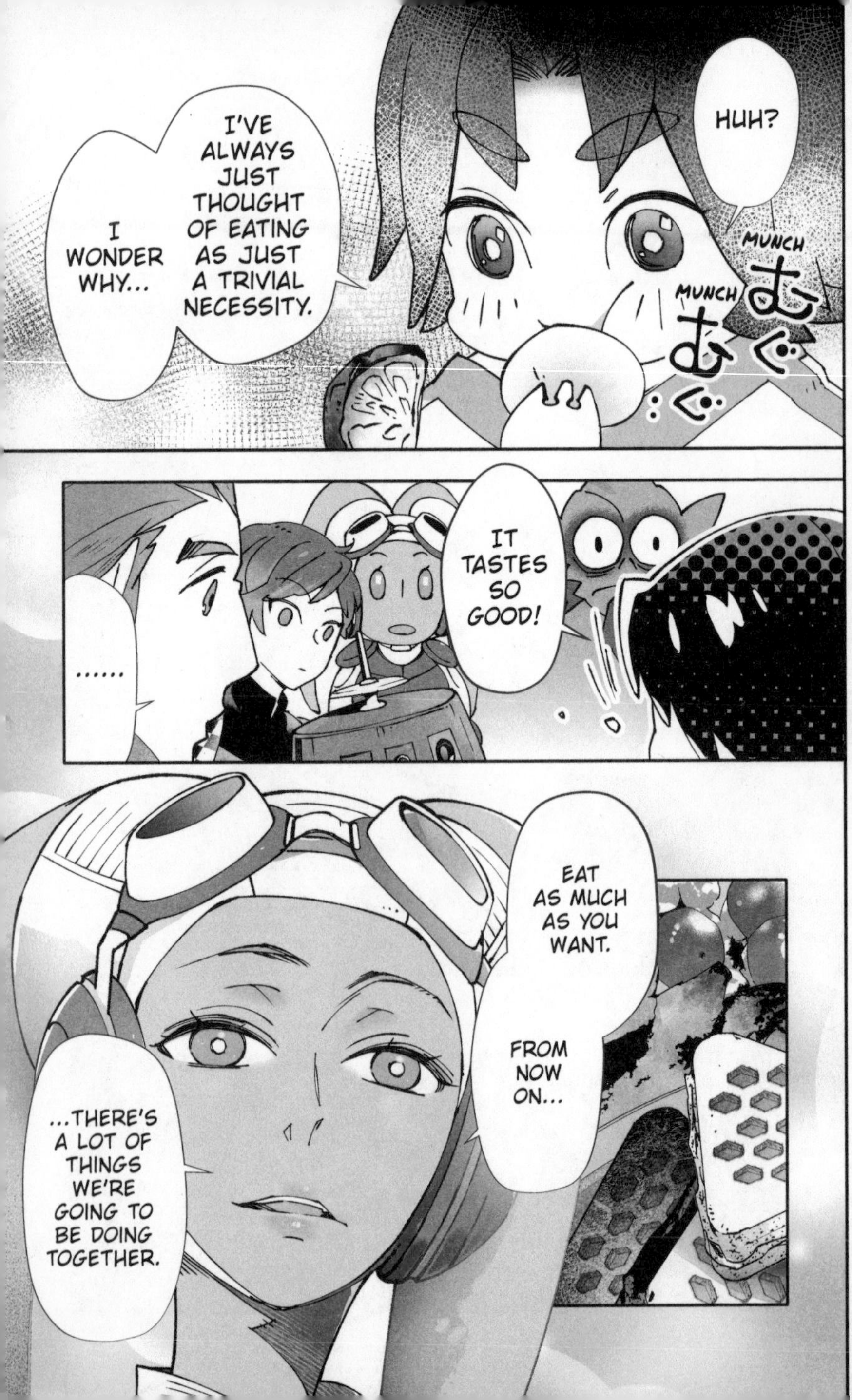
HUH?
MUNCH
MUNCH
むぐ
むぐ
I'VE ALWAYS JUST THOUGHT OF EATING AS JUST A TRIVIAL NECESSITY.
I WONDER WHY...
IT TASTES SO GOOD!
......
EAT AS MUCH AS YOU WANT.
FROM NOW ON...
...THERE'S A LOT OF THINGS WE'RE GOING TO BE DOING TOGETHER.

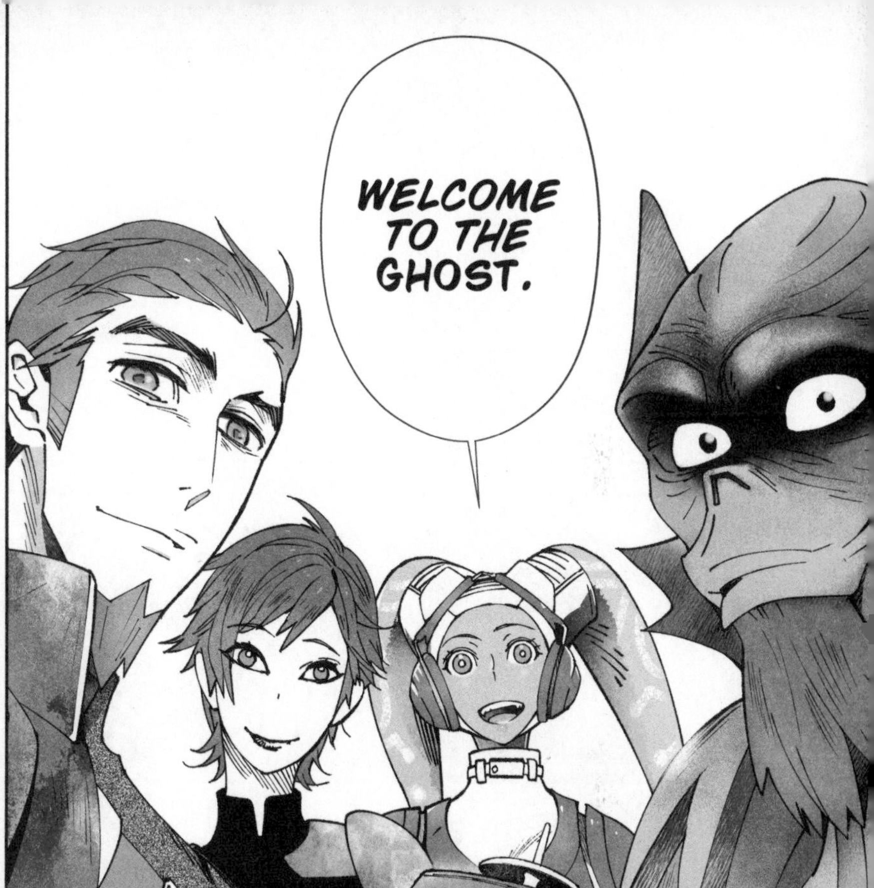
WELCOME TO THE GHOST.
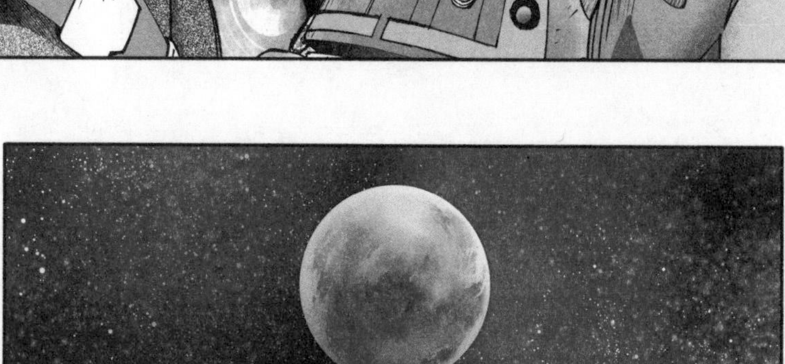

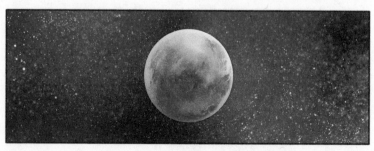

STAR WARS
REBELS
VOLUME 1 — END

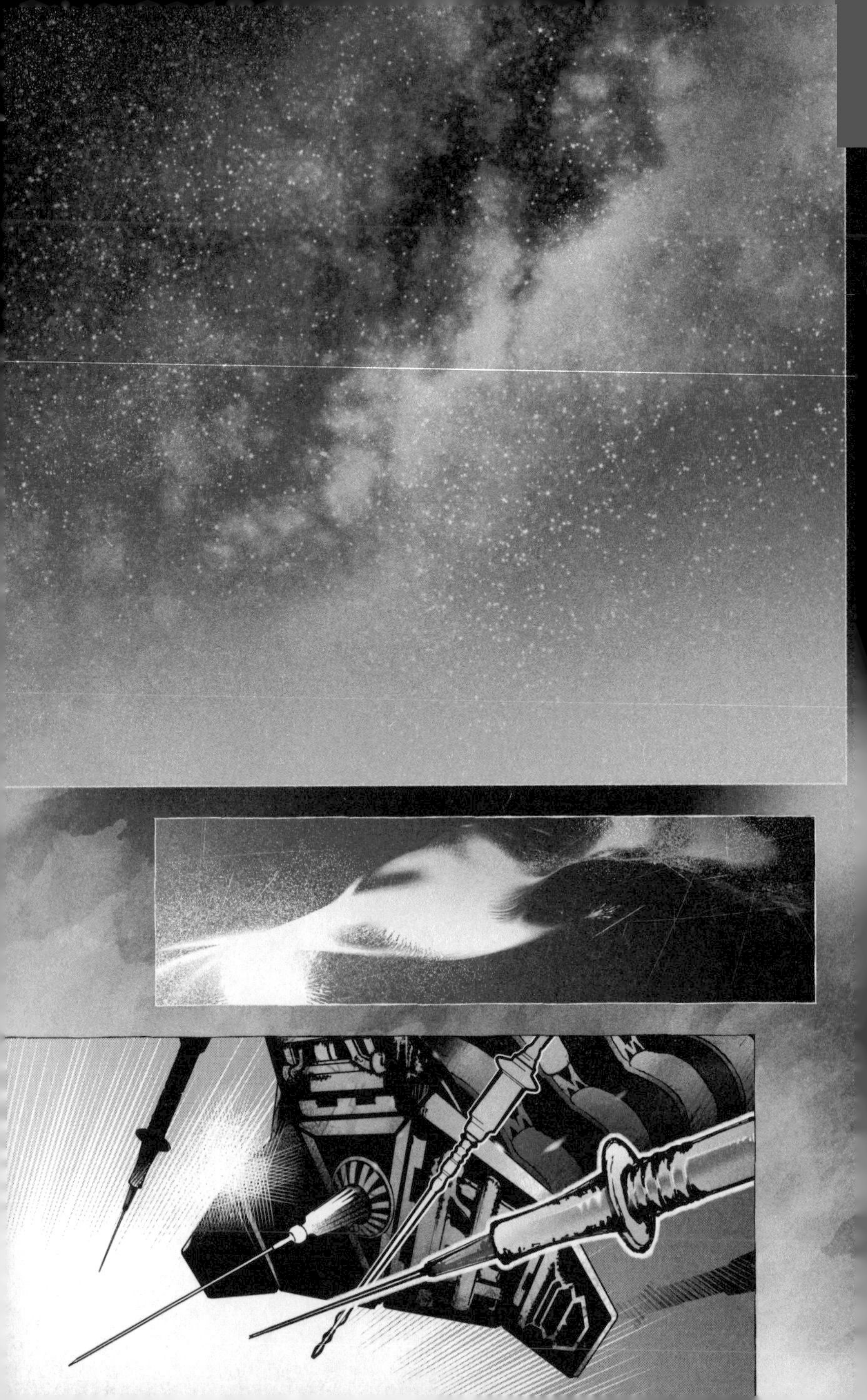

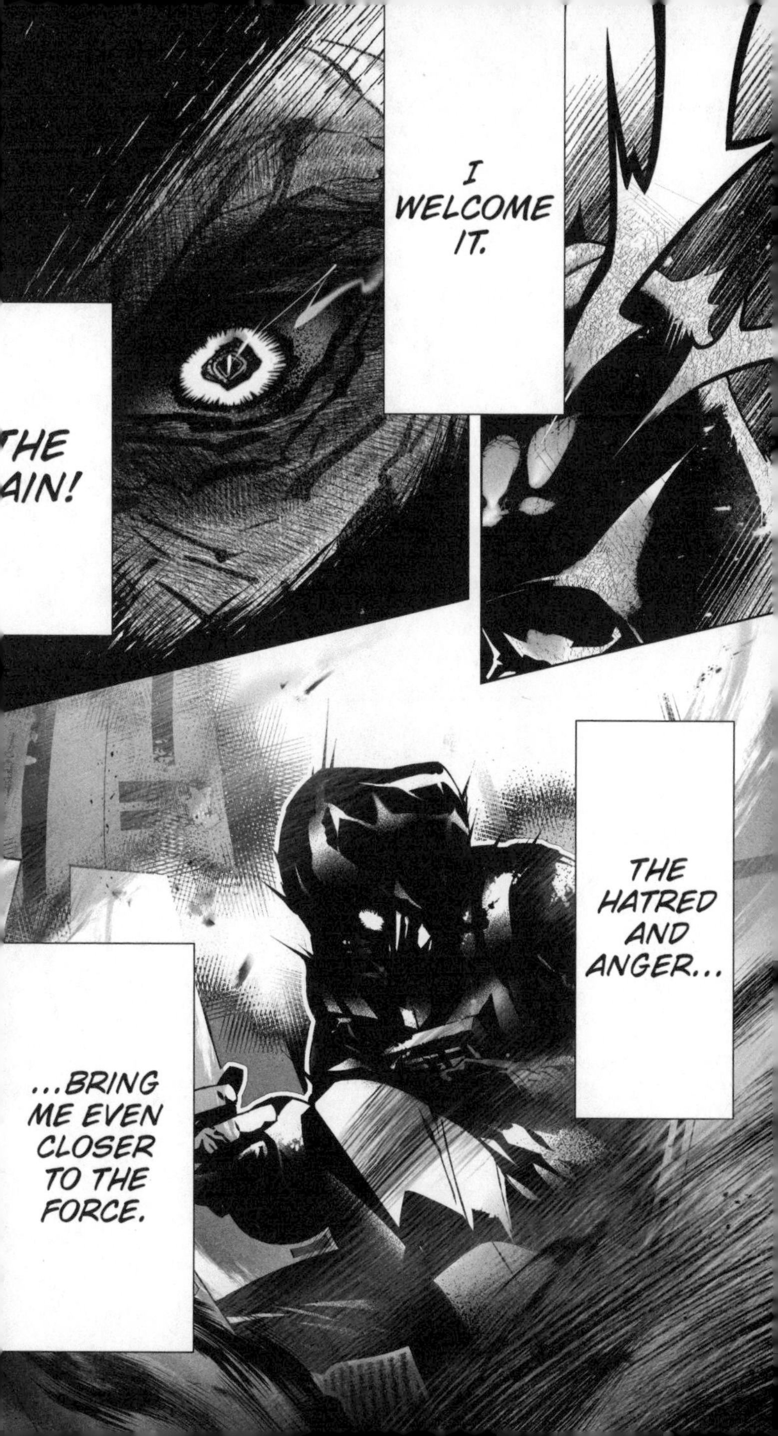
I WELCOME IT.
THE
AIN!
THE HATRED AND ANGER...
...BRING ME EVEN CLOSER TO THE FORCE.

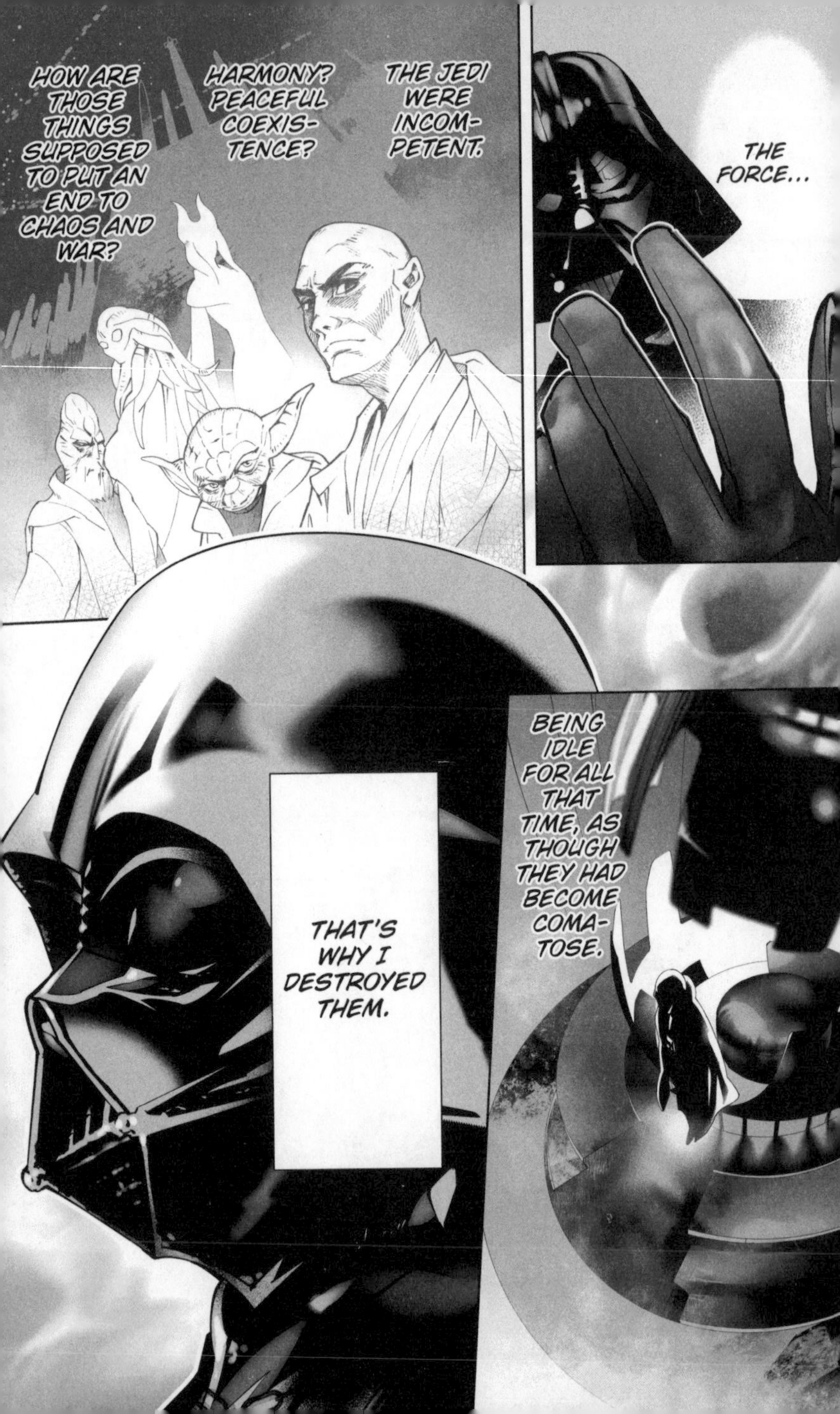
THE FORCE...
THE JEDI WERE INCOMPETENT.
HARMONY? PEACEFUL COEXISTENCE?
HOW ARE THOSE THINGS SUPPOSED TO PUT AN END TO CHAOS AND WAR?
BEING IDLE FOR ALL THAT TIME, AS THOUGH THEY HAD BECOME COMATOSE.
THAT'S WHY I DESTROYED THEM.

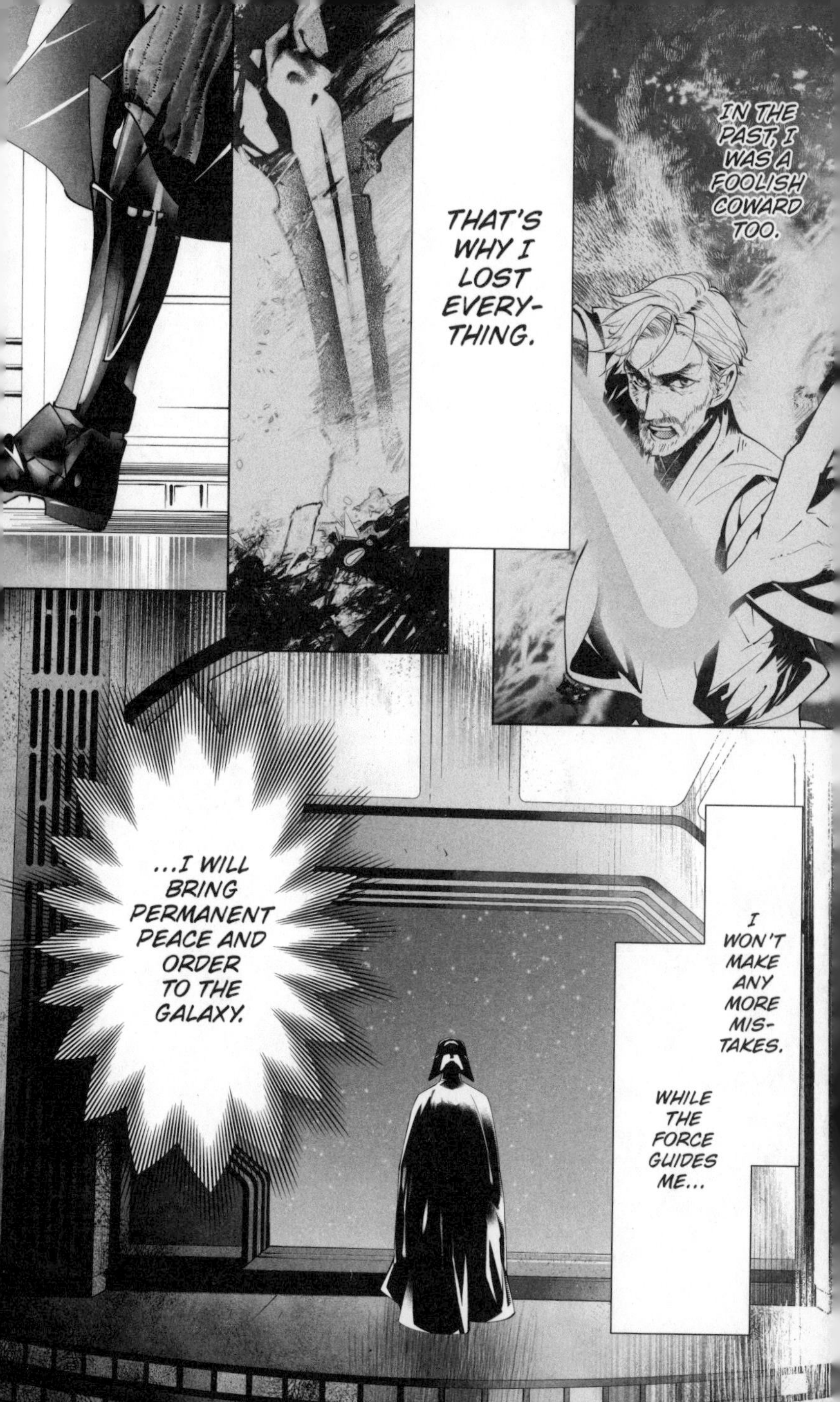
IN THE PAST, I WAS A FOOLISH COWARD TOO.
THAT'S WHY I LOST EVERY-THING.
I WON'T MAKE ANY MORE MIS-TAKES.
WHILE THE FORCE GUIDES ME...
...I WILL BRING PERMANENT PEACE AND ORDER TO THE GALAXY.

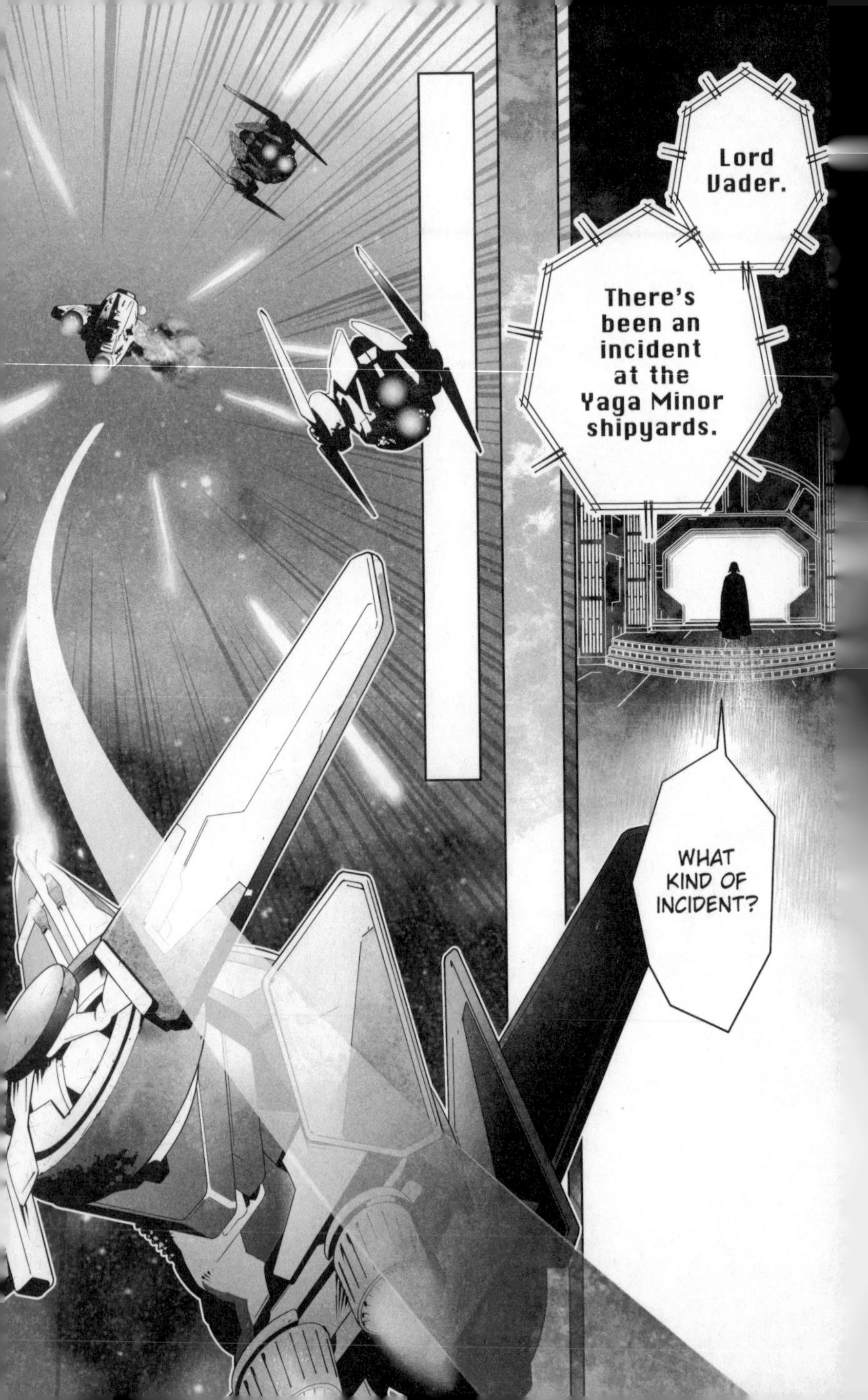
Lord Vader.
There's been an incident at the Yaga Minor shipyards.
WHAT KIND OF INCIDENT?

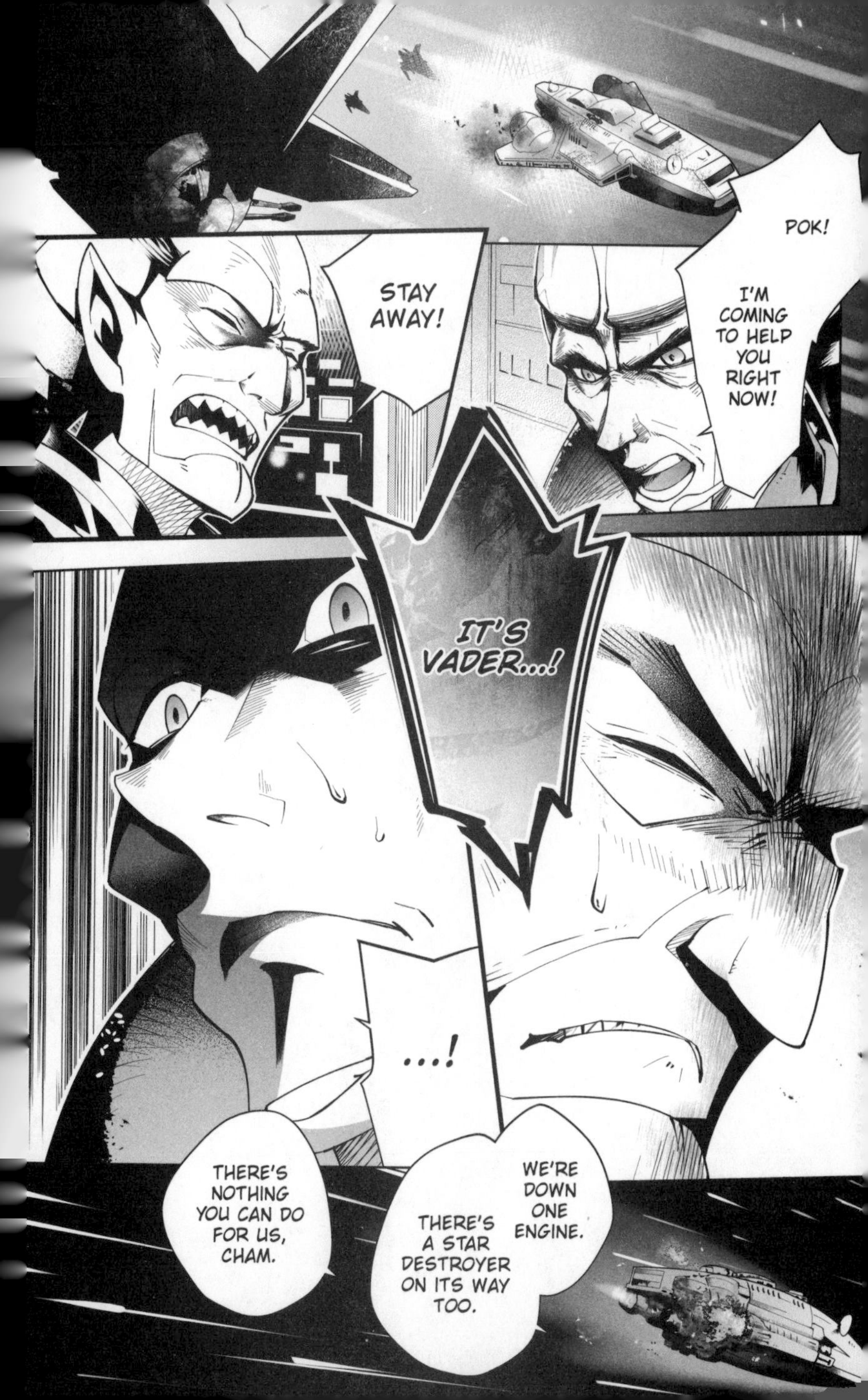
POK!
I'M COMING TO HELP YOU RIGHT NOW!
STAY AWAY!
IT'S VADER...!
...!
WE'RE DOWN ONE ENGINE.
THERE'S A STAR DESTROYER ON ITS WAY TOO.
THERE'S NOTHING YOU CAN DO FOR US, CHAM.

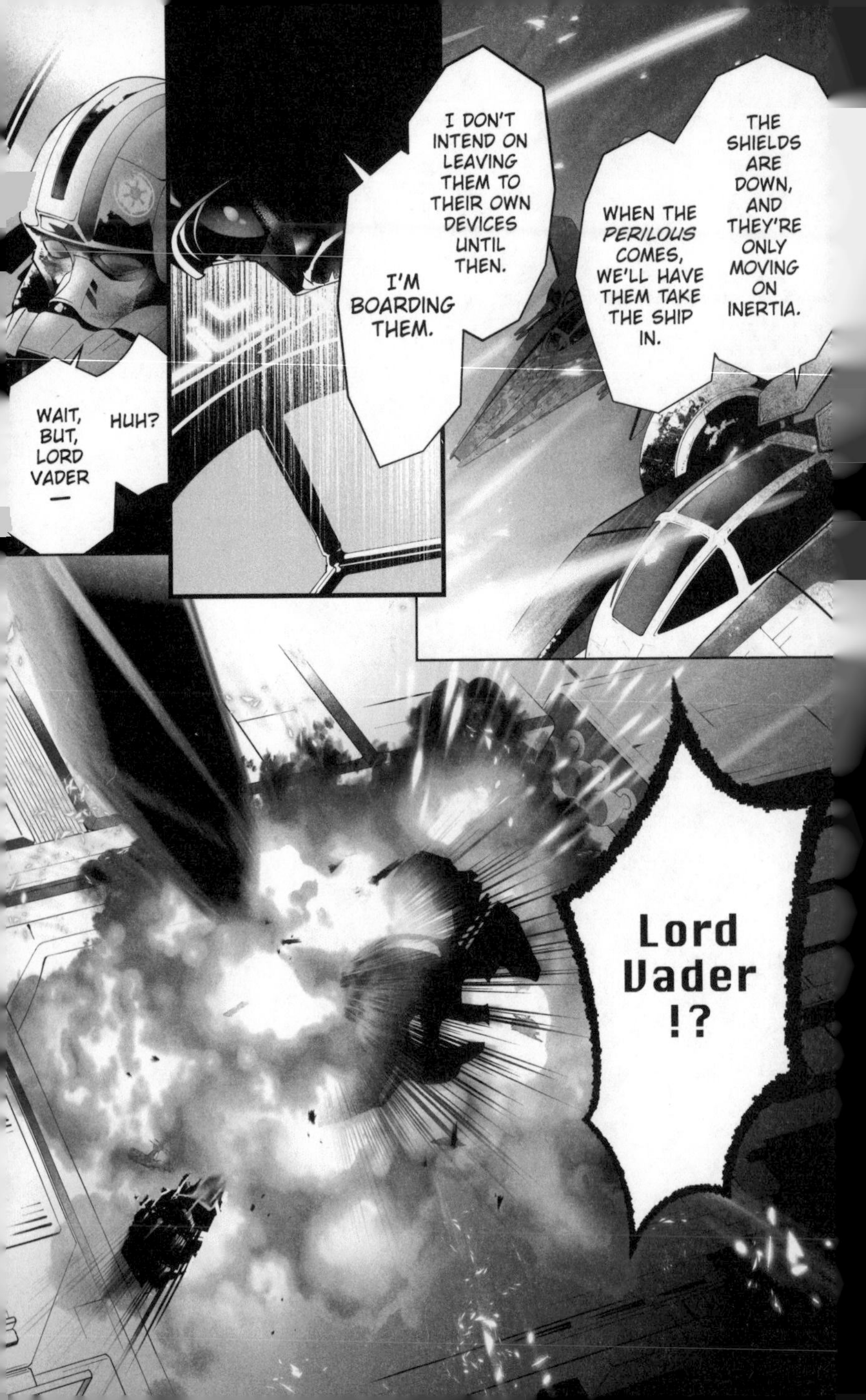
THE SHIELDS ARE DOWN, AND THEY'RE ONLY MOVING ON INERTIA.
WHEN THE *PERILOUS* COMES, WE'LL HAVE THEM TAKE THE SHIP IN.
I DON'T INTEND ON LEAVING THEM TO THEIR OWN DEVICES UNTIL THEN.
I'M BOARDING THEM.
HUH?
WAIT, BUT, LORD VADER —
Lord Vader !?

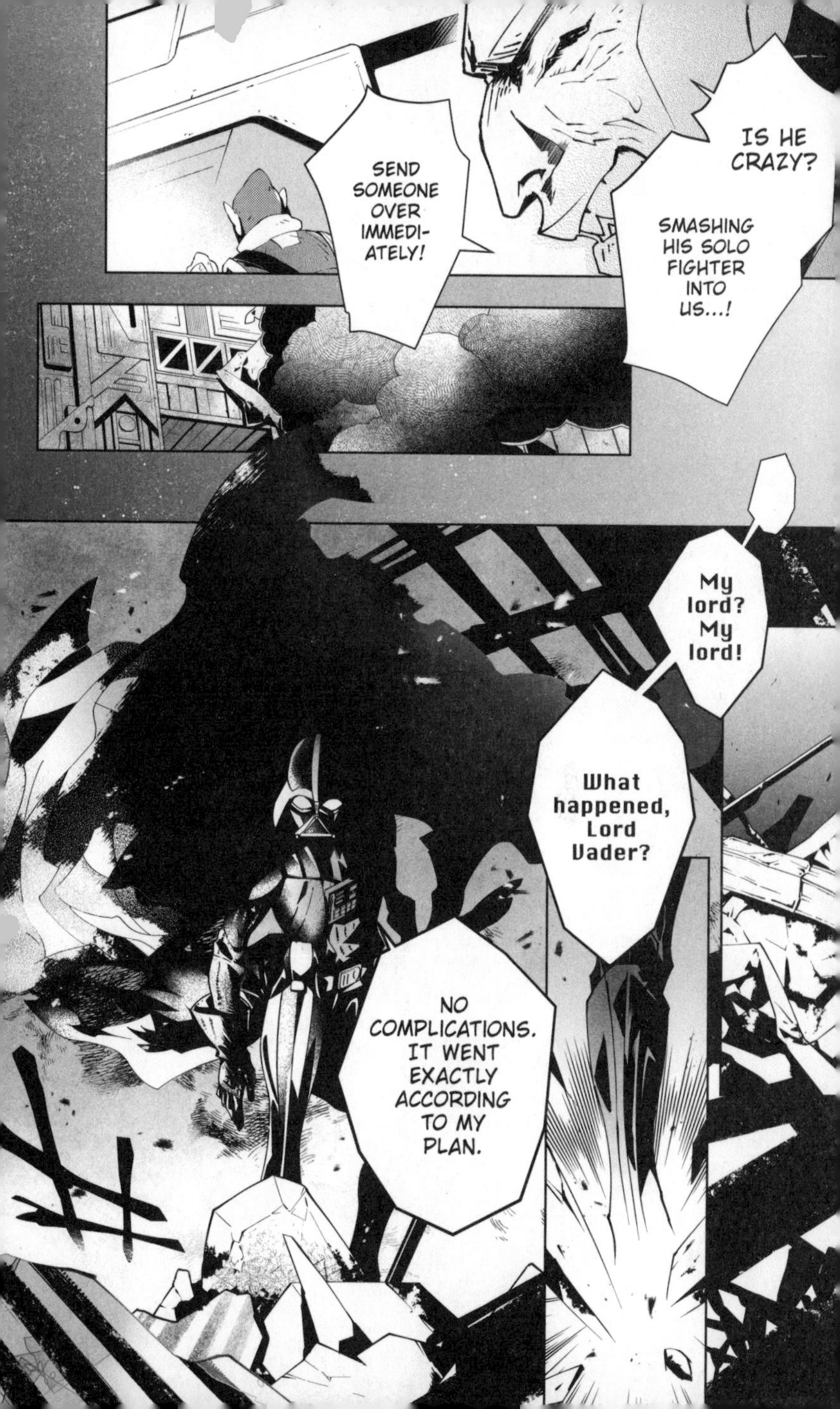
IS HE CRAZY?
SMASHING HIS SOLO FIGHTER INTO US...!
SEND SOMEONE OVER IMMEDI-ATELY!
My lord? My lord!
What happened, Lord Vader?
NO COMPLICATIONS. IT WENT EXACTLY ACCORDING TO MY PLAN.

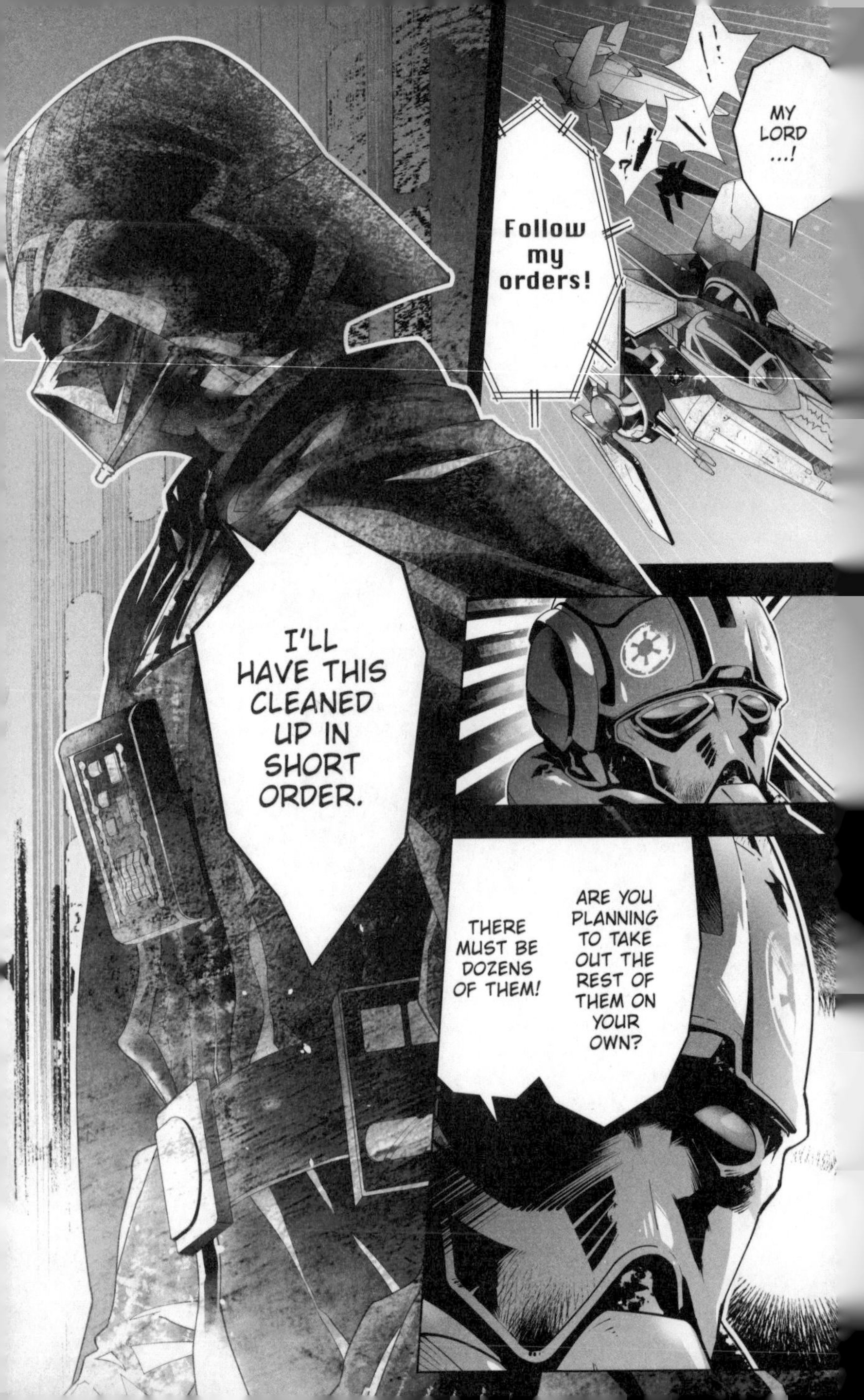
MY LORD ...!
!!
!?
Follow my orders!
ARE YOU PLANNING TO TAKE OUT THE REST OF THEM ON YOUR OWN?
THERE MUST BE DOZENS OF THEM!
I'LL HAVE THIS CLEANED UP IN SHORT ORDER.

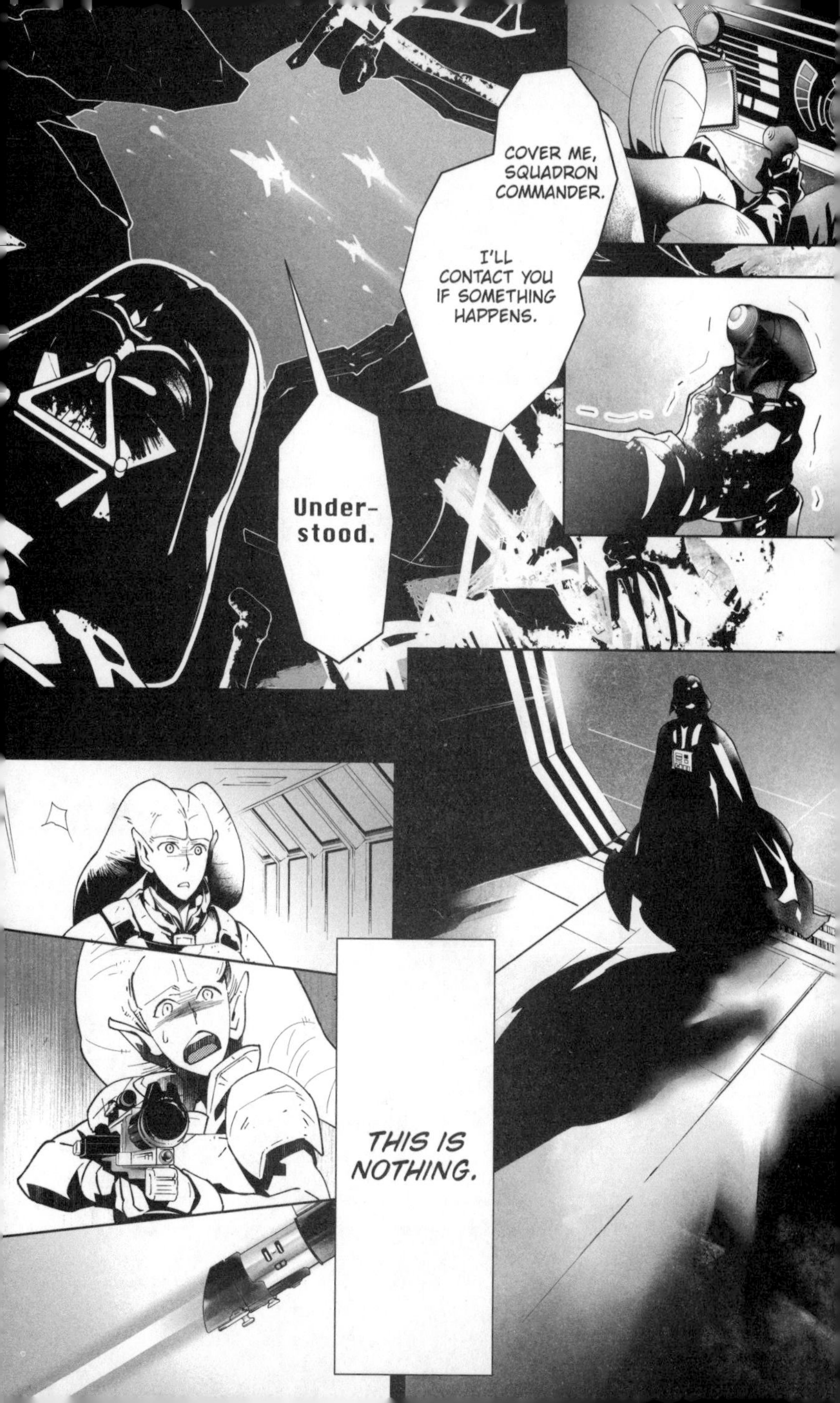
COVER ME, SQUADRON COMMANDER.
I'LL CONTACT YOU IF SOMETHING HAPPENS.
Under-stood.
THIS IS NOTHING.

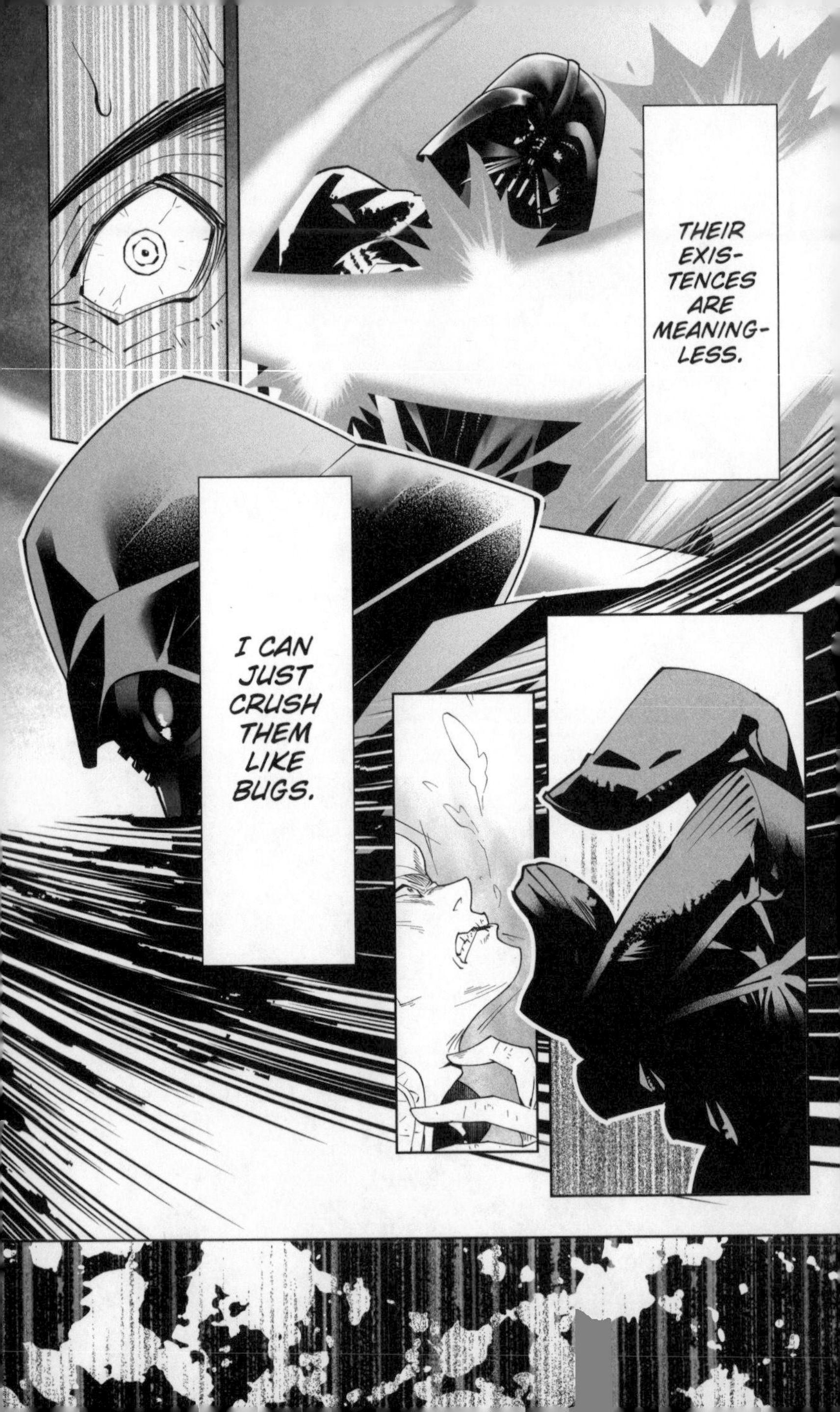
THEIR EXIS-TENCES ARE MEANING-LESS.
I CAN JUST CRUSH THEM LIKE BUGS.

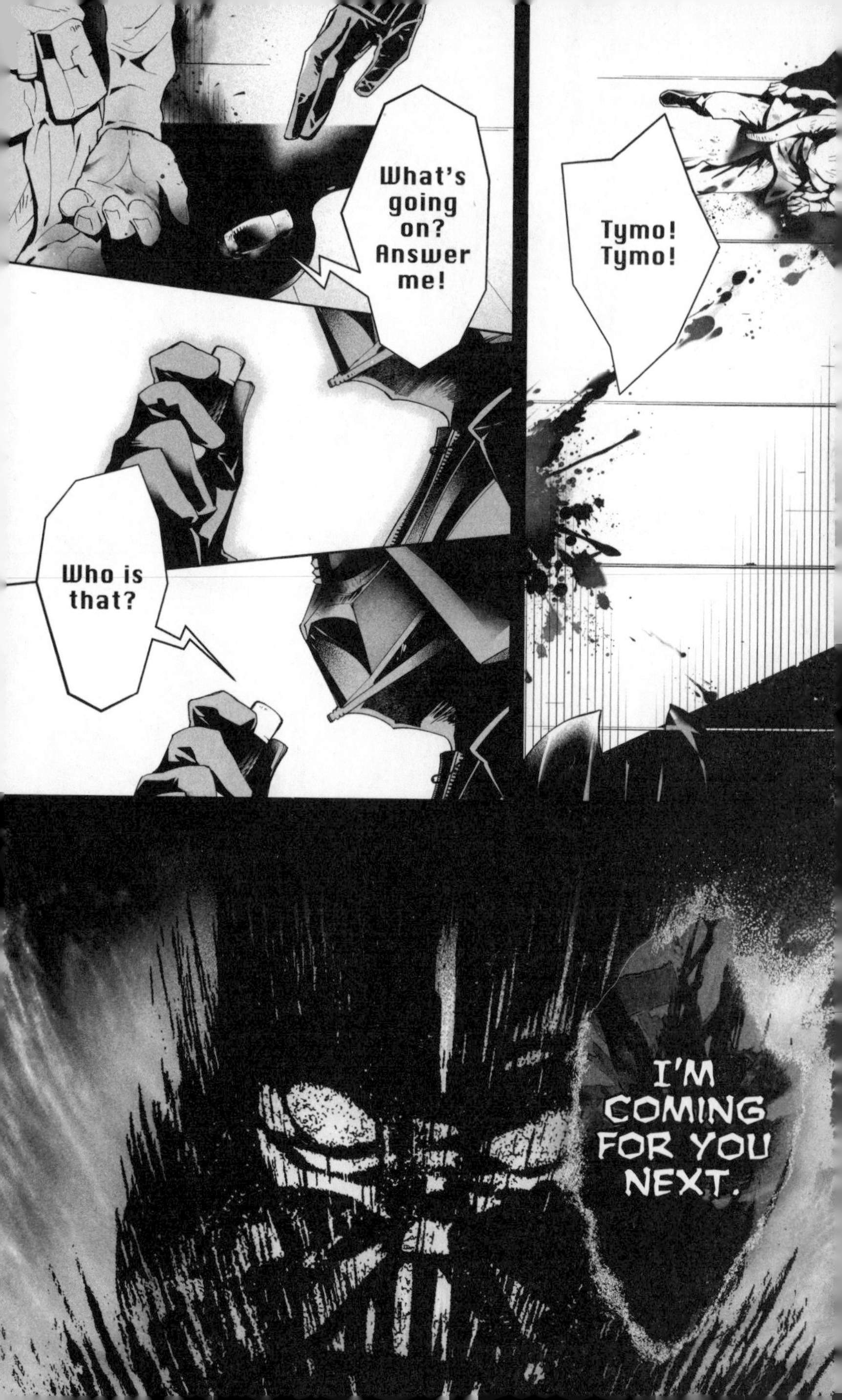
Tymo! Tymo!
What's going on? Answer me!
Who is that?
I'M COMING FOR YOU NEXT.

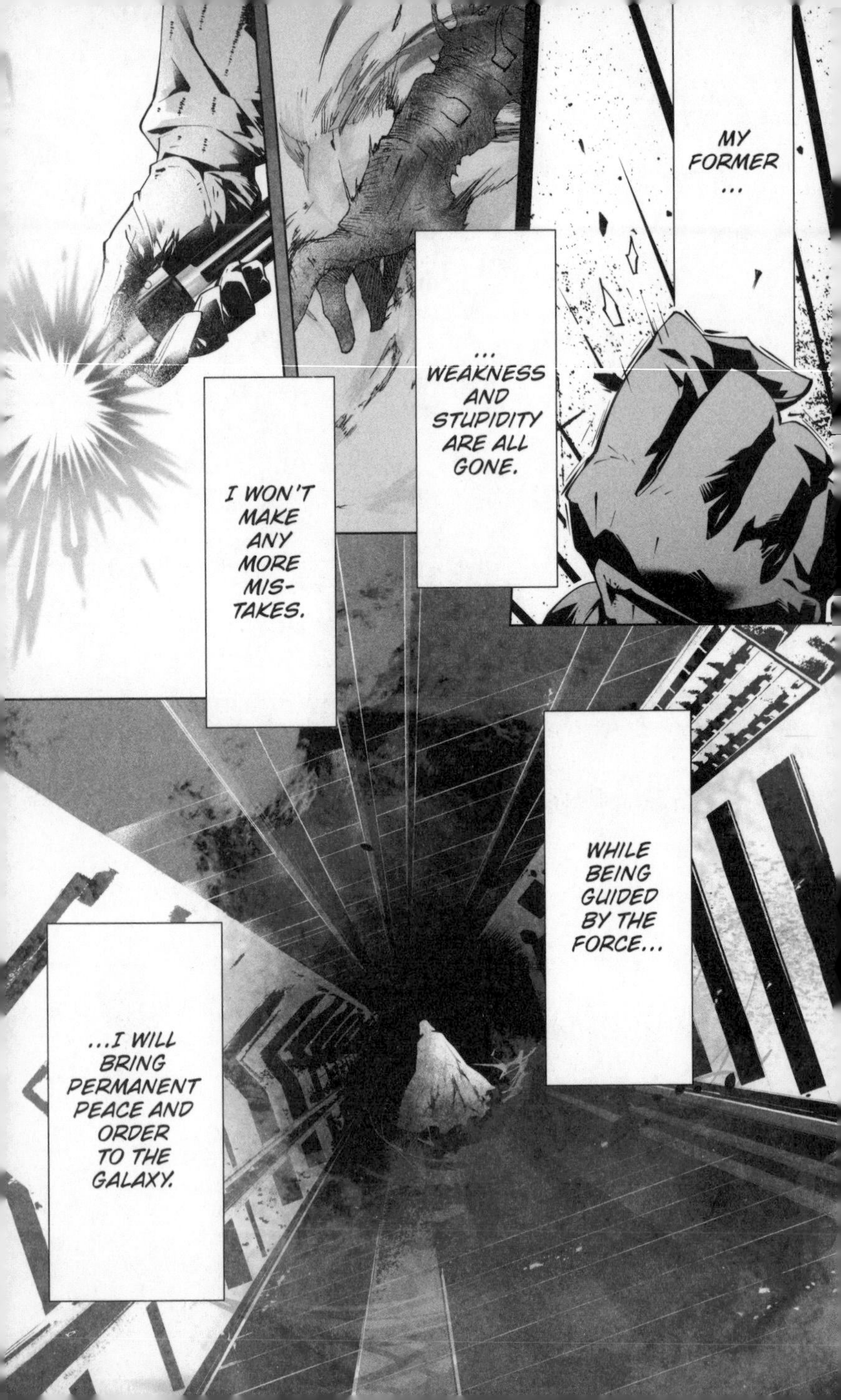
MY FORMER...
...WEAKNESS AND STUPIDITY ARE ALL GONE.
I WON'T MAKE ANY MORE MIS-TAKES.
WHILE BEING GUIDED BY THE FORCE...
...I WILL BRING PERMANENT PEACE AND ORDER TO THE GALAXY.

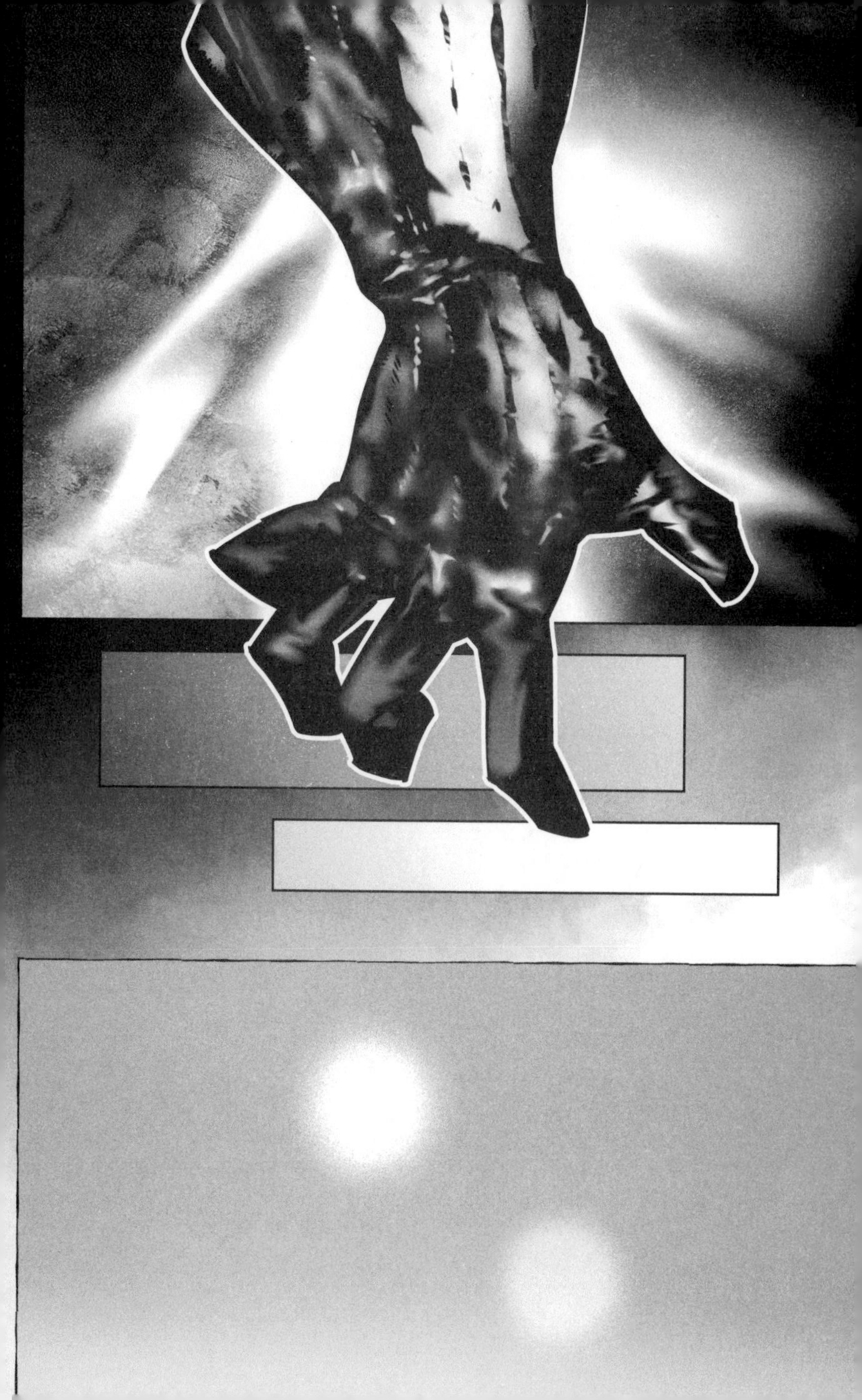

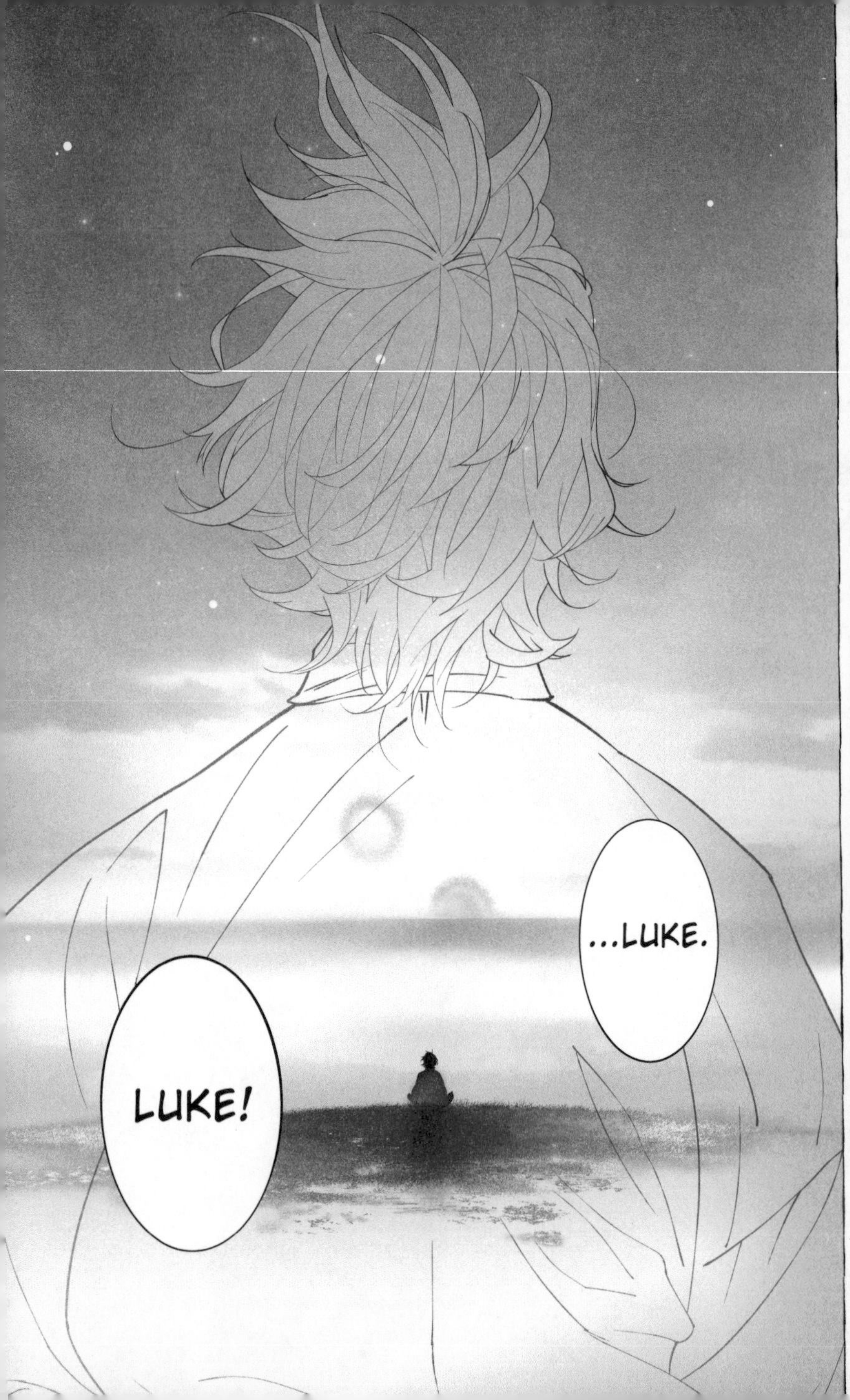
...LUKE.
LUKE!

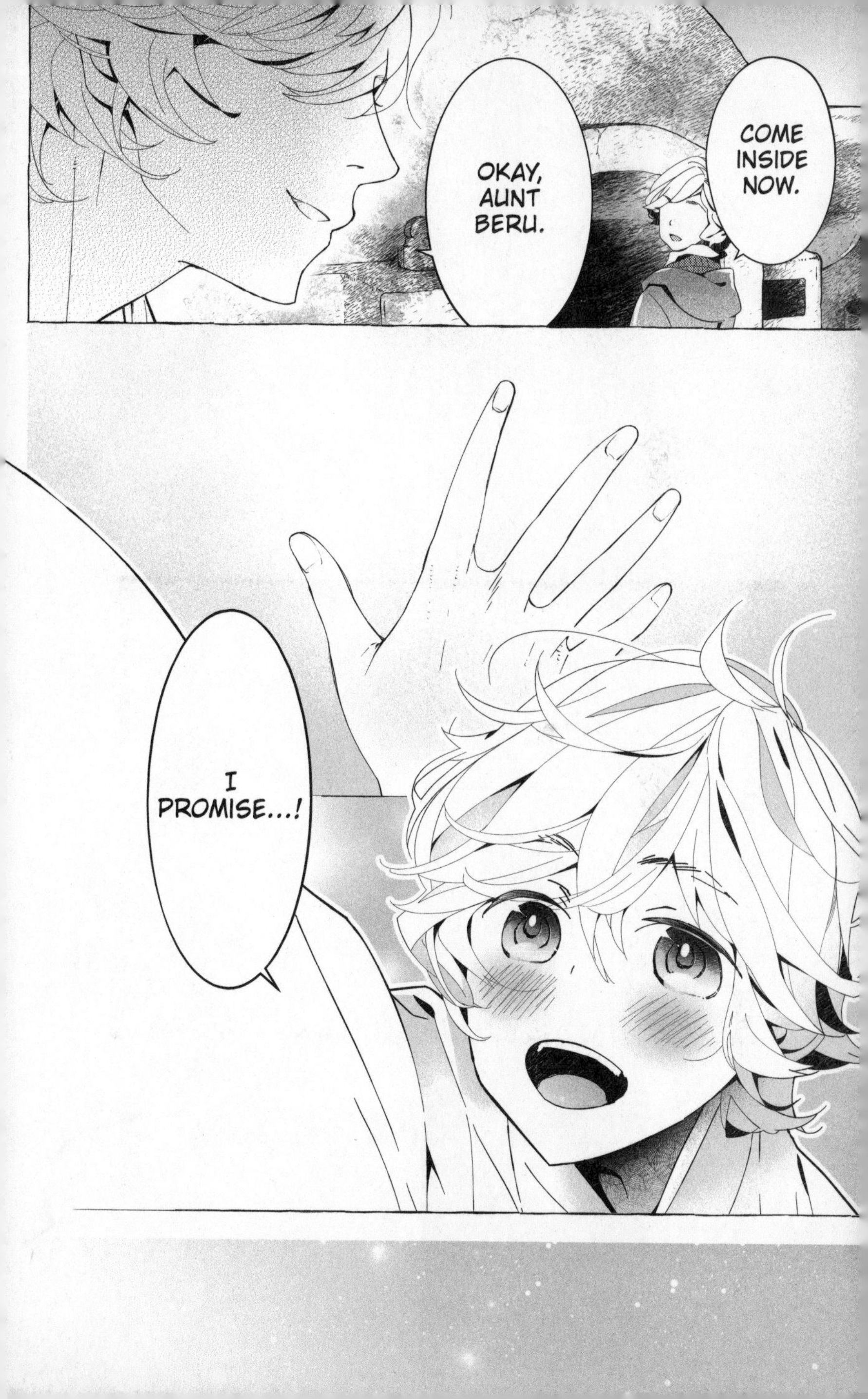
COME INSIDE NOW.
OKAY, AUNT BERU.
I PROMISE...!